Fall Irmgard:
Operation Irmgard

Dedicated to
All Six!

Fall Irmgard: Operation Irmgard

A Novel
by
Rand Charles

Published by PENURIOUS PUBLISHING

www.fall-irmgard.com

ISBN-13: 978-0-9967939-0-2
ISBN-10: 0-9967939-0-9

Cover design by Cathy Helms/Avalon Graphics

Cover photo © Corbis. Used with permission - 12066759.

Buch Eins

I

Todesfall in Paris
Mort à Paris
Death in Paris

Forward One Day

DAY TWO

1

Occupied Paris
Palm Sunday, 6 April 1941

Am Tag danach
Transmettre un jour
Forward One Day

DAY TWO—Paris—Sunday, 6 April 41—12:23 AM
It rained earlier that night. Damp streets glistened. Shafts of
moonlight veiled in wisps of clouds transformed the wartime blackout
to blue, as shadowy ghosts of budding limbs waltzed on the creamy
walls and sparkling windows of curfew-quiet Saint-Germain.
Saturday night had just become Sunday morning. The silent city, her
streets and structures, still held winter's chill deep in her sturdy
bones. A bitter Nordic winter, the winter of 1940–41. Old men, old
enough to remember the last German occupation of Paris seventy
years ago, had deemed last winter the coldest in history.

The war was over now for France, handily defeated by the
outnumbered German Wehrmacht in five short weeks. Still, it raged
in the flak-choked skies over England, while America held onto hopes
of remaining neutral.

In a breezeway just off the place Alphonse-Deville, an arched
entrance led to a courtyard. Dipped in black paint except for a tiny
spot on its crown, a blackout bulb dimly lit the white lettering on a
royal-blue sign, announcing, *Nur für die Deutscher Gemeinschaft*. For
the German Community Only. Under it a smaller sign in rune script
read, *Offizierslokal*. Officer's Club. On the granite keystone of the
archway, far enough from the street to avoid defiance of the blackout
code, a soft-blue neon script buzzed *Club l'Heure Bleue*. Part cabaret.

Part café chantant. All German. A Wehrmacht *Nachtlokal* stabbed in the heart of the French capital.

A heavy door sprang open. The quiet of the shackled city was rudely violated. The screamed punch line of a lurid joke spat in a high-pitched German squeal spilled out from the subterranean club and into the chilly spring night like an indignant fog. Next blared the quick zip of a kazoo, followed by riotous laughter and applause. German applause, in unison. Downstairs in the smoke-choked club, scores of German officers and businessmen reveled in the boisterous goings-on. For most it was a coven of inhibition like nothing they had seen back in Germany for years. *Ungeknöfpt.* Tunic buttons undone. An unbuttoned world of bellows and guffaws rather than the restrained snickers and snorts of the properly prudent Prussian. This was Wehrmacht Paris. And not yet Nazi Paris. Hopefully, not ever. And the Club l'Heure Bleue was the truest, warmest, and coziest of Wehrmacht Nachtlokals in all of Wehrmacht Paris.

"Then of course, there's the Paris brothels." Major Hans-Hubert von Hirschbach swigged the last sip of his Domfrontais, shook the Calvados sting from his head, and bellowed on. "Let's see, I arrived on a Tuesday. And on that Thursday, as great fortune would have it, I was selected as part of the thoroughly energized team Schaumburg put together to tour these glorious dens of repute." His voice then exploded from him as his dark eyes darted back and forth between the two men at his table. "Every damn one of them!"

He stopped to catch his breath. No one in Germany talked faster than Major von Hirschbach. Thick black center-parted hair was piled above dark movie-idol eyes. Manicured fingers moved around the rim of his cocktail glass as tenderly as they would some newly explored areola. Beaming, the machine-gun patter continued.

"We were duly charged, you see, with determining those establishments best fit for accreditation as Wehrmacht houses. Took us most of a week to designate a good forty bordellos with that distinction, five of the very best, of course, reserved for officers. And let me say, my friends, first-class places, these. Rolf, you and your adjutant here must give them a try."

Major Karl-Rudolf, or Rolf, von Gerz, smiled back at Hans-Hubert with a twinkle in his tired eyes. He nudged his adjutant next to him, Oberleutnant Gephardt Fechter, with his elbow.

"Gep here is the more practical of the two of us," Rolf said. "When it comes to women, I'd rather pay for their affections with fine wine and dinners."

12

Before his beer glass touched his lips, Gep blinked and smiled, interjecting, "I probably get the better deal then." Gep was a lean and wiry figure with cold eyes as blue as an Austrian mountain lake and short blond hair parted high on his elongated head. His rugged face bore a *schmiss*, a coarse fraternity dueling scar across a pockmarked cheek.

"Well, I assure you, gentlemen," Hans-Hubert blitzed on. "These girls—clean, classy things—all have French certifications and health cards." Feigning some momentous realization, he stopped suddenly and lowered his eyebrows. "Prostitute certification minister!" His smile and straight teeth gleamed under a hairline mustache. "How do you suppose one lands that job?"

Major Rolf von Gerz slapped his old university chum's back and chuckled. "Truly, a ministerial position you were born to fill, Hans, old rascal."

"Oh, good god, Rolf!" Hans barked, suddenly dead serious. "Where do you suppose one would apply the certification stamp?" Then he bellowed, breathlessly laughing, looking pleadingly at each of them to ensure they too were duly entertained.

"Oh, Rolf." Hans composed himself and caught his breath again. "Stay in Paris, my wonderful old friend. You and your adjutant Oberleutnant Fechter, stay here with me. Paris is Wehrmacht Walhalla, Rolf! All of us, the entire officers corps, we're gods among mere mortals as we strut through this amazing city. Why on earth would you want to return to miserable fucking Warsaw?"

"Hans, my friend." Rolf was a handsome and distinguished officer with piercing, veracious eyes, a strong square jaw and curly brown hair. "First of all, there's a war going on."

Hans-Hubert gave a jerk and a silly scowl. "A war. When did that happen?"

Rolf smiled. "We are fortunate, Hans," he said, purposefully. "We enjoy the gamesmanship of war while others suffer its grim reality."

"So, while war rages in North Africa and the Balkans, Rolf," Gep interjected, "your friend Hans here, and his minions, enjoy a quite luxurious Paris holiday at the expense of the Wehrmacht!"

"Well, you're half-right, Gep, my friend." Hans-Hubert shot him a quick wink. "But our little holiday is actually at the pleasure of the French government! I tell you the occupation of France was perfectly concocted." Hans put his elbow on the table and held up a thumb.

"First, we overvalued the mark against the franc. As a result, French goods became extremely affordable to Germany and Germans in France. Whether it's Abwehr officials like my team buying trainloads of wool or coal or cattle for the army, or tourist soldiers and businessmen buying silk stockings and champagne, French goods are flowing."

Rolf nodded his tacit understanding with pursed lips, but his attention was averted to the table at the back of the club where the striking American girl held court, surrounded by her entourage of dolled-up beauties. She was delicious. Cherries for lips, peaches for cheeks, and dark caramel eyes. *If only there were more time,* Rolf thought.

"Secondly," Hans-Hubert continued, adding his index finger to the raised thumb, "everything is paid for! Every building we occupy, every hotel, office or villa. Likewise, when my people buy goods and raw materials for the army, we pay for it all, with cash. French francs! Even the German soldier buying a coffee at a café or an apple from a street stand is expected to pay. And if he doesn't, he is arrested like any other criminal."

"And where does this money come from?" Hans continued, noticing the cigarette girl standing next to him, white ruffles and black taffeta sprouting long fishnet legs. Her back to him, he slipped his fingers under her short skirt and tapped her on her silk-pantied rump as he rattled on.

"Under the terms of the armistice, the French government is required to pay for all occupation costs to the tune of six-hundred million francs a day!" The girl spun around, and Hans pulled her to him with a waggish smile.

"French hoteliers, restaurateurs, owners of office buildings are all paid, full price. Most are doing far better than before we marched in, I can assure you!"

As he spoke he peered into the flat of cigarettes suspended from the girl's neck by a satin sash. Relieving the tray of two packs of Junos, he reached into his tunic pocket and withdrew a fold of cash. Hans' eyes never left Rolf and Gep as he slid a folded twenty-franc note into the top of her hosiery, his scoundrel fingers working it around to the inside of her thigh.

"So, who loses? The banks? Investors?" Hans asked, glancing up at the cigarette girl and gleaming at her pouty smile as she moved on. "When we took over, we forced the closure of the Paris Stock Exchange. An effort to keep the French economy from folding. We reopened it within a month, but not for security trades. Rather, for the purchase of government bonds. Bonds Vichy must sell in order to make continued payments on their obligation."

Hans lit a Juno and blew the smoke up into the club's recently frescoed ceiling. He started to speak, then simply chuckled his way through a three-pack-a-day cough. Zipping off a story was, of course, always more important than breathing, so on he stumbled.

"So, who loses? Merchants are prospering, agriculture and industry are thriving. Investors are happy. The only losers in this beautifully convoluted web are the peasants and the pensioners. Our unbridled consumption of virtually all French goods has created inflated prices and vast shortages. But you know the lower classes; those miserable souls are accustomed to hardship. They'll muddle through. Admittedly, however, if an element of resistance were to ever rear its head, it would come no doubt from their ranks. Most of them are just fucking communist anarchists anyway."

Rolf withdrew his own silver cigarette case embossed with a Prussian Eagle. He wriggled out an Ernst Udet and tapped its gold-tipped end on the table, still stealing glances toward the back of the room at the enchanting Adelaide Bridges. Earlier in the evening he'd been introduced to this urbane young woman and learned very quickly she was pure American sybarite. Brunette hair that caught the candlelight in soft hues. Lovely brown eyes that held a glint of both sassiness and vulnerability. And the *Grübchen,* Rolf thought, those dimples. How he delighted in them.

Still in the throes of his coughing spell, Hans flipped his lighter open, lighting Rolf's cigarette and averting the enchantment.

"We hold more than a million French soldiers in POW camps. Say some pain-in-the-ass peasant tries to start some French terrorist uprising? He is arrested, and any family member held as a prisoner of war goes into forced labor, or worse."

Hans stretched his arms out as he yawned.

"Is it not a beautiful thing to behold?" He cocked his head to one side. "Our occupation may have been a bitter pill for the French to swallow"—he smiled and tapped his middle finger on the table as he made his point—"but for a vast number of Frenchmen, it's been going down quite nicely with some very expensive champagne!"

The waitress approached them, and Hans-Hubert ordered another round of drinks. Rolf tried to refuse. Hans wouldn't hear of it, as he fired on.

15

"Civil administrative posts were filled by old chums of the general staff—lawyers, bankers, Kaiser-era civil servants—all spirited off to Paris, thrown into a uniform, and put into official positions," Hans said. "Positions SS and Party administrators would otherwise have filled. As a result, very few Party hacks and SS operatives have found a way to slither past shrewd old General Stülpnagel. But the SS! They use the registration of Jews to try to get a foothold in France. Still, I assure you, it's been an uphill struggle for them. And they are none too happy about it."

"You're being naïve, Hans." Rolf gave him a rueful look. "The SS, the Gestapo—they're all here. I just saw Kruder and his bulldogs come in."

"They're here, Rolf. But unlike in Warsaw, they're not in control of anything! And they can never be! That's why I need you, my friend—you and Oberleutnant Fechter—here. You're both fluent in French. Why, you were even raised in Paris, weren't you, Rolf? The more good people we can place in France, the fewer SS and plaster-saint Nazis we need. Let them occupy their time chasing down their miserable Jews while we run the war . . ." He held up his glass. "And Paris!"

"Hans-Hubert," Rolf said, "you are either criminally naïve or incredibly drunk. And probably both."

Hans held a finger aloft and waved it back and forth.

"I know you, Rolf. I know your breed." Hans closed his eyes and shook his head repeatedly. Opening them, he fired off. "You're like most of us in the Abwehr: we tolerate these Nazis, we placate them, but very few of us truly embrace them. Our ranks hail from nobility, from titled and professional soldiers. Their lot slithered from back alleys and beer halls; they're little more than vagabonds and peasants."

The long line of drinks was becoming his undoing. His own discomfort in the direction the conversation was taking made Rolf survey the nearby tables. *Who might be listening?*

"Look at you, my friend," Hans barked, loudly. "All of us. Officers in the grandest army in the world, yet we are such a circumspect lot. Cautious. Discreet. You both know, any public display of even the slightest degree of normal human emotion can be construed as 'weakening the Wehrmacht' and, thereby, as treason. Treason? Disconcerting to be sure!"

Fall Irmgard

Furtively, Rolf squeezed his friend's forearm. "It is, I'm afraid, what it is, my friend. You've had too much to drink. You're saying things you shouldn't."

"This is Paris, Rolf." Hans-Hubert tore his arm loose from Rolf's grip. "We're in a Wehrmacht club. Most of these chaps are attached to the Abwehr, like us. No Party snoops here. No golden pheasant Nazi mongrels sniffing our farts." Hans-Hubert grunted and snarled, curling one edge of his lip. "This isn't Warsaw, comrade! You can speak your mind here."

Rolf knew better. He was relieved as the band started playing. A recognizable tune, though the title escaped him.

"Here she comes again!" Gep was like a schoolboy at the sight of the saucy blonde chanteuse as she sauntered onto the stage. An ageless beauty, perhaps late thirties, probably mid-forties, possibly early fifties, stunning regardless. He joined the wave of applause as she blew kisses to the crowded room.

"She's Dutch," Gep gleefully shouted to Hans and Rolf over the crowd's roar, never taking his eyes off her.

Rolf was oblivious to Gep and the singer. Over Gep's shoulder the smoky sea of black silhouettes parted, and he could once again see the American girl at the back of the club. It wasn't her striking brown eyes as much as the look in them earlier that evening when they first met, officially anyway. A *we were meant to meet* look. She was returning to America on Monday; still a sudden warmth filled him as he recalled their brief meeting only an hour earlier.

"I regret we won't be able to become better acquainted, Miss Bridges," Rolf had said, clicking his Prussian heels together.

She gauged him for a second with a tilted glare and puckered lips, then said, "I'm afraid most German officers find me quite disagreeable. You wouldn't like me either."

"Why on earth not?" Rolf had asked.

"I'm not French, major. I'm American. We fight back!"

Rolf had felt a winsome smile grow in his eyes.

"And I, my dear, am quite certain I would be handily vanquished."

He had then taken her hand and kissed it softly, his eyes never leaving hers. As he released it, he felt the regret in the way her fingers gently lingered in his.

Smoke from his cigarette now burned one eye, but Rolf never lost sight of her. Her glance deflected his, and a tinge of anguish coursed through him as he watched her smile up at the sweet old man seated in the midst of this table of red-lipped beauties with bouncy curls and soirée updos. The man's laugh was a jolly, contagious thing, with his twinkly eyes and a big beaver-toothed smile. His tubby frame danced in his seat to the music, a finger leading the band. Der Herr Ritter, they called him. *Lord Knight indeed,* Rolf chuckled to himself. He knew this breed of German businessmen, *Altreichers,* rich and titled men from the grand old days. Be it cafés or churches, brothels or boardrooms, men of Ritter's ornery ilk possessed that rare quality of fitting in, flawlessly.

Suddenly the singer was singing, the swaying field of silhouettes all shifted, and Rolf's view of Miss "Call-me-Addie" Bridges from America was blocked. She was gone.

Their first day in Paris, his and Gep's. Her last. What was today? Saturday? No, it was past midnight, early Sunday morning. Tomorrow, she would return to America. Tragic. He should go back over to her. Talk to her. But he was so weary. Four days with barely any sleep. More than three glorious weeks remained in Major Rolf von Gerz's Paris furlough. There would be other girls, playful, insignificant things. Girls he wasn't *meant to meet.*

The singer moved through the crowd; her gentle touch floated across warm, flushed faces.

"They call her Sabina," an intoxicated Gep purred, leaning against Rolf. "Isn't she the most sinful creature? I can feel her voice in my stomach."

Sabina made her way through the tables and ultimately to theirs. She tickled Hans-Hubert's ear, mussed Rolf's curly hair, and then stopped behind Gep. Slowly, she nestled her sequined form between Rolf and Gep and kissed a whisper in Gep's ear. Rolf couldn't make out what she was saying, but its intent was quickly vivid on Gep's rugged face.

DAY TWO—Paris—Sunday, 6 April 41—1:51 AM

Major Rolf von Gerz reluctantly slipped out of the club, leaving his adjutant Gep Fechter and his old university friend Hans-Hubert von Hirschbach to close it down. Overcome with fatigue, it would be all Rolf could do to keep his eyes open long enough to get to the Hotel Lutetia, just down the boulevard Raspail. The long trip from Warsaw the day before was taking its toll on the Abwehr major. The party at the Club l'Heure Bleue had deteriorated into a "day at the races at Longchamps," where female jockeys hopped on the backs of Wehrmacht officers and whipped their steeds around the room in a pairs-elimination contest as the band played raucous racing music. Sabina rode her "big, muscled-up gelding; Gep *Fickter*," who promised to "prove himself anything but a gelding" once they'd won the purse, which had grown to twenty-two hundred francs by post-time.

As he was leaving, Rolf bid the American girl, Addie Bridges, farewell and bon voyage. A look in her eyes asked why he hadn't returned to her when he had the chance. It pained him. He found it difficult to turn and walk away. But he'd been such a fool with the most recent woman in his life. He couldn't, he wouldn't let it happen again.

Rolf handed the pretty French hatcheck girl his token. She retrieved his hat, top coat, and gloves from the shelves and racks where hundreds of upended Wehrmacht officers' hats were lined. Fingers of leather gloves spat from the side of most hat bills like so many dead gray ducks. Up in the l'Heure Bleue's courtyard, the fresh, cool air was a blessing as it slapped Rolf with enough brisk vigor to make the trip back to the hotel. He walked through groups of two and three officers talking, smoking, and laughing, and on out to the damp sidewalk.

The bright crescent moon in a now cloudless sky cast a *l'heure bleue* over all of blacked-out Paris. *The blue hour.* The metaphor for occupied France wasn't lost on Rolf, a city he'd loved so in his youth. His heavy boot steps were the only sounds to be heard as he cut across the tiny Place Alphonse-Deville. Halfway across the square he was startled by a tight group of shadows huddled against a tree trunk. Two young Wehrmacht soldiers had a dark-eyed French girl pinned between them. The one behind her had her skirt and coattails hiked up over his wrist. The other tore at her coat and blouse buttons, while both nuzzled and nibbled her neck and cheeks, carnage as much as sex.

Honor, Rolf thought. The first victim of hunger, and forlorn. He had seen it in Warsaw. A wonderful meal, some intoxicating wine, a little warmth, and now this lonely, hungry girl would let these beasts devour her dignity.

As he passed the orgy, the men snapped to attention. The girl just stared woefully at Rolf.

Look what your fucking war has done to me!

19

DAY TWO—Paris—Sunday, 6 April 41—7:20 AM
When the phone rang beside Rolf's bed, it seemed to him he had no more than laid his head on his pillow and fallen asleep. He lifted the receiver with one hand and simultaneously picked up his wrist watch with the other: 7:20 AM.

"Major von Gerz here."

"Major. I am Professor Baumgart at the Majestic Hotel, aide-de-camp for General von Stülpnagel. The general requests your presence in his office with all due haste."

"Yes, of course, Herr Professor. Might I inquire as to the nature—"

"Thank you, major." And the line went dead.

DAY TWO—Paris—Sunday, 6 April 41—7:38 AM
A block away in cabaret singer Sabina van der Gorp's room, two floors above the Club l'Heure Bleue, a peach-colored morning crept through the tiniest slits around the blackout shades and heavy velvet curtains covering the corner room's six floor-to-ceiling windows. Slowly, the room was filling with a soft glow. Gep lay naked in the bed on his back, his arms folded behind his head on a stack of embroidered green pillows. Sabina sat astraddle him, nude herself save the Oberleutnant's dress hat perched on one side of her head. Delicately, she moved the tan leather riding crop back and forth on Gep's pockmarked face as he toyed with the tiny bows, the color of a good Bourgogne, tied on the bulging straps running between her garter belt and her violet silk stockings.

"So, you're a morning person, are you, Herr Leutnant?" she asserted.

Gep quickly tore the whip from her grasp and slapped it on her fanny. "*Ober*leutnant!" he snipped with a sardonic smile.

She leaned forward to grab a tin of Panter Mignon cigarettes and a crystal ashtray from the bedside table, and Gep felt himself slip out of her. She clicked on the radio. After a few cracks and pops, the lonesome strains of "Où Sont Tous Mes Amants?" filled the dimly lit, high-ceilinged room.

"Not so much a morning person," he went on. "Rather, a Wehrmacht stallion."

Sabina sat the ashtray in the center of Gep's chest, nestling it in his thick, soft hair. "Oof! Indeed, you are," she quipped, her eyebrows

20

emphasizing each syllable of the sexy innuendo, "*Ober*leutnant *Fickter*."

Again he popped her with the whip. "It's Fechter, not *Fuck*ter, you vamp."

She smiled coyly and lit two cigarettes. Handing one to him, she coughed. Gep felt some of himself fall onto his abdomen.

"Look at the mess you've made," he groaned.

"I'm quite certain it's actually your mess, *mijnheer*," she quipped, wiping a wad of satin sheet over his stomach. She prolonged the process, playfully, thoughtfully. Then after a few moments, she added, "So." She arched one eyebrow. "Are you a spy, Herr Oberleutnant?"

"What a queer question."

"Oof, I think not. Aren't all of you German Foreign Office men spies?"

"Intelligence work isn't all espionage, Fräulein." He gingerly used the tip of the whip to toy with this nipple, then that. "Our work mostly consists of little more than reading and rereading stack upon stack of daily reports that have already been read and reread by others." He took a drag from the Panter, truly a *cigar*ette, a tiny cigar. "And by the end of the day, hopefully, we garner some useful tidbit of intelligence. That's my drab life, you adventurous little Mata Hari."

Suddenly, Gep grabbed her throat with one hand, his cigarette still wedged between his fingers. He took the crop's knotted end with his other hand and thrust it up under her chin, pushing her pretty head upward. The officer's hat tumbled from her head to rest on his shin.

"What about you? Are you a spy, Sabina?"

She looked down at him from the corner of her eye. "Oof." Again, she raised the eyebrow. "What if I were?"

"Then I should have to chain you to some dank cellar wall," he said, his chin jutting. "I would have to strip you naked."

Again he used the knotted end of the whip.

"Search you . . .

In here.

And in here.

And in here."

She squirmed and shuddered with each probe of the whip.

"Then I'd whip you and I'd beat you. I'd twist and pinch and I'd crush the most tender parts of you." He released her throat, sucked another drag on the cigarette, and moved its ash perilously close to her right nipple. Defiantly, her nostrils flared and she arched her back

21

slightly until her nipple just touched the Panter's long, spent ash. It broke away, cascaded down her stomach, and exploded into gray dust on his.

"I'd torment and defame and torture you until you willingly succumbed to my every inquiry and desire."

"Oof, Herr Oberleutnant! Then indeed. Indeed, I am a spy!" She quickly moved the ashtray back to the bedstead. "And you should begin without delay!" She snuffed out her Panter and took his to do the same, bending over to plant a gaping kiss on him, sucking his tongue deeply into her hot, moist mouth, when suddenly . . .

A tap at the door!

Sabina placed her finger over Gep's mouth. "Shush," her wet lips whispered. She licked his saliva from them and added, "They'll go away."

Another tap, a little louder this time.

Gep swatted her again with the whip. "Get the door, spy," he said, turning off the radio and taking his cigarette from her. "And put something on. It may be for me."

Sabina smashed Gep's head back into the pillows with her palm, bounced out of bed, and slung a flimsy floral silk robe around herself. She peeked out the cracked-open door and saw the club's prissy little Alsatian manager Xavier standing in the hallway.

"Forgive me, *mon cher*. An urgent message for the German."

Sabina looked over to Gep. He threw the sheets over himself and motioned with a wave of his fingers for her to open the door. Instead of Xavier, a tall uniformed German soldier burst into the room, clicked his heels, and snapped to attention as Sabina subtly placed the telephone's receiver back in its cradle.

"Herr Oberleutnant, a message from Major von Gerz. You're ordered to appear forthwith at General von Stülpnagel's office at the Majestic Hotel."

"Thank you, Feldwebel," Gep said. "That will be all, sergeant." The soldier left the room and closed the door behind him as crafty little Xavier struggled to peer inside.

Gep tossed the sheets off of himself. "Clean me, spy. And help me dress."

Sabina poured water from the chifforobe pitcher into the porcelain washbasin and tossed in a washcloth and a bar of soap. Stuffing a towel under her arm, she waltzed over and sat on the bed next to him, her languid body jostling wondrously under the floral silk. With menace in her eyes, she bit the tip of her tongue as she took the sopping wet cloth and let it drip over Gep's stomach and chest, delighting in his gasps. Gep's eyes never left her long, elegant fingers. Laboriously, she wet him with the cloth—his face, his arms, his stomach, his groin—then lathered him with the soap and rinsed him with the wet cloth again, while he lay there, smoking, grinning and imperious. As she toweled him dry, she thought about asking him for "a little *Trinkgeld* to help a struggling single woman get through this nasty war business" as she usually did to each morning's bed guest. But not this one, she decided. With this one, she needed to heed her instincts, become more than just another night's fuck. This one could be important. She placed her hand under the firm muscle of his upper arm, felt it slide over bone as she tugged and helped him roll toward her so she could towel off his back and rump. His eyes met hers and his jaw clenched.

"The commanding general's office," she cooed as she cocked that telltale eyebrow. "Oof, must be something very important."

DAY TWO—Paris—Sunday, 6 April 41—8:24 AM
"Major Karl-Rudolf von Gerz, Herr General."

"Show him in."

Rolf came to attention before the officious cavalry general. Von Stülpnagel looked up, stoically. He was a thin, sinewy man, tall, with dark hair and sharp chiseled features. His hard, leathery appearance was softened only by discerning eyes and a bushy chevron mustache.

"Major von Gerz. You favor your father."

"Thank you, Herr General."

"Please, at ease, major." General Otto von Stülpnagel rose from his desk and walked around to press Rolf's palm. "Karl. That was your father's name. Do you also answer to Karl?"

"Rudolf, or, Rolf, sir."

"Then Rolf it is." The general motioned for Rolf to take a seat and started to sit in the chair next to him, then suddenly added. "It's Sunday, isn't it? Would you like a coffee, Rolf? I'm quite certain my call must have awakened you."

"If it's no trouble, Herr General, yes."

"No trouble for me at all." The general placed a shaky hand on Rolf's shoulder and called out, "Wilhelm!"

The doors opened almost immediately.

"*Café* for the Major."

"*Jawohl*, Herr General."

23

Von Stülpnagel smiled and took his seat next to Rolf. "How is your father? Is he still alive?"

"Yes, sir. He's in a sanitarium in Berlin. A complete loss of all his senses. No memory of anything whatsoever. Healthy as a horse, physically. Chronic dementia, they call it."

"I'm sorry to hear that. He was a good soldier, your father. Never wavered. Always in control of his emotions, his men. I served with him, you know. With the 2nd Foot Guards and again during the war on the general staff of the 6th Infantry. He was older than I. How old is he now?"

"I'm forty-two, so he's seventy-five, I believe."

"Yes, twelve years my senior." Stülpnagel's gaze downward was accompanied by the slightest series of nods as he bit his lip, no doubt pondering Rolf's father's memory.

"He's the reason I summoned you, major. Your father. He was a man fully worthy of my trust. Loyal, tight-lipped, steadfast in his devotion to duty. A vanishing breed, to be sure." The general crossed his legs and placed his fist on his hip as he leaned forward.

"Can I assume you're the same sort of man?"

"Steel sharpens steel, general," Rolf answered, a gleam of pride in his eye.

"Indeed," Stülpnagel said, smiling. "Indeed it does. So you're an Abwehr inspector?"

"Since '38, sir. When Admiral Canaris took over."

"I read your dossier. Great work in Holland, von Gerz. I understand we are still utilizing that cell of agents to throw off the British."

"Yes sir, we are."

"And this recent nastiness in Warsaw. A woman, I understand."

"A white Russian, sir. Right under our noses." The thought of beautiful Tippi twisted knots in Rolf's stomach.

"Tragic." The general pursed his lips and shook his head.

"Yes sir, we could have put her to use as well, but the Gestapo . . ." The doors opened and the orderly entered, rolling a sterling service cart of coffee accompanied by sundry crystallized and cubed sugars, honeys, cookies, and a Delft demitasse filled with brownish cream. "Yes sir, it was."

The general nodded knowingly. "Major, I considered your father a close friend." He touched the tip of his pinky in the honey and put it to his tongue, dismissing his aide with a sweep of his fingers. "Friend. A word I neither take nor give lightly. Friendship, to

24

me, requires a bond of solid trust and an affirmed commitment. Once I choose to befriend someone, it is binding, eternal, only to be betrayed by you, never by me. My friends are therefore very few and very important to me."

"Quite admirable, Herr General."

"One such friend, major, a dear old soul, was villainously murdered this morning here in Paris," the general said as he poured Rolf's coffee himself.

"I am sorry, sir."

"His name was Konrad Ritter."

A scowl creased Rolf's forehead and his eyes tightened. "But I know this man. I met him only last night at a club."

"I am incensed by his murder, von Gerz." Stülpnagel's jaw clenched as he stood up. Walking to the front of his desk, he leaned on its edge and folded his arms. "Livid as well in my disgust over this situation. Not just because I lost a dear friend, but this dastardly event could have unfortunate consequences for the fragile occupation we currently enjoy in France."

Rolf gave the general a curious look.

"You have been in Warsaw, major. You've seen the course a hostile occupation can take. Granted, the Poles are a less civilized breed than the French. Consequently, the Polish occupation has required that we keep our boot firmly on the neck of Poland. But we hardly step on the toe of France. We occupy all of northern France, over a third of the country, with only a small fraction of the manpower being used in Poland. Why, quite confidentially, the police forces of France outnumber us three to one! Notwithstanding, the fact that we hold more than a million French prisoners of war in Germany truly serves to keep most terrorists docile. For now. In my command of this occupation, I have tried to maintain an atmosphere of rapprochement and generosity without displaying even the slightest degree of vulnerability or acquiescence. But it is all very fragile, this balancing act I play with the French. An egg on a pinpoint."

Rolf suppressed a growl in his stomach. He hadn't eaten since yesterday afternoon. A spontaneous reach for a cookie was stopped short by decorum. He plopped two additional sugar cubes in his coffee and stirred, never losing his focus on the general.

"You see, Herr Ritter was not only my friend, but our Führer, Adolf Hitler, was also close to the man. Or so I was told by old Ritter on many an occasion." The general smiled poignantly, remembering his friend, then bit down on his next words.

"I shudder to think what course of action I should be required to take if it turns out that my friend Konni Ritter was killed by a Frenchman; communist, Mason, Jew. Some lunatic from the asylum. It will matter very little. I shall be expected to retaliate, and will do so, I assure you, with harshness and severity unlike anything seen here in France so far. Severity you are all too familiar with from your time in Poland." He went to his desk. Pulling out an envelope, he returned as Rolf quickly threw back his coffee and stood to accept it.

"Major, I am placing you in charge of the investigation of Herr Ritter's murder. You are to have the complete cooperation of the military police, the French National Police, the Préfet, *and* the Gestapo." He handed Rolf the orders. "The Paris police are holding a witness who was with Herr Ritter at the time of his murder. An American woman. You should go immediately to the préfecture and get her statement."

Realizing the general was referring to Addie Bridges, Rolf concealed his astonishment as the general shook his hand again, warmly gripping his shoulder.

"Major von Gerz," he pleaded, a sad look in his eagle eyes. "Find my friend's murderer!"

"I shall, Herr General," Rolf said, saluting with a head bow and a click of his heels as he turned for the door.

"Major."

Rolf stopped and turned to face the general.

"Find the truth."

One Day Earlier

DAY ONE

2

Saturday, 5 April 1941

Club l'Heure Bleue

Ein Tag vorher
Un jour plus tôt

One Day Earlier

DAY ONE—Paris—Saturday, 5 April 41—3:51 AM

The lights dimmed slowly to a flickering, candlelit din. Laughter and conversation dwindled to a polite murmur, then collapsed into silence. The casual clink of glasses and glubs of poured wine. A snicker. A cough. And the haunting strains of a lone violin started the introduction to Sabina's last song of the evening. Or rather of the morning, Saturday morning; it was nearly 4 AM. A coronet, then a trombone, and finally a piano joined in, and an erotic melancholy settled over the cozy den. The club was still packed with Wehrmacht officers and German businessmen, most in a liquored stupor. A bright blue spotlight exploded through the smoky room, illuminating only Sabina's beautiful face. Bright auburn hair and green eyes were brilliant against her alabaster skin. Rhinestone ear bobs, a necklace, and a tiara with bangles that dangled down over one ear were all ablaze with sparkles in the spotlight. Her blood-red lips pursed and she started singing.

Her voice was deep, enticing silk, a warm breath that kissed the ear of every man in the place. The bartenders of the Club l'Heure Bleue, in black vests and white shirts, folded their arms and refused any insensitive barmaid's last-call drink orders. Tuxedoed waiters with their trays of dirty dishes all stopped in their tracks and moved this way or that to ensure they were not blocking the customers' view. The men in the band, in black turtlenecks and white fedoras or derby hats, ignored sheet music and keyboards and never took their eyes off of her. Even the club's crippled little red-coated bathroom attendant, an old veteran of the Great War who remained in Paris after the 1918

29

armistice, his weak heart pumping renewed life into his numb groin, smiled with anticipation as he hurriedly limped his way up the spiral staircase to once again take her bewitching cure.

Through the light, Sabina could see the first row of tables, make out a few faces. The club would be filled with Wehrmacht, Kriegsmarine, and Luftwaffe officers in their field-gray and blue uniforms. And most recently, over the last few weeks, there would be a few SS officers, some in their smart dress blacks. There were always a number of German and Ostmark businessmen sporting new French-cut suits and Parisian silk neckties. Seated in remote areas would be nefarious types with menacing eyes engaged in sotto voce conversations. A few women would be scattered here and there; German clerical or military workers from the Abwehr office around the corner from the club, and a large flock of French girls, some reluctant, but most willing escorts of rich Germans or Wehrmacht officers. But there was only one face Sabina was looking for. At a front table just to her right she spotted him, tonight's delicious young victim. He was still there, an SS Hauptsturmführer, a captain, tall and lean with a strong, muscular neck and a stern face with a smooth, boyish complexion, perhaps twenty-four years old, sitting with five other SS officers. She would be sure to look at him while she sang the next verse. Look only and obviously at him, into those big brown love-starved eyes.

He was unable to maintain eye contact with her! He continually looked away in an awkward discomfort bordering on virgin embarrassment! *Good,* she thought, nostrils flaring. *Wunder . . . schön!* Wonder . . . ful! The spotlight widened, moving slowly downward, illuminating Sabina's long, flawless neck, her tiny shoulders, the glittered pale flesh of her soft chest. The round form of her unbound and plentiful breasts rose under the supple ivory silk as she took in each deep breath. Impressions of her prominent nipples and the gooseflesh of her large areola pushed through the surface of the slinky fabric. Then, as she sang the next verse, they slowly disappeared.

None of the men noticed or cared in the least about the run behind the knee in her left silk stocking, hastily abated by haphazard stitching, or the makeup that soiled the straps, or the safety pins that bound the underarm hem of her gown. Women in the audience may have detected such imperfections, but not the men. Even the red passion marks on her neck and chest, all thinly cloaked in makeup, would go unnoticed. Not that homesick or carousing men ignore such cruel details. They are simply oblivious to them, captivated by the beauty in the beast. Sabina was the reason most had come, or returned, to the Club l'Heure Bleue. The *Arena Sabina*! And all they could see was the personification of the perfect feminine form before them, an *Aphrodite Germania*; a man's, especially a German man's, most pure and affective form of living, breathing art.

She slinked slowly off her stool and waltzed across the stage. Again, her chest heaved, her breasts and nipples surfaced in the silk and she started the song's sad chorus:

"Ich Weiß Nicht, zu Wem ich Gehöre."

The song was the lament of a woman who realizes she will never fulfill the hopes of one true love, but will accept the pleasures of a life filled with many short affairs.

I don't know just whom I belong to.

For Sabina van der Gorp, the lyrics were her life. Born in Rotterdam and raised in Amsterdam, she was the daughter of a Dutch prostitute and any number of possible men. Whoever her father was, he gave her a velvety voice, which her mother recognized had to be nurtured and perfected. Young Sabina was enrolled in fine music and voice schools and taken to church regularly to sing in the children's choir, despite the scornful stares by the proper women of the congregation. Her mother was ever hopeful that her daughter's future fame and fortune would someday buy her a well-deserved life of leisure, away from the drunken squalor and urine stench of Amsterdam's red-light *Wallen*.

By the time Sabina was thirteen, she was winning voice contests and talent awards. But even though she had gleaned a beautiful voice and fearless stage presence that must have come from her father, she was still her mother's daughter. By fourteen her figure was already more shapely than her mother's, and her childhood longing for a daddy's embrace gave her an unhealthy weakness for the company of pleasant older men. One such man took her under his wing. For nearly a year, every Wednesday after her regular classes he gave her voice lessons, along with an education in the erogenous areas of the male body, using his own less-than-appealing anatomy to practice upon. He taught her the nuances of touch. Her fingernails and fingertips, her lips, her tongue. When and where and how to be feathery, or frisky, or firm. And through his tutoring she became the most pleasurable young girl, and he the most pleasured of men.

But one Wednesday afternoon it was not Sabina at his door, but her cleaver-wielding mother who twisted the doorbell. Within a few short minutes, bloody chunks of meat from the young girl's voice instructor were strung from the foyer to the old man's upstairs boudoir.

With her mother in prison for killing the man, who turned out to be a local district governor's father, Sabina was singing in brown cafés throughout Amsterdam by night and, like her poor mother, working the Wallen windows by day. By the time she was sixteen, the Great War had started, and Sabina found herself in northern Germany, invested in unsavory sailor clubs and brothels in Hamburg and later in Bremerhaven.

Sabina stepped off the stage and strolled through the tables, the spotlight following her every sexy move. The slinky gown clung to the teardrop cheeks of her soft, firm rump and quivered slightly with each graceful step she took.

Floating from table to table, her finger's time-trained touch explored the ears, necks, chins and cheeks of the captivated men at the tables, sometimes running through their short, freshly pomaded hair.

Eight years after the end of the Great War, in 1926, during the fledgling Weimar Republic, imposed on defeated Germany by the Allies in the Treaty of Versailles, Sabina relocated to Berlin to sing in a number of cabarets. There, she found her real calling, but she was never truly successful, always stymied by her battle through two miscarriages and addictions to cocaine, whisky, and cheap wines, anything she could find that helped take away the pain and despair of her miserable life. Then, in 1928, she showed up broke, drunk, and desperate on Bruno Kestler's doorstep, the owner of Berlin's *Klub l'Huere Bleue*. He had opened his Berlin club in the Kreuzberg quarter two years earlier, finding relatively popular success. Bruno moved Sabina in with him, sobered her up, and very harshly kept her sober. He bedded her, but he nursed her and cared for her and quickly became the father figure she'd yearned for all her life. Over the years that followed, Sabina van der Gorp became one of the most wildly popular cabaret chanteuses in all Berlin.

Sabina moved on through the front tables, intentionally avoiding the young SS captain, moving right past him as though he didn't exist; all he would get from her now was a whiff of her Shalimar. Her eyes smiled. Like a tigress, she could sense his wanton exasperation. Making her way to some of the tables farther back, she noticed a pair of men in cheap, dark suits seated by themselves, men she'd never seen before. As she moved up to them, they sipped their drinks and looked at each other, feigning some very important conversation. They seemed to want no part of her.

Gestapo, she thought. Or no. Paris underworld figures who dealt in the French black market, drawn to the club by the Wehrmacht procurement activities of the Abwehr office around the corner, in the Hotel Lutetia. *What could these assholes be after?*

She moved behind them and caught Bruno's eye. With the lowering of one eyebrow and the slightest tilt of her head, she warned him to watch these two.

Bruno was a brute of a man, plump, pink faced, and stout for his sixty-four years, with huge mitts and fingers. And Bruno cared deeply for Sabina. Even to the point of having fallen in love with her. The success of the Berlin club made them both rich beyond anything they could have ever imagined, and when it seemed nothing on earth could stop them, Adolf Hitler's National Socialists came to power in 1933. Slowly, over the months and years that followed, every night became a dice roll. Brown-shirted Nazi Party storm troopers, most little more than unemployed bullies and enraptured Hitler Youth, were raiding clubs and cabarets throughout Berlin and Germany. Bruno never knew: Would the Klub l'Heure Bleue be harassed tonight? Would they even get to stay open? Or would they be closed down and remain so until huge piles of Bruno's Reichsmarks passed through dozens of Nazi officials' hands?

Two months open, two days closed. Five weeks open. Two weeks closed. With each reopening Bruno toned down the club's politics, but it was never quite enough. The club was continually harassed by these *verdammte* Nazis. Then finally, in June of 1936, Berlin's Klub l'Heure Bleue was closed for good. In anticipation of the Berlin Olympic Games, a hot summer night's parade of Hitler Youth hoodlums had marched in chanting they would cleanse the vermin dens of the German capital. With saps and sawed-off pool cues, they beat Sabina and Bruno, his girls and lady lads, and much of the clientele nearly to death. One of the hatcheck girls had even died later of her wounds. They broke sinks and commodes, crushed musical instruments, rent curtains and tablecloths, and torched a good third of the place.

The next week, Bruno and Sabina emptied their bank accounts and left Berlin forever. Bruno wanted to go to Amsterdam, another of Europe's few progressive cities at the time, but Sabina let him know he would go alone if he did. She'd vowed never to return to that dank, miserable place. So, they went to Paris. Bruno leased a failed club on the edge of the 6th arrondissement just off the Place Alphonse-Deville and opened his Paris version of the Club l'Heure Bleue. However, in Paris they were just another of the city's more than two hundred boîtes and cabarets, and average at best. Sabina's French was terrible and her thick Dutch accent crawled up the backs of her French audiences.

Then, in September 1939, when France declared war on Germany after the German invasion of Poland, Bruno was arrested and spent four months in Fresnes prison as a possible German spy. Sabina still held her Dutch papers and was left to run a nearly empty club, alone. But the war was a *drôle de guerre*, a phony war. The two enemies did little more than survey each other from either side of the Rhine, the French behind the fortifications of their new and impregnable Maginot Line, the Germans from their Siegfried Line. No shots were fired, and no offensives were attempted for almost a year. Through a sort of gamesmanship borne of boredom, the only thing that found its way across the Rhine were shouted vilifications, vulgar gestures, and ingenious and sundry ways of propelling receptacles of excrement, urine, or other disgusting concoctions across the river to the often wildly entertained enemy.

With the stealth of a lioness, Sabina moved back and forth behind the dapper SS captain. She would attack the boy from the rear, when he least expected it.

When Bruno was released from prison on Christmas Eve, 1939, he and Sabina struggled to keep the club going. For months she worked on improving her French and learning the lyrics of some of the new, popular French *chansons*. Bruno lowered the prices on his drinks and food to barely profitable margins. It was useless. A city at war with Germany, even if it was a phony war, cared nothing about a club owned by a German. Once again these Nazi bastards had ruined him. The l'Heure Bleue was a disastrous failure. On a rainy Wednesday night when the club was without a single customer, in a fit of drunken self-pity Bruno proposed marriage to Sabina and suggested they close the club, abandon his lease, and move to some nice Caribbean island or maybe to America, to start a new, quiet life together. The next morning without a word, Sabina was gone! He would never forget the day—May 9, 1940—because the next day the German army stormed its way around the impenetrable Maginot Line through neutral Belgium and Holland. This new German motorized *blitzkrieg*, or lightning attack, smashed through northern France, through the static lines of the world's largest military force, the combined French army and British Expeditionary Forces, an army comprising three million men. And within five short weeks, outnumbered ten to one, the Germans marched victorious into Paris on June 14, 1940.

And Bruno Kestler would be there to meet them with open arms. This time he would embrace these Nazi shit-asses. Every song or joke that ridiculed Adolf or his ilk would be thrown out or the lyrics changed to ridicule the defeated French or, better still, the turn tail British who tossed their weapons and war-making matériel onto the beaches of Dunkirk, high-stepped it through the swells, boarded any one of thousands of boats and dinghies, and scurried home to England.

Homosexual innuendo was *raus*! Out!

Lesbians, raus!

Raus with the politics!

Scantily clad lady lads? Raus! (The girls, of course, would stay).

This would be the perfect club for homesick German soldiers. Once they'd tried and tired of Pigalle and Crazy Horse, of the likes of the Sheherazades or Tamerins, they'd come home to the Club l'Heure Bleue. The songs, the conversation, the food, the drinks, the very smells, and even the beer they missed—all of this he would have in abundance in the Club l'Heure Bleue.

There was no way he could not be successful! But he had to find Sabina.

After looking for her for days all over Paris, Bruno was sitting in the Brasserie Lipp watching the city writhe and rush in panic, a continual growing procession of refugees pouring into and out of the city, ahead of the German advance. As the newspaper boys scampered down the boulevards shouting that the Germans had crossed the river Meuse, with everyone fully aware that nothing lay between them and Paris but the retreating French Army, suddenly Sabina reached around from behind and kissed him on the cheek, saying, "We're back in business, aren't we, *mein Schatz*?" His smile acknowledged her and she added, "And no more of this marriage foolishness, *klar*?"

"Clear," he agreed, and within weeks the club was packed with big-spending Germans, so much so that after just three days Bruno was able to have it declared for officers only. And after only two months, the Club l'Heure Bleue was expanded into the basement of the next building, a furniture store formerly leased by an Englishman, doubling its size and adding a restaurant upstairs, the Bistro Bruno, which spilled out onto the rue du Cherche-Midi on nice days, its tables overtaking the entire place Alphonse-Deville on glorious ones. Once again Sabina was on stage, and never before a more spellbound and appreciative audience.

The stoic-faced SS officer jerked slightly, startled by Sabina's warm fingers as they slid softly up the back of his neck and into his thick blond mane. The hairs on his neck, his arms, and his scrotum stood erect from the tingling rush of her touch. An involuntary double gasp from the young SS captain told her and the other SS officers at the table his heart had skipped a beat! The men laughed. The dour boy wanted to jump up, slap this old bitch; he was letting her make a fool of him, he thought. Verdammt! He was an SS Hauptsturmführer! But he realized in this venue, with all these Wehrmacht—regular army—eyes on him, such a reaction would only serve to make him look childish and bring him even further humiliation. So, he mustered a weak smile, wanting to make the impression to the others at the table that he was quite at ease with her folly. She pulled his flushed cheek to her. The side of his face was enveloped in her soft bosom. He could smell her breath as she sang on: cigarettes, garlic, and whisky, all cloaked in Jägermeister peppermint.

The muffled lyrics entered the boy's head through her breasts. Was that her heart he heard beating or his own?

She bent down and kissed his warm ear. Her tongue licked it. Tickled it. Entered it. The soldier gasped again. A warm tinge coursed through him like some fluttering bug; from his ear, through his heart and stomach, and into his groin.

Then her hot breath softly whispered, "I am *sooo* wet for you!"

Tonight, with little more than the snap of his fingers, this chiseled young SS captain could have bedded any two or three of thousands of lonely young Parisian women whose husbands or lovers had been prisoners of war in Germany for nearly a year. But when the club closed this morning, he would be in Sabina's perfumed bed. Almost every franc or Reichsmark the poor chap owned would be coaxed from him. And by noon she would be lying nude next to him on lavender sheets soaked with his slick sweat. A slight smile would come once again to her face as it had so many other times, and she would drift off once more into a deep, sated sleep.

As the song and the night came to an end, Sabina made her way back to the stage curtain and turned for the song's last verse.

The spotlight closed in on her. She threw the curtain around herself. Turned her head to her left shoulder. And raised her dainty chin.

A thrown switch. Candlelit darkness. A moment of absolute silence, peppered only with the crackling and popping of the cooling spotlight, as the violin finished the last slow, sad strains of the song.

Then, wild applause.

3

Der Major

DAY ONE—Paris—Saturday, 5 April 41—7:33 AM
The Berlin to Paris express gasped and groaned as it departed
Brussels; there would be no further stops before arrival in Gare du
Nord. Major Karl-Rudolf von Gerz relished the two hours it would
take. He had to get some sleep. Stretched out in his cabin with two
other officers, von Gerz struck an imposing figure. Average in stature,
his countenance projected him as a man who commanded most
situations in his life, even before he had donned a uniform. He had
curly hair and sculpted eyebrows that peaked as they approached the
crown of his chiseled nose. His handsome face was sleek and strong
with weary, winter-sky blue eyes and the slightest of cleft chins.

The conversation from the other officers had faded before the
train had reached the outskirts of Berlin. Finally, solitude for a few
hours sleep on the overnight train. But each time he dozed, an
explosion of pressure rocked his Pullman car, jarring him awake as
long trains with canvas-draped cargo rushed past them, stealing away
in the dark of night from France to Germany and on to Ostmark, the
eastern empire.

With each passing train, another of his loves was slammed to
mind. Including his daughter, there had really been only three women
in Major Rolf von Gerz's adult life. Two were now dead, and the
other was a Nazi tramp. He had to get them all off his mind. There
was a war to fight. Advance unit preparations to make for what could
prove to be the most decisive offensive of the war. But his mind kept
racing between his three beautiful women.

Charming Frieda. Seventeen years they were married. His
primrose memory of her was compounded with every passing day.
Six years now since her death. The face he tried to remember was the
one in the photograph he carried next to his heart, her chin resting on
a dainty hand-bridge of clasped fingers. Dazzling eyes, that lofty
smile, those cute dimples. But the face he saw in his frantic dreams
was the emaciated shell of her former, vibrant self, lying in her bed,
surrounded by her nurses. A weak heart and then *Wassersucht*, or
dropsy, her doctor called it. Six years now. And he had adjusted. He
kept himself occupied. Busy. Numb. As he would continue to do.

Another train slammed past. The car rocked. His ears popped. Tippi. Tippi Rostikov.

Only five days since her death. What was Tippi? Mistress? Love of his remaining life? Or just another British spy, brilliantly seducing her handsome Abwehr major? Potassium cyanide. Why did she wait? Why didn't he just jam the capsule in her teeth and mash her tiny jaws together? Hold her. Help her. Fucking Gestapo!

Another passing train. On the very heels of the previous one. Liesl.His daughter. The light of his life, his *little* Liesl. He couldn't even think about her now without becoming enraged. His Little Liesl, now an SS slut! And as good as dead to him as well!

He had to shake his women from his memory, from his life. And ban all new ones. Major Rolf von Gerz was a brilliant Abwehr counterintelligence agent, a distinguished Wehrmacht officer, but his fatal flaw was his constant need for the company, the adoration of a beautiful woman. He placed the blame on his mother. She had never once touched him that he could remember.

Three years old when his parents separated, they basically split young Rudolph's life in half. For the first ten years he lived with his mother in Paris. And from age five he rarely saw her, spending most of his time in developmental nurseries; kindergartens and early preparatory schools in the English and French countryside; conservatories of music, liberal arts, and history. His limited time at home in his mother's family villa in the exclusive 16th arrondissement of Paris was mostly spent in the cheerful service quarters above the garage with his governess and her husband, the gardener and chauffeur, where he learned the Polish language as well as what to him seemed a condition common only to the Polish, the warmth of a true family.

After his confirmation at age 13, Rolf had then been spirited off to Berlin, where for the next eight years his father, the Herr Oberst, or Lord Colonel, von Gerz took command of young Rudolf's upbringing, molding him into a Prussian gentleman soldier. And just as with his mother, Rolf rarely saw the man. But it was all perfectly fine. It had made him the man he was. Fluent in English, French, Polish and German. Lethal with a foil or a rapier. He could play almost any sonata, many from memory. Second in his class at academy. Fourth at university. Top of the class at officer's college. He was a strong, brilliant man. Just this one flaw. This longing for a woman's tenderness.

Major Rolf von Gerz was a pragmatic Prussian. The words of his father burned in his memory: *When we possess the insight to know our flaws and weaknesses, then so must we muster the wisdom and courage to control them.* And he would control this. He would always treasure the good fortune of his three dear loves, but there would be no more. Once he arrived in Paris, no more women, at least none with whom he could develop emotional ties. The war would take a turn in June. For better or worse? He wasn't sure. But it would require his undivided attention. He would savor his April holiday, then fight his war! Paris would be full of wonderful books, books impossible to find any longer in the Reich; French books, English, and even American books! And scores of quiet green parks and comfortable cafés in which to enjoy them. And cinema! Books and cinema would fill his free time on his Paris holiday, not women. There would be no more women in Major Rolf von Gerz's life!

He opened one eye. Buildings crawled slowly past. Squinting from the bright sunlight, he closed it again. The special express troop train from Berlin to Paris had left Berlin's Zoo Station at ten past midnight that morning, with as much commotion and fanfare as the Propaganda Ministry could create. A full trainload of Wehrmacht soldiers and officers, departing on their Paris holiday. The war was going that well for Germany that she could spare such a large number of men and advertise it to the newsreels. So many troop trains, heading west for this reason or that. Make them think that Operation Sealion, the invasion of Britain, would be imminent this summer. And take the world's eye off the clandestine buildup at the Polish border and the true target. Fall Barbarossa—Operation Barbarossa—the invasion of the Soviet Union, set for late spring. Of course, as he had just learned yesterday in Berlin, Barbarossa had now been postponed, pushed back to probably mid-June by the inept Italians in Greece and the anti-regime coup that had sprung up in Yugoslavia. *Developments in the Balkans are the Führer's top priority now. Resistance must be repulsed forthwith.*

Rolf opened an eye again and looked at his wafer-thin gold Edox watch: 7:41 AM. By habit he wound the watch. Had he even wound it yesterday? The train had slowed to a snail's pace as it pulled through some town on the outskirts of Paris. He'd probably dozed for the third time somewhere past the border. But was it even sleep? Or was it just his mind racing pell-mell through a dream world? He opened the eye again and the bright sunlight made him squint. Four cold, gloomy months in Warsaw, and he'd never once seen the sun. Paris, he thought. And with sunshine! Paris would renew him.

The last few days had been frantic. He had ordered his adjutant, Oberleutnant Gephardt Fechter, to leave Warsaw for Paris five days earlier. The young first lieutenant hadn't proffered even the slightest objection. Then Rolf could look through Tippi's things, undisturbed. *There simply had to be someone else involved,* he thought. *Someone local, perhaps in the translation staff, where she had worked. She couldn't have operated completely alone.* After two days of combing through her apartment in Warsaw, he gave up the search and released the evidence to the Gestapo.

After Tippi's death Rolf decided to detour into southwestern Poland to see his daughter. Their last visit had been Christmas at the Landjahr camp in Schneidemühl, where she was doing her compulsory year of training, learning about rural life and the process of establishing a proper rural home and garden so she could in turn teach German resettlement pioneers. She had foregone any university schooling in favor of this "new and important work for the Führer." Through her association in the Bund Deutscher Mädel, she applied for a position in *Ostraum,* the eastward expansion of Germanic peoples, through the Reich's Labor Service. Since her mother's death Liesl had been raised by the same Polish governess who had raised Rolf. Fluent, therefore, in Polish, she was now a unit leader assigned to a tiny Polish village.

Rolf had traveled by train to Krakow, where he purchased two rooms at the Hotel Europejski and requisitioned a car and driver to take him the hour's drive north to her village. Through everything he'd had been forced to coldly witness at the Warsaw Gestapo headquarters the last week with Tippi, he had been able to hold his emotions in check. But the minute he saw his daughter, he couldn't stop the tears in his tired eyes. He held her tightly to him. She was thin, but growing so womanly. *Mein Gott,* how she looked like her mother. But, as much as he loved his daughter, he hated what she was becoming.

"Poppi, I'm so happy here, doing our beloved Führer's work! Dr. Goebbels says we're not here to eradicate the Polish, just their lazy Polishness. And to help turn the Germanic Poles into good, productive *Deutsche Volk!*"

Since October she'd lived in this afterthought of a community, consisting of one block-long patchwork lane of brick and cobbles. Hers was a tiny apartment in a three-story cedar shake boarding house with a tethered cow in the yard. As proud as though she were treating him to an evening at Horscherer's in Berlin, she led him to the village market and deli. Little more than the front room of another old house, it was hardly larger than Liesl's apartment. They sat on handmade hickory chairs, nailed and leather-strapped together at a flimsy table covered with a green checkered tablecloth. They downed Afri-Colas and currywurst with very tough pierogi. And they talked. Or rather, she talked.

"Before I could teach them anything about the Führer or the Party or the German way of life, I first of all had to teach them about, of all things, toilet hygiene. *Mein Gott*, Poppi, can you imagine? Even the care of their babies. I had to teach them to wipe the little girl's bottoms backward instead of forward, away from their little *popos*. Heavens, Poppi. Can you imagine the disease?"

Rolf tried to let his delight in her happiness and enthusiasm cloak his disdain for her absolute lack of a single independent thought in that pretty head. She told him how she was charged with cleaning and disinfecting the vacated homes "of the most pitifully Slavic of them," to ready the houses for families of German pioneers who would soon resettle there. She was also charged with Germanizing the village's remaining Germanic Poles and especially their children of Aryan appearance or heritage. She had even started appearing in their school three days a week, teaching the German language and National Socialist doctrine.

With giddy enthusiasm she went on to say that the Polish families whose homes had been confiscated had been herded into agriculture camps a few kilometers away, where they would be held for use in the upcoming planting season while the legal details of acquiring their homes for the Reich were sorted out by Party lawyers.

Rolf had planned to spend a few days with her. Take her back to Krakow, for a nice dinner and a concert, Brahms' Fourth and Beethoven's Seventh, scheduled for the next night at the Wawel Kirche. But it quickly became a visit of less than an hour when Liesl told him, more in passing, almost parenthetically, "And, oh! Guess what, Poppi! I'm pregnant! Hopefully, I can give the Führer a son!"

At first Rolf was sure he hadn't heard correctly. When she repeated it, he exploded. His voice bellowed through the entire house, rattling the faded pictures on the wall, even the loose windowpanes danced in their frames. Upstairs, footsteps and creaking floors could be heard as everyone in the house rushed down the stairs and out the front door. The things he said to her: "your place of privilege in

42

Berlin society, abandoned and squandered . . . wasting your life in this pigsty of a village . . . National Socialist lemming . . . Nazi whore . . . SS slut!" Yet, she remained so calm and succinct in her retorts to each of his insults, just as her mother used to do, talking to him as though she were trying to calm some cranky child.

"But I don't know his name, Poppi. He was with the SS garrison in the next village. And I am nineteen now. Not eighteen. I had a birthday. You sent me that lovely card and beautiful *Schokoladentorte* from Warsaw. Remember?"

He was so angry he couldn't hold thoughts in his head. His heart raced. Chest ached. And the rage within him was being further fueled by this incessant composure she was able to maintain! He stood, but had to steady himself against the wall. He was afraid he was going to faint, or start wailing like some woman. He wanted to grab her beautiful neck and shove his leather gloves down her throat.

"But you don't need to worry, Poppi. You won't have to ever see him. Neither, for that matter, will I."

Instead, he just rushed past her, needing to get away from her before he killed her! But she followed him, continuing her haughty and vexing civility.

"I'll simply go on holiday in Bavaria this summer; they'll help me birth the little dear. They have wet nurses and everything. Then he will be taken and raised for the Reich. I thought you'd be happy for me, Poppi. Dr. Goebbels says it's our duty as good German women, you know."

His driver had jumped out of the automobile and snapped to attention when he saw Rolf storming out of the house. The last thing he remembered was shouting at the driver to "start that fucking machine!"

From Krakow, Rolf had spent two days in Berlin at Tirpitzufer, Abwehr army intelligence headquarters. He briefed his constituents on the capture—and suicide—of the *Warschau Fuchs*, the Warsaw Fox—one Tippi Rostikov, a sophisticated and erudite White Russian and one of the most elusive spies of the war so far. He had written the report a number of times on the long train ride from Krakow, had even disembarked the train in Prague for a few hours to walk the city and put his story together . . . more plausibly. All the while, thoughts haunted him of his adorable little girl being covered by some ghoulish SS peasant.

He learned in Berlin that along with his well-deserved holiday, he was also being given an assignment in Paris to serve as a consultant on Operation Felix, a military contingency planning the German invasion of Gibraltar. Spanish president Franco had refused to allow the Germans to attack through Spain, so Rolf was to help brainstorm another attack plan, Fall Blau, Condition Blue, an attack from the Mediterranean. His orders further stated the he was to take his holiday in Paris and report back to Berlin at 0800 hours on 28 April, where he would work with other Abwehr officers in preparation for an important Barbarossa meeting scheduled for 2 May in Krampnitz near Potsdam. So, now as he arrived in Paris, there were just twenty-two days left.

The cabin door opened abruptly.

"Major von Gerz! My old friend." SS/SD Sturmbannführer Alois Kruder motioned for the junior officers in the berth to dismiss themselves so he could sit across from Rolf and converse in private.

"I was always led to believe," Kruder continued, in his high-pitched, sinister voice as he brushed the leather seat off with his gloves and took a seat, "that cyanide was painless. Isn't that what they always told us, von Gerz? But have you ever watched someone die from cyanide poisoning?" Kruder parted the closed blind to peer outside. "This Rostikov woman of yours. Terrible. Watching her succumb to that cyanide capsule. You should have seen it, major. Absolutely barbaric."

"Much to your delight, no doubt," Rolf said, never opening his eyes. *Gestapo peasant!* he thought.

"Imagine my surprise. I boarded the train in Dortmund and passed by this berth, I don't know, four or five times now, completely unaware that you were even on board, cuddled up in here all nice and cozy."

Rolf said nothing, hoping Kruder would take offense and leave.

"Yes, Herr Major. I do delight in watching a criminal British spy die." Kruder settled further into his seat and removed his hat, tossing his gloves into it. "Although, I must admit, not as much when she turns out to be such a beautiful woman. But I am certain to see many more of them do so over what should no doubt be my long and illustrious career in our Thousand-Year Reich."

"Alois Kruder. The patriot." Rolf sat up and stretched the stiffness out of his neck and knees. "Why were you even in Warsaw? When I last saw you in Amsterdam, you told me you'd been posted to Paris."

"I go where I am needed, major."

"Doesn't speak well for your Warsaw comrades."

"So, you're having me on, then, are you major?"

"Anytime, Sturmbannführer." One corner of Rolf's mouth smiled as he added, "It would almost be worth the jail sentence."

"We must be civil to one another, major. We're on the same team, you know."

"I wonder."

"Now, major. I understand you were very close to this woman. She spoke quite highly of you. Told us that you were even seeing her socially."

"As you well know, I was feeding her disinformation. I had been doing so for months until you and your clumsy cowboys arrested her."

"Possibly. And possibly when we forced her hand, you were as surprised as she was." An empty cigarette holder bounced in his slit of a mouth as he continued. "You boys in your little Abwehr club are very efficient, aren't you? Catch a spy and issue her a cyanide capsule in case any real policemen catch on to her."

"I'm sure any capsule she had was issued by the British."

"All of us in the service of the Reich's security—the SD, the Gestapo, and even the intelligence apprentices in the Abwehr—are issued the same glass cyanide capsule, major. If you were a perceptive man, you'd have noticed the tiny moniker imprinted on the end of the glass. It seems her tiny jaw wasn't able to crush it completely, leaving us with that very profound evidence."

"I don't need your tutelage on a Reich-issued cyanide capsule, Kruder. If it was one of ours, then it probably fell out of your pocket when you bent over to kiss Heydrich's ass!"

Kruder snickered at the levity.

"I invested four months in that woman," Rolf went on to say. "I was close to learning her system, learning of any accomplices. All of which could have been of great value to the war effort."

"Perhaps you were." Kruder took the holder and twisted a Trommler cigarette into it, adding, "After all, she worked right there under your noses for months, didn't she, major? How embarrassing that must have been for the Abwehr, our great Prussian boys' choir. Perhaps you had to hurry up and subject her to the cyanide to cover your ineptitude . . . or even something else?"

"Face it, Alois." Rolf sat forward and looked Kruder in the eye. "We discovered her months before you or your cronies knew anything about her. We uncovered and penetrated her operation and used it to send phony information for much of the winter, and you and your henchmen never had even a clue what was going on until my adjutant made that phone call on your bloody tapped phone!"

"Oh, but no reason to get nasty, major." Kruder turned his head to the side and lit his cigarette, but his eyes never left Rolf's.

Mercifully, the train crept into Gare du Nord. Rolf stood and draped his coat over his arm, saying, "Hopefully, I'll see you in Paris, Kruder. We can continue this meaningless banter."

"Just one last question, major. We searched this woman very thoroughly when she was arrested. Inside and out, as one might say. We never found any capsule. I was wondering, with your *deep* affection for this woman, perhaps you could tell me where she might have—"

"That's enough, Alois!" Rolf said, sternly.

"I so enjoy this cat-and-mouse game with you, major. Too bad it's over . . . for now."

Rolf pulled his bags from the overhead rack and started out the door.

"The Abwehr fraternity house in Paris is the Hotel Lutetia, von Gerz," Kruder added, trying to stay up with Rolf. "I assume you'll be staying there. I'm told there's a club nearby that is all the rage with the Wehrmacht."

Rolf was out of the train and on the platform before the wheels had fully stopped. A swarm of field gray soldiers poured from the train like disturbed ants as Kruder shouted after him, "Perhaps I'll see you there!"

"Major von Gerz!" a voice called out. "Major! Over here, sir." A smile grew on Rolf's face as he spotted Oberleutnant Gephardt Fechter. He had grown fond of his adjutant over the past year, first in Holland and then in Warsaw. Oberleutnant Fechter was a sinuous sort with a chiseled face and a ruddy complexion. And he was a brilliant young intelligence officer. It had been Gep who had actually first shed light on the fact that Tippi might very well be the spy they had been searching for. In having the Abwehr intelligence analysts at Zossen lay out typing examples from each girl working in the translation Abteil and comparing them, he had uncovered a consistent mistake in Tippi's first few weeks of typing that didn't exist at all in examples of her later work. In the former she had repeatedly and incorrectly hit the *Y* key instead of the *Z* key on her typewriter. The first line of keys on a German typewriter spells QWERZ, unlike QWERTY on an English language typewriter. It was reason to suspect her. It had also put a strain on Gep's relationship with Rolf for a short time, until he tested her with some phony information and discovered from Abwehr agents in London the information had been passed along.

Outside in the warm spring sun, Gep motioned for the driver. "So, how's your daughter, major?"

Rolf rubbed the sunlight's sting from his eyes with his fingertips, trying to fully awaken himself. "The Führer would be very proud of her, Gep."

"But not her father?"

Rolf shrugged as they both ducked into the backseat and the driver stowed the bags in the boot. "What a waste of a beautiful and intelligent young girl."

"I'm quite sorry, major."

Rolf looked out the window. "What a glorious day."

"It's the first sunshine I've seen since I arrived. You brought it with you."

"There hasn't been any sunshine in my life for some time, Gep, my friend."

The car pulled away from the station and headed down the nearly deserted rue La Fayette. Rolf's memories of Paris from his childhood were of a city bustling with people and traffic. Now it seemed like a sad ghost, nearly devoid of life in the midmorning sun.

"Everything is arranged for you at the hotel, major."

"The Lutetia, I understand?"

"Yes, it's Abwehr headquarters, but they have maintained a few of the rooms for guests. Yours is a small suite."

"When is my briefing scheduled for Operation Felix?"

"Ach," Gep exclaimed. "You haven't heard. Our friend Felix is dead! Teletype came this morning. Direct from General Student. Operation Felix postponed again. Can't understand why. All the work we've done on Felix and Sealion. And then to just drop them. Something big must be up."

Rolf knew now why Felix was dead. Along with Sealion—the invasion of Britain—and a number of other contingencies. It was no doubt why there had been no declaration of war on America after FDR signed the Lend-Lease Act. It all came down to one word: Barbarossa. Gep was not yet privy to Fall Barbarossa, so Rolf quickly changed the subject.

"I hear there's a famous club near the hotel?"

"The l'Heure Bleue. Amazing place. There's a woman who sings there. Greta Garbo eyes, Lale Andersen's voice. Superb."

"So, you're already bored with the place?"

"Not at all, sir. I haven't been there yet. I hit the Scheherazade and Crazy Horse on my first few nights in town!"

"Then it's the l'Heure Bleue tonight for us, my friend."

"I guess you'll want to rest after your long trip, Herr Major?"

"And waste this wonderful sunshine? Not at all, Gep. I want to report in, throw my grip in my room, and splash some water in my face while you find us a nice sunny café. We'll order a bottle of Beaujolais, a couple of big Cubans, and spend the whole afternoon *sitzen und schwitzen*, sittin' and sweatin'! And that's an order, Oberleutnant!"

"Jawohl, Herr Major!"

DAY ONE—Paris—Saturday, 5 April 41 9:51 AM

"Rolf von Gerz, you old fighter!" Rolf had barely made his way into the black-and-gold marble-columned lobby of the Hotel Lutetia before he heard the voice coming from the bank of phones to his right.

"Hans-Hubert, you old dog!" Major Johann-Hubert von Hirschbach was an old university chum with whom Rolf had attended both officers college and intelligence school. Tall and thin, Hans was a dashing figure who always struck an erect, confident pose. As was the fashion of the day for young men with dark hair and features, he sported a hairline mustache that he accentuated with a pair of reading monocles attached to a small gold chain extending from a button on his tunic.

"Welcome to paradise, old friend." Hans handed some papers to the gray-aproned female assistant at his side and flicked her on her way with his fingers.

"You fellows *do* know there's a war going on?" Rolf quipped, pressing Hans' hand and grabbing his elbow.

"Why yes, but of course, the French women retreat every morning, but they're quite resilient, old chum. They regroup and wage a counterattack every night!"

"I'm certain you've taken a few prisoners."

"Indeed. But they're very tight-lipped, these gals from Gaul. Ultimately, however, I'm usually able to"—he raised his rascal eyebrows—"penetrate their defenses!"

Fall Irmgard

Rolf laughed and patted Hans on the shoulder. "You old scoundrel. We'll have to catch up, my unforgettable old friend."

"Afternoon briefing at six, old man. Cocktails at six-o-two! See you there."

Once he was shown to his room, which overlooked a cozy green courtyard, Rolf shed his tunic and blouse, drew back the drapes, and opened the tall double windows. The crisp spring morning felt good on this damp flesh. He went into the tiny bathroom, doused water on his upper torso, lathered his chest and underarms with soap, and washed himself. *Mein Gott,* how he needed sleep. But he mustn't. The day was too lovely. He ran cold water over his head, massaged his fingers into his scalp, and splashed water into his eyes. As he dried off he dropped an eyebrow and cocked his head to one side. He could hear faint music coming from the courtyard. Jazzy music. American jazz! *Niggermusik*, the Nazis called it, outlawed in the Reich for years. It was absolutely wonderful! Paris was like awakening from a bad dream, especially after repressive Warsaw. Except for a brief visit to his mother before she died, Rolf hadn't been in Paris since he was thirteen.

He went back to the window. The catchy tune brought a smile to his face and started his fist to bouncing back and forth to its beat, albeit with an all-too-German awkwardness, the same way it would if it were holding a stein of beer in some Berlin Stube. Searching for the music's source in the courtyard's many windows, he lit an Ernst Udet, took a deep draw from it, and blew the lingering smoke out into the courtyard's still morning air.

Then he saw her.

In the open window across the way, in the next building's courtyard and one floor below him, he could see the figure of a young woman wearing nothing but a lacy lavender brassiere and matching half-slip. She had her back to him, looking into a full-length mirror, holding a white dress covered with tiny red dots in front of her. He could just make out her face in the mirror's image. *Wie wunderschöne*, he thought. *How very beautiful*. She spun around and held the dress against her backside, looking over her shoulder into the mirror again to get a perspective from the rear. Her brunette hair was pulled up in an ivory comb at the back of her head, but a few ribbons of hair had loosed themselves and hung down over her left eye and at her temples, turning shades of chestnut and auburn in the sunlight. The attractive brunette was talking to someone else in the room. She

49

was a very thin thing, but her bosom filled the brassiere to nearly overflowing. When she turned around, she immediately noticed Rolf. Startled at first, she covered herself with the dress. Then slowly, she dropped her arms and just glared at him, defiantly.

Time froze between them across the courtyard's peaceful calm. They stared at each other for an uncomfortable, glorious eternity. Then, methodically, never taking her eyes off him, this beautiful creature slowly drew the drapes.

And the wonderful jazzy music stopped.

4

Madame Bellier

DAY ONE—Paris—Saturday, 5 April 41—8:53 AM
Madame Bellier bounced and kicked her bony self from her right side
to her left on the old canvas cot next to the living-room wall. Her
flannel gown, the muslin sheet, and the purple crocheted throw all
wadded and wrapped themselves more tightly around her. Particles of
dust rose from the commotion like disturbed gnats and glistened,
swirling in the sheets of morning sunlight that sliced through the
window blinds. She shouldn't be listening anyway, she thought. But
she shouldn't be sleeping, either. It was late morning. Madame Bellier
had work to get out. It was Saturday morning. Her customers would
need their crisply ironed shirts and collars and kerchiefs for their
Saturday night soirées. Of course, a few moments' sleep would do her
some good; she hadn't slept all night. Because *they* hadn't slept all
night. But Mélina was madame's only daughter. She had to know.
Know everything. So, she unwrapped herself again and rolled back to
her side, cupped her tiny hand to her ear, and put it against the wall.
Again, they were at it. *Sacrébleu.* The panting. The pounding. The
infernal screeching song of the old bedsprings. *Are they rabbits?* she
thought.
      Madame Bellier hated the Germen. All the Germen. But if
there was one German she should hate above all others, it would be
this big, redheaded *Boche* that lay in the bed in the next room, having
his way with her daughter, her married daughter! And in Madame
Bellier's bed, no less! All night long she'd listened to their whispers,
wails of passion, whimpers of longing. She could hear every word,
every groan and gasp. But not once had she heard Mélina tell him.
Madame knew she wouldn't tell him. There was still time. His train
didn't leave until eleven. Mélina should tell him. Tell him now. Get it
over with.
      "I want to die. I can't go on. I can't live without you."
      "My love, you must be strong. You must be strong for both of
us."
      Madame could hear the German getting out of the bed.
      "If you're going to marry a German officer, you must quit
being so damn French! Use your heart for loving, but use your head

for living! This war can't last another year. The Englander can't make it through another winter. You have to stay alive for me, just as I will do my best to stay alive for you. But I'm just saying, if something should happen to me, you know what to do. Go to Herr Ritter and . . ."

"Darling, shh," Mélina said. "Maman can hear. She has a watchdog's ear."

"She's sound asleep. I will take care of you. I will take care of you and your mother. But you must be strong while I am away."

Madame wiped a tear from her eye. It was just from being up all night. Her fatigue was letting her emotions escape from her. She turned her head away from the wall. She did indeed hate all the Germen. But not this one. Not this dear, wonderful man, this Ruti. Mélina's Ruti. And he would have gladly married Mélina months ago if he could have, but the German general had forbidden it. German soldiers were not allowed to take French wives. And besides, Mélina was still officially married. But when Ruti returned from the war, they'd go to Switzerland. That was their plan.

Suddenly, Ruti entered the room, naked as the day he was born, and went into the bathroom. Madame could see him through the web of crocheted yarn in the throw over her head. He peed a forceful stream that resonated loudly though the entire flat, perhaps the whole building could even . . . *Jesus and Mother Mary*, Madame thought. There he stood, completely exposed to her, scratching his scrotum. Surely he couldn't see her open eyes through the throw. *Mon Dieu, the boy is a chestnut stallion!*

Her composure regained, she reached her tiny hand under the cot and touched the two cases of wine hidden there under the quilt. Madame had busied herself every evening before she retired hiding all the wonderful bounty *cher* Ruti had bestowed on them. A half-meter wheel of Camembert and a full wooden case of Pont l'Évêque was stacked behind the towels in the linen closet, along with two brown paper bundles of fragrant charcuterie bound in string netting, and a pair of huge *jambon du pays* smoked hams. At the back of every drawer or cabinet in the little flat lay one or two of the seventeen cartons of American cigarettes, Chesterfields, another Ruti miracle. Such things could be sold or traded to get them through next winter if the need presented itself. For it would be a winter without their *chevalier allemand*, their cher Ruti, who had kept them relatively warm and their bellies full when most other Parisians were suffering so. But even more important, behind the photos in her family album she had carefully folded and hidden the 4300 francs, 160 unrestricted Reichsmarks, and four ration booklets. As she looked across the front room, lined with racks of freshly ironed clothes and paper-wrapped shirts and dresses, standing at its place of honor in the center of her mantle was her new electric iron, another, and probably the most important of cher Ruti's many gifts. No longer would she have to wait for her six stove irons to warm, the terrible heat wilting her and every other living thing in her tiny flat during the summer.

No, Madame hated the Germen, but she hated to see this German leave. As much as Mélina, she wished he could stay in Paris forever. This man knew how to take care of his women. If he were only French, and *Catholic*, he'd be the perfect man! He was nothing like that miserable dog Maurice, Mélina's husband. And so, Madame had to admit, there was another German she had at least some regard for. The German who fired the shell into the forest of Sedan that blew Mélina's Maurice into a million bloody pieces last year. That German will always be in Madame's prayers, along with cher Ruti. God must somehow forgive her for her hatred of this beast, Maurice. He didn't marry Mélina, he enslaved her, whipped her with that strap like she was a misbehaving horse. "Missing in Action." That's what the war department said! Phooey on them! All they found of the hideous Maurice was his bloody ID plate. If they would only pronounce him dead, Mélina could draw his pension!

Madame knew she should also give thanks to Mother Mary each night that her husband, Monsieur Bellier, wasn't alive to learn that such treatment had befallen his only daughter. Why, Monsieur would have sliced Maurice's belly open like the hogs he butchered for ten years at Abattoir Le Clair. No, just like this German boy, Monsieur Bellier knew how to take care of his women. He died at Vimy defending them in the Great War, when Mélina was just a baby. Unlike these modern-day Frenchmen. Phooey on them, anyway. Cowards one and all! How on earth did over a million French soldiers surrender? This is what the other women in her parish said, under their breath, of course. Over a million prisoners of war in Germany, and their poor women, some of them must beg on the street . . . or worse. Why, in her husband's day 999,000 would have died defending France and her women and children, before the rest would even consider surrender. But these modern Frenchmen, well, phooey on them all. They were . . .

"Why in the name of God almighty didn't you tell me before now?"

It was Ruti, shouting, making the whole house tremble.
Madame sat up in the cot, thinking, *Mon Dieu, she must have finally told him!*

"I didn't want to burden you. I didn't want you to be off God-only-knows-where"—she stopped to sob and catch her breath—"and have to be worried about me *and the baby.*" Madame could hear his footsteps scurrying around the room. Now there was hopping. "Why are you getting dressed? You don't love me anymore because I'm pregnant. You're going to leave me, forever. Oh, no. No!"

"You know I love you, Mélina. You are my life. But now our child is also my life. Can you understand that? You spring this on me in our last hour together. I have to make further arrangements. There's more to think of than just us."

"But what about me?"

A loud knock came at the front door. Madame sprang like a cat from the cot and stubbed her toe as she hurried, then hopped over to answer it.

"Go away!" she whispered, forcefully.

Another loud knock. Ruti entered the room, mostly dressed this time. He grabbed the door handle. "Madame," he politely said, as he moved her aside and opened the door.

Before them stood a ten to twelve-year-old boy with a flat cap and an envelope in his hands. He stepped back, startled by the big uniformed German.

"Message for Madame Mélina Vaugeois?"

"I'll take it," Ruti said, stepping out in the hallway and closing the door behind him. Madame raised the blind on the window just enough to see Ruti hand the boy a five-franc coin and tell him, "Wait for me downstairs, and there will be a lot more of this for you."

The boy's eyes lit up. "But of course, monsieur!"

Ruti returned to the bedroom, and Madame Bellier hopped straight back to her cot, her sore ear pressed hard against the wall.

"It's from Addie, the American girl who introduced us." Mélina sniffled. She was a small girl, like her mother, with her father's blond, nearly white hair. Through her sniffles and sobs, she continued. "She wants me to come over to her apartment this afternoon, after your departure."

"That's good, *Liebling.* You should go. I want you to go."

"Yes, that's good, Ruti. That's wonderful. Because she's going home tomorrow to America. So, two of the most important people in my life are leaving me. Leaving me forever!" She dropped the letter and her shoulders wilted as she threw her head back and gave herself up to her tears. Her robe slid down her arms and into a pile around her heels.

Ruti finished dressing and watched his beautiful young darling— red, swollen eyes and love marks and grief shingles in rosy splotches all over her delicate body—lose complete control of herself. Fully dressed, he moved in front of her. She seemed startled as though awakened from a nightmare, then threw herself around him.

"Ruti, we have an hour. You must give me this hour; it's our last together!"

"It is no longer our hour, my love. It belongs to our child. There are things I must do now, before I leave. As a mother, you must give the hour to me, to our baby. None of this will be any easier an hour from now. Quit being a selfish little girl and be a strong mother, for me. For your child, Mélina." He reached in his bag and pulled out a framed sepia-tone picture they'd taken together a fortnight ago at Studio Harcourt. On the back of it he'd handwritten something.

He started reading, but threw the frame on the bed, looked into her eyes, and recited his tender message to her instead.

You hold my heart in your dainty palm,
No matter where, how far or how long,
I'm gone.

Ruti kissed Mélina and held her naked body tightly in his arms. She sobbed. He gritted his teeth. Slowly, he slid down the soft flesh of her torso to his knees and kissed her stomach. "Ruti, why?" Mélina wailed, forcing her fingers through his curly red hair. "Why does God do this to people?" Quickly he stood up, took her face in his hands, and kissed her, a long, agonizing kiss as though it could stop time and be etched in the hard granite of their memory forever. He kissed her until his lips burned from her tears and the hot breath of her sobs. Then he pulled away from her and held her out before him.

"All my love, Mélina. Forever!" he said, and he quickly tossed his bag on his shoulder, picked up the heavy suitcase next to the bed, turned his back to her, and left the bedroom. Sobs became a scream as she threw herself onto the bed. He stormed into the front room and stopped suddenly. Not turning around, his hand reached out toward the cot. Madame Bellier poked her tear-soaked kerchief deeply into her palm with her thumb and touched her trembling finger to his.

"Madame. Adieu," he said. And Wehrmacht Leutnant Rutgers Heht went out the front door, down the squeaky stairs, and into the sunny Paris morning wondering how on earth he'd let his life become so complicated. Now all of his plans must change. Everything must be moved up. Now, there were even more loose ends he had to tie up before he caught his train, *five* hours from now.

5

Meine Freundin die Ami
Mon ami l'Ami
My Friend the American

DAY ONE—Paris—Saturday, 5 April 41—10:03 AM
"You like it? It's the newest thing from America," Adelaide Bridges
said, turning the volume knob up on the record player. "Well, it was
new last summer. I bought it before things became so horribly
impossible. But do you like it?" She took her dress off over her head
and continued talking while trapped in the process. "Isn't it just the
cat's meow? It's 'Shorty George' by Count Basie."

"It's divine, belle amie," Yvette Debonnet said, helping her
with the dress and tossing it on the huge pile on the bed. Yvette was a
tall girl with a long, pleasant face and dishwater blond hair, rolled
under in an inverted delta behind her head. "What about this one? Are
you sure it is too big for you?"

Addie Bridges held up the summer sundress, white cotton with
red Swiss dots. "I've lost at least two dress sizes since our German
friends arrived. So many of these wonderfully expensive ensembles
just swallow me . . ." She took the dress to the mirror and held it up to
herself. Addie was a twenty-seven-year-old all-American beauty with
brunette hair curled and pulled up in ivory combs in bunches on top
of her head. Her eyes were a brilliant brown with naturally long dark
eyelashes. She had dimpled cheeks, pouty Betty Boop lips, and a cute
upturned nose, the tip of which danced with each word she spoke.
"But I do so love this little number." She turned around and held it
behind her, glancing over her shoulder in the mirror to see how it
looked from behind.

"I'm just certain it would be a tent on me. I'm so tiny now,
Yvette. It would make me look like one of those poor dears that prowl
behind the Gare du Nord. But you're so wonderfully tall; on you,
Yvette, it would look simply divine. You might just let out the hem
and—" Addie gasped and quickly swung the dress around in front of
her. Across the courtyard she could see a man, naked from the waist
up, staring at her from his window. A rush of defiance suddenly
coursed through her, and she slowly dropped the dress and stared

back boldly at the man. He was, after all, quite dashing. Slowly, she pulled the drape closed, never taking her eyes off him.

"What is it, Addie?"

"Nothing, just a Peeping Tom from the Lutetia." She turned off the record player and handed the dress to Yvette. Addie pointed to the bedside table where a huge ivory Philco tabletop radio sat next to the lamp. "Do be a dear and switch on the radio, please." Yvette pushed her palms into the mattress, walked her rump over to the head of the bed, and did so. A pop, a few cracks, and Jean Sablon's faint voice singing "Vous Qui Passez Sans Me Voir" grew louder as the radio tubes warmed. Addie was slipping into some red pleated pants. She stopped. A ragdoll slump and a longing smile came to her pretty face. "Oh, that reminds me so of the good days in Paris, Yvette, before everything turned to *merde!*" Her eyes grew wide as she said the French word for *shit*. She wriggled into a peasant blouse and added, "I'm so very glad you could come over this morning, Yvette." A gesture at her wrecked apartment, where every inch of floor was covered with piles and stacks of books, fashion magazines, phonograph records, and mountains of clothing. "There is simply no way I can pack all of these blasted things now."

"When did they tell you, belle amie?" Yvette sat on the bed and pulled her knees up to her chin, resting her cheek on them.

"I found out only yesterday afternoon when the livery men delivered the crates." She pointed to the two slatted wooden crates in the center of the floor.

"Two shipping crates into which I must pack six years of cherished Paris memories. It's simply barbaric, Yvette! These hideous Germans and their beastly war!" She pulled the letter from its envelope and showed it to Yvette.

Thursday 3 April, 1941

My dear Ms. Bridges,
My most humble apologies, as I must inform you that although your steamer from Lisbon to Havana departing on 1 May allows four (4) in-hold shipping crates for their luxury-class guests, unfortunately (as I have only this day discovered) your Danish vessel from Cherbourg to Lisbon departing on this coming Monday allows for none (0)! I was, however, through much and quite difficult negotiation, able to convince

*them to allow you two (2) crates in-hold. For this
concession, regretfully, they will require an
additional 800 francs payable to the shipping
chandler upon boarding. (Not to worry, as he shall
forward to me my commission.)
Merci & bon voyage,
M. Jacques van Brunt
Agent de voyage*

"That man is an utter shit, Yvette!" Addie exclaimed. "I could
just scratch his eyes out! This is nothing but highway robbery. I am
absolutely convinced this Monsieur van Brunt has been the one who
has sabotaged every aspect of my travel plans since day one, and not
them like he always says, rolling those big ugly eyeballs, not even
having the guts to call *them* Germans!" Addie looked at her friend
with teeth clenched. "Geez! I could just scream, Yvette! I'm not
going to get away from this miserable country with ten francs in my
purse!"

"Belle amie, you know I'll gladly give you all I can," Yvette
whined.

"Oh, no, darling! No." Addie put her arms around Yvette and
hugged her. "You dear, swell girl, that's not what I meant. Not at all.
I'm just angry. I don't need any money. Well . . ." She mimicked a
cute, wide-eyed Betty Hutton face she'd seen in the movies, rocking
her head back and forth and adding, "Now, as a matter of fact, I just
very well may!"

They both laughed and she added, "No, darling, I invited you
over because as you can see now there is simply no way I can take
everything I'd planned. Why, I have over forty pairs of shoes. And
that brings up another problem. What on earth am I going to do with
little Fifi? She has such a fragile constitution. How will she hold up
on the trip?" The little Yorkie heard her name, scampered across the
room, and leapt into Addie's lap.

"She's a dog, Addie. She'll be fine."

"You think so? I was going to ask if you'd keep her."

"You know I would, chère amie. But I can barely keep my
daughter fed."

"Forgive me, Yvette. Such a crass girl! How rude of me." She
could see tears welling in Yvette's eyes. "Don't worry, darling. Your
sweet husband will be released soon and you'll be fine. I just know
it."

"I so wish you could stay, belle amie. I'll be so lonely without you."

"As will I, Yvette. You're such a swell friend." Addie gave her a hug and wiped a tear from Yvette's cheek with the hem of a wool skirt on the bed. "But I absolutely must go, Yvette. That dastardly Mr. Roosevelt and his wicked Lend-Lease conspiracy with Britain. I just know it will lead America into this dreadful war. Every morning for weeks now I have bounded from my bed to check the early edition, quite certain I'll read that Herr Hitler has declared war on America. I shudder to even think about it. And now! Last week that horrible Mr. Roosevelt confiscated all those German ships. And my daddy can't send me another cent! The US treasury has blocked transfers to German-occupied Europe. If I do get out of France, it's going to be just under the wire. This all makes me a nervous wreck, Yvette. I need a drink!"

In the tiny kitchen she poured two small glasses of Amontillado. Handing one to Yvette she continued, "Oh! And this you haven't heard. You know Gretl, the German girl that works at the Foreign Office in the Hotel Lutetia? Addie placed her hand on Yvette's forearm. "You absolutely mustn't repeat this to anyone, but she told me the entire coastline from the Pas de Calais to the Pyrenees is going to be closed off next week and become a restricted zone like the *Departement du Nord* is now! If it happens tomorrow, I won't be able to get to Cherbourg to catch my freighter for Lisbon without some special *Ausweis* permit that would probably have to be signed by old Adolf himself. Gretl thinks it will be midweek. But I'm so afraid, darling; it seems that everything is just closing in around me."

As they returned to the living room, Yvette sipped her sherry and asked, "Why don't you just go tonight?"

"I would if I could, but my travel permit is good only for Sunday. Besides, I'd miss the little fete the German girls have put together for me at the l'Heure Bleue tonight. You *are* going, aren't you? Tell me you are!"

"Oh, belle amie, I hate that place so," Yvette said, folding the clothes Addie had given to her and stacking them on the bed. "So many Germans. Would they even let me in?"

"I'll leave your name with the doorman, yours and Mélina's. Tell him you're there for my bon voyage party. He'll let you in."

"I'll come, Addie. But only for you and only for an hour or so."

"You're a swell girl, Yvette. And my dearest friend of all," Addie declared as she helped Yvette stuff clothes in a laundry sack.

"I sent a message with that little rascal downstairs to tell Mélina she should come here straightaway just as soon as Ruti leaves. When the boy gets back, I'll get him to carry off the clothes we've collected for you."

"What about this pile?" Yvette asked, pointing to a haphazardly constructed mountain of clothes in the room's corner.

"I'm saving those for Mélina. They're just some dowdy old things. I lamented over giving her some of my nicer things, but I'm afraid doing so may cause her undue ridicule from that bourgeois lot she runs with. I'm giving her my bicycle though. She can sell that old rattletrap she uses."

"Mélina is well below our class, *chérie*."

"She's barely of the working class, much less ours. What do you think, Yvette? Would I cause her grief if I gave her some of my finer things? My daddy says that when you give peasants a taste of the finer life, it only serves to bring them misery when they realize they'll never see so splendid a life again."

"I don't know that her clothes would be the worst of her problems. You do realize Mélina is pregnant."

"Take that back, you beastly girl." Addie gave her wrist the slightest slap.

"No, belle amie. It's true. The big German is the father. The little dear will be a *Boche* baby. A little redheaded goose-stepper!"

"Does she have family in some far-off part of France where she can go away and birth the little bastard?"

"No, she has no one. Her poor mother will probably have to midwife for her. She'll be shunned and ridiculed throughout her neighborhood and parish. You should have never introduced her to the German, Addie. To be frank, you never should have brought her into our circle of friends."

"I know, Yvette. But when I saw her in that line at the Kommandantur Office, the poor dear had been there for three days. I just fell hopelessly in love with her."

"Paris is full of 'Mélinas', Addie."

"I know, mon chère. And God bless them. And God bless you, Yvette. You're such a strong woman. And God bless dear little Claudette."

Yvette had married her childhood sweetheart four years earlier and given birth to their daughter, Claudette, ten months later. Her husband, Claude, who was called up when war was declared two years ago in September, had been taken prisoner last June and had spent the last ten months in a POW camp in the Rhineland.

"How will we ever get through next winter without you, belle amie?"

"Oh, darling, the war will be over by then. You know me, I'm just an old worry wart. America has stayed out of the war for nearly two years. Who am I to think they'll ever enter it? Those poor British souls could never hold out another winter. And when it is over, there will be coal enough for warm, cozy toes every night, plates full of hot beef and pork, mounds of butter, and cases of wine, enough bounty for three full meals a day! Won't that be glorious?"

"Mon chère, belle amie. I'm going to miss you so much." The trembling in her lower lip moved immediately to her pretty chin, and she burst into tears, holding a green sweater to her face.

Addie sat next to her, embraced her, and started crying herself. "I'm going home, Yvette. I'm so happy! Please be happy for me."

"I am happy for you. Are you happy?"

"Of course I'm happy."

"Then why are we crying, Addie?" Yvette asked looking up, tears rolling down her cheeks.

"You're right. We must stop this, immediately. We have work to do!" Addie smiled and her own lip started quivering as she added, "Besides, that sweater's alpaca!"

They laughed and Yvette stood up. "It's after ten. You don't have much time. I'll help you pack." She walked over to the six tall stacks of phonograph records in the floor. "What about these phonograph records?" She picked one up and its stack tumbled over and spilled across the floor.

"Damnit, Yvette!" Addie rushed over to her and took the record from her, adding, "Please, forgive me, darling. But these records are my most treasured possessions. You mustn't even touch them. You just can't imagine how important they are to me. I'll pack them myself."

The girls hadn't worked more than twenty minutes when a knock came at Addie's door. A tall, regal woman in a Red Cross cap, cloak, and lapel pin greeted them as the door opened. Her hair was perfectly coiffed, her nails manicured, her shoes were saddle-throated beige leather of the quality and fashion very few could afford nowadays. The Red Cross wasn't this woman's job, Addie quickly surmised. It was her pastime. There were now so many of these noble souls in France. She was probably some countess or baroness, volunteering for the Red Cross as a way to do her part, and to keep from going mad, while her husband, the count, had been locked away in some prisoner of war camp in Germany for nearly a year. The stately and very charming woman was winded and seemed befuddled. The faintest hint of steam rose from her shoulders.

"I'm looking for Madame Vaugeois, Madame Mélina Vaugeois. Would either of you be Mélina Vaugeois, or if not, is she here?"

Yvette was behind Addie, draped around her like a cape, her arms around Addie's waist, her cheek against Addie's ear.

"I'm so terribly sorry," Addie responded, "but no. She's not here."

"Her mother, one Madame Bellier, was quite sure she was coming here."

"Indeed, she is," Yvette said.

"But she has yet to arrive," Addie added.

"Oh, my," the woman said, looking at her tiny diamond watch attached with a looped gold chain to her cloak. "It's past eleven. I biked all the way here from the 18th." She raised her eyebrows, "if you can imagine. The Métro is crammed with people. I don't know, tomorrow's Palm Sunday? Could that be it? Anyway. Do you suppose she'll be long?"

"Her bicycle is in repair," Addie said. "So, she probably walked. She could be another hour or more."

"Oh, my."

"What's wrong? Why do you need to see her?" Yvette asked.

"It's private business. It's . . . war business. I must tell her directly."

"Would you care to come in and wait for her? Excuse the mess, but I'm—"

"*Merci*, but I am afraid I can't." Again, she looked at the dainty little watch. "I have a benefit luncheon this afternoon I absolutely must attend, and look at me, I look a fright."

"You can tell us," Yvette blurted out. "We'll tell her. We're like sisters, aren't we, Addie?" Yvette pulled back and looked at her.

"Yes, indeed we are, like sisters," Addie replied, nodding to Yvette.

"No. I'm sorry. That's out of the question. I've already been through that with the girl's mother, this Madame Bellier." The

63

countess shook her head and closed her eyes, adding, "And excuse me for saying so, but that woman is a cantankerous shrew!"

Both girls chuckled simultaneously. Addie had always cruelly referred to Mélina's mother in English as "Madame *Bellyache*!"

"My poor dear woman, you're simply going to have to tell us," Addie said, placing her hand on the countess's warm shoulder. "Mélina could make a hundred stops before she gets here. It could be hours."

"Oh, my."

"Darling, you can trust us," Yvette added. "Believe me."

"You're an American?" the countess asked, looking to the embassy sticker on Addie's door.

"Yes, I am," Addie answered with a smile.

"Then, you'd have no reason to report me?"

"Of course we wouldn't," Yvette interjected.

"Okay, but you must tell Madame Vaugeois the minute she arrives."

"We will, indeed."

The countess reached inside her cloak and withdrew an appointment card. "We believe, or rather, the Red Cross believes they have found Madame Vaugeois's husband, and he is alive!"

Both girls' mouths dropped wide open.

"Mon Dieu!" Yvette exclaimed.

"Isn't that glorious news?" the countess exclaimed, a smile radiating from her lovely face.

Addie looked at Yvette. "Isn't that glorious news, Yvette?

"Oh, Mélina will be . . . overcome."

"The poor man was burned beyond recognition and has languished in a state of comatose shock in some sanitarium in the Rhineland for the last ten months. Tell madame to bring some pictures of her and Monsieur Vaugeois to the Red Cross office Monday morning at nine." She handed the card to Addie. "This is the address. And thank you both for your help. Please excuse my rude expedience, but I simply must take my leave. Ciao."

Once the door closed, Yvette took Addie's hands and held them to her lips.

"Poor Mélina. She'll be devastated, Addie."

"Is she sure she's pregnant?"

"Positive."

"She'll be suicidal!"

"Oh, how dreadful, Addie!"

"Yvette, we can't tell her. Not yet."

"Addie, we have to, we promised."

"Just think, Yvette, think of all poor Mélina has had to endure today. Ruti has left her. I'm leaving her. I promise you, that hasn't sunk in. When she waltzes in here and sees me all packed and ready to go, it will hit her like a ton of bricks. Let's wait, Yvette. Let's give her some time."

"But her mother knows something's up. She'll tell her the Red Cross came here for her. I simply won't lie to her, Addie."

"Please, mon chère. Please, don't tell her. Just until tomorrow."

"No, Addie. She has to know."

"You ghastly girl, Yvette! You're going to completely ruin my bon voyage party!"

DAY ONE—Paris—Saturday, 5 April 41—12:46 PM

Mélina took nearly two hours. Yvette had already departed. Fortunately, Mélina had carried the letter from Addie inviting her to visit once Ruti was gone. She was stopped by a gendarme who questioned her reason for being on the street alone. Without the letter she very well may have been hauled in. Unaccompanied Frenchwomen who took leisurely strolls around the city of light without a purpose or purposeful destination were regarded as suspect. Then, of course, her detention was further protracted, it turned out, by "her beautiful eyes," as the scoundrel policeman coyly quipped, tugging the curl out of the end of his mustache and letting it spring back with a wink of his eye.

"Mélina, you poor darling. You look a fright." Addie ushered her in and seated her at the kitchen table.

"Addie, I'm so sick with anguish." Tears still rolled down her face. She held a sopping wet hanky in her hand, but chose the hem of her skirt to dab her red eyes. "I'm so lonely. He's only been gone a few hours and I'm already so forlorn." She looked around the room, and her sweet face contorted in pathetic sadness. "And now you're leaving me too."

Addie held her friend's trembling hands in hers.

"Yes, I'm leaving, darling, but I'm not gone yet. Let's please, dear, not bury the cat until he's dead. We have tonight. The German girls are throwing me a party at the club. And I want you to be there."

Mélina started shaking her head.

"I want you to be there, Mélina, for me, sweetie, and for you. It will do you good."

Mélina blinked her red eyes and sniffled, finally nodding reluctant agreement.

"I'm sorry, Addie. You're my best friend and I kept this from you. I'm pregnant."

"Yvette told me. I'm so happy for you, Mélina. Truly, I am. Won't it be wonderful? You and Yvette in the park. Your children playing and running together."

"She's your friend, Addie. Once you leave, she'll never see me again. I don't think she's ever been to the 18th in her life."

Addie took her own hanky and started wiping Melina's face.

"Posh!" she declared. "Yvette loves you dearly, silly girl. You'll be wonderful friends. You and your baby can just come to Saint-Germain to play, dear."

"Addie, I love you so, but you don't know my life. I work so hard every day washing and ironing. My times with you and your friends were like living a dream. With the dream gone, and now a baby, I'll be trapped with my doting mother and mountains of dirty clothes."

"And dirty diapers, darling. Don't forget the dirty diapers!" Addie became Betty Hutton again, crossing her pretty eyes.

Laughter burst from Mélina.

"Isn't that better?" Addie hugged her and could still feel trembling in her tiny body.

"Oh, Addie. This terrible war has already widowed me once. Now I could be widowed again. I don't think I can face that. The only thing that keeps me going is knowing I'm pregnant and that when the war is over, Ruti and I will be wed."

Addie heard nothing after "widowed me."

"Mélina," she softly said. *Only one way to do it. Just blurt it out.* "The Red Cross came today. They say your husband is still alive."

The look Mélina gave her could only be described as furor.

"NO!" she screamed.

"Yes, it's true. They left this card and asked you to come to the Red Cross office Monday morning."

"No, Addie. He's dead! My god, no. What do I do?"

The only blood left in her face was in the splotches under her eyes and in her red nose.

"What would you do, Addie?"

"Mélina, it's not like it's the Kommandantur!" She grabbed her shoulders and added, "It's the Red Cross, darling." Addie shook her head and pursed her lips. "Don't go!"

6

Der Herr Ritter
Le chevalier seigneur
The Lord Knight

DAY ONE—Paris—Saturday, 5 April 41—10:27 AM

In the Year of Our Lord 1522, during the infancy of Martin Luther's reformation movement, there rose up a rebellion of the lesser knights and lords in the south of Germany. This Reformist rebellion was quickly dashed by knights of a higher order, loyal to the emperor and to the church. Yet, there grew from these beginnings a legend of one imperial knight, so ruthless and cavalier in his dealings with the reformists, it was said he had grilled and eaten the very hearts of the vanquished.

Two years later an uprising of peasants was also crushed by this league of imperial knights. And the knight's draconian legend grew manyfold. Sojourner storytellers and doomsday monks spread wild tales of his carnage and bestiality. Within months the juggernaut of the knight's legend wrought sheer panic in peasant villages throughout the land. The most innocent distant thunder and lightning would be rumored as the approaching pounding hooves of his fire-breathing steed and marauding army.

Such was the ancient legend of der Ritter von der Krumme. The Knight from the Krumme.

One of the young kepi-capped pages at the Hotel Ritz, in his maroon tunic and white gloves, took two steps at a time as he scurried up the stairway to the second floor of suites. The boy had announced the telephone call in the lounge, in both restaurants, and in the lobby, but to no avail. Every room in the hotel had newly installed telephones, but this German found ensuite telephones "a barbaric invasion of boudoir privacy" and had the hotel engineers remove it. Down the hall the uniformed garçon could hear a phonograph playing some dull, sad music. "Only a German could listen to such drivel," he mumbled. Sure enough, as he got closer the music was coming from number 208, the room of the stupid Boche he'd been trying to find for the last ten minutes. He knocked harshly at the door.

"Téléphone pour vous, monsieur."

The truth behind the legend of the Ritter von der Krumme was personified in a Frankish lord from the Haus von Stendal. He was indeed a knight and had profited greatly from both his true, yet much less-than-legendary exploits as well as the self-perpetuating legend itself. Such that this first Ritter von der Krumme decreed that each firstborn son of his lineage was to inherit the legendary though infamous title.

Through the generations each new Ritter von der Krumme amassed great and compounded wealth and real holdings. Then, in the late nineteenth century the thirteenth Ritter von der Krumme squandered, frittered, gambled, and drank away the entire von Stendal fortune in less than twelve years. So that when the fourteenth Ritter took the title it was completely worthless. Nonetheless, this undeterred young knight, like his fourteen-times-removed grandfather, was a self-driven, shrewd fellow who vowed to take up his legacy and cut his own swath through life. For what he lacked in a sixteenth-century title and means he would make up for in twentieth-century cunning.

The door opened and the snippy hotel page was greeted by an old white-haired gentleman with laughing blue eyes and the most contagious of endearing smiles. The page couldn't help but smile back. "A call for you, monsieur."

"Merci, my dear lad. Tell the caller it will take me a few moments," the old man said in perfect French and handed a coin to the boy. "Old bones move slowly, you know."

The page looked at the coin in his gloved palm and his eyes widened. A shiny German two-Reichsmark coin! *Sacrébleue*, he thought. For such a tip he'd be glad to carry the Boche's crippled old ass down to the phone.

The boy stepped back, bowed, and clicked his heels, a performance he knew Germans liked. "I am at your service, monsieur."

Konrad Victor Johann Sebastian von Stendal *der Ritter von der Krumme* closed the door and slowly shuffled through his sitting room. He was a smallish man with a barrel chest, huge tummy, and spindly legs. His bulk made his posture overerect, always, seemingly, in the attitude of falling over backward. He grabbed his newly shined top hat, his Marengo topcoat, his cane, and his satchel, as he would leave for the day after taking the call.

Konni Ritter, as he was called, was a spry little man. A body with seventy-three years on it and a lithe and youthful spirit, his rident, handsome face didn't look a day over fifty. He had a vivacious lust for life. His droll, witty presence made everyone around him love life as well, a rare quality in men of the privileged class, especially Germans. Hence, his overwhelming success as a businessman of the Thousand-Year Reich. Konni was most proud of his relationship with the great German Führer, Adolph Hitler. Hitler developed an affinity for Konni almost immediately. He liked Konni for three reasons: First, Ritter was witty and convivial, one of the few men outside the inner circle who could get away with levity in the presence the Führer. Second, Hitler was ecstatic about Konni Ritter's idea to make all German automakers use the same interchangeable parts for all automotive vehicles produced in Germany, both civilian and military. In this way, when a generator from an army truck went on the fritz, it could be quickly replaced with one from any automobile or farm truck in the area! It was an idea Konni had put to the Führer in their first meeting in the lobby of the Hotel die Post in Augsburg in 1932, a year before Hitler became chancellor, and again at a gala in 1933 at the groundbreaking of the Reich's first stretch of Autobahn. It went without saying that the third and probably most important reason for Herr Ritter finding favor with Hitler was that Konni let the Führer take all the credit for the idea!

When Hitler first made his automotive parts standardization policy a decree at the Berlin Auto Show in May of 1934, Konni was there in the audience. When the Führer said, "All chief automobile parts of any manufacturer's car are to be standardized as a part of the Reich's seven-year plan," Konni had a wide smile from ear to ear. The next year Hitler placed Konni as an initial member of the *Wirtschaftsgruppe Fahrzeugindustrie*, the Automotive Industry Economic Group, WiGruFa for short. While WiGruFa's duties included allocations of raw materials and assignment of parts production, its primary goal was to bring all automakers around to accepting the Führer's automotive parts standardization policy, and leading the charge in that regard was Konni Ritter. Further to his finding favor with Hitler, Konni was to serve as the liaison officer between WiGruFa and the Wehrmacht.

After war was declared, standardization goals took a backseat to the need for increased vehicle production, much of which was coming from Moravia, Bohemia, Poland, and now France. And even though the practicality of a one-part-fits-all policy became a pipe dream, it was still one that Konni Ritter moved toward every day, especially in France, where vast shortfalls could quickly be filled by manufacturers like Citroen, Renault, and Peugeot.

The old knight now waddled over to the *Voix de son Maître* phonograph machine with its black and silver logo, a cute terrier dog peering cock-eared into a gramophone trumpet, hearing *his master's voice*. Ritter's liver-spotted hand gently lifted the phonograph needle from the record and abruptly ended the strains of "Pavane," by Gabriel Fauré, the great French composer! The record continued spinning irregularly on the phonograph's plate as he had failed to engage the motor's brake.

Once out in the hall, Konni Ritter closed the door behind him, fiddled with the key until he got the door locked, placed the key into his vest pocket, and started his short, choppy walk down the hallway.

Suddenly, he remembered the spinning phonograph. He stopped, planted his cane, and his little feet started the pitter-patter process of turning around. Halfway through, he stopped. His head jerked downward and his little fists bounced as he blurted out, "Zum Donnerwetter!" He continued shuffling on down the hallway, deciding to let the phonograph plate's mechanism unwind itself down to a stop. Once again he would have to fully crank the blasted phonograph player's handle when he wanted to listen to another record.

In the vast velvet-clad lobby, a salon quartet played "Simplemente Triste" as Konni shuffled his way through the sea of people. The hotel telephone operator gave him a booth number, he entered and mostly filled the cramped booth, closed the glass door, and lifted the receiver. "Hallo," he said. "Here is Konrad der Ritter von der Krumme."

"Mein Gott, I've been waiting for an eternity!" the man's harried voice on the other end of the line said.

Konni Ritter recognized the voice. "I'm sorry, I had to put away my skate key and my riding wheel! What do you want?"

"I must see you, it's of the utmost of urgency. I left you a package at the front desk yesterday, did you—"

"Ja, ja," Konni said. "I have it. Now, what on earth is so blasted urgent? Why didn't you just come up and see me when you were at the hotel yesterday?"

"You weren't there, you infernal . . . And now I think I'm being followed. It's of the utmost importance, Herr Ritter. I must see you, now."

"Ja, ja. But I am rather sure, good man, there is no need for all this drama."

"I must see you." The man was frantic. "Where can you meet me?"

"I was just on my way out for an important meeting. It will consume most of the afternoon. I can meet you at the club. Tonight. Nine o'clock. When you arrive, tell the doorman you're there to see me.

"But the club? What club?"

"Somewhere on the Left Bank. Blasted, I don't remember the street, rue Chéri something or other. Just tell your driver the name. The Club l'Heure Bleue. He'll know it. Later, then." Konni abruptly hung up the phone just as the caller was saying, "I don't have a fucking driver, you . . ."

What on earth could this imbecile want now?

The doorman at the Hotel Ritz hailed him his "Germans Only" limo, allowed to be on the street after curfew.

"*Bonjour*, Herr Ritter," the driver said, twisting around to greet him.

"Pierre, is that you again?"

"Oui, monsieur. At your disposal." He flipped his flat cap at Konni and returned it to his head, adjusting it in the rearview mirror. "We drew straws, and I won! So, Pierre is your driver today, monsieur."

"*Très bien*, Pierre. Très bien indeed."

"Where to, monsieur?" Pierre started the car and pulled out from the curb.

"We have a very busy day, Pierre. First to the Hotel Lincoln to pick up a young lady. Then to the Club."

Fall Irmgard

"Forgive me, monsieur. It isn't noon yet. Very early for clubbing, isn't it?"

"It seems my negotiation skills are in vogue on even the most basic of levels. I had to settle a delicate problem for my friend Bruno."

After the Great War, at a time when other middle-aged men cursed the workings of the newfangled technologies—airplanes, motorcars, wireless radios, and the like—Konni Ritter was intrigued by them. During the height of Germany's automobile boom of the late 1920s, he invested in a carburetor company in Köpenick. A friend's company, a dear friend, once, but now, very much estranged.

In the backseat of the limo, Konni unlocked his satchel and flipped through the six dark-green file folders it contained. Oh, my word, yes, there it was, he assured himself, the large gray envelope that had been delivered to his room yesterday morning. He hadn't remembered putting it in his satchel. He scolded himself for becoming such an old woman. But, he felt, it was quite necessary for an aging businessman starting to show signs of his senility to make sure things had been put in their proper place. Yes, he thought, putting the key back in his pocket without relocking his briefcase; sure enough, there the envelope was, filed in their proper file folder, the one with the heading in silver ink that read:

F. IRMGARD

7

J.E.I.P.
Jeder einmal in Paris
Tout le monde une fois à Paris
Everyone Once in Paris

DAY ONE—Paris—Saturday, 5 April 41—11:47 AM
Ernst Schneider was a Gefreiter in the 15th Panzer Division, soon to
be attached to the DAK, General Erwin Rommel's Deutsches
Afrikakorp. Corporal Schneider's unit had earned a two-week holiday
pass in advance of deployment to Libya, and he and six other men in
his unit had scurried immediately off to Paris. *JEIP.* Every German
soldier knew the acronym. *Jeder einmal in Paris.* Everyone Once in
Paris. And every soldier couldn't wait for his turn. Most of three days
to get here from Ostmark, a day to register and find lodging (a
Soldatenheim, soldier's barrack in the rue de Bellechasse), and now
nearly a week of his precious two was almost gone.

And Corporal Schneider had not shit even once!

The frantic traveling, the rich foods, the baguettes, the wine,
late-night walks through Pigalle in a drunken stupor; he'd thrown up
plenty of times, but not one single shit. He'd gone to the apothecary
yesterday and taken a laxative, but still *Nichts!* Nothing. Perhaps one
little turd the size of a butter bean last night, but nothing else since
he'd laid a log that a thoroughbred horse would have been proud of in
the men's room of the Café Relais in Graz just before his departure
for Paris.

For the last twenty minutes, he'd sat in the toilet room of the
Brasserie Le Coq Rouge just off the boulevard Raspail in the 6th
arrondissement. His legs were asleep. His hemorrhoids felt like a
baboon's ass. With a frustrated "Scheisse" he arose from the toilet,
started to flush it, and then flapped his fingers at it, admitting,
"What's the use." Once in the dark little hallway, he glanced out into
the bar he saw something incongruent that made him stop, clear his
head for a second. His mind flashed back to his youth, when he was a
boy back in Hohenholte, Germany. His father, the village carpenter
and handyman, had repaired some rotted windowsills in the church
and rushed off to the pub, leaving young Ernst to paint and clean up
the mess. After twenty minutes or so, Ernst had looked up and

couldn't believe his eyes. A huge stately eight-point buck stood in front of the altar, proudly, as if he belonged in church today. His father had left the door open. Ernst thought, *You aren't supposed to be in here. This shouldn't be happening.*

But now, this was happening. Through the doorway's veil of hanging beads, Ernst could now see that the French bartender, just a boy, really, not much older than twelve, had his penis in his hand and was pissing a little into a beer glass, and then into another and another. He then filled the glasses the rest of the way with beer as the two waiters watched and chuckled.

Ernst quietly slipped back into the toilet room. He flushed the toilet loudly, ran water over his hands, and made as much noise as possible coming through the hallway and out into the brasserie, whistling along with the strains of Josephine Baker's "J'ai Deux Amours" coming from the radio. Giving the boy behind the bar a coy smile, he followed one of the waiters out to the sun-drenched tables on the sidewalk. The waiter had set two of the seven St. Omer beer glasses from his tray onto the table in front of Ernst's six Afrikakorps comrades. As he reached for the third, Ernst tipped the tray over onto the waiter. Quickly, he grabbed one of the glasses from the table and smashed it into the waiter's face. Gefreiter Schneider was trained in hand-to-hand; he knew to rest the solid base of the glass in the heel of his palm so it didn't break, leaving him with severely lacerated tendons *and* constipation. Ernst could feel the bone in the waiter's face give way under the heavy glass, like the dented shell of a hardboiled egg. The waiter cried out in pain, "Mon Dieu!" He fell to the ground, slamming his heels again and again on the cobblestone and screaming, a sliver of his orbital bone having punctured a sinus.

"The *Schweinehunden* are pissing in the beer!" Ernst shouted, pointing at the young bartender's frightened face staring out between the *Menu* and the *Chaud* painted in white script on the brasserie's window. The two round tables the group of soldiers had pulled together when they first seated themselves at the Le Coq Rouge, some forty or more beers ago, went flying into the street as the Germans stormed the brasserie. The last of them got his shin tangled in one of the chairs. He kicked it free and then, smarting, threw it through the pub's window. The other waiter dropped the tray of Pernod and Vichy water he'd just collected for an old French couple seated outside. He darted out onto the boulevard Raspail. Looking back to see if he was being followed, he ran headlong into a school of French girls on bicycles. Five of them, then six, then seven, eight, and nine crashed onto and over him. Two other tables of German soldiers, mostly Schütze, or privates, having heard Ernst, joined in the fracas. Half went after the waiter in the street, the rest rushed into the pub.

At a table farther away from all the excitement, seated on the sunny side of a large ash tree, Rolf looked at Gep and slapped his legs as he stood up. "Is this Paris, or are we back in Warsaw?" Gep was standing too, smiling and saying, "Aren't you glad we had the wine!"

Rolf nodded toward the street. "You get that under control; I'll go inside." Gep ran to the pile of girls and bicycles and soldiers trying to get to the waiter just as two French gendarmes in bleu de travail capes did the same, their whistles screeching in a series of short, continual blasts. Boot heels had already been driven through bicycle spokes and into the waiter's cut-up face. Gep pulled the soldiers off one at a time and told them to come to attention. He then directed three more arriving gendarmes into the pub.

Just as Rolf rounded the huge trunk of a chestnut tree at the pub's doorway, a little girl came running out and headlong into him, screaming, "*Meurtre!* Murder!" She looked up at Rolf, saw his uniform, and panic besieged her little face. She shrieked and tore herself away from him and shrieked again, bolting into the hat shop next door. Blood-curdling, her second scream shivered up Rolf's very spine. As he rushed on into the pub, he saw two of the Wehrmacht privates holding the frantic proprietress, one saying in terrible French, "You see, you see we do froggie boy go piss the beer!" The boy, obviously her son, was on the floor on his back. A grenadier had his heel on the boy's ear, smashing his cheek against the floor, his frightened face a bloody, snotty mess. Saliva bubbled from his lips as he screamed to be set free. Two Oberschützen, PFCs, pulled hard on his arms with their boots in his armpits. Ernst and one of his comrades rested all their weight on his knees. Another sat backward on the boy's stomach and was unbuttoning his trousers, his HJ dagger between his teeth. And still another was kneeling down and screaming in the boy's face, "We now cut off your *Schwanz*, you *Scheisskerl!*"

"HALT!" Rolf shouted. "Come to attention!" He grabbed the collar of the Schütze with the knife and slung him across the floor, upsetting tables and chairs just as the gendarmes ran in. "I said come to attention, *sofort!* Immediately!" The soldiers all snapped to attention. Ernst quickly shouted, "Permission to speak, Herr Major?"

"Do so." The woman ran toward her son, then stopped, dropped to her knees, and quickly kissed Rolf's hand and held it to her cheek, chanting some rapid, inaudible prayer. Then, sobbing uncontrollably, she quickly crawled over to her son.

"He pissed in our beer, Herr Major. I witnessed it myself."

"So, you saw this thing happen?"

The woman started shouting, "I told you to stop, Pierre. I begged you. And now look."

"Jawohl, Herr Major, I saw it."

"Good, you'll file a report at the gendarmerie." Rolf then turned to the gendarmes and told them the same thing in French. Ernst's face melted. Now he'd waste the rest of the day at a police station! Constipated!

As he had taken control of the situation, the gendarmes deferred to Rolf for further orders. "Arrest the boy! And the two waiters," Rolf continued in French. The woman leapt up from her son's side, pleading with the major. "And close this establishment pending determination of the appropriate fines."

"Oui, oui, monsieur," the gendarmes said as they helped the boy to his feet. Rolf dismissed the Germans, and after they had left, he told the boy's mother, "A few years' working in Germany, building roads and bridges with other boys who need a little settling down." His knuckle touched her cheek. "He'll be fine, I assure you." As he walked out the door, he slapped his gloves on his leg, "Now, where is that Gep?"

A crowd of French passersby had gathered at the broken window. They dispersed as Rolf walked out and Gep appeared from their midst.

The two of them walked up the boulevard Raspail.

"You shouldn't have told her that," Gep said, taking issue with Rolf's handling of the affair. "You very well know, major, all three of them will be executed at Romainville by week's end."

"And deservedly so for the two waiters. They put the boy up to the deed, I'm quite certain of it. But I'm ordering labor service in Germany for the boy. And my commands are usually honored at even the highest levels."

"Why waste your influence on a contemptible French brat?"

"He's just a boy, Gep. Two or three years' mixing concrete in a labor camp will serve to transform him into a respectful citizen of the Reich." Rolf was becoming vexed by Gep's contradictory tone. "Of that, I am also quite certain."

"I'm not disputing your rationale. I'm just pointing out there are elements in the regime who would look on that sort of farsighted judgment as dereliction. The Nazi hawks, major. They just want blood."

"I answer only to my superiors, my conscience and my best judgment. And I am certain, my young friend, my decision would find favor with all three."

"I admire your noble nature, major. Just be fully aware that it can be dangerous."

Rolf smiled defiantly as they continued down the sidewalk, French pedestrians avoiding eye contact with them and moving this way and that to avoid them. *Sans regard.* That aspect of occupied Paris was no different from Warsaw.

"If we're taking in the Club l'Heure Bleue tonight, we should eat an early lunch."

"You're the tour guide, Gep. Where's lunch?"

"Superb smoked salmon at La Coupole."

"Sounds good, but Gep?" Rolf added. "Nothing but bottled beer for me, alles klar?"

"Quite clear, Herr Major," Gep answered, nodding his agreement, eyebrows raised and mouth cocked to the right.

They strolled a little farther and Rolf noticed Gep chuckle to himself. "What is it?" he asked, smiling.

"Ach!" Gep snorted. "We should probably avoid the foie gras!"

8

Süße Suzi Rupp
Douce Suzi Rupp
Sweet Suzi Rupp

DAY ONE—Paris—Saturday, 5 April 41—11:51 AM
"Don't worry about Sabina," Bruno said, lighting his Jägerlust cigar. "I told her about this new kid. The situation. She'll come around. Eventually." He held his lighter's flame out to Konni Ritter. As his cigar started to glow, Bruno added, "What choice does she have?"

"Bruno, my friend, you are a pragmatic man." Konni took Bruno's wrist to steady the flame. "A reasonable . . ." His lips popped with each puff he took. ". . . and pragmatic man." He looked up at the huge club owner and smiled. Smoke drifted from his clenched, soda-bleached teeth.

"Eight years now with National Socialism, Herr Ritter. Pragmatism and a shiny lapel pin are what keeps us able-bodied nowadays."

"And prosperous, don't forget prosperous, Herr Kestler." He put his hand on Bruno's shoulder and shook him, nodding and smiling. "You know from your days in Berlin, once these Party fellows get their hook in you, they don't stop until they get what they're after. You were right to come to me."

"I still don't have to like it."

"Bruno, my friend. I assure you, it will all work out."

"So, where is our new Nazi nymph?" Bruno asked, just as club manager Xavier du Bois darted out from behind the stage curtain.

"She said she needs just a few more minutes," Xavier said, handing a list of the new girl's music choices to Enrico at the piano, then stepping off the stage and taking a seat with Bruno and Konni. Xavier was a wisp of a man with deeply set eyes and a skullcap of baldness on his tiny head. His thin black suit and plain black tie were always crumpled and covered with a dusting of dandruff. The suit was a summer cut he wore year-round. And the pants had the faintest gray stripe in the fabric, unmatched. But in his own way, Xavier du Bois was as vital to the l'Heure Bleue's success as Bruno and Sabina had been. A tiny Alsatian barely five feet tall, he was a bundle of nerves and energy, always fidgeting, mumbling, always up to some scheme or other. He kept everything in order. Food inventories, liquor and liqueurs, champagne and wines, cigars and cigarettes, everything was kept organized and plentiful. And at a time when "plentiful" was sometimes next to impossible. Xavier always gave Bruno exactly what he asked for.

"This is going to be terrible," Xavier said, pouring himself a sip of Calvados. "Sabina will leave us. I just know it. I should have never come to you, Herr Ritter. I'm just terrified everything will come undone. What on earth will we do if she leaves us?"

"Settle down, du Bois. Sabina won't leave us," Bruno answered. "But this little twat had better be good. If not, I'll be kissing Dutch ass for a long time. After all, we're stuck with this new bitch now, regardless."

"I am sorry, monsieur," Xavier said, his breath caught. "I fear for poor Sabina. I fear the dear woman may do something to herself."

Bruno looked at Konni, then leaned around and looked Xavier in the eye. "Better to herself than to us, du Bois."

It was actually Xavier who had run into the club and announced to Bruno he had heard on the radio that the German blitzkrieg had begun. Before that moment Bruno had never really known him. The little shrimp had been in the prewar club a few times and tried desperately to befriend them, especially Sabina. But he was regarded as insignificant and basically ignored. Until that bright May morning almost a year ago.

"The Germans are coming, monsieur. And I can have everything in place the moment they arrive. Leave it all to me. I'll work for nothing—the food I eat, the wine I drink, that and nothing more until they arrive. And then, only for a mere percentage of the profits from the bar . . . from the food and from the bar. Just fifteen . . . No, no, no, of course, twelve percent. Twelve percent. That, and of course any rebate arrangements I can negotiate with my vendor friends and my sundry contacts in the south and in Alsace. That and twelve percent, monsieur. We have a deal, no?"

Bruno just gave him a rare smile and a big, meaty handshake. "Ten percent," he told the little man. "You can make any side deals you want."

And the stars were suddenly aligned for one of the most lucrative business arrangements of the occupation. Neither Bruno nor Xavier knew it could all happen so fast, and so perfectly. It didn't take until autumn for the German Army to march into Paris. Only five short weeks. And who could have foreseen the Hotel Lutetia just around the corner from the club would become the headquarters of the Abwehr, housing offices for fifty or more officers and as many support staff, including more than twenty German women. Who knew the exchange rate would be doubled between the franc and the Reichsmark, so he could buy everything in cheap francs and sell it for inflated marks!

Yes, everything had been perfect. And Bruno, the pragmatist, knew that's when it usually started to turn to *scheisse!* In recent weeks, he was beginning to wonder if he wasn't correct.

SS and Nazi Party civil administrators were starting to arrive in Paris. The occupation of France was run entirely by the German Army. But,trains from the Reich were dumping scores of Nazi Party officials into the city to fill the void left by the army's continual departure. Officials who were finding reasons to be involved in this bureaucracy and that. Racial edicts were starting to be announced. French government administrators, bankers, and employers with government contracts were being *advised* to release their Jewish workers.

The Propaganda Ministry arrived just after the fall of France, but used the competent members of their staff for print and publishing. The l'Heure Bleue's Propaganda Ministry inspector for all things musical was Reinhard Rupp, who actually had been schooled in music in Dresden and could see very easily past Bruno's guise of translating the titles of Nazi-banned songs into French so they could be performed without implication.

"Reinie the Heinie!" Xavier called him. He was the first true by-the-bloody-book Nazi administrator either of them had been forced to deal with in Paris. Bruno hated the man and avoided him for fear he might be compelled to take a cricket mallet to the back of Reinhard's greasy head. He was Xavier's to handle, Xavier's to argue with, Xavier's to buy off. Herr Rupp had come to the club for the first time four weeks ago, wearing the typical red swastika armband. Xavier masterfully coddled the Nazi and found ingenious means of payola. But each payoff was only good until the next visit. The last two times Reinhard visited, he was in a new French suit and donned only a swastika lapel pin. And week ago, with Bruno in attendance, the Nazi noose was tightened.

"Oh, but no, my diminutive Alsatian friend, you've completely misinterpreted my meaning. We must go forward one song at a time. Your club is frequented by illustrious members of our brave armed forces. I would be remiss if I let even one tune of questionable origin or intent slip past me, now wouldn't I?"

Bruno had leaped from his chair, knocking over the table. "Get out of my club, Rupp!"

With Xavier at his wits' end, Bruno enlisted the help of Konni Ritter, and within a few days Konni learned this Nazi administrator was like all the others. There was always some element of graft or other lurking in their unreasonable demands. In this case it was a so-called *niece* who wanted to break into show business in Paris.

Her name was Suzanne Rupp. She was a twenty-three-year-old gray-eyed, baby-faced china doll with jet-black hair. She walked out onto the stage in a short skirt and a puffed-sleeve white blouse. The music started. It was the intro to "Keiner weiss, wie ich bin, nur du." Suzi started singing and everyone smiled. Her crisp voice was high-pitched and quivered in the popular tremolo style of Édith Piaf and Erna Sack.

"Back in Vienna she was known as *die süße Suzi Rupp,* Sweet Suzi Rupp," Konni whispered as he poked his elbow into Bruno's ribs.

The song finished; they all applauded. Suzi did a cute impromptu tap dance and bowed to them, fanning out the skirt. Then she turned and did the same for Enrico at the piano. And when she did, they could see her intentional nakedness beneath the skirt.

Konni raised both his palms and shrugged at Bruno.

"Not in my club," Bruno said. "Take her shopping!"

"But my dear man," Konni pleaded. "Your other girls expose their 'charms' now and then."

Bruno shook his big head.

"Bruno?"

"If she works for me, she's never to give them so much as a bare shoulder without my permission."

Suzi's next song was "Sagt dir eine schöne Frau, Vielleicht." Bruno let her sing a few bars and stopped her.

"I am sorry, my dear," he said, hoping Sabina was somewhere in earshot. "Forgive me the interruption. Your singing is divine, but that song is one of Sabina's signature pieces. I can't let you continue with it. Perhaps something else?'

"Something French, maybe?" she asked, in her cute little girl voice.

"Of course, please."

Fall Irmgard

As Suzi started the third song of her audition, Xavier glanced over his shoulder, hoping to see Sabina. The kitchen door was askew, and he could see a woman's long red fingernails keeping it so. Politely, he excused himself and went out the front door, upstairs through the courtyard, and down the service entrance, where a short hallway ended at a longer one that ran from the kitchen of the bistro next door to the club. And at the club end of the hallway, holding the door barely open, stood Sabina, barefoot in a sable fur coat. Suzi's nightingale voice was perfect for "J'Attendrai," and her French was spot-on perfect. Xavier tiptoed up behind Sabina. She was nearly a head taller than him and had always excited him beyond his wildest imagination, but also intimidated him. She despised him and constantly threatened and bullied him.

"She doesn't even compare to you, ma chère," was what he heard himself tell her.

Sabina spun around, her teeth clenched and her eyes full of fire. The coat swung open, and he saw she was wearing nothing but white cotton panties underneath. She grabbed his face and squeezed it with one hand, holding his testicles firmly in the other. Squeezing his cheeks together harder, she bent down to stare squarely into his wrinkled fish face. "Don't you say another word to me," she said, in a forceful whisper. "You despicable little *stront!*" Her spittle splattered his face as she continued.

"After I slit that fat old dandy's throat and his little Nazi cunt's, I'll have doomed my soul to hell, du Bois. So, if I slit your scrawny chicken gullet too, it will be of absolutely no consequence to me!"

Eyes wide open, she found the end of his tiny penis and pinched it! She smashed his head against the wall and bit his chin, hard, drawing blood. His open mouth sucked in her hot, angry pants of breath from her flared nostrils. He gasped deeply, twice, and quivered. Through the trousers' fabric she felt wetness in her hand. Looking down at it, she scowled and wiped it on the front of his cheap suit jacket.

"You queer, pathetic bastard!" She bit the tip of her tongue and flicked her knuckles hard into his groin. As the little Alsatian doubled over in excruciating pain on the floor, Sabina van der Gorp scurried off barefoot down the hallway and through the kitchen past the oblivious staff, sable coattails and bare breasts swaying in her haste.

9

An der Brücke
Au pont
At the Bridge

DAY ONE—Paris—Saturday, 5 April 41—11:36 AM
First in rolling wisps, then in fluffy puffs of smoky gray, the clouds
came rushing in, low and heavy from the French coast to the west. As
a Paris spring day is prone to suddenly do, within moments a single,
solid bank of dark, menacing clouds approached, almost low enough
to touch. Relentlessly, it tumbled into Paris and within minutes the
beautiful sunny Saturday wore a cruel gray veil.

By the time Fabien Lemay reached the Pont Royal, the bleeding
had stopped. Yes, he was certain of it. His fist was sticky now, no
longer wet and slimy, and the blood was drying between his fingers.
What had been a warm wetness running down his inner arm and
along his side under his coat was cold now and becoming sticky. The
bleeding had stopped. As a distant clap of thunder rumbled through
the buildings of the once again gloomy city, he looked to his left and
could see only the bottom two-thirds of the Eifel Tower, the rest
swallowed up by the stealthy gloom. Suddenly, he ran headlong into
one of the dozens of people scurrying across the bridge to find refuge
from the pending storm. "Pardon," he warmly said, tipping his cap, as
he continued on across the bridge to the river's right bank. Once
down on the Port du Louvre he saw a few straggling sunbathers lying
here and there on their blankets and towels, one playing "Les Roses
Blanches" on a concertina, all hopeful the sun would somehow return.
Another louder clap of thunder, and slowly, reluctantly, they too were
scrambling for cover.

Fabien dipped his kerchief in a puddle and climbed atop the
bridge's concrete bulwark, up under the structure, where he would be
protected from the rain when it started. He would wait there for the
German. He would wait with dread. What would he tell the German?
The German would be furious.

How had it all gone so wrong? Fabien had once been a highly
regarded businessman, a securities broker of respectable character and
unquestionable integrity. And now look at him. Fighting like a gutter

rat. Forced to deal with the lowest form of Paris' hoodlums and gangsters.

The Paris Stock Exchange was one of the world's grandest. And Fabien had served as a stockbroker for more than thirty years. Of course he was not one of the distinguished floor traders, a prestigious position held by a select few: the *agents de change*, the Parisian parquet brokers. He was instead a *coulissier*, a curb broker who had developed a clientele of mostly working-class and small-business owner investors.

When the Germans first occupied France, they ordered the Paris Stock Exchange closed. In the panic of the French defeat and the country's partition, most investors heeded their brokers' advice and moved their securities to the vaults of Châtel-Guyon in unoccupied Vichy France. But Fabien Lemay had other advice for his most trusted clients, and most had followed it. Fabien's family had lived in his house in the 9th arrondissement for more than two hundred years. His great-grandfather was a trader in precious metals and stones. In the early nineteenth century a twelve-square-meter vault was installed in a false end of the building's cellar. While other Paris curb brokers headed to Vichy with their clients' securities, Fabien held the stocks and bonds of more than eighty of his clients in his camouflaged cellar vault, safe from the occupiers, yet still quite accessible. And of course, as the bitter winter and food and coal shortages took a terrible toll on most of the city's working class, Fabien went from trading on the Paris stock market to trading for many of his clients on the black market, a very profitable undertaking, but a very dangerous one.

His eyes closed, Fabien laid his head back against the buttress, gasped, and then smiled. At least he would live! The knife had only severed the flesh over his ribs. He spit in his hand. His saliva was bloodless. It had not entered his lung or any other organs, he was sure. It was a small knife. Fabien had seen it before. This man, Victor, had shown it to him. The knife had torn into Fabien's ribs; he felt it even sever bone. So sharp, razor sharp. Fabien's bloody hand had gained a solid grip on the knife during their struggle, averting Victor's attack. But Fabien's knife was long and sharp. He felt it hit the flesh over Victor's hipbone and slice into his leg-joint. And when it sliced across Victor's face, Fabien saw it sever the left eyelid and eyeball, saw the eye split like a grape, then suddenly gush with blood. That was when Fabien made his escape.

Victor, that snake! Try to steal the envelope in Fabien's hand. The last of his clients' securities. Desperation made Fabien trust people like Victor. He wished now he had known the German earlier. The gangster, Victor would never have needed to be involved. Now Fabien must flee! The German would help him and his family get out of Paris. For a man of such high standing, procuring a *laissez-passer* that would permit him to cross the frontier into Vichy was a small matter. After all Fabien had done for the German, he was certain this favor should be granted. He would wait for him here under the bridge where they usually met, give him his final instructions about the change of plans in Lyon, and ask—no, demand—the German's help.

As Fabien wiped the blood from his forearm with the kerchief, the hairs clung, wet and red tinged, to his skin, then here and there they broke free and stood erect again, leaving thin red lines of blood behind on his arm. A light rain was falling steadily now. Everyone on the quay was gone except an old man with a walrus moustache pulling a green wheeled trash barrel, cleaning up the trash left by sunbathers. The rain suddenly increased to torrential sheets. The old man limped hurriedly under the bridge, pulling the barrel behind him.

Oblivious, Fabien Lemay's mind was consumed with thoughts of Victor. What would Fabien do now? Now that he had disfigured and nearly killed Victor, second in command only to the gangster boss, Guy de Forney. Of course. Fabien could use this to his advantage. Perhaps the German would now come after Victor! Perhaps— It was at that moment that the mustached trash sweep shoved a dagger into Fabien's right nostril. He shoved it so forcefully and so deep that an inch of the knife's point stuck out from the top of Fabien's head. The cunning sweep then withdrew the blade just enough for it to become dislodged from the bone of Fabien's skull, and quickly stirred it around inside his cranium, scrambling the broker's brain. Confused by flashes of dark and light and sound and silence, Fabien fell from the bulwark a jerking, cavorting heap on the damp cobblestone.

The assassin withdrew the blade. Quickly, he found the soft flesh under Fabien's sternum and shoved the knife into the body, hard and upward, then with the heel of his hand he jammed it, handle and all, deep into the chest cavity. Fabien was a motionless corpse. The old sweep bent over and buttoned his victim's jacket, hiding the chest wound. He removed the Wehrmacht-issued gloves he'd worn, threw them into the Seine, and tore the envelope from Fabien's dead grasp. Looking around to see if he was being watched, he raised his coat collar against the cold, pulled down his wet brown cap, grabbed his broom and the wheeled trash barrel, and scurried spryly off down the Port du Louvre into a driving rain.

10

Fall Chesterfield
Opération Chesterfield
Operation Chesterfield

DAY ONE—Paris—Saturday, 5 April 41—11:53 AM
Ruti Heht's first stop when he left Mélina's was the *Soldatenheim* just
down from the École Militaire. An office building formerly owned by
a British law firm, it had been converted into a dormitory for visiting
German soldiers. He and the messenger boy carrying his duffle bag
exited the Métro station in the center of the square. Ruti carried the
heavy suitcase without the slightest lean in his gait. The boy fought to
tote the duffle valiantly, but mostly just drug it. At the door of the
makeshift barracks, he gave the lad another tip and told him to meet
him at Gare Lyon at 3:45 where he would have further instructions
and gratuities for him. Once in the lobby of the Soldatenheim, Ruti
deposited his grip as well as the large strapped and locked suitcase
with the orderly-cum-concierge to hold for a few hours. A private at
the front desk noticed him and called out, "Leutnant Heht. I have a
message for you." He took the envelope from a cubbyhole behind him
and handed it to Ruti. "I know you're leaving today," he went on.
"But it's from the office of the SD. A man named Kruder? I hope it's
nothing, but I had to be sure you got the message."

"He's an acquaintance of mine." Ruti smiled. "He probably just
wants to bid me adieu."

From the bank of servicemen's phones along the wall in the
Soldatenheim hallway, Ruti rang up the SS offices on the avenue
Foch.

"Kruder here."

"You're back."

"Leutnant Rutgers Heht. I thought I might have missed you."

"My train leaves at four. So, you couldn't let me go without
wishing me farewell?"

"I wish that were the case. I need to see you."

"Is something wrong?"

"Probably not. I just need to ask you something about a matter
that has suddenly arisen. My office. In a quarter hour."

"I don't see how I'd have time."

Fall Irmgard

"You'll need to make time, Herr Leutnant."

Ruti slammed the phone in its cradle. Then slammed his doubled-up fist into his palm as he stormed out onto the rue du Bourgogne.

"Rutgers, my young friend," Kruder announced from his desk.

"So, how was Warsaw?" Ruti said, setting down his hat and draping his coat over an opposing chair.

"Dreadful." Kruder lit one cigarette with the remnants of a spent one. "It's still winter there."

"It's always winter there. Did you catch your terrorist or Jew, or whomever the hell it was?"

"Let's say it was a worthwhile visit." Kruder extinguished the spent cigarette stub in a crystal ashtray on his desk. "You seem distraught, Rutgers. Is something the matter?"

"I have a lot to do before I depart, and this wasn't on the list."

"I'm certain it wasn't."

"What do you want, Kruder?" Ruti asked with tight, stern eyes.

Kruder took a pack of cigarettes from his tunic pocket and tossed it across the desk at Ruti. "Forgive my rudeness. Would you care for a smoke?"

Ruti looked at the pack of Chesterfield cigarettes.

"American?" he said, smiling at the Gestapo officer.

"But of course they are, Leutnant. Frankly, I would have thought you were the one responsible for them being in France. You see, they're turning up everywhere recently."

Ruti lit a Chesterfield with Kruder's, holding his arm steady as he did, looking into his empty eyes.

"Then we'll all enjoy some good smokes for a while."

"So, you know nothing about these?"

"Of course I don't," Ruti remarked, a resolute smirk on his face.

"How would you suppose they made their way to Paris, Rutgers, my friend?

"Maybe the British dropped them on one of their flyovers, trying to win over the hearts of the French."

"Or maybe they were confiscated by the Abwehr and are being used to barter on the black market," Kruder suggested. "You work in the procurement office. I would think you'd be just the sort to pull off such drama as this."

"Oh, I don't think so, Kruder."

"And why is that?"

"Because if that were true, I'd be offering one to you."

"You're quite the wiseacre, aren't you, Herr Leutnant?"

"Is this why you've interrupted my very busy morning?" Ruti asked as he stood up and took his coat off the chair.

"No. I wanted to wish you a bon voyage. By the way, where are your new orders taking you?"

"You know that a German soldier can't talk about his orders to anyone other than his immediate superiors." He grabbed his hat and stuffed it under his arm. "Besides, you're Gestapo, Kruder. If you need that information, I'm certain you can get it."

Ruti took the pack of Chesterfields from the desk. "May I have these?"

"Are you sure you want them in your possession? They're contraband."

"Arrest me."

Kruder smiled. "Sure, take them. They'll be my bon voyage gift to you."

"Then to you, Sturmbannführer Kruder, I say *danke schön* and adieu."

Ruti turned and started to walk away as Kruder called out, "Heht?"

Ruti turned back around.

"Heil Hitler."

Ruti stopped buttoning his coat and stomped his heel, then, raising his right arm in the obligatory fashion, added; "Yes, quite, Heil Hitler."

Ruti's next stop was the Deutsche Occupation Bank, where he withdrew a package from his safe deposit box and turned the key over to the officer in charge, saying that he'd been redeployed. From there, he visited Credit Suisse, where the package was placed in the deposit box he'd set up in Mélina's name. After he closed it, he took the key and placed it in an envelope along with a letter he'd written when he left Kruder's office. Stuffing the envelope into his inner tunic pocket, he went to a bank of phones on the mezzanine level.

He dialed the number and listened to the double-buzz meter as the connection was being made.

"Hallo."

Fall Irmgard

"I just wasted ten minutes of my life answering troubling questions of our friend from Warsaw," Ruti said, looking this way and that, then adding. "It seems he's back in Paris."

"You mean Kruder? Yes, I know. I saw him."

"I think he knows."

"Why do you say that?"

"He offered me a smoke. A very rare brand."

"Is that all?"

"It's enough. If he keeps snooping around, he could stumble into everything."

"He's just fishing."

"I think we should wait."

"No, that's impossible. Everything's in place.

"I don't like it."

"Proceed as planned. He's inconsequential."

"The Gestapo is hardly inconsequential."

"Nobody knows anything. Do your job."

"I'll do my fucking job!"

As Ruti walked down the Champs Élysées, he thought back to when it all started to turn sour. Back to when everything started crashing in around him.

Four weeks earlier, on March third, a week before the American Lend-Lease proclamation was ratified by the US Congress and signed into law by Roosevelt, the American steamer *Louisa* was sailing as part of a convoy headed to Britain with foodstuffs and medical supplies. She experienced mechanical troubles that crippled her 170 kilometers off the southwest coast of Ireland, and there she was left behind, her cargo considered non-vital. The British destroyer *Scander* came to her rescue that night with plans to tow her to port. When it arrived under cover of darkness, German U-boats of wolfpack 117 struck the *Scander* with two torpedoes. Within eight minutes of taking on ballast, she broke up amidships and sank seven minutes later. The wolfpack picked up four of *Scander*'s able survivors. Scores of corpses and disabled crew members incapable of motioning for rescue were left floating in her frigid slick. Meanwhile, two U-boats surfaced alongside the *Louisa*. She was boarded, and, as she was a ship flying the flag of a neutral noncombatant, the crew was told it would be shuttled aboard U261, transported to the Irish port at Baltimore Harbour, and set free. The *Louisa* however would be sunk. The four British survivors were to be sequestered in the hold of U186,

91

passed over to the hold of the refueling tanker early that next morning, and turned over to the Abwehr in Bremerhaven for questioning before being sent to *Marlag und Milag* Westertimke, the German Kriegsmarine camp for combatant POW sailors.

It was during the proclamation of these orders by the captain of U261, who served also as commander of wolfpack 117, that his ensign handed him *Louisa*'s manifest. He took the clipboard and looked the three manifest pages over and saw nothing on the first two but long lists of foodstuffs; the third was completely blank. He shook his head and shrugged. The ensign pointed to the last item on the second page.

Suddenly, the captain rescinded all orders. The ensign was told to take charge of the manifest, tell no one about its contents, and return to U261. The *Louisa*'s crew of fourteen, the four survivors from the *Scander*, along with seven armed German Kriegsmarine sailors who would act as guards for the lot were all ordered immediately back aboard the *Louisa*. And that dark, overcast night, U261, along with four sentry escort U-boats from wolfpack 117, towed the *Louisa* at top speed 385 kilometers to the German submarine base at the French port of Brest.

Once back aboard U261, before locking it in the ship's safe, the ensign looked over the manifest again. The first two pages contained twenty-five and twenty-six lines respectively of varied items ranging from cooking oils, lima beans, cornmeal, and sugar, to Ovaltine, dehydrate of lemon, Ralston's cream of wheat, and thousands of cases of canned pork from the Swift meat company in Chicago, Illinois, branded as PREM. But the very last entry on the second page of the manifest was 960 cases, 48 cartons to the case—46,080 cartons in total—of American Old Gold brand cigarettes. And on the third page of the manifest, one single, final entry at the very top, visible only when the manifest was taken out of the clipboard, listed 960 cases of American Chesterfield cigarettes.

When the *Louisa* reached Brest that next afternoon, the ensign gave the manifest over to the port quartermaster, one Leutnant Arnold Felden. The ensign then returned to the refueled U261 and, along with the other four U-boat escorts, rejoined wolfpack 117, now redeployed in the North Sea.

Quartermaster Felden looked over the three pages of the manifest, boarded the ship, and took inventory. Within twenty minutes, he determined he'd need nine three-ton Lorries to move the ship's cargo inland. He then had the cargo off-loaded from the

Louisa, proffering strict loading instructions about which numbered wooden crates went into each truck. While this was being done, he went up to the quartermaster's office to have someone in the secretarial staff type up triplicate carbon paper copies of the manifest. A cute freckle-faced beauty from Luneberg flirted with the handsome Leutnant as she quickly typed away. His captivating green eyes were framed by dark, short-cropped hair and an intricately groomed Balbo beard. Within ten minutes, fluttering like a schoolgirl, she handed him the finished triplicate carbon copies, without a single mistake. Also, she handed him the original manifest he had given her. *Both* pages.

Just after dusk that evening, led by one Gefreiter Karl Schwarz, an eight-truck convoy left Brest for the Abwehr Groupe OTTO procurement warehouse in the freight yards at Porte de la Chapelle on the outer edge of Paris. A ninth truck, led by Quartermaster Felden himself in a black Peugeot, departed the docks of Brest on the heels of the convoy, delayed under the guise of paperwork difficulties. At the submarine base checkpoint, Leutnant Felden demanded and was swiftly granted clearance in hope of catching up to the rest of the convoy.

At 3:35 AM the next morning, headlights off, a lone French Ford truck and a black Peugeot 301 pulled up the long gravel lane leading to an isolated farm twelve kilometers outside of La Roche Guyon. And 950 cases of Chesterfield cigarettes were unloaded into the nearly empty hay barn of farmer Jean Rains. Monsieur Rains, his teenaged son, his three daughters, his wife, and his mother-in-law all helped unload one case at a time, restacking and camouflaging each with hay. Quartermaster Felden slipped both farmer Rains and the truck driver ten one-hundred-franc notes as they all shared a cherished bottle of Pomme Prisonnière. The rest of the sweat-covered unloading crew moved ten cases of American Chesterfields into the family's cellar, then went to the well house, where each took a turn at a shower and a swig or two of Pays d'Auge cider.

Four hours later the black Peugeot pulled up at the procurement headquarters in the square du Bois de Boulogne in Paris, the heart of the Abwehr's military goods procurement operation. Quartermaster Felden took the signed, dated, and stamped two-page manifests, original and copies, from Gefreiter Karl Schwartz, who was waiting for him in the lobby. Giving a halfhearted salute to the Oberschütze guard at the staircase, Leutnant Arnold Felden bounded up the stairs to the third floor and the office of Wehrmacht Procurement Records Department operations chief and Abwehr Leutnant Rutgers Heht.

Ruti's desk chair scraped on the marble floor as he rose and pressed Arnold's palm. Ruti motioned for his friend to be seated and went around the desk and closed the office door. When he returned there was a new, crisp pack of Chesterfield cigarettes standing upright on his desk like some American magazine advertisement. Arnold had two Chesterfields from his own pack in his lips. Lighting them and handing one to Ruti, he blew the smoke up toward the schoolhouse light high in the office ceiling and said, "So, Ruti, my friend. I need to enlist your help in finding a market for a half-million packs just like this one!"

"Sorry, Arnold. I have neither the time nor the guile."

"You'll have to find the time and the will." Arnold leaned forward and placed his forearm on the desk. "You owe me, Ruti. You know you do."

Ruti gritted his teeth, closed his eyes, and nodded reluctantly.

"A half million packs? Fifty thousand cartons? We can't move that in Paris undetected. We will have to go to the provinces. To Vichy. Twenty to fifty cartons at a time. It will take us years."

"You know as well as I, we can get ten, maybe twenty francs a carton. A million francs between us. Find a way, old friend."

"Arnold, I'm being reassigned in April. I don't think I can get this placed by then."

"Sure you can. Your black market contacts are second to none. I'll check back with you the first if the month." Quartermaster Felden stood up to leave. "Get me fifty thousand francs now. The rest before you leave."

He grabbed Ruti's forearm and shook his hand.

"I know you won't let me down."

DAY ONE—Paris—Saturday, 5 April 41—12:48 PM
Soaked to his core, Ruti dashed through the driving rain down the steps to the Port du Louvre and rushed along the Right Bank of the Seine. He was late. Hopefully, the broker was still there. As he came up to the huge bulwark under the Pont Royal, he was startled by a gendarme bending over a body in the set back under the bridge. The policeman quickly stood up.

"Halt. Don't move," he demanded.

Ruti held up his palms to the gendarme. "I don't know anything about this." Ruti smiled at the young gendarme. "I'm just in a hurry. I have a train to catch."

Fall Irmgard

"You stay right there. You're not going anywhere." The policeman pulled his pistol.

"I'm a German officer. You can't talk to me like that."

"You're a possible witness to a murder. You'll do as I say."

"You mean this fellow is dead," Ruti said, moving over to look at the corpse. "What happened?"

"Don't come any closer."

The gendarme barely finished the sentence before Ruti had him in an armlock and drove him into the stone wall. The air in the officer's chest exploded from him as a deep sigh. In one smooth motion Ruti hyperextended the policeman's arm at the elbow, dislodging the pistol. As he kicked it in the Seine, the big, powerful German drove his elbow backward, hard into the policeman's nose. In a daze, the gendarme grabbed for his whistle, but Ruti tore it from him and drove the side of his head into the wall. Ruti hoped he hadn't killed him, as the man hit the cobblestone hard when he fell. Quickly, he looked at the corpse.

"Scheisse!" Ruti exclaimed, examining the dead man's face. It was indeed Fabien Lemay. He searched all around, looking for a briefcase, a package, perhaps an envelope. Something that would hold the last of the securities and information about the change of plans. Nothing. Just a corpse was starting to swell, its mouth, nose, and the back of his head were thick with clotting blood and swarming flies.

11

die Liga der Herren
La ligue des seigneurs
The League of Lords

DAY ONE—Paris—Saturday, 5 April 41—3:10 PM
In the lobby of the Hotel Ritz, Willy von Kanderstein sat looking at
his pocket watch as the hotel's salon ensemble played the elegant
"Albéniz Tango." A lobby waiter passed and Willy grabbed his arm,
ordered another brandy, and nervously adjusted his tie. Every time the
tall polished brass and beveled glass revolving door spun another
person or two into the gilded lobby, Willy looked up from his
Nouveaux Temps newspaper hoping to see the man he'd traveled two
days to meet. And as each strange face rushed past him, he grew more
frustrated.

Willy von Kanderstein, along with his silent partner, owned and
operated *Lodei Vergaser GmbH*, the Lodei Carburetor Company,
producers of automotive carburetion and fuel-injection systems based
in Berlin-Köpenick, an industrial suburb on the southeast outskirts of
the German capital. Over the past five years, Lodei Vergaser had
tripled its output of fuel systems and parts production. But the
increased volume had taken a toll on Lodei's production machinery.
In January the company's main press had to be replaced at a cost of
over three-hundred thousand Reichsmark. Willy and his partner were
making good money. But they were both spending it by the
wheelbarrow loads. Their little company maintained lavish hotel
suites in Rüsselsheim, Cologne, and Stuttgart. As financing was being
arranged through Dresdener Bank for the purchase and installation of
the new equipment, representatives from the Hermann Göring
Konzern approached Willy, offering to completely reequip the plant,
for free! All Willy had to do was sign over forty percent of the
company to HGK GmbH. Willy's partner, who owned twenty-five
percent of Lodei Vergaser, refused to give up his part of the shares
without considerable remuneration. Willy turned them down, but the
Göring people approached his partner and negotiated a separate cash
deal with him. By the end of the week, the Hermann Göring Konzern
had a twenty-five percent stake in Lodei, and Willy von Kanderstein

was working for the SS. Since then, Willy and his longtime friend and partner had become estranged, albeit in a civil Prussian way.

When Willy's former partner waddled through the tall revolving doors, Willy jumped up and startled the old man.

"Zum Donnerwetter, Willy!" Konni Ritter exclaimed, grabbing his chest. "I believe my silly heart may have stopped!"

"I must talk to you, old friend."

"Willy. Let me catch my breath." Konni held his palm out to Willy and took some deep breaths. "This has been an exasperating day. You have absolutely no idea."

"Please have a drink with me, Konni. I must talk to you."

"My good man. I am already late for a very important meeting."

"Please, Konni." Willy grabbed Konni's arm to keep him from walking on. "For the old times. Drink with me."

Konni handed his cane and hat to an unsuspecting lobby waiter carrying a tray of dirty glasses.

"Yes, then. I suppose I could use a drink. A drink to the old times, Willy." The waiter awkwardly took his overcoat and their drink orders.

"I'm desperate, old friend," Willy said, lighting the next in a string of Haus Neuerburg cigarettes. "These bastards are killing our— my company. My family's company."

"I'm sorry for you, Willy. But you're the one who first made the deal with the devil. All I did was follow your lead."

"Indeed, Konni. The perfect word. The devil. The Göring Konzern owns twenty-five percent of my company, yet they run everything! I've infected my people as well with this hideous plague. I'm the president of the company. Yet my salary is the sixth highest! Five people—people who never show up at the factory—make more money than I do. And the highest-paid employee? Who is it? None other than Hermann Göring himself!"

The waiter appeared with their drinks. Willy extinguished his cigarette and took a few deep breaths trying to compose himself, looking vacantly up at the huge crystal chandeliers in the hotel's lobby. The waiter placed a clean ashtray on the dirty one, set them both on his tray, and returned the clean one to the table as he turned to leave.

"And our big, roomy factory? They've crammed twice the machinery into it they should. One whole third is already producing fuel system component for Messerschmitt. And they've started using French prisoners to do some of the work. These men are soldiers, they're not factory workers. They're unskilled. But Lodei Vergaser pays the Konzern the same for these prisoners as we do our skilled workers. The prisoners don't get a pfennig! It all goes to the SS. And now I have uniformed SS men walking the factory floors. SS men in my factory, intimidating my people."

Konni sat back and took a sip of his drink and asked, "Willy? What on earth would you have me do?"

"You can help me, Konni. You've always had the Führer's ear. You can ask him to put everything back the way it was. We'll go to the back to the Dresdener people. We'll get our loan. We'll get our company back."

"Willy, you poor fellow." Konni looked at his watch. "This is not some back-alley Party hack. It's Reichsführer Hermann Göring. There's simply nothing I can do, my good man. Besides, I'm no longer a part of the company."

"Yes, you got your money, didn't you?"

"So then, Willy, sell your remaining interest."

"I tried to. What did they offer me? A paltry million marks. Seventy-five percent of a company doing over four hundred million a year in sales for a mere million marks? It's robbery!"

"So, negotiate with them, Willy. Make a demand and meet them somewhere in the middle."

"I have nothing to negotiate with. They discovered . . ." He took a sip of his drink. "Somehow, they found out about my little tête-à-tête. They threatened to expose everything to my sweet Theresa. Those arrogant, flippant Frankfurt lawyers. They hold all the cards."

"Then I'm afraid, Willy, that you must accept your lot."

"You can't abandon me, Konni. Look at me. I drink a liter a day. I can't eat. I can't sleep. I'm going quite mad, Konni. You must help me."

"I'm sorry, my friend. I can't help you." Konni looked again at his watch. "Now, I simply must take my leave. My best to you, old friend." He smiled and put his hand on Willy's shoulder.

"Yes, smile you bastard." Willy jerked his shoulder aside. "Just like the Reichsführer's Nazi lawyers. Smile at me and pander to me. You're out of this pickle, aren't you? What do you care? I got nothing! Nothing but an SS factory paying me a monthly salary I used to go through in a weekend! A company that won't see a pfennig of profit for the entire thousand year Reich! But you got your money. You backstabber. Look at you! I'm ruined and you're living it up here at the Ritz." Willy's voice grew louder, until he blurted out, almost screamed, "You did this to me, you bastard!"

"I believe I have finished my drink, and my conversation with you." Konni stood and snapped his finger at the waiter. "I hope your lovely wife is well. And I wish you great success in your new business endeavor." The waiter handed Konni his coat, hat, and cane as Konni told him to put the drinks on his tab. Konni turned back to Willy, tipped his head, bowed, and with the slightest click of his heels bid Willy von Kanderstein, "Au revoir."

"I'll get you, you bastard!" Willy said as two huge men in tuxedos quickly approached him. Shaking uncontrollably, Willy held his palms out to them and said, "Okay, I'm leaving." He chugged the last of his drink and stormed out the tall revolving doors and onto the place Vendôme into a cold, swirling drizzle.

DAY ONE—Paris—Saturday, 5 April 41—3:23 PM
For the past seven months, on the first Saturday of each, the suite of rooms at the far end of the hall on the second floor of the Hotel Ritz was secured by a very astute American lawyer from Houston, Texas, known to everyone in the oil business as Bentley Henderson, attorney at law. On each occasion the hotel staff had the suite rearranged for a meeting of nine people. Two Louis XIV settees were removed from the elegant stateroom and replaced by eight tall winged-backed fauteuils. The chairs were arranged in a semicircle in the center of the room, and beside each chair was a cherrywood end table with a beveled glass top. On each table sat two packs of American cigarettes one Lucky Strike and one Camel; a Meissen china ashtray molded in the form of a bathing Japanese geisha; a pocket-size, mahogany five-pack case of Havana cigars; a small brass lamp with a domed green fluted-glass globe; and a bottle of each attendee's liquor of choice. This time there was also, in the center, a leather-padded desk chair and a cast-iron ashtray stand in the shape of an overly gleeful Negro servant, his face made of finely polished black onyx, his ghoulishly large lips white alabaster and his eyes ivory discs with inlaid opal for pupils. In his right hand, he held a pewter and amber ashtray, and a little higher, in his left, a small pewter serving tray just large enough for one crystal drinking glass.

When the knock came at the door, Bentley Henderson did little more than raise his index finger and a frail, doting woman in a plum pinstriped suit with a tightly drawn hair bun rose from the secretaire directly behind him and went to the tall double doors. She opened them and bid entrance to the somewhat mystified old man at the door. Bentley Henderson lit a Lucky Strike as he held out his diamond-laden hand, gesturing for the old man to take a seat next to the Negro ashtray stand.

"Gentlemen," Bentley Henderson said, in his slow, overtly showy Texas drawl. He took a long and very dramatic drag from his cigarette and blew the smoke upward to disturb and mingle with the thick swirling pall that had already collected above the circle, turned an ominous green patina by the eight desk lamp globes.

Konni Ritter looked around at the men in the circle. There were no faces. The yellow light from the desk lamps showed them only from their shoulders down, illuminating their tailor-made Park Avenue and Savile Row suits and their shiny black shoes. Occasionally, a face would glow here and there for a second when one of them took a drag on their cigars or cigarettes.

"I'd like to introduce, for those of you that don't know him, a man I am going to refer to as Mr. Knight. Now, that's not Mr. Knight's real name. No, he's got one of them big fancy-ass German titles than runs on long as a young bull's dick. But Mr. Knight, as ya'll do know, has been an extremely good friend to the varied and important American business interests in Europe represented by all of us in this room." He stopped and scratched behind his ear while inhaling deeply through a big clenched, toothy grin, still more woodsy drama.

"Now, Mr. Knight? This is one of those you-can't-believe-your-lying-eyes type meetings. What I mean by that is, this meeting never took place. And these old boys you see around you here? Welsur, they aren't really even here. Bentley leaned forward in his chair. "Mr. Knight? Would you like a drink?"

"Doch, ja . . . yes, perhaps a Cointreau," Konni said, adding a big smile as a shield to the intimidating proceedings.

"Miss Garland?" Again with the finger flick. The secretary called out from her desk in French: "Garcon, a Cointreau for the gentleman, s'il vous plaît." A boy of maybe fifteen appeared like a ghost from a dark corner of the room and took a bottle from a wheeled silver bar.

"Miss Judy Garland?" Bentley inquired with a wide-eyed smile and bounce of his head. "Star of stage and screen? The Wizard of Oz?"

Konni shook his head.

"Never heard of her? No? You Nazzi boys need to get out a little more." The uniformed attendant poured Konni's drink. As he did, Bentley smiled and whispered to Konni, "Don't worry. He don't speak no English."

The ghost returned to his darkness and Bentley continued.

"Anyway, Mr. Knight, I want to tell you a little story." Bentley Henderson patted Konni's shoulder as he started walking around the circle. "When I was a boy, I was the baby of seven kids, six of us was boys. I had a big sister. She could whup any two of us. Now, my daddy was a poor man. He farmed a little rice and run cattle on about seven sections. Now, in south Texas? An old boy got a little dab of land like that? That is a poor man, Mr. Knight. So, growing up in a big family? I was extremely fortunate to learn the most important lesson of my life at a very early age. When you are the little guy . . ." He paused intentionally. "At the far end of the table?" Another long pause. "Mr. Knight, you never get nothing but backs and necks! You never get no breasts, you never get no thighs or drumsticks. Not even any of them little bitty drumsticks comes off the wing? Lord, you'd think a mama'd be sure her baby boy got some of them little bitty drumsticks comes off the wing, wouldn't you, Mr. Knight? But nope. No, sir. Just backs and necks. And God bless her, Mr. Knight. Because you see? All my tender young life I had to nibble and suck what meat I could off of backs and necks. So, when I grew up, I made me a vow, Mr. Knight. I vowed I would never again in my life be the little guy at the far end of the table. Nor would I let any of my people, or the people I represent, be the little guy at the far end of the table. No backs." He looked down at Konni. "No necks." He raised his eyebrows and emphatically shook his head. "Never again. For me or any of mine, Mr. Knight."

Bentley sat back down and looked Konni in the eye. "Do you understand what I'm saying to you, sir?"

Konni took a sip from his glass and leaned back in the chair, trying to bolster a little of his own drama. He wasn't used to not being the one in control of a business meeting. And he didn't like it. "My good fellow," he said, his English thickly accented. He took another sip of Cointreau. "I suppose I do have one somewhat important question for you."

"But of course, Mr. Knight. What would that be?"

"What language are you speaking?"

Laughter in the room re-erupted each time it had almost waned, as "Miss Garland," try as she might, found it impossible to bring herself under control. Konni too was caught up in the fray and was wiping the tears from his eyes.

"Mr. Knight," some other faceless voice interjected. "In the past you and your, well, let's say your friends, have been very helpful to all of us in this room. And not without a fair amount of risk, I might add. Over this past year, the German government has administered tight controls on the ability of foreign businesses to convert profits into international currency. We feel like it is only a matter of time, possibly just days, before America will be drawn into this war. As a result we have come up with a—"

"Mr. Knight," Bentley harshly interrupted. "What my esteemed colleague is trying say, without all the boring detail, is that we would like to know if you're up to another go at it?"

Konni's bewildered look led Bentley to add, "We want you to do some more work for us, Mr. Knight. And as far as your fee goes, well sir, the sky's the limit!"

"I'm very sorry." Konni shook his head. "I lost contact with Irmgard. I'm quite certain she's been arrested or worse."

"You're a resourceful fella. So, get a replacement."

"Back then, the war was just folly. But now, since the invasion and occupation of France, it's all virtually impossible. And in my position, with my responsibilities here in France..."

"Mr. Knight, we'll just go ahead and take that as a *no*."

"But I simply can't do it."

"Thank you, Mr. Knight. I trust you will keep anything we discussed here today in the strictest confidence." He turned his back to Konni and added, "Miss Garland, if you'd be so kind as to show Mr. Knight out."

Bentley Henderson nodded toward the door where "Miss Garland" stood holding it half-open. "We wish the very best to you, Mr. Knight."

12

Unglaublich blauen Augen
D'incroyables yeux bleus
Incredible Blue Eyes

DAY ONE—Paris—Saturday, 5 April 41—7:15 PM

The restaurant attached to the Club l'Heure Bleue was called Bistro Bruno, and the namesake adored his two-meter-tall, cream-white, neon script sign that defined his fare as *Kuche der grosser Reich*, Cuisine of the Greater Reich. It upset Bruno to no end that he had to kill the sign just after twilight each evening due to the blackout restrictions. Luftwaffe bombing campaigns in Britain throughout the winter had caused retaliation, not only in Germany but also on the French coast and in Nord, the restricted zone of occupied France around Lille. As recently as mid-March, huge Luftwaffe losses over England had caused heightened alert status.

As the days of spring grew longer, with France on German War time, an hour ahead of pre-war Europe, the purple glow in the western sky was all but gone before the creamy script above the Bistro Bruno went dark. It was at that moment tonight that Werner Heitner walked slowly across the place Alphonse-Deville. After ringing up Konrad Ritter at the Ritz this morning, Werner had walked from the rue Oberkampf, backtracking through shops and department stores, cutting back and forth through huge evening crowds scurrying along on busy boulevards and crowded lanes. He was a thin man with dark-blue eyes and a Führer mustache. Smartly dressed in a brown pinstriped suit with a dark-brown fedora, his appearance had been badly wilted by the long cat-and-mouse walk, certain the best strategy was to keep moving. He stopped across the street from Bruno's and looked at his reflection in the shop window. Glancing around, he stuffed his floppy shirttail back into his trousers and adjusted his suit coat more squarely on his round shoulders. A deep breath of self-assurance and he followed a group of couples through the restaurant's wisteria-draped breezeway and into the courtyard, toward the side entrance.

Down the street a dark-blue Renault Vivastella pulled away from the curb and drove up to the breezeway. One man got out and the other drove around the block to the restaurant's main entrance on the rue du Cherche-Midi.

Werner gave the maître d' Konni Ritter's name and was seated at a reserved table in the back. He looked over the eight pages of house specialties, his daring eyes darted from this *wurst* to that. The menu at Bistro Bruno contained selections ranging from lachsschinken and buttered *vollkorn* bread with Dutch pea soup to Vienna's own Wienerkalbschnitzel and every Prussian or Hessian, Saxon or Silesian, Bavarian or Bohemian sausage, schnitzel, potato, or kraut combination imaginable. But his mind was on more important matters.

Werner Heitner was a traitor, both to his imperialist upbringing and to his elitist lifestyle. His father Adalwolf was a distinguished horn smith artisan from the tiny Austrian village of Telfs on the Inn River west of Innsbruck. For generations Heitner artisans had handcrafted buttons, combs, music boxes, and clock pieces from animal horn and hoof as well as from tortoiseshell. Werner was the youngest of Adalwolf's three sons and the only one without the slightest interest in the family business. In 1913, with his father growing senile, Adalwolf's eldest son, Max, assumed command of the company. For years, Max had taken a serious interest in the new rennet casein artificial horn materials being used in Germany under the brand name Galalith. Casein was an early plastic derived from the combination of whey protein in milk and rennet extracted from a calf's stomach (not unlike a cheese making process), which was then mixed with a formaldehyde solution. The resulting product was a hard, dyeable, easily polished type of plastic that could be molded and fabricated much more easily than horn or tortoiseshell. Casein's discovery was fabled to have been the result of a clumsy cat owned by a turn-of-the-century French chemist that knocked a saucer of milk into a bowl of formaldehyde. *Voilà!*

Max Heitner moved the family business to Innsbruck and created *Katz und Teller Kunsthorn Fabrik AG*. By the start of the First World War, the Heitner brothers had grown the tiny artisan business of their father and grandfather's day into a mass-production marvel. And when Max met a dapper and convivial German army officer and automotive industry enthusiast on a skiing trip to the Salzkammergut, *KuTKF* Incorporated of Innsbruck, as the company was expediently referred to, would become even more successful. The next spring, in 1914, the world was at war, and through Max's ski-trip association with the same German officer, one Herr Konrad Ritter, KuTKF acquired contracts with the German and Austro-Hungarian armies for automobile and airplane knobs, switch ends, and underwear and uniform buttons.

During the last year of the war, while his brothers worked in the factory young Werner, only nineteen at the time, attended university in Vienna, consuming his loving father's benevolence with a voracious appetite and duping the old man into believing in each winsome change in aspirations that prolonged his education and increased its cost. Werner was especially interested in music, though he lacked the initiative to play anything, and after his first year, he became devoutly interested in Karl Marx and the tenets of socialism.

The company fell on difficult times in the inflationary period of postwar Europe and the worldwide Depression. Max and his other brother Friedrich both worked diligently to find contracts to keep KuTKF in business while Werner demanded more and more from his ailing father to support his playboy student lifestyle.

When Max finally convinced the old man to stop funding Werner's folly, Adalwolf Heitner's youngest son returned to Telfs, bitter and daunted. Within weeks Adalwolf died and Max forced Werner to work in the factory, where he learned the business and finally earned his way. Werner quickly learned enough about casein to see that it was a dying substance. Werner's interests lay in phonograph shellacs. He wanted the family's production medium to change to the new Bakelite plastics that were taking over the phonograph record production industry.

The popularity of Bakelite was blossoming in the 1920s, and Max had designs on taking the company in that direction as well. Bakelite's more durable, malleable, and, most importantly, nonconductive properties made it the substance of choice for automobile, electrical, and radio parts. Konni Ritter promised to help Max get contracts with the Wehrmacht as well as with German automakers like Daimler, Opel, and Ford if he retooled for Bakelite production.

A clause in Adalwolf's will required unanimity of all three brothers in all KuTKF major decisions. Werner refused to agree to the change without being allowed to branch off into phonograph reproduction with KuTKF financing. An impasse resulted. And on an icy winter night as Max and Friedrich returned from Mittenwald, their Maybach drove off a mountain and, along with their chauffeur, both older brothers were killed. An investigation determined some sort of acid, probably from a leaking battery, had eaten through the car's brake lines. While everyone from the authorities to his sisters-in-law suspected Werner, no proof was ever unearthed. So, in 1927, Werner Heitner became sole proprietor of KuTKF, and by the next year he was living off the Casein fabrication profits, as well as those from the handful of bone artisans back in Telfs. He was making only feeble efforts to move into Bakelite and was doing little more than toying with phonograph record manufacturing.

Konni waddled his way to Werner's table in the back of the restaurant.

Werner rose and pressed Konni's hand.

"It's good to see you again, Herr Ritter."

"Frankly, we'll just have to see about that, won't we?" Konni took his seat and asked of the maître d', "A Bitburger, if you will, my good man."

"Of course, sir. I'll tell your waiter."

"So, Werner, still the Marxist, are you?"

"My god, man! Are you daft?" Werner looked around with incredulity.

"Young fellow, I had nothing but the highest regard for your family. I considered Max the best sort of friend and I had immeasurable respect for your very dutiful brother Friedrich, may God rest their souls. But you, Werner, you are nothing like them. I am certain you were pushed by events during your university days, influenced by its leftist culture. But you cannot, in these dangerous times, stand so defiantly against these people. They will catch you, they will behead you, and, most importantly where I am concerned, they will relentlessly come after anyone who finds himself in your association. Therefore, as you have little regard for anything short of your foolish ideals, I haven't the slightest regard for you!"

"And Herr Ritter, I could care less. But you, sir, will continue to do as I require, because, old man, if heads do roll, I assure you, yours will be among them."

"I never chose to be involved in this scheme of yours. You imposed yourself on me."

"I believe it all started when you came to me with need of your first fake passport, didn't it, Ritter?"

"Indeed. With your brother's death, unfortunately, it did."

"And it was a flawlessly perfect job, was it not?" Werner leaned across the table, his voice barely a whisper. "And each credential since has been as well, has it not?"

"They have. Your people have always been the most skilled artisans."

"And did this mysterious woman of yours ever run into any troubles of any sort?"

"None." Konni looked down and sighed. "That we know of."

"No, none. And that brings me to one of the reasons I am here. I don't think this woman died like you led me to believe. I think she's quite alive, old friend. And I think that she's back in Switzerland."

He was interrupted by a waiter, who set down a dish of tiny Stellendam shrimps and Konni's beer. When he left, Werner continued.

"You got the package I left for you at your hotel? I expect it to be delivered, just as before. And I assure you, the consequences of your failure will be fatal!"

"The package cannot be delivered," Konni said, sipping his beer and stabbing a few shrimps with his fork. "The woman is dead. And you, sir, are out of the espionage business. As am I." With the shrimp popped in his mouth, he smiled at Werner. "Allow me to give you some advice, young fellow," he continued.

"No!" Werner interrupted, pointing his finger in Konni's face. "Let me give *you* some." Werner stood to leave. "Keep looking over your shoulder, old fool. I want you to see it coming!"

Konni shook his head. "Go back to beautiful Austria," he said, chewing. "Live to be an old man with grandchildren on your knee. And in doing so, permit me to do the same!"

Werner swept up his coat and hat and as he left he bent down and whispered to Konni, "You won't live through the day!"

His coat collar up to his ears and the bill of his hat tipped down over his eyes, Werner walked briskly out of the bistro's courtyard and down the darkening sidewalk along the rue d'Assas. In the place Alphonse-Deville the dark-blue Vivastella pulled away from the curb and slowly followed him.

13

Gute Reise
Bon voyage

DAY ONE—Paris—Saturday, 5 April 41—9:41 PM
At the l'Heure Bleue Hilda and Lorraine danced a sexy tango to
"Schreib Mir einen Brief." Both girls wore black stiletto heels. Hilda
donned tuxedo pants and white evening suspenders that loosely
covered her tiny bare nipples. Lorraine wore only heels, a top hat, a
waistcoat with tails, and ivory silk panties. After a first few bars of
the song, each girl chose a man from the audience to dance with.
They avoided German officers, finding instead businessmen. Over the
last week, throughout Paris, dancing had been outlawed by the High
Command due to the terrible beating the Luftwaffe was taking over
Britain. But in the Club l'Heure Bleue, it was simply a part of the
show.

Bruno set three glasses on the table in front of Konni, Reinhard
Rupp, and Suzi and filled each with champagne.

"I'm quite anxious to see my niece's l'Heure Bleue debut, Herr
Kestler," Reinhard said, patting the top of Suzi's hand with his own
and smiling.

"As I am anxious to see the club operate very smoothly from
now on." Bruno forced a smile and added to Suzi, "You should get
back stage, my dear. You have less than ten minutes."

The bubbly girl sprang from her chair, threw back her
champagne, and kissed Reinhard's pasty cheek, then hugged Konni's
neck. Smiling and asking for "*Gluck*," *luck*, she was gone. Bruno
clamped his huge mitt on Reinhard's shoulder as he moved past him,
adding, "Our deal is solid, Herr Sonderführer."

The Propaganda Ministry official cringed only slightly, saying,
"Indeed, our deal is solid."

Bruno walked away, gritting his teeth. Every aspect of the
l'Heure Bleue was a serious matter to him. A successful club didn't
just happen. It was willed, and the l'Heure Bleue was commandeered
by Bruno Kestler's strong will. A genius of ambience and setting a
night's mood, he understood the important role light and dimness,
motion and fixture, music and silence all played in creating what he
demanded. How each effect was a muse for its creation and how

maintaining it throughout the evening was a fragile process that could all very easily come crashing down. Every nuance was important—the temperature, the décor, the arrangement of the tables, the flowers, the candles, and especially the music, its timing, and even its sequence. Bruno made every such decision with the greatest care and maintained each with the strictest vigor.

He felt that each hour should consist of five minutes of overture music, fifteen minutes of show, and thirty minutes of what he liked to call *Konverzationsmuzik*. Music that was conducive to polite socializing and, of course, heavy drinking. That would leave ten minutes an hour for the band members to smoke and pee.

Overture music was chosen from lively, popular pieces, something that told the crowd the show was nigh; tunes like "Night Train to Warsaw" or "Gypsy Wine," the latter of which the band started playing tonight after the polite applause for the tasty tango.

Bruno became suddenly upset that the reserved four-top table two rows back and to the right of center was still empty. He searched out Xavier and asked him why. The show was starting soon. He wasn't going to have people waltz in to a front table and interrupt the show.

"Very important guests, monsieur. Very important."

"I don't care if its Adolf himself. If they're not here in ten minutes, they're losing their reservation. We have people lined up to get in tonight."

"But Monsieur Bruno. Impossible. The tables must be held."

"Who is it, Xavier?"

"A very important man. A man who prefers to remain anonymous."

"Xavier, who is it?"

"Him." Xavier pointed with just the tip of his finger to a group of four men entering the club, led by one of the usherettes in a sheer black blouse and long, flowing panted-skirt.

"That's . . . "

"Oui, monsieur."

"The gangster? What's his name? Forney?"

"Oui, Monsieur Bruno. Guy de Forney."

"What's he doing in my club? Two of them are Germans. Who are they?"

"I do not know, monsieur. Gestapo, maybe?"

Bruno glared at Xavier, who could only shrug as if to say, "What could I do?"

***

"*Vive la paix*" was the toast offered by Guy de Forney after everyone's glass was filled, "*Long live the peace.*" He was said to be the most beautifully attired and most dangerous pheasant in all of Paris. Tonight he wore a burgundy tuxedo with matching black velvet lapels, butterfly tie, cummerbund and button studs, and brilliant black spats. To his right sat SD-RSHA Sturmbannführer Kurt Hummel of the avenue Foch Gestapo headquarters. On his left was Victor Roche, de Forney's right-hand man who tonight wore an eye patch over a freshly wounded eye and walked with had a pronounced limp. Across from Monsieur de Forney sat Sturmbannführer Alois Kruder, newly arrived from Warsaw only this very morning.

"What is it the French call it?" Kruder asked. "Our presence here, the occupation?"

"They call it *l'affreuse chose*, I believe," answered Hummel.

"Yes, *l'affreuse chose, the terrible thing.* But you don't concur with that sentiment, do you, Monsieur de Forney?

"I have . . . adapted, shall we say."

"It was of course a terrible winter, don't you agree?" Hummel raised the glass of champagne again with two fingers and sipped.

"On the contrary, it was a lovely winter," de Forney contradicted. "A winter where people paid exorbitantly for warmth and food. A winter where people needed more of what I have to sell."

"Then I propose another toast, gentlemen," Kruder said, rising over them to refill their glasses.

"To this *l'affreuse chose*, to this terrible thing."

Sheepishly, Xavier smiled at Bruno across the room. Bruno just turned and walked away.

Xavier was famous for upsetting Bruno, but conflict waned quickly as Bruno knew he needed his business manager. Many things had gone perfectly to bring about the club's success, but none more than the conspired web of inventory resupply and clandestine payoffs this little man was able to weave.

No one could have foretold that Xavier's brother, Lorenz in Saarbrucken, had a truck, and a brother-in-law in the local Gestapo as well as a first cousin who worked with the Grepo Grenzpolizei (border police) in Metz, officially at Novéant—Neuburg an der Mosel, the newly annexed Moselle region of France. Within weeks, barrels of German *beer*—Radeberger and Berliner Kindl, Tucher and

Dortmunder Union—as well as crates of tiny Nürnburgers and Münchner Weissewursts, Krakauer, and Thuringian sausages were loaded in from trains in Saarbrücken onto the Opel trucks of Spedition Lorenz, iced down, and delivered to Paris, to the Club l'Heure Bleue and Bistro Bruno.

And it all came twice a week for free! Because on the return trip, each truck was packed with hundreds of cases of French wines, laces, fashions, and perfumes. Booty purchased with francs at huge exchange-rate discounts and sold for Reichsmark on the black market in German cities.

Every night at the Club l'Heure Bleue, the show started with a lively, extended rendition of "Musik! Musik! Musik!" during which each singer and member of the band could be introduced. On this particular evening, it would not include Sabina. She refused to ever share the stage with the new little twat! So her part was taken by Suzi.

As the show started, the first in almost a year without its star singer, Sabina snuck out from back stage, avoiding any well-wishers, and slid along the back wall to join her friends at one of the six-top tables in the rear of the club hosting Addie Bridges' bon-voyage party. The party table consisted of Konni Ritter at one end and Mélina at the other. Seated behind the table against the wall were Addie and Yvette along with two of Addie's German girlfriends who worked at the Abwehr Office in the Hotel Lutetia, Gretl von Reinsdorf-Vilmer and Hedy von Rohrbach. Like most of the German girls working in Paris for the Wehrmacht, Gretl and Hedy were the daughters of Germany's titled elite.

Sabina wriggled herself in between Yvette and Addie. She took Mélina's drink out of her hand and offered it up as a toast to Addie.

"So you're really leaving us, are you?" Sabina almost shouted, being purposely disruptive as the show was just starting. "Well, bon voyage, Addie, my dear American friend." Glasses were clinked and sips taken. "With your departure I will once again be the most beautiful creature in the neighborhood!"

"Oh, but Sabina, darling," Addie offered. "You always have been."

Sabina handed the glass to Mélina saying, "Here, toast Addie and take a swig, gloomy puss!"

"Sabina, you remember Mélina . . ." Addie started the introduction, but was interrupted by Sabina.

"Ruti's Mélina?"

"Yes, she came for my party."

"Tell me, my dear," Sabina asked, leaning across the table toward Mélina. "Is it difficult to walk upright after that big stallion has a roll with you?"

Mélina started crying and rushed out of the club, saying, "I'm sorry. Addie. I just can't do it."

"Mélina!"

"Let her go, Addie," Yvette said. "She can just make the last Métro. I'll talk to her tomorrow for you."

"Sabina! That was most uncalled for!" Addie scolded.

"Perhaps, but necessary. This is a party, not a wake!"

The disruption brought Xavier to the table. "Shush. The show has begun, Sabina. We must be respectful of the other performers."

Sabina lowered her head and forcefully whispered, "Oof, we must be respectful, darlings."

Xavier scowled and scraped his left index finger over his right, gesturing his shame on her.

"He's quite queer, you know, Xavier is," she added.

Hearing her insult, the little man threw his head in the air and pranced away.

"Why, I know for a fact the man is queer!" Konni whispered, feeling it was time the party began in earnest.

"How do you know that, Herr Ritter?" Hedy asked, hugging herself around his arm and smiling at the other girls.

"It's been made obvious to me for some time. You see"—he bent down as if to tell a terrible secret—"the silly sissy just giggles like hell every time I kiss him!"

Libation-fueled suppressed laughter became chortles and squeaks. Bruno heard the commotion and made his way over to the table.

"You should be up there, Sabina," he said, angrily.

"Never, while your little tramp is on stage."

"But Sabina, love. You simply must," Addie pleaded. "Darling, this is my last night at the club. Do be a swell girl and go on stage." Addie took Sabina's hand in hers and kissed it. "Please sweetie, for me."

"Yes," Sabina said, tapping Addie on the nose. "Indeed. I'll do it for you. Only for you."

"Then you better hurry." Bruno's whispers were really just his deep voice, gone deeper.

Sabina pointed at him and added, "And just for tonight."

Bruno shook his head and moved along.

"Well, I say, isn't that that gangster fellow sitting over there?" Konni asked, shaking his pointed finger, then snapping them in the air while he tried to remember. "Guy something or other?"

"Guy de Forney," Yvette answered. "The Corsican. He's a racketeer and even a murderer, they say."

"Yes, that's him. Why, I should introduce myself to that fellow. I'm told we have common business interests. In today's gray economy, one can never have too many associates, you know."

Feigning a playful zeal, Sabina slinked quickly over behind Konni and told him, "Take care, my sweet darling. That beastly vermin might slip up behind you and slit your throat . . ." She stuck her left thumb into his mouth from behind him, pressing it deep into his tongue, grabbing his jaw with the rest of her fingers. The long thumbnail on her right hand then slid forcefully along the width of the old man's throat. "Like a butcher slits a fat pig's throat!"

"Sabina, darling. You're hurting him!" Addie scolded.

Konni gagged and pushed her hands away.

"Yes, Sabina, really," Konni added with a trumped-up fluster. "You're creating a most unsightly stir, my dear. And frightening me and the other girls!" He grimaced. "That didn't come out as intended."

Again, the girls struggled to subdue snickers as Sabina quickly jumped around beside Konni and cocked her head to one side. She cupped the bewildered old man's chubby cheeks in her palms and baby-talked. "Sabina wouldn't hurt a hair on Sweet Suzi Rupp's sugar daddy, would she?" She kissed his lips, his nose, and his forehead, and quickly slinked across the room toward the backstage doorway.

Konni turned to the others at the table with a goofy smile. They all burst again into suppressed giggles. He looked in the smoked-glass mirror paneled wall behind him and could just make out in the darkness that his mouth, nose, and forehead bore perfect impressions of Sabina's bright-red lips.

The song "Musik! Musik! Musik!" proceeded, each performer had a stanza or two, the last of which was to be sung by Sabina's replacement, Sweet Suzi Rupp. But when Subina entered the stage the only one surprised was Suzi. She just forced a smile and looked away.

The girls at the back table all started applauding when they saw Sabina, and their applause moved like a wave from the back to the front of the audience.

During the interlude before the show continued, as the band played "Bei Dir war es immer so schön," the hostess escorted Rolf, Gep, and Hans to their reserved table in the center of the club. She was a pretty young French girl in a black evening dress and pleated hat adorned by a long black feather that curled around to tickle her opposite cheek. Seeing them, Addie noticed the man she'd seen gawking at her in the window. The tiniest flutter danced in her stomach.

The men had just ordered drinks when Hans noticed the girls at Addie's table.

"Look who's hiding back there," he quipped.

Rolf and Gep followed Hans to the girls' table, and as introductions were made around, Rolf's blue eyes smiled as Hans came to Addie.

"Miss Addie Bridges, allow me to introduce Oberleutnant Gephardt Fechter and Major Karl-Rudolf von Gerz."

"I kiss the hand, mademoiselle." Rolf clicked his heels and took Addie's hand.

She coyly quipped, "I believe we have already met, haven't we, major?"

The others all looked at each other, exchanging their surprise. Rolf rose up from the kiss with smiling eyes.

"I happened to catch the major window *licking* this morning," she quipped. Tell me, Major. Did you see anything you liked?"

"Paris is a beautiful city full of many lovely treasures, Miss Bridges." Still holding her hand, he placed his other over it and added, "Yes, I have been duly impressed by everything I have seen since I stepped off the train this morning. And please, call me Rolf."

His nickname delighted her. She took her hand slowly away and said, "Then you can call me Addie, Rolf."

"Addie is returning home to America," Gretl said. "She leaves Monday."

"How regrettable," Gep said. "Paris will be saddened by your departure, mademoiselle."

"Like they say, *après moi*," Addie quoted.

"So, an American who knows her French history," Hans quipped. "Louis XV, I believe. '*After me*, the deluge.'"

"I was referring to the song, Hans-Hubert. So you're vindicated, I am indeed *just* a silly American girl."

"Touché," Hans feigned a death blow, staggering.

"How long have you been in Paris?" Rolf asked, his eyes having never left hers.

"Six years now. I came as a student in '35 and just never left. And I will miss it so." Tears welled in her luscious brown eyes. Rolf was their captive. "And I'm going to miss all of you so very much."

"Then why must you leave?" Rolf asked.

"Because I am quite certain"—she wiped her eye with her napkin—"my president is going to draw us into this nasty business and I'll be turned into a prisoner of war. And I, unfortunately, do not speak a word of German."

"Why," Konni blurted out, "I'd never let something like that happen to you, Addie, my dear!"

"But of course you wouldn't, darling." Addie reached across and patted Konni's hand. "You're such a swell friend, Konni."

"Adelaide, you can rest assured it wouldn't take me but a few weeks to teach you German!"

"You're incorrigible"

"You're welcome to join us, gentlemen." Gretl's invitation lacked sincerity.

"Thank you, but no." Hans took the hint, uncharacteristically. "But we'll be just over there if any of you beauties decide you do need a man's company."

"But we have a man's company," Yvette said, tilting her head, her rolled-under curls bouncing delightfully. She pulled Konni's hand up to her cheek.

"And he's the perfect man."

Konni jutted his chin and raised his head, saying, "Indeed."

"He's handsome."

"It's a curse," Konni added.

"He's humble."

"To a fault!" Konni quipped.

"And, he's . . ."

All the girls said it in unison: "*Harmless!*"

"Completely!" He grimaced and shook his head. "Or, I, I'm what?"

When the laughter settled, Hans and Gep bid the party *au revoir* and returned to their table, leaving Rolf to say his good-byes.

"*Enchanté*," Rolf said, bowing slightly and scanning the table.

"I regret we won't be able to become better acquainted," Rolf told Addie, clicking his Prussian heels together.

She gauged him for a second with a tilted glare and pursed lips, then said, "I'm afraid most German officers find me quite disagreeable. You wouldn't like me either."

"Why on earth not?" Rolf asked.

"I'm not French, major. I'm American. We fight back!"

Rolf felt a winsome smile grow in his tired eyes.

"And I, my dear, am quite certain I would be handily vanquished."

He took her hand and kissed it softly, his attention glued to her big, glistening eyes. As he released it, he felt the regret in the way her fingers softly lingered in his.

The first performance that evening was Sweet Suzi Rupp in a stirring rendition of "Regentropfen," raindrops. She was dressed in a white peasant blouse and a blue, full dirndl. Girlish, springy blond curls had been pinned under a milking cap, and she was seated next to a mocked-up window with fingers of water trickling down the glass. Her tiny voice and teary gray eyes gave the song the perfect mix of innocence and sorrow. A lump had to be cleared from nearly every throat in this den of merry-makers and adulterers, who for a poignant moment were forced to think of their wives and sweethearts back home in Germany.

Tears of pride rolled down Onkel Heinrich's face as he joyfully watched sweet little Suzi's premier performance. The sentiment, however, was completely lost at Monsieur de Forney's table.

"Monsieur de Forney." Kruder leaned over the table toward the stern-faced Corsican dandy. "The SS will soon be making its presence known in Paris."

Kruder stabbed a Kalamata olive from the dish on their table and disgorged it between his teeth.

"My mission here in Paris over the next few months," he said, spitting the seed into his palm and dropping it in an ashtray. "is to establish an auxiliary police force. A special unit of French *faux policiers*, let's call them. *Special policemen.* Men with a conservative and like-minded constitution. Men who could enforce the law of the Reich and, quite frankly, the will of the German state on their less-than-cooperative French brethren. Men not unlike those that circulate around and report to you."

"What's in it for me?" De Forney admired his manicure.

"Money, monsieur. Power."

116

"I'm not a political man, Herr Kruder." He twisted one of the many rings on his fingers and added. "Just a simple businessman."

"You're too humble, sir. You're a very shrewd and successful businessman."

"Merci," de Forney said, holding up his glass to them, then taking a sip.

"But forgive me for saying so with such unbridled candor," Kruder continued. "You are small potatoes, monsieur. Completely insignificant."

"Excuse me?"

Dieter Fuchs was the head bartender at the Club l'Heure Bleue. He was a tall, bald Frankish version of Sir Winston Churchill. Not only did Dieter do magic tricks off and on through the night while the band played lively tunes like "Schönes Wetter Heute," but during interludes he would come out and mimic Churchill, poking fun at the British prime minister, another highlight of every evening.

"MontTY?" Dieter's Churchill character said, entering the stage with long lit cigar twitching in his thick lips, a telephone in one hand while the other held a receiver to his ear.

"MonTY? This is WinSTON. Why are you back in CaiRO? You were supposed to take back Benghazi a week aGO!"

Xavier's high-pitched voice could be heard from back stage.

"Sorry, Winston, old man. Can't hear you quite so well. Bad connection, I guess. You and de Gaulle must be back in Paris already!"

"When do you depart, Addie?" Hedy asked.

"I actually leave Paris tomorrow afternoon. I travel by train to Cherbourg, where I stay the brief night at some tiny hotel. Then, early Monday morning I sail by Danish freighter, of all things, to Lisbon, arriving three days later."

Through the crowd, she could see Rolf talking to Gep and Hans-Hubert. His elbows on the table, he was rubbing his big, beautiful hands together and telling some wonderfully adventurous story.

"It seems," Addie continued, her eyes still diverted, "according to my remarkably astute travel agent, the entire coast of France is mined and the freighter must skirt along just offshore through some marked passage all the way to Spain, which adds an extra day or more to the trip, not to mention a ghastly element of drama."

Through the smoky silhouettes, she noticed Rolf looking at her. He glanced at Gep and Hans, and seeing that they were watching the show, he looked again at her and smiled.

"Then on the first of May"—she smiled back, slightly, then tossed her head and continued—"it's off by steamer to Havana, and from there, another week of boat and train travel and I am finally home!"

From his perch against the wall, Bruno watched over tonight's crowd as he always did, but his eyes continued to find themselves transfixed on the American girl. He liked this young Adelaide woman and really hated to see her leave. She'd been coming to the club since back in the lean days. But what he liked most about her was the way she talked. Her French was impeccable, slow and dignified; no doubt her English was the same. But it was the manner in which she spoke, a mesmerizing cant that completely entranced him and, to be sure, everyone else she met. There was a lilt in every few words that seemed to be tossed from her pretty lips with the slightest backward tilt of her head and a hardly noticeable dipping of one of her shoulders or the other: "*Darling*, you simply *must* inquire at the préfecture about this *atrocious* charge being leveled against your *dear* father." And it was genuine. Probably the way her mother and her mother's mother had talked. And, oh, how it released the beast in Bruno! That flawless skin, that smile that lit up gloomiest day, those perfect teeth. And those enchanting, unforgettable dark-brown eyes. How he'd like to *take* her to his room and *turn* her upside down and *taste* her all *fucking* night long!

The set ended with Sabina singing "Le Cheland Qui Passe," and her accented French and deep, silky voice were the perfect touches for the mystic tone of the song.

"The woman is pure vamp, truly she is," Gretl noted. "But when she sings, she becomes somehow so elegant."

Addie ducked her head and whispered, "But isn't there just the tiniest place in every girl's heart that wishes she could live just one day with Sabina's lusciously wicked abandon?"

"You're all such soft, tender dough," Konni interjected, sliding an olive-oil-soaked ring of squid down his throat. "But alas, in one *Augenblick*, one short blink of an eye, you'll all turn to crusty old toast like my mean old *Hausfrau*."

"She has to be a true dear to put up with the likes of you," Gretl argued.

118

"Oh, but she's a mean old cracker, that one. I tell you. Why, a few nights ago she banished me to my room with no supper and no sex!"

"What did you do, Konni?" Addie asked.

"Why I went upstairs, I put on my ascot and my paisley jacket, splashed on my toilet water, and marched right back down and told her by all the gods *im Himmel*, I was the man of this castle and I was going to have my way right here and now!"

"And what did she do, pray tell?"

"Why, she let me make my supper!"

"Konni, you're intractable."

Even Xavier got into the act himself. Coming out in a black-and-white-striped shirt and a red beret, he pranced up behind Dieter's Winston Churchill character. Pulling a Union Jack handkerchief from his pocket, he blew his nose to the sound effects of a long slide on the trombone. Dieter feigned being startled as Xavier quickly stuffed the British flag hanky back into his pocket.

"Pierre," Dieter's Churchill asked Xavier, "where have you been?"

"I went out to meet the German Army, Monsieur Winston."

"What on earth did you say to them?"

"Table for a hundred thousand, messieurs?"

"Herr Kruder!" Guy de Forney set his glass down forcefully on the table, pulled a scarlet hanky from his sleeve, and dapped his lips. "I am not a man who takes well to insult. Even from the Gestapo."

"Forgive me, monsieur." Kruder lit a cigarette and blew the smoke out the side of his mouth. "I am a blunt man. My intention was only to make an important point. Fact is, the people around you are little more than pimps and prostitutes, criminals and thugs. Small-timers, monsieur. There is a much higher pedigree in the lot one finds around Monsieur Hugo Sturekov, your adversary, I believe? While commanding a gang of cutthroats just as dangerous as yours, Sturekov is connected to illustrious vintners and canners, as well as miners, rail companies, metal millers. The deals you make with the Wehrmacht through the Abwehr's Bureau Otto offices are trivial, a thousand francs here, ten thousand there. Sturekov makes hundred-million-franc deals with the Wehrmacht and does so regularly."

"So talk to Sturekov?"

"Sturekov has nothing to gain in joining up with the SS. But you, monsieur, you have a great deal to gain."

Kruder leaned forward with his elbow on the table.

"Allow me to be even more succinct. I'm not asking for your services, monsieur." Kruder pulled a pack of Chesterfield cigarettes from inside his tunic and placed it on the table. "I'm demanding them. You and your crew will work for us. Or the Gestapo will have to start a very nasty investigation."

Guy de Forney stared angrily at Victor, his astonished, one-eyed associate.

"It appears as though I should consider becoming a policeman," de Forney said.

Kruder shook a Chesterfield from the pack and offered it to de Forney. He lifted his champagne glass and added, "Vive la paix."

"So, Konni, where were you for so long?"

"Went outside for some fresh air. All this smoke is brutal on my old eyes. By the by, truly a multitude of stars out tonight. Should be a glorious morning. Why don't we all take a stroll later, watch the sun come up from the Alexander Bridge? Wouldn't that be tip-top?"

"I don't know if I'll be able to, Konni," Hedy said.

"How about you, Addie? One last time?"

"We'll see, my darling," she answered, sweetly. "We'll see."

Konni noticed Victor Roche leave de Forney's table and head to the bathroom, the old man excused himself from the party and followed him. They stood at the urinal. Victor peed, Konni tried.

"What happened to Fabien, my broker friend?" Konni asked.

"He was evidently eliminated."

"Did de Forney have something to do with it?"

"I couldn't say."

"I need the rest of the cigarette money. I need it tonight."

"It won't be forthcoming."

"Do you realize this could bring down the wrath of the German Reich on you and your boss?"

Victor buttoned his trousers. "Monsieur Ritter, it appears that it already has."

The night progressed. The drinks were many and inhibitions became few. At one point, Hans found himself at the girls' table, draped around Gretl and Addie. Certain that Rolf was watching, Addie poured on an overdone affection for the boorish cad, all to

120

Hans' delight. Rolf simply turned away. He wasn't about to have anything to do with someone he found himself so attracted to.

Not again.

Not ever again.

Buch Zwei

II

die Untersuchung
L'enquête
The Investigation

14

Palm Sunday, 6 April 1941

Alexander III

DAY TWO—Paris—Sunday, 6 April 41—9:51 AM
Inspector Luc-Henri Saint-Ruynon was a Paris policeman of the highest character and reputation. He was a decorated gendarme when he was called to duty in the Great War. Within weeks of the 1918 armistice, he took a bullet in his back at his left shoulder and a second on his left heel. The former had healed quite adequately, but his heel, was an entirely different matter. For the most part, the heel and its tendons were shattered or missing. Attempts were made to build a heel with bone from Luc-Henri's hip, which proved useless and did little more than create a third painful malady for the disabled young soldier. Yet as many of the most diligent and ingenious of the human species are prone to do, over time Corporal d'Armée Saint-Ruynon found a way to walk again. He did so by strapping a thin bend of green willow bark with a wadded clump of cloth in its crux to his calf and his foot, stuffing and cinching it all up in a tall laced boot and locomoting himself along with a series of plants and twists and hops. And he had done so with such verve and valor over the twenty-two years since his injury that, coupled with his ingenious police skills, he rose through the ranks to inspector in the Paris Préfecture of Police more rapidly than some of the most agile of his comrades.

Inspector Luc-Henri's office was adjacent to the long bank of interrogation rooms on the préfecture's second floor. One such room was just off his office and was supplied with a one-way mirror looking in. The American woman, one Adelaide Bridges, had given him her statement and had been instructed to keep herself seated in the room as some German investigators were coming to get their own statement. Luc-Henri watched the beautiful young girl through the window. She was a much-frazzled sight. Her hair was mussed and had fallen out of place from a number of elegant tortoiseshell combs that girls of her class wore on evening soirées. Her eyes were swollen from crying and fatigue. Her nose was red, and unbeknownst to her, the slightest smear of lipstick blemished the right side of her chin. A black wool coat with astrakhan collar and cuffs lay across her lap, blotched and matted here and there with black patches of the old man's blood. She'd arrived at the préfecture more than four hours ago and was in shock. It took the better part of an hour to get her tremors under control with blankets and coffee. By the time he had finished his interview with her, she had composed herself. The inspector was impressed with her grasp of the French language and found the enchanting cant of her speech very elegant and endearing. He was certain this American girl had known life from the highest rungs of society. An event such as she had just experienced would have been unlike anything she had ever known before. He was almost apologetic when she became frightened and agitated as he told her she would have to wait for the Germans. But then, he thought, who wouldn't be?

"They're here, sir." The voice came over Luc's desk intercom. He pushed himself up and grabbed one of his canes as the door to his office opened. The secretary let the two Germans in and departed.

"Bonjour, inspector. I am Sturmbannführer Alois Kruder. I'm here to take the witness to Gestapo headquarters. This is my driver. I don't know his name. You are ordered to turn the witness over to me immediately." Kruder looked at the woman through the window. "Is this the witness?"

"Oui, monsieur. She's an American, though. The American consul must be notified as she—"

"That won't be necessary. We'll notify them when we have finished our interrogation."

"Forgive me, monsieur. But as a citizen of the United States, she is entitled to—"

Again the intercom buzzed. "Inspector, there are more."

"More what."

"Germans, sir.

Again the door opened and two regular army officers entered the room.

"Good morning, inspector. My name is Major von Gerz and this is my adjutant, Oberleutnant Fechter." Rolf shook the inspector's hand and, noticing Kruder, smiled and moved over to him.

"What brings you to the préfecture on Sunday morning, Kruder?"

"As you may or may not be aware, von Gerz, an important member of the German business community has been assassinated, and this woman is a material witness to the crime. I am making it my duty to lead the investigation into this murder, and I will be escorting the girl to avenue Foch for proper interrogation." Kruder reached for the door, but Rolf leaned against it and shook his head. A glorious smile grew on his face.

"I am afraid Sturmbannführer, you have made some unwarranted assumptions. You see, I am the one in charge of Herr Ritter's murder investigation."

"Under what authority?"

"The highest in Paris."

"Stülpnagel? But this is a civil matter. The military administration has no authority in state matters!"

"The general has authority over all matters in Occupied France. As well, Herr Ritter has served on WiGruFa, the Reich automotive commission as liaison to the Wehrmacht for more than three years. His death is therefore very much a military matter."

"If such orders exist, let me see you produce them."

"Kruder," Rolf said, reaching into his tunic pocket and handing over the orders. "You have no idea how much it pleases me to show you these."

It appeared to Rolf that Kruder was tasting belched bile. Kruder said something under his breath that Rolf took as "soft-witted old fool."

"Did you say something, Sturmbannführer?"

"It appears your instructions are in order. You may proceed with your investigation, major."

Rolf put his hand on the interrogation room's door handle just as Kruder grabbed it.

"Pity, von Gerz," Kruder said under his breath. "You have no idea the pure pleasure I derive from interrogating beautiful young women!" Then he coyly smiled. "But wait, I guess you actually do, don't you major?"

"Keep in touch, Alois."

Addie was startled when Inspector Saint-Ruynon opened the door and entered the room, followed by Rolf and Gep.

"Mademoiselle Bridges, permit me to introduce Major . . ."

"Oh, Rolf. Thank God it's you." Addie's posture melted with relief at the sight of Rolf. She sprang to her feet and rushed to his arms.

"You know each other?" Luc asked, bewildered.

"I met her yesterday, she was . . ."

Addie's body wilted and started slipping from Rolf's grasp.

"She's fainted!"

"Get her into my office. Here. On the divan."

They laid Addie down, and she was immediately revived as Luc poured water from the pitcher on his credenza into his handkerchief. Rolf took it from the inspector and wiped her harried face, including her smudged chin.

"I'm sorry. I just haven't slept for two days. And then, that horrid scene. Poor Konni, I . . ." She started to cry. "Oh, Rolf. Take me home, please. I must get some sleep."

"I'm sorry, Miss Bridges, but I must get a statement from you. It has to be now. It can't wait. There are possible details that are fresh on your mind that may be lost if we wait."

"But Rolf, darling, I don't have a mind. My mind is mush. I'm at my wits' end. Please take me home. You simply must take me home. I implore you."

"I have a motorcar downstairs. As soon as we're finished, I will take you home straightaway. I promise you. It won't take half an hour. You can lie right here and give your statement."

"But I'm so very tired, Rolf." She turned her head away, resting her chin on her shoulder and her cheek on the divan. "I'm just . . . so . . ."

Luc hopped and twisted his way over to them and handed Rolf a glass of brandy. Holding it to her lips, Rolf asked over his shoulder, "There was another witness. A German soldier, a grenadier?"

"Oui, major." Luc answered. "He's being held a few rooms down."

"Gep, go to him. Order him to meet us at the scene of the crime at . . ." Rolf looked at his watch. "At 14:00. Then get back here as quickly as possible. We'll let her calm down for a few minutes until you return."

"Jawohl, Herr Major."

He turned back to Addie. "Take another sip, Miss Bridges."

She closed her eyes. Sulked. Then whimpered, "I will. But call me Addie."

"Okay, Addie. Take another sip."

She did as instructed, then laid her head back on the arm of the divan and covered her eyes with her forearm, Luc's handkerchief still wadded in her palm. After a few minutes, Gep returned, a stack of filing cards in his hand. He sat at the inspector's desk, pencil at the ready. Luc-Henri nodded to Rolf as he turned on the tape recorder.

"Now, start from the beginning." Rolf took the glass from her and turned to hand it to Luc as he said, "Take your time, and tell me what happened."

"I had to change my shoes. Bless his heart, the sweet old thing loved to walk us to the Alexander III Bridge and watch the sun rise over Paris. We hadn't done so since autumn. Winter was just horrid. But none of the others could go. So, I told him I would go with him. For old times' sake, you know? He loved to show us off. He simply adored us all."

"When you say us, who are you—"

"The girls. You met them all last night. On rare occasions Sabina would join us. We would leave the club just as the slightest hint of dawn was showing so we couldn't be accused of breaking the curfew. Then we'd all strike out together, usually still quite tight! We'd lock arms and walk, or rather waddle—he didn't walk, you know, he waddled. We would mimic him. All of us doing that darling little waddle of his. That's why he called us his little . . ." She sobbed twice and started crying as she said, *"Duckies!"*

She took the handkerchief and wiped her swollen eyes. "I'm sorry."

"That's fine. Proceed, Addie."

"Anyway, like I said, last night I had to change my shoes before I could go with him. It's much too far to walk in heels. So, I hurried around the corner to my apartment and was back before he'd finished his cigarette. And then we just started walking . . ."

A thumbnail moon hung low on the dark western horizon and stars twinkled overhead in a crystal-clear sky made even more vivid in the quiet, blacked-out city. In the east, dawn was the faintest purple glow. Konni and Addie left the club and slowly walked up the ghostly quiet boulevard Raspail. Konni had gone outside several times during the evening to get some air and noticed the clear night sky teeming with stars, certain it would be a brilliant morning.

Neither said much.

"Are you cold?"

"No, I'm fine."

"You?"

"I'm still glowing from all the alcohol."

"The walk will do us good."

It did. By the time they switched to the rue de Grenelle, the cold, fresh air had sobered and refreshed them. They moved at a comfortable pace for Konni. It took the better part of an hour to reach the Esplanade des Invalides. Dawn was just about to burst over Paris as they made their way onto the bridge.

"I'll never forget you, Konni," Addie said, resting her cheek on his shoulder. "You've been like a father to me."

He smiled at her. "I would have preferred 'lover.'"

"Always the flirt. Even when I was certain everything was going to cave in on me, there you always were, ready to make me laugh."

"My dear, that's because I so love your laugh."

"You're having me on, aren't you? My laugh is dreadful, isn't it?"

"Your laugh is fine. It's your dimples. They're quite adorable, you know."

"I get them from my mother."

"So I've heard."

He pulled her to his side, and they both stood silently and watched as the sun broke through the buildings and rooftops and chimneys to climb and sit on the frosty shoulder of Paris. Sunbeams danced and sparkled off the black waters of the Seine. The cream-colored statues and banisters along the Pont Alexandre III were all cast in an orange glow, their gold inlay glistening against the brilliant stone.

"You're one of the strongest and most gallantly independent young women I've ever known, Addie."

"Thank you, my swell darling. You'll never know how proud it makes me to know you feel that way."

"You must promise me to come back. To Paris. To me."

"But of course I will, Konni. You had stepped out, but all of us, the girls—even Sabina—we all pledged to return to the l'Heure Bleue exactly one year to the day after the war ends. You must be there too. Promise me, now."

"I'm getting old, my dear. May not have that many years."

"You've decades left in that sassy soul of yours. You must be there. For me?"

"For you, duckling," he said, touching her on the nose. "I'll be there for you."

"Good."

"Now, give us a kiss." He pointed to his cheek. "Then do be a good girl and see if you can fetch me a taxi. I've tuckered completely. Far end of the bridge there's a stand. Hail me something, dear, even a carriage. Something to get me onward to my hotel. Here, give me back my briefcase so you can hasten along."

Addie kissed his cheek and handed him the satchel. "I'll be just a jiffy . . . duckie! You wait here and enjoy the sunrise and do try to rest." And she scampered off to the Right Bank.

Halfway across the bridge, the sunny, silent morning was broken by the clap, patter, and thunder of automobile tires on the cobblestone as a dark-blue French Matford lumbered around the turnoff of the Cours-la-Reine and onto the bridge. Addie couldn't help but take notice of the car. She saw the driver's steely face and his bushy gray Kaiser mustache, which wrapped around his serious frown like a silver horseshoe. She was perplexed at first, expecting to see uniformed Germans, as on Sundays only Germans were allowed to operate automobiles. As the Matford raced past her, she tried to see who the passenger was in the backseat, but to no avail; he was just a ghostly silhouette hunched over behind the sun's glare on the glass. She hadn't gone another ten steps when she heard the screech of the car's brakes. When she turned around, she saw that the man in the backseat had jumped out and was dashing toward Konni. Then she saw the flash of a pistol firing, followed a mere second later by the gun's report. Konni was slumped against the bridge railing, one hand clutching his chest and the other his briefcase, his elbow supporting him on the banister. Another flash fired, another report, as the man ran across the street and grabbed for the briefcase.

Addie screamed, "No! No! Please, God, no!" as she watched Konni slide against the stone railing to sit down hard on the sidewalk. Behind her she heard the shrill sting of a whistle and a man's voice shout, "Get down!" What sounded like a bee buzzed past her ear followed by another, much louder rifle report from behind her. She fell to the sidewalk and quickly peered around to see a uniformed German grenadier, no doubt a night watchman on the bridge, run a few steps, then stop and fire again. When she turned back toward Konni, Addie could see that the grenadier's second shot had run true. The assassin was nearly knocked off his feet as he tore the briefcase from Konni's grip. Files and papers went flying across the bridge. Holding his side and dragging one leg, the assassin dove back into the car as it sped off toward the Left Bank with his legs still hanging out the door.

The grenadier was up next to Addie when he fired another shot, shattering the car's back glass, causing it to swerve suddenly. It bolted across the center median and tore off down the quai d'Orsay, with the assassin's legs finally inside and the back door slammed shut.

Addie leapt to her feet. She and the grenadier ran to Konni's side. The old man was slumped over against the bridge column, his chin on his chest. The front of his top coat was soaked. Blood oozed from his mouth as he tried to talk.

"They've murdered me!" he mumbled.

"No, darling! No!" Addie pleaded as she sat next to him and pulled him to her. Her hat was hanging at the side of her head from one pin. She tugged it loose and tossed it aside. "You're going to be all right, Konni. I'm just certain of it."

"They've murdered me. The villainous . . ." He coughed and spat blood over Addie's cheek. The grenadier's whistle shrieked in repetitive blasts trying to summon any other duty guards or policemen within earshot.

"Where's the honor? Villains! Why murder me? Why, Addie?"

"Stop that bloody whistle!" she screamed, reaching up and grabbing the soldier's pant leg. "I can't hear him!"

The grenadier did as instructed and, seeing a gendarme running toward them from the far side of the bridge, knelt down in front of them.

"Darling? Do you know who did this to you?"

Konni reached up and grabbed a handful of Addie's hair and pulled her to him. His voice was broken and fading.

"Again, darling. I can't hear you."

The soldier bent in and tried to listen as well.

"Please, louder." She started crying uncontrollably. "Please, Konni."

Again he said the word.

"NO!" Addie screamed. "NO! NO! Please God, NO!"

"Death's chill came over him at that very moment. It passed right through me. I felt it, like a wisp of cold breeze when you open a window." Addie looked up at Rolf, her beautiful brown eyes pleading with him for understanding. "I tell you I could feel it. Truly I could." She looked at Gep and Luc as well. "I knew he would die. I knew it when I first hastened to his side and saw all that blood." She inhaled deeply and her lip started trembling. "Then sure enough, that dear, sweet, darling man . . ." She sobbed and continued, "died right there in my arms." Her voice rose to almost a whimpered shriek as she spoke the last word.

"Was it a name?" Gep asked.

"I don't know. But surely it must have been. It sounded like *ear*." She tugged at her earlobe. "The English word *ear*. But it was two syllables, and it was so faint. It was the last wisp of breath the poor dear could muster. I just couldn't understand him."

"It could have been the German word *Ihr*," Gep interjected.

"I don't speak German," Addie said. "I wouldn't know." She looked down. "And that's it." A quick gaze at Rolf. "Now, please, Rolf. May I go home?"

"The word can mean a lot of things: your, her, or they, their." Gep looked at Rolf, then back to Addie. "It depends on how it's used."

"No," Inspector Luc-Herni forcefully interjected. "It's a name!"

They all looked at him, astonished.

"A German name," Luc continued. He started nodding and bit the side of his lower lip. "I'm certain of it. There was a file in Monsieur Ritter's satchel. The name is Irmgard."

DAY TWO—Paris—Sunday, 6 April 41—11:02 AM

Rolf asked the inspector to join him and Gep in their investigation of Herr Ritter's murder, admitting that they could not proceed without the help of the Paris police. After instructing Gep and Luc to meet him a half hour later at the property room to go through Ritter's things, Rolf escorted Addie down to the waiting car and joined her in the backseat.

She leaned her head on his shoulder as the driver took a shortcut through Saint-Germain along the rue Saint-Sulpice to Addie's apartment. At the intersection of rue Bonaparte, the driver slammed on the car's brakes, avoiding a horse-drawn fiacre moving much too quickly across their path to stop.

Rolf was just quick enough to throw his hand over her face, protecting her as they both were slammed into the back of the automobile's front seat. Addie screamed. The incident over, Rolf righted her and picked up her purse from the floor; returning its spilled contents, he came to a train ticket and his heart suddenly raced.

"Are you all right?" he asked her.

"I guess I'll live, if I can ever get some sleep."

"Miss Bridges," he started, dreading what her was about to tell her.

"I told you," she cuddled up next to him and put her head on his shoulder. "Call me Addie."

133

"I am afraid I have to impart what will quite surely be upsetting news."

"Is our way is blocked?" She sat up and stretched to see in front of the car.

"No, it's much worse than that."

"At the moment, Rolf, darling, nothing could be worse than coming between me and my pillow."

"I must unfortunately require that you remain in Paris until the investigation of Herr Ritter's—"

"ABSOLUTELY NOT!" She bolted upright in the seat. It was as though she'd become a different person right before his eyes. "You cannot do this to me! I refuse to permit it! Do you hear me! I am leaving, and there is nothing you can do!"

"I'm terribly sorry, Addie. But I have to insist. You're a material witness in a—"

"I hate you! Do you hear me? You beastly man! You hideous man!"

Rolf grabbed her arms to keep her from flailing at him.

"And stop calling me Addie!" she added.

"Look at me." He grabbed her smeared cheeks and forced her to do as he commanded. "Look at me! It is only while I am conducting this investigation. When it is concluded, I will see that you get home."

"Oh, really, major? And just how will you do that? Do you realize how many Germans have lied to me? For eight months I have been trying to go home. 'Not to worry your pretty little head, Fräulein. I'm sure something can be arranged, Fräulein. These things take time, Fraulein.' At least you Germans had the decency to placate me with this feeble excuse or that. The French officials just shrugged and blamed everything on you guys!"

"I assure you. I will get you home."

"Why am I to trust your word? It's taken me eight months to get all the paperwork, this Ausweis, that permit. And then the passage I needed to get home. And you're telling me, 'Don't worry, Addie. I'll get you home.' Like it's simply a matter of putting me on a train and waving ta-ta. Do you think me daft?"

"Miss Bridges. I am a major in the German Army. I am also a member of the Abwehr, the German Intelligence Service. I can assure you, if I want to put anyone"—he shook her, growing more vexed with her as each word came out of him—"ANYWHERE in the world, I can do it with little more than my signature! Do you understand me?

Now, I am not asking you, I am *commanding* you, explicitly, to remain in Paris until I release you. I can place you under arrest if I think I need to. I can place guards at your door. Is that what I have to do?"

"Oh, Rolf, darling, please forgive me. I do so want to trust you." She nudged herself back beside him. "I want to believe you," she cooed, "but what if we wake up tomorrow and we're at war? What happens to me then? Even you wouldn't have the power to protect me, then, Rolf."

"I assure you. There will be exchanges. Dignitaries and VIPs. If war is declared, I will ensure that your name goes on the list."

"Promise me," she begged, looking up into his eyes. Now she had transformed herself into a frightened child. "Promise me, Rolf darling. Please. Look me in the eye and tell me 'I promise.'"

"You have my word, Miss Bridges."

She raised her eyebrows, entreating him to say it exactly as she had requested.

"I promise."

She leaned her head back on his shoulder and closed her eyes.

"Rolf?"

"Yes, Miss Bridges."

"Call me Addie."

15

Lyon, Vichy France

Der Börsenmakler
Le courtier en valeurs mobilières
The Stockbroker

DAY TWO—Lyon—Sunday, 6 April 41—11:28 AM
Leutnant Rutgers Heht crossed the frontier into Free France at 6:10
the previous evening wearing his Wehrmacht uniform and bearing a
military *Ausweis* naming him as being attached to the Armistice
Commission offices in Marseilles, where he said he was due to report
Monday morning at nine sharp. His passage through Vichy customs
proceeded with little difficulty. He then disembarked the train a few
stops before Lyon and purchased a storage locker. In less than a
quarter hour, Ruti exited the men's room wearing green corduroy
trousers, a tweed traveling jacket, and a brown flat cap. A little less
than two hours later, after a completely forgettable meal of leek and
turnip soup accompanied by an aspic sandwich laden with a clear,
oily goo that was probably expected to pass for some sort of
mayonnaise, he boarded another train and continued his journey
onward to Lyon. Just after ten PM he checked himself into the tiny
hotel across the plaza and just down the street from the Lyon train
station, bearing a Swiss passport that identified him as Thomas
Widner. Next to printed courier type that read, *Occupation*, written in
blue fountain pen ink by a supposedly official hand, were the words
Courtier en Valeurs Mobilière. Stockbroker.

Sleep had been difficult, but had finally overtaken him in the
morning's wee hours. Awakened by church bells, he showered and
dressed himself. He was to meet the "balding, quite less than ordinary
little man in a red bowtie" at ten thirty this morning in the mezzanine
café of the train station. As had been expected and planned, the
station and the café were both all but deserted on a Palm Sunday
morning. Ruti took a seat next to the wrought-iron banister where he
could oversee the entire station and watch for the man, a French
stockbroker from the Lyon Exchange, who would be carrying a faux-
leather pasteboard suitcase edged with lighter orange trim and
covered with travel decals advertising some of the most popular

European destinations and hotels. Identical to the one Ruti was to bring to this clandestine meeting. The one Ruti had taken from storage at the Soldatenheim in Paris, the one he had left in the train station locker last night.

Soon, the 'balding, quite less than ordinary little man in a red bow tie" did enter the station. Ruti watched him as he came up the stairs to the café. He did so all too lightly for Ruti's tastes, because, like Ruti, he was not carrying the decal-laden suitcase despite his instructions.

"Monsieur Fox," Ruti said, leaping up from his chair, startling the little man with his candor and size. "Surely you remember me. Thomas Widner?"

"Yes. But of course, Monsieur Widner. Of course, I do." Ruti was shaking the little man's hand, squeezing a wincing frown from the broker's confused face.

"Please, join me, won't you?" Ruti motioned for the sleepy waitress at the bar, who was resting her pudgy cheek on her palm. "What will you have?"

"Perhaps a café au lait."

"Wonderful choice. One for me as well, please."

"So tell me, how is your lovely wife?" Ruti didn't like the way the little man's eyes darted around the station. He now relished the fact that his cautious instincts had been well served.

"She's quite well, thank you."

"And your child, what's his name?"

"Yes. He is, uh . . ."

The French stockbroker went completely blank. Ruti was ready to push him over the banister and say he'd slipped, when the assigned name came to him.

"Oh, uh . . . you mean little Michael? He's fine. Thank you for asking."

Ruti had enough of the charade. "You're not the man I met with in January."

"He lost his nerve," the little man said, trying to muster his own.

"You were supposed to bring something, weren't you? A suitcase?"

"I understood Monsieur Fabien would come himself this time. A fellow broker from Paris."

"I'm afraid he won't be coming. Got himself killed Saturday."

The little broker started crying. "I, too, am being followed, monsieur. They will kill us both."

"De Forney's people?"

"I don't know, perhaps."

"Not a problem."

"I admire your bravado, but you don't know these people. They come from the shadows and slit your throat. You wind up in a gunny sack, tossed in the river. In a year they find you downstream. A bag of wet bones!"

"I know Monsieur de Forney and his comrades. I deal with them on a regular basis. I assure you, he will not interfere with us."

"Regardless, this man is a cold-blooded killer. And you are his associate?"

"I'll take care of him."

"Unless you're with the Gestapo, I can assure you, monsieur, we are *not* safe. Your accent sounds odd, but it doesn't sound German. You are Swiss, perhaps."

"Pomeranian, and I'm a fucking officer in the German Secret Service!"

The broker gently placed his fingers over his mouth.

"Now, where's the money?"

"In my office safe, monsieur. Locked away."

"How much?"

"Six millions francs, the agreed-upon—"

"That's all changed. We need Swiss francs. I'll take four million. No less. I can move the securities in Marseilles for that amount."

"Then I am afraid, monsieur, you must do just that. So much in Swiss francs is impossible. It would take weeks. My investors would not stand for it."

"Then your investors lose the right to own fifty million francs worth of securities for a mere fraction of the risk. And that de Forney goon will kill you and throw you in the river the minute he sees you leave your office with the suitcase full of money, whether you plan to bring it to me or return it to your investors."

The little man started whimpering, his face contorted in fear, his eyes darted this way and that, his mind grasping for some feasible answer.

"How long will it take you to get to Switzerland and back?"

"I don't know, monsieur." It was a whispered wail with a barely audible shriek at the end. "Wednesday? Wednesday afternoon."

"Noon Wednesday. Right here. Get me a hundred thousand in Swiss. On top of the six million French francs."

"But the assassin that awaits me, monsieur?"

"He'll be eliminated before you're back in bed with you wife."

Ruti gave the broker instructions to have the money with him when he returned in two days. If he did not, Ruti would kill him himself. He left the station and was pleased to see the assassin across the street. And now he was following Ruti instead of the little broker. Ruti stopped at a storefront alcove, where he waited. He withdrew a small standard-issue Wehrmacht mirror encased in tin and watched de Forney's man slink along the building in the gray silent city.

In three swift motions, Ruti's service dagger stabbed the man in the cheek, the throat, and the chest before the poor soul knew what hit him. In a mere matter of seconds, Ruti dragged him into the shadowy darkness, removed his coat and everything from his pants pockets. He noticed a tattoo of a buxom woman on the man's forearm and pulled the arm out of the shadows to look at it more closely. With four quick slices from his bloody knife he removed the tattoo and folded it in his handkerchief. A quick kick to the victim's head before he left, and in a few minutes, Ruti was back in his hotel room going through the man's wallet.

16

Der Beweis
La preuve
The Evidence

DAY TWO—Paris—Sunday, 6 April 41—12:43 PM
Inspector Luc-Henri led the German Oberleutnant down the hallway, explaining the property rooms were downstairs, in the basement.

"They keep them there to curse me."

The process required Luc to descend six flights of stairs, three floors. Gep moved at Luc's side, ready to catch him if necessary.

"There's an elevator down in the next annex. I use it coming upstairs. But it's very far; believe it or not, this is faster."

As the two men completed each flight's decent, they stopped on each landing and Luc got around to explaining his wound. He took a chair next to the corridor window, cracked it open, and lit his pipe, offering up his tobacco bag to Gep, who shook his head and lit his own Juno.

"A ludicrous Docteur Frankenstein surgery. Convinced me I'd walk like normal in a year. Instead, my recovery was delayed three years by his butchery. I'm told he was relieved of his manhood by a scorned lover. By the grace of God! *I may never walk again,* I told myself, *but I still have good wood in my shorts!* Ha! So, the doctor be damned, no? It has made me a better policeman. Backtracking in my condition is quite troublesome."

Luc and Gep entered the brightly lit property room, where they studied the contents of Herr Ritter's valise. Papers of various degrees of dampness were spread over three large tables.

"My men are still fishing documents from the river downstream, as far as the Bois de Boulogne."

Gep pulled a leather wallet from his jacket pocket, untied it, and withdrew long tweezers from its pouch. Gently, he separated a few documents and held them up. The third one caught his eye. It was from a member of WiGruFa, the German automotive board. The letter writer was thanking Ritter for interceding in the wiring harness matter and promised a few cases of champagne de Venoge & Cie— "Frightfully adequate stuff, this"—and the keys to his lodge in Tirol for any purpose and for any requested period of time.

Another was from an Austrian radio housing manufacturer appealing to Ritter for six barrels of Bakelite. Another was from the Ford Motor Company in Cologne confirming an appointment with the director of operations in the electrical components department.

Gep moved to Ritter's wallet. He opened it and started removing its contents, again with the tweezers. A card declaring its holder *en résidence* at the Hotel Ritz, Ritter's identity card, and an Ausweis, declaring his occupation as automotive industry executive. There was also a French Automotive Committee identity card with the old man's entire name handwritten in beautiful script next to a set of official blue ink stamps, one reading simply *Carte Blanche*.

Luc looked over Gep's shoulder, quietly, alertly taking in every nuance of Gep's interest in this paper or that. Gep took an immediate liking to Luc. It was more than just a respect for a war veteran and his affliction. He could sense a consternation in Luc's eyes and his expressions. Others would have been annoyed by Luc's hop-skipping behind him as he moved from table to table, item to item. But not Gep. He even waited until Luc got into place before studying a piece. Luc was the kind of policeman, the kind of detective, Gep hoped to be someday. Someday after the war. Someday when Gep was working in Linz or Graz, he would have "a man in Paris I can consult about this matter."

Finally, the file folder. Gray cardboard, thick and worn on the edges and along the spine. German brand, imprinted with the most delicate of silver filigrees branding it from Stein und Söhne, Leipzig. A Wehrmacht Prussian eagle was stamped on the jacket along with the word *Geheim*. Secret. One leaf of the folder was raised above the other, and on the inside was penned in white ink *F. Irmgard*. All the other folders on the table were olive green, and their headings were typewritten on strips of white paper then glued in place on the raised leaf.

"The *F.*, monsieur?" Luc asked. "It has some special meaning in German?"

Gep wasn't comfortable telling him the obvious. He preferred to come up with other possible explanations.

"It could stand for anything. A first name? *Frau?* Mrs. *Fragen?* Question. Just guesses." But Gep knew the single *F* in military jargon referred only to *Fall*.

Fall Irmgard.

Condition Irmgard.

Operation Irmgard!

17

Die Wächter
Le veilleur de nuit
The Watchman

DAY TWO—Paris—Sunday, 6 April 41—2:04 PM
Schütze Hermann Kaas had been posted to Paris in July of 1940, a
month after the cessation of fighting and the French collapse. He had
an exceptionally wonderful assignment, working ten hours a night, as
watchman on the Alexander III. The good fortune of his Paris posting
had little to do with Hermann and everything to do with his father,
Captain Richard Metgers-Kaas, a member of a Brandenburger
paratrooper unit dropped into Holland a full day before the invasion
and responsible for upsetting Dutch communications ahead of the
assault.

Young Hermann was not a bad soldier. He loved his country
and assumed his duty to defend it proudly. He just *wasn't* a soldier.
Hermann Kaas was a writer, a young man of letters, a philosopher,
and a thinker. In being such, he had an untimely and unhealthy
propensity for free thought and therefore a dangerous contempt for
the Nazis. At the cost of a severely broken nose and near
imprisonment, during his university days in Heidelberg he had
admonished a gang of Hitler Brownshirts for their attempt to storm
the campus library and burn all the books. Hermann told them
burning all books rather than the select few their Party deemed
unpatriotic simply proved they weren't even good National Socialists,
but rather little more than ignorant anarchists. This incident and
others along the übereducated lad's path to soldiering made his
dutiful father realize the best way to keep his son alive, and his
family's honor intact, was to find Hermann a posting to a more
civilized theater of operation. So, twenty-two-year-old Hermann
found himself on guard detail on Palm Sunday morning, patrolling the
beautiful Alexandre III Bridge.

From it, Hermann could see for a kilometer in both directions
down the Seine. His rectangular sentry routine took him back and
forth from one end to the other and along each side of the magnificent
structure. A full round took Hermann ten minutes. There was really
nothing to guard, Hermann soon realized. His nightly assignment was

more about catching curfew breakers and having a German presence
on the Seine. So, except for the occasional pair of drunken lovebirds
sneaking from the nightlife of the Right Bank to the smaller civilian
hotels on the Left, Hermann's night was usually uneventful. That is,
of course, until early this morning, when Wehrmacht private
Hermann Kaas shot his first human being.

Parisians strolling along the Alexandre III Bridge after Palm
Sunday mass were diverted from the northbound lane by a score of
gendarmes and long white barricades. Heads poked up and out of the
passing crowds, crowds that had grown much larger than they should
have been. Because the word was out!

A German has been murdered!

*A British assassin did it! It was a bomb, my sister in the 5th
heard it!*

It was a Frenchman that pulled the trigger! God help us!

About fucking time!

*The man was a general in plain clothes! They'll line us all up
now, you wait and see!*

A pair of small motorboats manned by the National Police
raced up and down both banks of the Seine looking for and retrieving
every scrap of paper or trash all the way downstream to the Pont de
l'Alma.

When Rolf's Voisin limousine sporting Wehrmacht flags on the
fender pulled up heading the wrong way down the northbound lane,
two of the gendarmes lifted the barricade to allow the car through.
Schütze Hermann Kaas stepped up to the curb and saluted as Rolf
hurried past him to the spot where Konni Ritter was shot.

"Move these people to the other side of the bridge," Inspector
Luc-Henri commanded of the gendarmes, "and keep them there."

Gep shook the grenadier's hand and told Hermann to follow
him to where Rolf knelt, studying the nick where the bullet had gone
through Ritter and hit one of the painted limestone supports in the
bridge railing.

Hermann told the three investigators that he had been at the
north end of the bridge when he saw the car come from the east and
turn south onto the Alexander III bridge

"I noticed the woman and the old man perhaps ten minutes
earlier, standing on the bridge's east promenade, but paid them little
mind. The sun was up, curfew was lifted. But the car was a different
matter. As it turned on to the bridge from the east along Cours-la-

Reine, I was about to salute, when I saw the two men in the car were not Germans, not German military anyway. They looked French. The man at the wheel was in his mid-fifties, wore a walrus mustache and a tartan flat cap. He had dark, close-set eyes. The one in the back was very tall, hunched over, I couldn't see his face. He seemed to be scolding the first man, seemed to be upset that I had seen them, or that I was there at all. That's when the car sped up and I took down the registration plate numbers."

Rolf looked at Gep as the grenadier handed over his *Soldatenbuch* with the plate numbers written on the cover.

"Very thorough." Rolf was impressed with this private. "Go on."

"I continued watching them, so I could see which way they went after they left the bridge. Then they stopped where the old man was. The man in the backseat jumped out and fired a pistol at the old man. It was a Luger, I'm certain of it. That distinct report. So I readied my weapon and started for the scene. The woman was in my line of fire. I sent a volley over her head to try to scare the assailants. I shouted at the woman to get down, and when she did I fired once more. I know I hit the shooter in the hip. He was knocked off his feet. But he continued to fight for the old man's briefcase. Then the papers went all over the bridge and into the river. As the man jumped back in the car, I sent another volley into the back glass of the automobile. I believe I hit the driver as well. The motorcar drove away erratically. They went west just off the bridge."

Hermann went on to tell them he was sure the victim was a close friend or relative of the woman's. "I summoned some gendarmes from the other end of the bridge, then tried to listen to what the old man was trying to say to the woman. I'm not sure, but it sounded like he was calling her Irmgard, or saying the name anyway. The woman was speaking English to him. I found that unsettling. I don't speak English, so I don't know what the woman was saying. Assuming she was possibly British, or Canadian, I thought the old man may have been also, but he was definitely German. I checked his credentials."

"What type of automobile was it?" Rolf asked.

"It was a Ford. The Strasbourg type."

"A Mathis?"

"Yes, a Matford, dark blue."

18

Wegen Todesfall geschlossen
Fermé à la mémoire
Closed in Memoriam

DAY TWO—Paris—Sunday, 6 April 41—2:43 PM
An orange earthen flask of Zeer Oude Genever, the juniper-flavored Dutch gin, sat in front of Sabina van der Gorp. *Dutch Courage*, it had been deemed a century before at Waterloo. There were two cases left under the bar of the four she'd received in December through Xavier's Alsatian contacts. The little stront had hoped it would foster favor with her. Pathetic little shit! She had treated him humanely for a few days, but had thrown an empty Genever flask at him when he pestered her about it one time too many.

The saucy Dutch chanteuse sat alone at one of the club's glossy black-lacquered tables. The front door was open as well as the back door leading to the kitchen. A floor fan sat in the back hallway, venting the previous night's stale scents of smoke and sin into the Parisian winds. Shafts of daylight from the open doors gave the club a jarring nakedness. The only sound was the roar of the hall fan and the monotonous hum of a ceiling fan that had been left turning last night. Sabina watched it as it carried the remains of a limp pink bon voyage balloon around and around on its string like some fluttering soft cock. Mindlessly, she picked at the red wax Bols seal on the side of the gin bottle. Sleep had been impossible for her the last few nights. Bruno had needed his cork popped early Friday morning; it had been almost three weeks. Friday night, there was the young SS captain. Then last night, the German Oberleutnant *Fickter*. Certainly no sleep last night.

She was fully dressed except for her house slippers, the kind that don't really have a right or a left but, with wear, develop both. On the wrong feet. She didn't care. And while she was alone she really didn't mind either that there was a tear in her eye. Sabina would miss that jolly old dandy. Most men, she felt, were really nothing more than the "bastard offspring of rats and lemmings." But Konni Ritter was different. He was one of those rare creatures who brought light to the dullest and dimmest of gatherings. And now he was dead. And there was little to suggest that she wasn't behind it in some way. But what could be proved? She threw back the last of the gin in her glass and delighted in its hot, sweet sting. Another was poured, and suddenly she craved herring and a tiny Panter Mignon cigar, neither of which were closer than her room, upstairs.

The call had come that morning from the Lutetia. A German investigator would be there sometime after three with questions about Herr Ritter's last hours. There would no doubt be questions about her treatment of the old man last night. And the row she had that afternoon with that little squealing pig, Xavier. *"After I slit that fat old dandy's throat and his little Nazi cunt's, I'll have doomed my soul to hell, du Bois. So, if I slit your scrawny chicken gullet too, it will be of absolutely no consequence to me!"*

What should she say when they ask? What should her answers be? I loved him. I fucked him. I hated him. Perhaps in some strange way I even killed him. But then there was one other thing she could say about the old Ritter, something she couldn't say about any other man she'd ever known, except Bruno.

I liked him.

DAY TWO—Paris—Sunday, 6 April 41—2:57 PM
Bruno ordered a German car and driver the minute he heard about Ritter's murder. He was at the préfecture before eleven, demanding to know what had happened to his friend. No one would talk to him. No information could be shared with anyone other than immediate family. When he returned to the club, he stormed past Sabina, and summoned Xavier immediately into his office. Slamming the door, he grabbed the little Alsatian by the ear and twisted it, weakening his knees until he fell into a chair.

"What do you know about this, you little cunt?"

"Nothing, Monsieur Bruno," Xavier cried, grimacing, his good ear cocked to his shoulder. "I assure you."

"You drew him in, didn't you, some mischief or other, with that redheaded kid. Rutgers Heht! I watched you." Bruno was furious. His bulging eyes glistened. Tears streamed down his face. "You got that poor old man into something that got him killed. What was it?"

"I am quite sure I don't know, Monsieur Bruno," Xavier squealed. Bruno hammered the base of his free hand on Xavier's head, jerking on the ear as he did so. Xavier's screams shook the office door.

"Tell me the truth!"

"I'm telling you the truth."

146

"What about all these American cigarettes?" He grabbed the Alsatian by the collar and stood him up. "Was Ritter involved in that?"

"No, not at all."

"What then? What was it?"

Xavier squirmed, hesitated. He had to give Bruno something, something to make the guilt on Xavier's face disappear. "There was maybe this one thing!"

"What, you Dreckskerl! Tell me!"

"Monsieur Ritter. He had friends, no? I had friends. Friends who needed Herr Ritter's friends."

"Quit talking in circles. What do you mean?"

"He had very artistic friends, no? Friends that could get papers. Papers my friends needed."

"False documents?"

"False? Perhaps. Perhaps altered, no?"

"And where the hell did you get any friends?"

"Oh, the man with false papers, monsieur. He has many friends. Identity cards, passports, laissez-passer? Such a man has many friends. Jews, mostly. Some others. Monsieur Ritter, he was a valiant man, your friend. Saved many people. Mostly Jews. But still people, no? And he took nothing in return."

"Don't say anything about this to the police or the Germans. If it comes out later, so be it. But don't let them hear it from you. If you do, I assure you, you'll be arrested."

"Oh, Monsieur Bruno, you know Xavier. Xavier is the deaf mute. Xavier's lips are sealed." He pursed his lips together and used his imaginary key to lock them.

Bruno rolled his eyes and went on. "False papers are worth thousands of francs today. Are you telling me, Xavier, you made nothing on these so-called friends?"

"Oh, Monsieur," the little weasel said, smiling childishly. "You make the joke on Xavier, no?"

DAY TWO—Paris—Sunday, 6 April 41—3:16 PM
The café-bar of the Hotel Lincoln opened at noon on Palm Sunday, but only for its guests. Party Cultural Minister Reinhard Rupp and his diminutive niece, Sweet Suzi Rupp, sat sipping coffee at the window table, where sunlight was refracted in prisms of purples and blues. When SS Sturmbannführer Alois Kruder marched into the café, one would have thought based on Reinhard's immediate pandering that

Adolf Hitler himself had arrived. The corpulent Nazi official's coffee saucer was resting on his tie so that as he jumped up to give the Nazi salute, coffee spilled all over the table.

"Please, be seated, Herr Rupp." Kruder gave his own quick Hitlergruß, as a waitress quickly cleaned up the mess. He then turned to Suzi.

"And this lovely creature must be the famous Sweet Suzi from the saucy side of Vienna, so I am told."

The overdone butterfly flutter of Suzi's eyelashes wasn't lost on either of them.

"I am honored to meet you, Herr Sturmbannführer," she cooed.

"But of course you are, my dear." He motioned for her to scoot over to the chair next to the window so he could take the seat beside her.

"If you will, I would ask that you both excuse my abrupt nature, but it is just that, isn't it? My nature. So it can't be helped, can it?" Kruder snorted proudly and smiled.

Agreement was immediate and profound.

"I understand." He stopped and turned in his chair to look directly into Suzi's dark-gray eyes, placing his palm on top of her thigh. His cold fingers absorbed the warmth from her firm flesh through her thin cotton skirt. "That you." A pat on her thigh. "Are now employed." Another pat. "At the l'Heure Bleue."

She smiled sweetly at him.

"Why, yes I am, aren't I?" She said, drawing her shoulders up to her ears and smiling at her uncle, who closed his eyes and nodded emphatically. "Last night was my premiere."

"Yes, I saw you, my dear," Kruder went on to say. "Now, I need to ask a very delicate favor of you."

"Why, I would do anything. Of course, Herr Sturmbannführer."

"But of course you would, you darling girl." Again he patted the girl's leg, then kept his hand on it. He suddenly noticed the quartered remnant of a toast point on the plate in front of him. He picked it up and studied it.

Reinhard watched him, then gave Suzi a puzzled look.

"If you're hungry, Herr Sturmbannführer, we could order something for . . ."

Kruder shook his head.

"Just"—he twirled the toast around and looked up at Reinhard—"checking to see what side it's buttered on!" The SD investigator's eyes went cold and steely, his smile grew sinister.

Certain there was nothing but solid bone between Reinhard's ears,
Kruder was about to explain the metaphor to them both when the
obese Party minister cajoled like a barking seal. "We are thoroughly
ensconced in the Party, both of us. And we will follow our Führer's
commands to the ends of the earth!"

"And beyond!" Suzi added.

"And my commands, as well?"

"Definitely."

"Most assuredly."

"You see, Herr Rupp, I need to know that I can count on her not
to disappoint me, and count on you not to dissuade her in any way.
Regardless of how ugly this all becomes."

"I would never dissuade her in any endeavor necessary for the
advancement and security of our glorious Reich."

"And I, sir"—Suzi placed her hand over Kruder's and squeezed
it—"will never disappoint you."

"Good." Kruder smiled. "Good. Then this is what I need. There
are people at this club, this l'Heure Bleue, people I want you to
watch. People who don't butter their bread on our side, if you will."

"But Herr Sturmbannführer," Reinhard implored. "I could close
the place down with just the snap of my fingers. There are vile and
sordid goings-on in that place, and I would be—"

"No, not at all." Kruder interjected. "That day will no doubt
come. But no, not now. I just want the girl to watch them, the little
one, the Alsatian pipsqueak, Xavier. And the owner, Bruno Kestler.
And there's that woman, the singer."

"Sabina." The delight in Suzi's voice was apparent.

"Yes, Sabina. Watch their comings and goings. Try to
eavesdrop on their conversations. And report everything to me.
Everything. Spare me nothing. Then I have one other task. Very
important. There's a Wehrmacht major, newly arrived in Paris. Von
Gerz is his name. And his ugly lapdog, an Oberleutnant Fechter. Get
close to the major. Use all your charms. I assure you the man is not
the least bit immune to them."

Kruder moved a strand of hair back in place on Suzi's head.

"Do whatever you have to. Blow in his ear. Muss his hair. Sleep
with the man." Kruder looked intentionally for rage in Reinhard's
eyes as he went on. "Suck his fucking cock. I don't care, but become
the woman of his dreams. And tell me everything you hear from him.
Spare me nothing. You do this, and I can assure you rewards beyond
your wildest dreams. So, are you both still . . . ensconced?"

"More than ever." The girl was indeed a thorough Nazi.

"Yes," Reinhard said after swallowing hard. "Heil Hitler!"

"This is my card. If anything happens, day or night, call this office. Tell them it's urgent. They always know where I am and can reach me at a moment's notice. If I don't get back with you within fifteen minutes, I'm dead."

DAY TWO—Paris—Sunday, 6 April 41—3:37 PM

Squinting the daylight's brightness from their eyes, Rolf and Gep entered the l'Heure Bleue through the open front door and descended the stairs. Xavier sprang up in front of them before either could really see him.

"Bonjour, gentlemen. I am Xavier du Bois. I am the manager of the famous Club l'Heure Bleue. We have been expecting you. If you will be so kind as to follow me, I will take you to Monsieur Bruno, the owner of the club."

Bruno Kestler impressed both Rolf and Gep as a very straightforward man of few words. He explained his relationship with Ritter, having met him in 1934 in Bruno's Berlin club. He liked the man immensely. And considered him friend and confidant. He told them Ritter was a man with no enemies. A man who made only friends. Bruno explained what he knew about Konni's business dealings, working with the Reich automotive parts standardization commission in a liaison capacity to the Wehrmacht.

"I assure you, you will discover that Herr Ritter's murder was a mistake, gentlemen. A case of mistaken identity. A matter of being in the wrong place at the wrong time. No one in their right mind would have cause to murder my friend. This is *not* the work of some clever assassin or conspirator. This is the fuckup of some imbecile!"

Xavier had nearly wet his pants by the time the German investigators got around to him. And his frazzled nerves were quite apparent. Trying to play the ignoramus wasn't working at all for him. Each of the major's questions caused him more consternation and grief. It was obvious he knew more than he was letting on. And after they threatened to take him in for more thorough questioning, the little Alsatian burst into tears. It was the perfect deflection. Give up one thing, to hide the rest.

"Oh, monsieurs, she said she'd kill me! And she'll do it!"

Fall Irmgard

Gep remained with Xavier while Rolf talked to Sabina. The situation had become *delicate,* and he was forced to confess he had enjoyed an evening of copious delights with the Dutch singer the night before.

"May I pour you a drink, major?"

"No, thank you," Rolf said, as he took a seat across from her.

"Where's the other one, the Oberleutnant? My lover?"

"He felt it best to recuse himself. I believe the word he used was 'awkward.'"

Sabina let out a guffaw, then cocked her head and looked pensively at Rolf, holding her cigar between her fingers and gently moving the hair from her forehead with the tip of her thumb. Smoke from her Panter swirled around her head.

"Oof, you're the one, aren't you?"

Rolf gave her a puzzled stare.

"The one who put the cream in Addie's panties!"

He snorted a suppressed chuckle and shook his head. *The profane Dutch!*

"I'm here to talk about Herr Ritter."

"You've talked to Xavier, no less. The little *stront!* He told you I threatened to kill Konni. So I did. So what? I was pissed, major. Konni pissed all over me bringing that little Hungarian cunt in to sing at the club. *My* club!"

"Suzi Rupp?"

"Yes, Suzi the *cunt!* So I made a threat. *Gelul!* I wouldn't kill that old man any more than I would my own mother. I loved him. Like every other woman who ever met him, I loved that old fool. I was just drunk and pissed. Just like I am now. Besides, I have quite the alibi, don't I, major? Ask your friend, Oberleutnant *Fickter!*" she laughed loudly and threw back her head, having to steady herself, almost falling out of her chair.

"But I'll tell you this, *mijnheer.* That little shit, Xavier? By the way, he's a Jew, you know. Saw it myself, his little bald *Schwanz—* they can't hide from that, can they? So anyway, if he, if Xavier, should ever come up dead someday, then major. Then yes, you need to come and question me. Indeed. Come and question me for sure then!"

151

19

Monday, 7 April, 1941

Das Entgleitung
L'escapade
The Slip

DAY THREE—Paris—Monday, 7 April 41—05:18 AM
Rolf sat up suddenly in his bed. A chill ran through him. *The ticket!*
The train ticket to Cherbourg that had fallen from Addie's purse. He
looked at his watch: 5:18. Hurriedly, he dressed and bolted down the
stairs and out the front door of the Lutetia, startling the sentries. He
had let the investigation consume him, turning the clues over and over
in his head. This and his horrible weariness gave him an uncalled-for
trust in this possibly manipulative American woman. He had
completely overlooked the fact that she was not scheduled to leave
Monday, as she had told him, but Sunday, yesterday. His boots
echoed in the empty early morning streets. *Départ 6 Avril, 1941—*
15:20. April 6th. Sunday night. Last night, you imbecile! Not Monday
night like she said. Something had bothered him all day. After the
evening briefings, he had taken a few drinks with Oberst Oskar
Rheile, the Abwehr chief of counterintelligence in Paris, and retired
early. All the traveling had caught up with him. He had even lain
awake in bed, analyzing himself, cursing his weakness for attractive
women, and his woeful credulity.

He rounded the corner at rue du Cherche-Midi and hurried the
short distance to her building. Angrily, he twisted the bell and
pounded on the door of the concierge loge. One of the Lutetia's
sentries had followed him, concerned by the major's rage. A light
switched on, the door bolt shifted, and the terrified face of the
building's night-capped concierge peeked out the door. Rolf pushed
him aside and charged up the stairs to the third floor. A baby started
crying on the first, and a woman in a hairnet poked her head out on
the second. At Addie's room he banged on the door. "Fräulein
Bridges! Open the door!" Again he banged, directly upon the red
American embassy sticker that told intruders, especially Germans,
this apartment was held by a citizen of the United States of America.

"Open this door immediately!"

The concierge and the sentry appeared, and the little man unlocked the door.

The room was completely empty except for a sofa and a few empty beer boxes full of trash in the center of the floor.

"*Gottverdammt!*" Rolf exclaimed, looking at his watch: 5:25 AM.

He turned to the sentry. "Go back to the hotel, get my driver, and tell him to have the car at the front door at five forty-five! Go, quickly."

The landlady appeared, perplexed, a scowl on her red face. "What is all this, anyway?"

"What were her travel plans?"

"Who?"

"Don't waste my time, madame! The American girl. What were her travel plans?"

"I'm sure I don't know, major. She was departing France from Cherbourg. It has to be a merchant ship, though. There are no longer any passenger lines out of French ports. And I know she is catching a steamer out of Lisbon on May 1st. That I do remember. Out of Lisbon on May 1st." She said the last sentence to his back as he hurried down the stairs.

20

Der kleine Schlingel
Le petit coquin
The Little Rascal

DAY THREE—Paris—Monday, 7 April 41—08:04 AM
Gomer Bisset was twelve years old. His family had lived in the house
on the rue du Cherche-Midi for more than a century. With the death
of his grandfather just after Gomer was born, the building had gone
into probate. According to Gomer's father, for more than twelve
years, the building had to be rented from his grandfather's estate until
some tax dispute was settled. "This sort of legal thievery is the curse
of France," Gomer had heard his father say many times in the lad's
short life. As a result, three of the building's top floors were rented
out in order for the Bissets to keep the family legacy.

And all three were currently held by single women. Or rather,
women who currently lived alone, to be more precise. In the case of
two of them, their husbands were prisoners of war and the women
were put to caring for themselves mostly from their men's pensions.
For these two women, rents had to be reduced and Gomer's father had
insisted on a rent reduction from the probate court in lieu of the war
and his gracious act and all. After almost a year, the matter was still
under consideration.

In the case of the third room, the single woman living there was
an American. A very beautiful American, with the most perfect teeth
the boy had ever seen. Each tooth was identically set and matched
against the next, and all were the clean, polished color of his mother's
pearl necklace. Surely, American women must spend a fortune on
tooth powder.

What Gomer liked most about living in a house with so many
single women was the way they always needed his help to run errands
and move things for them. He was only twelve, but he was very
strong. The strongest boy in his class. He had carried the American
woman's bags and a trunk all the way downstairs and pulled them to
Gare Saint-Lazare only yesterday. Her name was Mademoiselle
Bridges. He learned that "Bridges" meant *ponts* in French. Americans
had such funny names.

Fall Irmgard

Gomer was making himself quite rich working for all these single women. A few centimes here, a franc or two there. But he preferred working for the American most of all. She had very rich friends, and most important, she had connections with the Germans. And the Germans were of course the richest of them all! One of her German friends, a big redheaded officer, gave him five francs . . . three times! And for doing little more than carrying a heavy suitcase for less than an hour! Gomer would miss Mademoiselle Bridges. She had returned to America. Gomer was sad. But perhaps all was not lost. Because he understood two German women from the Hotel Lutetia were taking the apartment. So now there would be four single women who would need Gomer's strong back. No, make that five! For this very morning, Gomer was on his way to the building around the corner, the one above the nightclub, where he was to tap quietly and not knock on door number 203, on the second floor, at precisely eight o'clock.

Oh, merde! Gomer was late!

He ran to the corner as fast as he could, pulling his green wooden wagon. Tugging it into the building's foyer, he tiptoed quiet as a mouse up to the second floor. The door to apartment 203 opened before he had time to tap quietly. The woman known as the great singer Sabina stood before him. She was very old and wore a shiny robe with lots of flowers on it. She was kind of pretty, but very old. And her breath smelled like his father's.

She held her finger up to her lips and frowned at Gomer. This meant he was not to say anything and stay quiet as a mouse. She slid the heavy brown suitcase with two dark straps around it out into the hallway and held up two fingers, mouthing the words *deux heures*. Gomer understood exactly what she meant and started lugging the suitcase down the hallway. It was heavier than he'd expected. Nearly as heavy as the American woman's trunk. It would take him longer than he'd planned, it being so heavy. He would have to explain to the singer that he had undercharged her for such a heavy object. She was rich, after all. She sang for the Germans so she had to be rich like them. The redheaded German had paid him fifteen francs and his suitcase wasn't nearly as heavy. Twenty francs would be his demand.

So now, Gomer had just under *two hours*, deux heures, to get the heavy suitcase to the Gare de Lyon. A very long way, and a lot of it would be uphill! But for a strong boy like Gomer Bisset, not so difficult. And for twenty francs? Some men worked all day in Paris

155

for less. Gomer was a lucky boy to live among so many single women. Lucky indeed.

Suzi heard the unusual scooting, scraping sound in the hallway and opened her door just in time to see a boy lugging a suitcase. It had to have come from Sabina's room. Was she leaving? She kept her door cracked while she hurriedly dressed herself, one eye never leaving the hallway, watching for any movement at all. Perhaps Sabina had already gone. She had to make a decision. Follow the boy or find a way to see if Sabina was still in her room. A phone call! No. She could simply ignore it. She had to go to her door. Knock and listen for any sound coming from within.

Quickly, she grabbed her sugar bowl and dumped its contents in the kitchen sink, then scurried over to Sabina's door. After a few taps, Suzi was startled to see the door open. Sabina stood erect in a robe and makeup and growled, "What do you want?"

"I'm sorry, love, but I'm out of sugar. Would you—"

"Do I look like an épicerie? Leave me alone!"

Suzi let a few minutes pass before she felt comfortable enough to follow the boy. She stood in the place Alphonse-Deville and looked up and down the rue du Cherche-Midi and the boulevard Raspail. No boy was to be found. The lad had barely been able to carry the heavy suitcase down the hallway; there was no way he could have dragged it out of sight so fast. Someone must have picked him up. As she went back into the building, she tried to think of a way to find out what was going on. She would definitely leave her door cracked open, just to keep an eye out. After all, it was her duty now. She had orders!

Upstairs Sabina stood in front of the huge windows in her room, looking down at the little Nazi bitch in the street. She had her fist resting on one cocked hip and her Panter held up high by her ear; her hand moved slowly back and forth. Cigarette smoke rose in zigzags toward the ceiling. Angrily, she bit her lip, then took a drag on the Panter and let its smoke escape from her red lips and float up across her oblivious face, her eyes never leaving Sweet Suzi Rupp. A stray piece of tobacco clung to her tongue. She opened her mouth and moved it to the edge of her top lip, then harshly spat it away.

156

DAY THREE—Paris—Monday, 7 April 41—9:54 AM

Curiosities abound in wartime Paris. A wooden beer case was as
regular a sight as a step stool in front of restaurant sinks. Street
sweeper broom handles were often sawed off a quarter. And
children's wagons—red and green and blue—filled with luggage
were commonplace in and around the many train stations of the
occupied city. Boys were taking over their missing fathers' service
jobs in Paris. Boys were becoming dishwashers, street sweeps, and de
facto neighborhood porters.

It was just before ten when Gomer arrived at Gare de Lyon. He
pulled his wagon, just one of scores in the busy station, into the foyer
and located the men's room on the west side of the station. The big
clock at the front of the foyer told Gomer he had less than five
minutes to get into position. With gentlemanly guile he ducked and
twisted and elbowed his way through the crowd, then followed a bald
Chinaman, who held the door for him into the restroom.

Leave your wagon at the sink. Second stall from the wall. Take
your suitcase in and leave the door unlocked. Duck into the first stall.
Take the suitcase you find there. Return to Sabina and collect your
fee. Those were his instructions. And he followed them to the letter.
When he left the first stall, he noticed the Chinaman immediately
slipped into the second stall after him.

As Gomer left the bathroom with a very light, probably empty
tan suitcase in his green wagon, the Chinaman exited right behind
him carrying the brown suitcase belted with two dark straps.

21

Marseilles

Die Vereinbarung
Les arrangements
The Arrangements

DAY THREE—Marseilles—Monday, 7 April 41—10:00 AM
"Just as before, monsieur?" The desk clerk and owner at the tiny Hotel Poseidon high on a hill overlooking the old port of Marseilles winked to this obvious returning spy. The man spoke well-practiced but pathetically accented French. He was not French.

"There will be a woman. A blonde. She is to be treated like royalty. Her stay here is to be completely incognito."

"But of course, monsieur. You know you can trust us." What was this spy up to now? Was he German? Some Nordic for certain. Red hair. Probably Scandinavian. Or perhaps he was just another rich Jew trying to escape Nazi Europe? The woman was blond, did he say?

"No one is to enter her room," the redhead sternly demanded. "No housekeeping. Daily changes of sheets and towels are to be announced and left in the hallway. She will order room service by phone, it is to be delivered to her door, announced, and left in the hallway. You are to ensure she receives anything she requests. No questions. No registration. Are my instructions clear?"

"Impeccably, monsieur." German, for sure!

"Here's two weeks in advance. Your highest rate." A wad of francs was slapped on the desk, cold blue eyes never leaving the clerk. Another wad hit the desk. "*Pourboire* for the chambermaid, the room service waiter, the cook, security."

A stack of francs twice the size of the other two was pulled from the man's jacket and slid into the clerk's desk. "And for you. Your wife, your children, and grandchildren." The redheaded German grabbed the desk clerk by his collar. The blue eyes turned black.

"One mistake. One of your people talks to their husband or wife or priest. Anything happens to this woman, you won't see the light of the next day."

The German closed his eyes and inhaled deeply. Composed, he released the hotelier and straightened his collar.

"Now I have one other request. For this, I need to hear some of your ideas."

"Why, any way I can be of assistance, monsieur."

"The woman who will be staying at your hotel is French. She's being tailed by the Gestapo. I need to get her out of the hotel after a short stay without being seen."

"So, you are asking me to risk my life to protect this French woman? I must ask, monsieur. What has this woman done wrong?"

"She fell in love with me."

The hotel owner's French heart melted his shoulders and tilted his head, sweetly.

"Then monsieur, of course. I am French and so I understand completely." He slipped into his dangling suspenders. "I know just the man who can help us."

DAY THREE—Marseilles—Monday, 7 April 41—10:55 AM

"I'll need passports and laissez-passers for both parties," the tour agent said. "As well as transit authorization forms. They are issued by the police."

"I will have what you require. I only need to ensure there will be two places on that ship for us." The big redheaded evacuee smiled at the travel agent as he fanned out a thousand francs and placed the money on the agent's desk. "And no surprises."

"The fare is two hundred francs each, monsieur."

The redhead placed another four hundred francs on the desk.

"There are many people trying to depart France, monsieur. It may be difficult to secure . . ."

A fist full of francs was suddenly in the agent's face.

"But for you, there will be two places on the ship to Barcelona, I can assure you of this."

The redheaded man left before he had a chance to see the agent's charming smile.

DAY THREE—Marseilles—Monday, 7 April 41—11:44 AM

"Are you certain of this, monsieur? All of it?"

"Yes, all of it."

"You make me cry. It's so handsome."

"Just do it. And shave everything as well."

The barber flapped the apron out and let it drift down over Ruti. He watched in the mirror as the barber started with scissors and then moved to shears, operated with the same scissor like mechanism. In a matter of minutes, his heaping pile of red curly locks was scattered on the floor. Next the barber whipped up a shave lather with a tortoiseshell-handled brush. Within seconds, a thick lather covered his head and beard, even his eyebrows. Ruti smiled and his big white teeth looked suddenly yellow on the blue-eyed snowman in the mirror.

22

Along the Normandy Coast

Die Verhaftung
L'arrestation
The Arrest

DAY THREE—Normandy—Monday, 7 April 41—10:58 AM
The captain of the Danish tramp steamer *Thorbjorg* looked in the
mirror and liked very much what he saw. His sea legs kept the
handsome image steady, even in the choppy swells. He *was* a dashing
fellow, dark eyes, salt-and-pepper beard, and indeed he *did* favor
Errol Flynn. At least the French girl in Cherbourg last night thought
so. Such a taut, young body. He wished he had another night, so he
. . .

 "Captain," the radio signalman said, peeking his head around
the corner of the radio room. "We're being called in to port at Saint-
Malo. A German major will board us there."
 "Do you think it's the cargo?" the captain asked, turning his
head slightly in the radio operator's direction, but never taking his
eyes off himself.
 "*Lort!* I think it's the woman, captain."

 Addie lay sleeping sprawled across the tiny trundle bed pulled
out into her cramped cabin. She hadn't undressed any further than her
ivory camisole after she was shown to her cabin earlier that morning.
Within moments of closing the cabin door, she collapsed and fell
sound asleep in the lumpy little bed. Mouth wide open, head turned to
her right, with every few breaths she emitted a slight whistle. In the
nape of her neck, almost camouflaged in its own chestnut hair, a tiny
black nose snorted, then nestled itself deeper into its haunches. The
Yorkshire terrier suddenly raised its head and growled.
 The fierce pounding at the door startled the dog. She leapt high
into the air and landed on Addie's chest, barking repeatedly.
 "Miss Bridges! Open this door!"
 Addie tried to pull herself from the deep cavern of glorious
slumber she'd tumbled into. More pounding. More infernal barking.
 "Open this damn door now!"

She raised up from the bed but couldn't get her eyes open. They were sealed shut from the nearly comatose sleep she was struggling to awaken from. She felt blindly toward the pounding, found the hatch pin, and slid it sideways. The door flew open, knocking her back into the bed. The little dog became enraged, snarling and barking fiercely at the intruder.

The door wouldn't open more than a few feet, blocked by her travel trunk with three suitcases and two stacks of hatboxes on top of it.

Rolf crammed himself inside.

"Get up and get dressed, Miss Bridges."

"Rolf?" She still couldn't get her eyes open. "Is that you?"

"You're under arrest."

"Rolf, no!" She reached blindly toward him.

"You have five minutes to get dressed."

"No, please, no!"

The door slammed shut.

When he returned to the cabin, Rolf found her awkwardly tugging a second suitcase into the ship's hallway. Her mink coat was misbuttoned and her hair was hastily stuffed under a brown satin wedge cap pinned clumsily in place.

Rolf grabbed her forearm and pulled her up erect.

"You won't be needing those where you're going."

"Rolf, you mustn't act so harshly. You're frightening me." The little Yorkie leapt into Addie's arms.

"Harshly?" He pulled her to him gnashing his teeth. The dog snapped at him. "You have no idea how harsh it is going to be for you, Miss Bridges."

"Rolf, we need to talk. I need to explain."

He grabbed the frantically menacing dog from her and handed it to his driver, who had joined Rolf on the ship. "The dog stays too."

It bit the driver and leapt back into Addie's arms.

"Du miese Köter!" the driver exclaimed, putting his wrist to his mouth and sucking on the tiny wound inflicted by the *damn mongrel*.

"Oh, you poor dear. I'm so sorry." She reached for the man's wrist. He jerked away.

"Fifi! You bad dog. You go hide right this minute." It disappeared into her coat, nestling itself in an inside pocket. Its nose wriggled back and forth out between the buttons until the little creature could just watch further goings-on.

162

Fall Irmgard

"Please, Rolf. We can't just leave her with these sailors. There's no telling what they'll do to her. And I have to have the bags. It's all I have in the world."

"*Verdammt noch mal*, I said no!"

The Danish captain and a few of his crew members watched from the upper deck as the German major's driver lifted the two suitcases he had lugged out of the ship onto a small boat. Carrying a stack of hatboxes wrapped in twine, the major led the mink-clad woman carrying her purse and four hatboxes of her own by the arm, moving faster than she could shuffle in heels. Behind them came two crew members carrying her trunk.

"Good riddance," an ensign snorted. "What about the crates down below? They could have some nice things in them for my Loretta."

"We'll take them on to Lisbon," the captain answered.

"But the Germans have her now. She'll never see Lisbon."

The tender revved its motor and turned inland toward Saint-Malo.

"We have more important cargo to see to. Prepare to get underway."

The dashed crew member flipped his cigarette over the side. "Lort!" he said. *Shit!*

The black Voisin C28 limousine sped over the rolling hills of the Breton and Norman countryside. Standing as tall sentries along the highway, a countless string of huge chestnut trees brought a dizzying number of explosions of shade and sunlight to the car's plush velveteen interior.

"I'm sorry, Rolf!" Addie continued. "Please, listen to me. I should have trusted you. I know I should have. But I was just so frightened. It has taken me so very long to arrange everything. I was sure this was my only chance to get home before America enters the war."

"Well, you're certainly right about that now." He was seated next to her in the backseat, his hat's bill pulled down over his eyes. "There damn sure won't be another chance!"

"Rolllllffff," she squealed his name in a singsong of shrieks, holding her face in her hands. "Please don't treat me so. Please. I promise you. I'll never give you reason to distrust me again."

163

"You intentionally deceived and defied me. I know better than to give people like that a second chance. A few months in a cell at the *tribunal militaire* will serve you well, my dear."

"ROLF! PLEASE!" Her hanky was sopping wet with tears. She used the back of her gloved hand to wipe her snotty nose. When she turned away and sobbed, Rolf looked at her. Her breath made rosettes of fog on the window glass. Little Fifi squirmed her way out of Addie's coat and started licking her, whining. Addie composed herself enough to turn back to him and say, "Fifi needs to do her business." She sniffed into the glove as the little Yorkie wagged about fiercely at the word "business."

"She'll have to hold it."

The dog was beyond consoling, turning circles in Addie's lap and jumping up to her ear, whining.

"He says we have to wait, darling."

Fifi licked Addie's ear eagerly.

"No, no, no, he's not a bad man, Fifi," Addie cooed, pouting her pretty lips and kissing the little dog. Her eyes glanced at Rolf as she went on. "He's a very good man. He's just cross with mommy right now."

"Mein Gott!" Rolf exclaimed, slamming his palm against the glass partition separating the backseat from the front. "*Anhalten!*"

The driver slammed on the brakes and the car fishtailed to a stop. They all got out and the little dog sniffed around for a few short seconds, then squatted and peed. A few more seconds of sniffing and she squatted again and did further, more substantial "business."

"See, I told you," Addie said, looking at Rolf. "I told you he was a good man, Fifi!"

The car hadn't traveled a hundred meters when Addie looked over at Rolf. Again, the whimper-laced words, "Rolf, darling. I'm famished. I haven't eaten anything since yesterday morning. If I have to spend God knows how long in some ghastly jail cell, I simply must have something to eat."

Again, Rolf slammed his hand on the glass. When the car stopped, he got out, slammed the back door shut, and jumped in the front seat with the driver. The transmission of the long, beautiful car whined as it pulled back onto the road and sped down the deserted highway.

Fields of white apple blossoms sprinkled with pink peach buds blanketed the Norman countryside. The springtime sun was winning its battle with the thinning gray clouds rushing in full and fluffy now from the coast. Spring thaw had come to the Calvados. The meadows were lush green pillows where short-legged cows were fatting themselves, hooves sunk deep in the mud, fat bellies dragging in the thick, cold grass that had gone through and oozed from them, their swaying tails painting their creamy haunches a gooey greenish black.

Climbing up from the lush valley, the midnight-blue and black Voisin limousine entered a nameless Norman village. The big car squeezed through narrow lanes and crept slowly around sharp corners meant for little more than oxcarts. Church bells tolled the noon hour. The driver stopped the car directly at the front door of a boulangerie. He got out enough to stand on one foot, his right hand never leaving the steering wheel, and asked something of the baker inside. Returning to his place behind the wheel, the driver then slowly backed the car up to the last intersection and turned toward the pealing bell. After a short wind between more stone and crumbling stucco houses with sparkling windows and crisp lace curtains, a small square opened up before them. With a slight screech from the brakes, the car stopped in front of the Café du Normand.

The driver leaned against the stack of suitcases strapped to the limo's trunk and lit a cigarette. Rolf took a seat in the sunshine as half the café's customers realized they were suddenly finished with their lunch or stuffed it in their shirts, deciding quite abruptly to take it to go. Addie went inside the café to do some business of her own.

When she returned to take her seat across from Rolf, he was bewildered by the way she had freshened and composed herself. She was as beautiful as the first time he saw her. The table was laden with Camembert; sliced apples sprinkled with lemon juice and raw sugar; a bowl full of tiny whole *crevettes*, a creamy pink sauce drizzled over them; and a plate of sliced cheeses and hams, sliced baguettes, and a big, cold demicrock of Normandy butter covered with a flat sheet of onionskin paper.

"Your last supper, so to speak," Rolf quipped, pouring her some wine.

"Perhaps." She nestled herself in her chair and unfolded her napkin, adding, "Or maybe our first date?"

A cute smile.

Suppressing his own, Rolf looked away, shaking his head. He snapped back around.

"You still don't understand what you've done, do you? Your sudden composure demonstrates quite clearly you think this is all just folly."

She looked up at him as she sipped her wine, her big brown eyes pleading otherwise over the rim of the glass.

"Rolf, darling, I—"

"Enough with the darling!" He curled his lip and clenched his jaw.

She grew defiant. "What would you have me do? I sobbed like a schoolgirl for fifty kilometers; that didn't help. I apologized and swore not to ever deceive you again. I deserve to be punished, Rolf. I insulted and embarrassed you. I know. But not jail. I'm sorry, but I know you. I size up people immediately, and I'm always right. The first time I looked in your eyes, I knew what kind of man you were. You won't put me in jail."

"You're in for quite a shock, Miss Bridges." The waiter brought two more beers as ordered. Rolf slapped some cheese and ham on a sliced baguette and grabbed one of the beers to take lunch to the driver.

Addie reached across and softly touched his forearm.

"You won't put me in jail. I know you, Rolf. I think I've known you my whole life."

Mein Gott, he thought as he stood up. *Diese Augen, die Grübchen!* He had to get away from those beautiful eyes and those dimples!

"You don't know me. You're about to find out what happens to people I no longer trust. From now on, Miss Bridges, I assure you, you'll be watched much more closely."

As he walked back to the car, that French phrase came to mind. *Double entendre.*

23

Die Jungen
Les garçons
The Boys

DAY THREE—Île-de-France—Monday, 7 April 41—1:54 PM
The dark-blue Matford crept slowly to a stop in a forest opening just above the banks of the Seine a hundred kilometers outside Paris. The two boys got out and stretched and yawned in the warm sunshine. A chorus of songbirds mixed pleasantly with the roar of the river below them. Jean-Pierre and Vincent Brisbois smiled at each other. The brothers had done it! Mission accomplished! The car was exactly the make and color they'd been ordered to *find*. It had been an arduous undertaking. Days just to locate it. Then . . .

It was just before dawn last Friday. Vincent Brisbois carefully opened the barn door and he and Jean-Pierre slipped in. Vincent tied a rock to a string and slipped it down the open spout of the gas tank. When he retrieved it, maybe fifty centimeters of the string was wet. He smelled it. Tasted it. It wasn't rainwater, it was fuel. Problem one was solved. Quietly, they lifted the motorcar's hood and problem two stared them both in the face. As with most cars remaining in French hands, whether by hook or by crook, few had keys to prevent theft or confiscation by the Germans. Owners simply unclipped the distributor cap and took it in the house, hid it in the cookie jar or in the back of a linen drawer. So now the boys had to find a distributor cap and coil wire. Another full day to walk back to Paris, over twenty kilometers away, to the only place one could easily find an abundance of automobile parts.

In the darkness of Friday night, the two boys stole their way along the fence line, grabbing the fence occasionally to catch themselves from tumbling down the rocky incline created for the very purpose of keeping their sort out. The German automobile impound out in Saint-Ouen was adjacent to the freight yards, in a lot fenced by high barbed wire. An occupied populace without fuel had no need to burden themselves with storage for their dormant automobiles. So, the Germans took possession of all but the most vital vehicles, those owned by medical doctors, police and fire departments, and of course the wealthiest and most politically connected, including black-market underworld gangsters the German administration deemed important.

Vincent was sure he wasn't exaggerating when he guessed there were over three thousand automobiles in the lot. It wasn't well lit, at least not at the back. The guards and dogs stayed at the front gate, a kilometer away. They located a green Matford just three meters from the fence. Jean-Pierre cut the barbed wires with his snips, they coiled back like springs, and the boys shot under the fence. Quietly, Vincent raised the hood. In the darkness he found the distributor cap with his hands, felt his way along a wire down to the first cylinder, snipped that wire short at the distributor cap, then found cylinder number two, followed it up, and snipped it off a bit longer than the first cylinder. The wire on cylinder three was cut little longer still, and so on. In less than a minute, he was back under the fence with the distributor cap and coil wire, as well as an ingenious system of placing it correctly on the other car. The boys hurried on down the gravel incline and into the shadowy refuge of the freight yard, where they would hunker down under a freight car and sleep until sunrise, when the curfew was lifted.

So, now it was Monday afternoon. Mission accomplished. Jean-Pierre straddled the headlamp and sat on the Matford's fender like a horseman, leaning back, closing his eyes, and soaking up the wondrous sunshine. They had stolen the exact car. A dark-blue Matford, functional. Their part of this gallant mission to strike terror in the ranks of the German occupier was finished. Their dead father would indeed be very proud of them. And age was not important. The brothers were sixteen and seventeen, and look at their daring deed! A smile came to Jean-Pierre's creamy-cheeked face. The boys would bring such pride to their village.

Vincent Brisbois walked around to the back of the car. He took out the rock-and-string fuel gauge and dipped it in the tank. Withdrawing it, he smiled and headed back toward the front of the car to join Jean-Pierre and tell him they'd hardly used any fuel getting the car overland to the assigned meeting place.

The first bullet tore into Vincent's hip at his left leg joint. Severing his artery, blood shot from the wound as the shot's report echoed through the forested valley. Silenced songbirds roared in the still air as their wings lifted them away. Vincent fell to the wet ground, screaming and clasping both his hands tightly in a struggle to put pressure on the sharp, stinging wound.

Fall Irmgard

Jean-Pierre leapt instinctively from the car's fender and ran, an all-out stumbling, frantic struggle for the river. Four quick shots from a Luger hit him in the back, and he flipped over the embankment and fell onto the rocks below, facedown in the river. The man with the Luger, in a dark wool overcoat and a brown beret, came from one side of the car tracks leading down to the clearing. Another man, wielding a Mauser, came up the other side of the tracks from the woods behind the car, followed by a third. The two of them, the first in a fedora, the other in a tweed flat cap, took Vincent by the arms. Ignoring his screams and wailing, they opened the back door and threw him in the car. One of them just stood there watching the boy writhe in pain in the backseat, screaming for his life, for his mother. The man with the Luger came up to the other window and stared at the dying boy himself. When the backseat was blood soaked enough to suit them, the first man flung the car door open and tugged and jerked Vincent by the arm until he fell back onto the ground, into the very patch of black, bloody grass he'd been lifted from. The two men on either side of the car stepped away from it as the third man with the Mauser fired off another round that crashed through the Matford's back window. The fedora took a screwdriver and changed the license plate on the car.

Two of the men lit cigarettes as they walked back along the tire tracks into the woods, the screwdriver and license plate back in the coat of the one, the Mauser on the shoulder of the other. The man with the Luger still at Vincent's side knelt down beside him. He took a large piece of sharp flint rock and dashed it along the boy's knees and shins, tearing into Vincent's trousers and flesh. After tossing the stone into the river, he placed the Luger in the boy's limp hand and grabbed the weak child by his sweaty hair. A toothpick moved from one side of the man's mouth to the other as he looked into the lad's terrified, dying eyes and coldly said, "Go to sleep, boy."

24

Hôtel Lutetia
Abwehrleitstelle Paris
Siège du renseignement militaire de Paris
Military Intelligence Headquarters in Paris

DAY THREE—Paris—Monday, 7 April 41—6:12 PM
The newly installed iron bars on the windows and at the main
entrance of the Hotel Lutetia matched those on the Bank of France
and the tribunal militaire across the street. *Iron bars on Lutetia.* This
metaphor wasn't lost on the French. Lutetia is Latin for Paris! But to
the Germans, it was just the new order of things. A security necessity.

One of the Lutetia sentries rushed to the limousine as it pulled
up along the boulevard Raspail. He was taken aback by the very
attractive young woman in a mink coat who extended her hand as she
rose out of the car. Rolf leapt from the other side of the car, said
something in German to the sentry, pointing at the luggage tied to the
back of the car, then coldly took Addie's arm and escorted her into
the hotel, little Fifi tucked away in her coat. The wrought-iron
elevator was barely large enough for both of them. Rolf stood behind
her, feet wide apart, hands folded behind him as the elevator groaned
its way to the top floor. He was struck with the vivid aromas of her
hair, floral scents, oranges and peaches.

The Lutetia had been taken over entirely as a workplace for the
Abwehr, almost all of the rooms had been converted into offices, save
the few on the fifth floor where he and Gep were staying. Before the
Germans took over the seventh, top floor of the hotel, had consisted
of tiny *dame de compagnie* rooms, servant quarters for aristocratic
clientele. Now they were being used by the Germans for document
storage. Rolf and Addie passed one padlocked door after another to
the end of the long, angled hallway where Gep stood in the open
doorway at the last of the rooms. His smile was grimly sinister. Addie
peeked in, removing her hat, and sniffed the room. Rolf's fingers
snapped loudly as he made a make-it-snappy gesture toward the
cramped chamber.

"My god, Rolf. This isn't a room, it's a closet!"

The fabric-clad walls were buckling in one corner, the low,
slanted roof was cracked and water stained around a tiny slit of a sun

window, barely the size of a baguette. On a blond side table with intricate dark wood inlay sat a large china pitcher filled with water, a single crystal drinking glass, and a large white china washbowl with pink and green raised ribbons and bows around its middle. In the bowl stood a laced pouch of Lutetia soaps and a corked bottle of bluish shampoo. The room was almost entirely consumed by a gray Wehrmacht-issue cot. On it a crisply ironed and folded set of sheets and a small silk pillow were stacked on a bare and stained duvet. A room hastily thrown together by men, a few things having been mercifully collected by women.

"Bath, exercise, and meal privileges will be earned and will depend entirely on your behavior. As will your length of stay." Addie's head shook slightly as Rolf went on. "The least bit of trouble from you, Miss Bridges, and you will be removed to the Cherche-Midi prison across the street." Rolf stepped aside as the sentry from downstairs entered the room and dropped a stack of newspapers on the cot, pushing the shiny pillow onto the floor. "Some reading materials," Rolf went on to say. "And when you're finished with them, you can spread them on the floor for your little dog's business."

Gep stuck his head in and took the top newspaper off the pile. He stretched it on the floor, folding it perfectly so the dog couldn't miss soiling the large picture of Il Duce, the Italian dictator Mussolini, ranting on the front page. "There you go, little doggie."

"What about my business?" Addie sobbed.

Rolf lifted the head of the cot to reveal a small bidet and slid a blue porcelain pot from under the bed with the toe of his boot, leering at her. The driver and another guard brought her luggage into the room, not stacking it so much as wedging it at the end of the bed. Then came Gretl, carrying Addie's hatboxes. She set them on the floor and neatly put the pillow back on the cot. As she backed out of the room past Rolf, she silently mouthed the words *I'll check on you* to Addie. Rolf snapped around and the fat, flustered girl slammed herself wide-eyed against the hallway wall, then scurried away.

"Welcome to your new home, Miss Bridges," Rolf stated coyly.

"This isn't home." A tearful breakdown was building in her face as she motioned at the room with her outstretched hand. "I don't have room to even turn around."

"I'm sure you can give it a woman's touch."

"But I'm an American. You can't do this to me. I demand to see Tyler Thompson at the US consulate immediately!"

Rolf so delighted in it all as he closed the door.

The hasp folded closed, the lock slid over the bolt and clanked as it snapped shut.

"Rolf, NO!"

Down in the hotel ballroom where morning and evening briefings were held, Gep cut a swath through the thick pall of smoke as he delivered Rolf a brandy. The two of them sat in matching high-backed, winged chairs with carved pecan wood claws for arms and legs. A side table and a gold-and-onyx shaded lamp separated them.

"So, Gep." Rolf took a sip and exhaled, blowing this terrible day from his head. "What did you discover while I was away?"

Gep leaned his elbow on the chair's arm and peered under the lamp at Rolf.

"I checked with some of my people in Berlin. In a communiqué this morning, I learned just how well connected the old man was. Ritter sat on the automotive parts standardization commission. His singular objective was to seek agreement from the various parts manufacturers on standardizing, and failing that, he had the leverage of raw material supply. It was a weapon he kept sheathed for the most part, being the sort of man who felt his sharp wit and charm could be more persuasive. But he did draw on it a few times, especially in regard to Bakelite, a hard plastic used to produce nonconductive electrical parts, steering wheels, telephones. The company that manufactures this Bakelite has complete control of the market, and its consumption is on strict allocation. Automotive allocation is controlled entirely by this auto parts commission. And of course, one Herr Konrad von Stendal der Ritter, Konni Ritter"

"So, Herr Ritter could make friends by controlling this raw plastic powder," Rolf interjected, without looking around the lamp at Gep. Then he added, "Or enemies."

"Exactly." Gep folded his paper.

"Anything else, Gep, old man?"

"One other important thing, for sure."

"Ach, good." Rolf set his brandy on the table between them and crossed his legs, lighting a cigarette. Nothing from Gep. Concerned, he looked under the lamp that separated them. "What is it, what else have you discovered?"

"That you, sir, have fallen for this American woman."

"That's nonsense, Gep. I'll have none of it!"

"Is it?" Gep moved the lamp out of the way. "Any other person in France—hell, in all of Europe—who pulled a stunt like that would be in a jail cell this very minute. And we both know it."

"I'll have the woman in chains in the morning!"

"Yes." Gep laughed. "And I'm the k-k-k-king of England!" German officers took cruel pleasure in poking fun at the British monarch's stammer. "Admit it, major."

"I'll do no such thing. The woman is American. She has certain rights."

"Rights she relinquished when she broke German law by disobeying you."

"So, take her away, Gep. Do with her as you will."

"I don't want her in jail any more than you do. I just want you to admit she's . . ." Gep looked around the gilded room as he searched for the word. "Special to you."

Rolf stewed.

"Major, let's go up there and release the poor thing and be done with it. We have more important issues to worry ourselves with."

Rolf swirled his brandy in his snifter.

"No." He gazed into the glass. One eyebrow arched and he shook his head. "No, she stays where she is."

25

Der Dienstdolch
La dague
The Service Dagger

DAY THREE—Paris—Monday, 7 April 41—8:08 PM
Inspector Luc-Henri tugged and pulled himself out of his car before
his tweed-jacketed driver could make his way around to assist him.
The two guards standing sentry at the door to the Hotel Lutetia
snapped their arms out and crossed the barrels of their rifles, blocking
the French police inspector's path. He displayed his ID and bounced
his hand deep into his coat pocket to extract the calling card of
German major Karl-Rudolph von Gerz.

"Moment," one of the sentries said as he disappeared into the
hotel. The remaining German guard and Luc-Henri stood
uncomfortably for a few moments, until the other sentry returned and
nodded his approval. The guard's unspoken offer of assistance was
denied with the subtle shake of Luc-Henri's head and a quick 'merci'
as he gyrated himself up the steps into the hotel. Once inside, he was
met by an orderly holding the major's card.

"If you'll follow me, please," the orderly chimed in French.

They made their way down the portico to the hotel's large
smoking room where Rolf sat visiting with several other officers.

"Inspector," Rolf exclaimed at first sight of Luc-Henri. "Good
to see you." He excused himself and pressed Luc's hand.

"You look preoccupied. You have new information?"

"It is very possible."

"We can't stay here. Policy." Rolf led him down the portico to
a lobby table next to one of the Lutetia's Palladian windows. They
took seats and Luc glanced outside, past iron bars and an unsettling
blur, onto the street. Each square pane of window glass had perfectly
cut wax paper inlaid over it, letting in daylight but not snooping eyes.

Presently, Gep arrived just in time to light Rolf's cigarette.

"Oberleutnant, perfect. The inspector was just about to share
some news about our investigation."

"I am not actually sure if this is related or not, but it involves
this weapon and so, perhaps . . ." From his briefcase he withdrew a
long object wrapped in clear paper. "A local stockbroker was

murdered sometime Saturday. He had been stabbed through the cheek and the heart, then this murder weapon was thrust into his chest cavity and left there. Intentionally."

Luc unwrapped a German service dagger with an SS insignia embossed on the handle. "Two gendarmes discovered the body, at the Right Bank buttress of the Pont Royal. It was during a pouring rain. One policeman remained with the body while the other went to summon help. It was then that a German officer, after being told he was under arrest as a possible witness, attacked the policeman, critically injuring him. The German was a burly redheaded fellow. This is all we know."

"This happened Saturday?" Rolf said, turning the glassine wrapped dagger over in his hands.

"*Oui,* sometime in the afternoon as best we can figure. The earlier part of the day was very sunny with many people on the quay. It would have had to have happened after the rain started, after one o'clock. The victim was drenched."

"Do you think your gendarme can tell an SS officer's chevrons from a regular Wehrmacht officer's?" Gep asked, motioning for one of the same from a waiter as he pointed to the other drinks on the table.

"If you could give me some examples, possibly, yes, he just may be able to." Luc closed the flap on his case and hugged his arms around it as he went on. "But there is more, much more about this murdered stockbroker. You see, an investigation of the man's home discovered a safe, a very well-hidden safe. A ransacked and quite empty safe."

"Would this man have kept large sums of cash around?" Rolf asked, handing the murder weapon to Gep.

"Possibly. But more than likely, he would have kept a stash of securities."

"Securities are registered," Gep interjected, looking back and forth at both of them. "They're not easily negotiable."

"In France, monsieur, registration of stocks and bonds is mostly nonexistent. A Frenchman's privacy is more important to him than a stock's security. Only recently"—he looked over the top of his glasses—"with *guidance* from Germany, are all Frenchmen being required to register their holdings. Not just stocks and bonds, but gold, jewelry, and art as well, which I must say, with all due respect, I personally find disconcerting. So, this too could be cause for this broker's safe holding a larger than normal stash."

"What about taxation?" Rolf asked. "How can your government be assured all assets are taxed without some sort of registration?"

Luc shrugged. "Taxation is a matter of honor to a Frenchman." Smiling, whimsical eyes rolled as he skewed his mouth and continued. "In the case of our recently deceased stockbroker friend, Monsieur Fabien Lemay, the fact that the securities he traded were all quite negotiable, as negotiable as any thousand-franc note, was obviously the man's death sentence, to be sure."

"How so?" Gep asked, unfolding his arms, shifting up in his chair. "How would anyone other than his clients even know about this secret safe?"

"Allow me to explain the brokerage system in France. Just like in other countries, there are large very reputable brokerage houses with centuries of tradition. *Parquet* houses if you will, brokers with floors so to speak." He smiled sweetly. "But there are also other, smaller brokers working on the fringes of the exchange, quite within the law, completely licensed, but working on a smaller scale. These we call *coulisse* brokers, working from the *wings* of the brokerage stage, if you will. Monsieur Lemay was a member of the latter."

Luc returned the dagger to his satchel and crossed his legs.

"Our investigation has shown the man had actually taken over his father's business some thirty years ago. Like most *coulisse* brokers, Monsieur Fabien Lemay had a very close-knit clientele, a small group of people, mostly of the tradesman and shop-owner class who wanted a piece of the big boy's pie. He was trusted to help this group of people reach these aspirations. This safe was used to secure financial instruments for many of his clients, which demonstrates the degree of trust these people placed in him."

Gep scribbled frantically on a note card. Luc hesitated politely to let him catch up.

"Then the Germans . . ." He cleared his throat. "Excuse me. Then your army came to Paris. Most all of the larger brokerages moved their customers' securities to Vichy. In the case of the smaller brokers, those who held their customers' securities for them were rare. Most émigrés preferred to stuff everything in their shirts and simply flee. But Monsieur Lemay's clientele were shop owners and artisans, people who both lacked the means to escape the German Army, but also, more than likely had nowhere to go. So they remained in their shops and businesses, ever hopeful it would all work out. German officials then closed the exchange here in Paris. It remains closed to this day, except for trades in government bonds. So

176

they all sit and wait, relatively secure in the knowledge that the safest place for their treasured life's savings was just around the corner in Monsieur Lemay's secret safe, unregistered, unknown, and therefore safe from . . . from you, from the German administration."

"So, have any of these clients come forward?" Rolf asked.

"Oddly enough, only two. Both are shop owners, Catholic gentiles. Both say they had sold most of their holdings in the winter, for a fraction of their true value. Lemay brokered the deals. But the clients have no idea to whom they were sold. These men had families to feed during a very difficult winter and frankly didn't care. There only remained for these two people a paltry few treasures, but enough to make a new start when the . . . when the war is over."

Luc inhaled deeply and sighed. "Alas, so now, the remains of their treasures are lost to them. Stolen away. And their trusted friend and broker, murdered."

"How do you see this tying in with the Ritter murder?"

Luc shrugged. "I'm not sure is does at all. But I am sure that you will agree it certainly could."

26

Tuesday, 8 April 1941

Die grauen Mäuse
Les souris grises
The Gray Mice

DAY FOUR—Paris—Tuesday, 8 April 41—9:00 AM
Rolf would make his next interrogation of the Ritter case the easiest.
Two of Ritter's "little ducklings," and friends of Addie's, worked for
the Abwehr at the Hotel Lutetia. Like the other three-hundred or so
Nachtrichtenhelferinnen in occupied France, the girls were daughters
of German aristocracy and business and industrial leaders who
applied for and received postings to occupied Paris to serve as file
clerks, mail sorters, and typists for the Wehrmacht officer corps.

Gretl von Reinsdorf-Vilmer and Hedy von Rohrbach entered
Rolf's small office as instructed at precisely 0900 hours. Both girls
were wary yet somehow also eager to be of whatever assistance they
could. They took their places across from Major von Gerz and
Oberleutnant Fechter. Rolf remembered the girls from the l'Heure
Bleue Saturday night and told them not to be frightened. He just had a
few questions for them. The first question was if the girls were aware
of Herr Ritter's murder.

"Oh, my goodness, yes," Gretl answered, leaning forward in the
chair. She was the shorter of the two, with a manly build and a square,
pudgy face.

"Oh, my goodness, yes," Hedy repeated almost immediately.
Hedy was definitely the pretty child in the room, tall and trim, with
long, dark eyelashes, brown eyes, and natural blond hair. But Rolf
and Gep would soon discern there wasn't much more than dense bone
behind those beautiful eyes.

"We just loved him so!" Gretl interjected.

"*Loved* him," Hedy added, only with her own more wide-eyed
emphasis.

Rolf looked at Gep, then went on.

"You were both at the l'Heure Bleue Saturday night, at Miss
Bridges' table?"

"*Ja, genau*. It was Addie's bon voyage party. She was returning home to America."

"Ja, ja. Genau." Hedy *was* nodding more emphatically than Gretl.

"I believe we had the pleasure of being introduced to you that night by Major von Hirschbach?"

More magpie *yeses* and *exactlys*.

"And of course, Herr Ritter was there."

Seven yeses and three exactlys, two of which were very dramatic and peppered with more wide-eyed nodding.

Rolf sat erect, stretching his back.

"I now need to inform you both that it is standard procedure in a murder investigation to talk to witnesses one at a time. So, I will start with you, Fraulein"—he nodded at Gretl—"and will ask you, Fräulein von Rohrbach, if you would be so kind as to wait out in the hall until we call for you."

Gep turned a spontaneous snicker into a polite cough. *Well done, major.*

"Ja, ja," Hedy said as she stood up. The tall mockingbird in her loose-fitting gray smock silently opened the door, tiptoed out, and pulled the door very slowly and very quietly closed.

"Now." Rolf rubbed his hands together and sat back in the chair. "I guess my first question is how you girls got into the club in the first place?"

"Hans-Hubert gets us in." Gretl smiled proudly.

"Major von Hirschbach?"

"Jaaa." It was a three-syllable "ja" that needed more nodding. "He says we can come on Saturdays if we stay all night until curfew is lifted at sunrise. And we're not girls, major. I'm twenty-two and Hedy is twenty-three."

Rolf cocked his head back and frowned. "I see."

"Hans-Hubert says the general doesn't allow Nachtrichtenhelferinnen to go to clubs because he doesn't want us fraternizing. It's to protect us. But he, Hans-Hubert, says, 'What the general doesn't know won't hurt him!'" This made her wag her sizable tail in the chair and smile again.

"I would not expect anything less from Hans-Hubert."

Gretl smiled, then chuckled.

"When did you first meet Herr Ritter?" Rolf asked.

Gretl went on to explain she and Hedy had both arrived from Hanover in August of last year, 1940, two months after the victory

179

over France. Like the rest of the Nachtrichtenhelferinnen in Paris, they were on a two-year work visa and had been immediately assigned to the Abwehr office at the Lutetia.

"Within a week of arriving, Hans-Hubert got us in at the l'Heure Bleue, so it would have been late August when we first met both Addie and Herr Ritter. The sweet old man was in Paris about every other week on business. Something or other to do with automobiles. He was always meeting with the most important people, including Wehrmacht officers."

She nodded to the water pitcher. Her eyes asked, *may I?* Rolf nodded and handed her a glass. Filling it, and gulping like a thirsty mare, her sweet eyes moved back and forth between the major and his adjutant as she drank. Smiling, she caught her breath and continued.

"We were quite the consortium. Me and Hedy, Herr Ritter and Addie, the two French girls, Yvette and Mélina (but they very rarely came to the club), and then of course, Sabina. Sometimes."

Gep took the names down, very neatly printed them, each on its own lined vanilla filing card, the growing collection of which he kept rubber-banded together in his tunic.

von REINSDORF-VILMER, Margrette (Gretl) *Deutsche
von ROHRBACH, Hedwig (Hedy) *Deutsche
DEBONNET, Yvette *Französin
VAUGEOIS, Mélina *Französin
van der GORP, Sabina *Holländerin
BRIDGES, Adelaide (Addie) *Amerikanerin

The last one he had already made out.

Rolf wrote each name down in his new Moleskine, giving each its own set of facing pages. Gep would later alphabetize his list. Rolf liked the chronology of the order in which each witness had been interrogated. The two differing record-keeping systems complimented each other.

"But it was really Addie who kept the gaggle together," Gretl went on to declare. "The French girls were her friends and though they took quite easily to Konni Ritter (and who wouldn't), they were much slower to accept us, what with the war and all. But after a while, they did."

"What did you do?" Rolf inquired.

"Romped about, mostly. The way girls do. Or, I guess, waddled about is more true to the point. Herr Ritter didn't romp, did he? Luxembourg Gardens, the races, sunny Sundays on the quays, the cafés, bathing in the country, picnics. The rest of that summer and then autumn were positively tip top! 'Tip-top,' Konni always said that. It's English. 'Tip-top!' Then winter came. It was the worst winter I've known in my entire life. Too cold and messy to even get out of bed, much less do anything. There were times when Hedy and I had to spend the night here at the Lutetia, curled up on the file-room floor. We share a dormitory in the 5th you know. And the poor French girls. They nearly froze to death. Yvette and her little girl spent one whole week in bed with Addie and her little dog. Never left the apartment. Konni acquired a ration of coal for Addie's building. Still, they only had heat for two hours a day. Addie told us there was one night that her cheek actually froze to the pillow! We laugh now, but it must have been terrible."

"What was it about this old man that created such a coterie of young beauties?" Gep asked, an incredulous frown on his face.

"Konni was just such a dear and generous man. He brought us all the most darling set of Kunsthorn Heitner combs for our hair." She turned her head to this side and that, pulling her blond hair back behind her ear, modeling a set of the combs for them. "They're terribly expensive. All handmade in Austria of tortoiseshell and ram's horn and ivory. For Christmas he gave us each an ornate little box with six sets of combs lined up, three and three. A box to everyone, the French girls, even Yvette's little daughter! They must have cost him a fortune."

Rolf jotted down the name of the Austrian combs, Kunsthorn Heitner. He had seen them somewhere, probably on his wife's dresser. Still the name troubled him.

"The other French girl, Mélina. She has a German boyfriend. Oh, *Scheisse!* I shouldn't be telling you that, I think. It's not allowed. But Hans-Hubert knows. So I guess it's all right. Anyway, he was able to get coal for Mélina and her mother. He's quite the find, that one. He was able to get food too, when it seemed . . . His name?"

HEHT, Rutgers *Deutscher LEUTNANT

"No, he's only been dating Mélina since before Christmas sometime. I think they met through Addie. I really don't remember. Anyway, sometimes we would all go to the cemetery and strip down to our bloomers and . . . Yes, Ruti knew both of them, Hans-Hubert and Konni. But I don't think they were chums or anything. You see, Ruti worked for Hans-Hubert at the Procurement Bureau. We really don't know what any of you do, you're all so mysterious. But he bought supplies for the army. That's all I really know about him."

"Did you see Heht recently with Konni and Hans-Hubert?" Gep asked.

"Lately? Not so much with Hans-Hubert, but I did see him with Konni. On Saturday. Hedy and I were on our break and we took a walk down the boulevard. Silly girls, we got caught in the rain. So we ran under one of the awnings on the place Alphonse-Deville and we saw Ruti jump into Konni's car. And they seemed to be quarreling. At least Ruti did. He seemed quite cross. But Mélina says Ruti is like that. He just blows off steam sometimes. He is really just the dreamiest guy."

Gep asked the obvious.

"I don't know, they just drove off and we ran back to work. Yes, Ruti was with him. But Ruti wouldn't hurt anybody. Especially not a fellow German. Do you think?"

Rolf's next question caused a furrowed look of surprise from her.

"Yes, as a matter of fact, Ruti is *redheaded*," she replied. "How did you know that?"

The interrogation of the young and quite beautiful Hedy von Rohrbach took a total of four minutes. In that time Gep recorded forty-six *ja ja*s and thirty-one *genau*s, establishing her positive and cooperative spirit, as well as vaulting her to the top of Gep's dating list.

27

"Old Shatterhand"

DAY FOUR—Paris—Tuesday, 8 April 41—6:12 PM
The driver opened the limousine door for Rolf in front of Hans-Hubert's villa in the wedding-cake canyons of palatial estates in Saint-Germain-en-Laye. Gep came around the car and met him at the stoop. Hans-Hubert's eagerness to show off his extraordinary digs was hopelessly on display when he opened the door before either had a chance to knock. The Prussian playboy stood there, regaled in his English hunting jacket and purple paisley ascot.

"Welcome, gentlemen, to my humble abode." He led them down the long beveled-mirror-and-chandeliered hallway lined with gold-leaf, cabriole-legged pedestals and tables filled with oriental treasures and ornately vased fresh flower arrangements. In the library Hans poured each of them a cognac and took a seat in a red ribbed-velvet lounge chair.

"You always had impeccable tastes, old friend," Rolf noted, seating himself across from Hans. *Tastes that always went far beyond his family's means,* Rolf remembered, playfully.

Gep wandered around the room, admiring the original works of the likes of Delacroix and Rouault that filled every available space on the villa's green silken walls.

"Completely adequate, I'd say." Hans was in perfect form, nose in the air, pinky up. "It was owned by some British Jew or other. Available therefore on two counts, I would guess. I abide the cramped clutter for a degree of privacy."

"For a taste of cramped camping, you should try one of those tiny rooms at the Lutetia," Gep quipped, walking over to join them.

"I'm certain it's dreadful, but you will both recall, I offered to put you up here several times. I have plenty of room."

Rolf smiled. "Gep and I will be returning to the war soon. I can't have us becoming too tender-assed."

"Delighted you brought that up." Hans flipped open a teak cigarette box and made offers around. "That's exactly why I asked you to join me for cocktails."

Rolf knew his old friend all too well. His airs were more act than earned or acquired through rearing. Throughout their academy and university days, von Hirschbach's roguish and extravagant behavior strained his family's less-than-abundant purse strings to the point of breaking. It was doubtful that things had changed.

"I have convinced Oberst Rheile and the old man"—Hans was referring to Admiral Canaris, commander of the Abwehr—"after some miserable failures, to allow me to have a go at America. Up to now, we have, for the most part at least, employed a bevy of imbeciles and traitors to get ourselves established in the United States. Germans, Spaniards, and Central Americans who sold us a heap of rubbish about their connections and ability to melt into their assigned social and business communities, only to have been met with FBI shackles the minute they stepped off the boat, or else they darted straight to the authorities to turn themselves in, begging for asylum, to be sure."

Obviously, Hans had very recently refilled his gold-plated cigarette lighter. Rolf could taste the oily fuel flavor in the first drag of his cigarette. A quick swig from his glass and he settled back into his chair, about to be, no doubt, duly entertained by whatever it was his old chum was up to.

"Trust me, there are plenty of German Americans who want to see us win this war. We need only to plant some of our people there to help organize them. So I, gentlemen, have worked for months finding not foreign agents with a relentless desire and questionable intentions to go to America for us, but actual Americans with the proper convictions of heart and conscience. There are six of them. Canaris, as I am sure you know, won't allow us to work them as one group, so I have set them up into three two-man teams. The first team arrived here from Lisbon last week and is at our training facility in Brittany. The next team arrives in a few weeks.

Hans-Hubert's coy smile was a bellwether. "So, my esteemed comrades—"

"Hold on, Gep, old boy. Here it comes," Rolf quipped.

"It occurred to me the minute I saw you walk into the Lutetia. Remember, if you will, I talked to you Saturday night at the club. Of course, I was a little tight. But I want you to join me in this little operation. Training and preparing these fellows for what they're about to find once they land in the States. You'll be perfect for this. You both speak brilliant English. And I learned only yesterday that you, Gep, studied in Virginia for some time."

"Three years, Virginia Commonwealth." Gep's pride was difficult for him to repress.

"Hans, you know we have commitments, Gep and I, back in Berlin and Warsaw."

"Warsaw! Rolf, Warsaw's a shithole! And frankly, from what I hear, so is Berlin nowadays. It doesn't have to be a permanent assignment. A few months, just while I'm training these teams. I can get the old man to alter your orders. And you can wrap up this murder investigation you're working on, surely in the next few days. From what I hear, it's obviously some de Gaulle terrorists. What do you say, old friend? Join me in my little game. A few more months in Paris. How bad can that be?"

Rolf swirled the last of his cognac in his glass and stared into it. The rolling flow of the sheer curtains over the open Palladian doors were rustled by a steady, cool breeze swirling in off the garden. Gep's glare was almost painful to bear any longer.

"Like you said, Hans. Let's take care of this current assignment with regards to the Ritter investigation, and then we'll see. I will admit, though, I do see Gep being of exceptional value in your training of these men. I won't stand in his way." Rolf felt down in the sofa and withdrew an earring. He clasped it in his palm.

"I know you have a keen mind, Gep," Hans cajoled. "I look forward to our working together."

"I merely light the major's path."

"Quite brilliantly, I might add." Rolf's endorsement was sincere.

"I have moved my timetable up. Now that America's entry into the war is imminent, we have no time to waste."

"So, Hans-Hubert," Gep said, setting his empty glass on the coffee table. "I recall the code name for the installation of agents in Britain was *Fall Lena*. Would the name you're using for this American team therefore be Operation *Lena-Sue*?"

Hans snickered. Rolf just shook his head.

"Actually, I'm quite proud of the name I have chosen, even if the old man has yet to concur. *Fall Shatterhand*. Isn't it just spot-on?"

"Old Shatterhand. The gunslinger in the Karl May western novellas?" Gep asked rhetorically. "I think I prefer Lena-Sue."

Rolf held up the diamond earring. "So, Old Shatterhand? This yours?"

"You boys know how it goes." Hans chuckled, the roguish twinkle returning to his eye. "A late night. Ding-dong. 'Hansie, love? Sorry to barge in so late and all. You haven't found a diamond earbob lying about, have you?'"

DAY FOUR—Paris—Tuesday, 8 April 41—10:32 PM
The l'Heure Bleue waiter, with his shaved, naked chest, scalloped
collar, bow tie, and smooth ivory suspenders, set their drinks on the
cocktail table in front of Rolf and Gep. When the music started, a
commotion at the front door drew everyone's attention. It brought a
few officers to their feet for just a second, until they saw him.

Bruno gave him the stage name Little Blackie Brown. He was
just over four feet tall and looked as if three feet of that were legs! He
was dressed totally in white; white patent leather tap shoes, baggy
white slacks, a white undershirt, and a white dishwasher's cap.
Against all the snowy white, his jet-black skin and sleek muscles
glistened and shined in the brilliant spotlight like handsomely
polished ebony. It all started in the coat-check room out at the club's
entrance. Everyone could hear it, the rapid tapping to the music, but
no one could see him. Heads turned throughout the club. *What is
that?* Suddenly, he exploded past the throng of people waiting at the
bar.

He tap-danced through the tables to the frenzied delight of
everyone as the band played the peppy "Rhythmus". A one-man,
three-ring circus! Cartwheeling over this table and backflipping over
that he went, his huge, bright smile never leaving his cheery face.
With the grace of a panther, he jumped up on a tabletop that Xavier
was practiced in clearing of drinks in a timely fashion. Young Mr.
Brown tap-danced wildly, his legs and arms kicking and whirling past
guests' astonished heads. As the song's finish drew near, he sprang
from a front-row table to the top of the piano, then did a flip onto the
stage. Each of his whirls and twirls brought the room's fevered pitch
to an even higher level.

Bruno liked to watch the audience while Mr. Brown performed,
hear their choruses of *oohs* and *ahhs*, watch their smiles, their eyes
grow wide, then wane, then grow even wider with each of Brown's
astonishing acrobatics. The huge club owner was always amazed at
the way their clapping became almost painful for them as they
seemed to want the applause for this flip to be louder than it had been
for the last. *Enraptured.* That was what Bruno saw in them each
night. *This,* he thought, *is the face of Germany that old Adolf must see
from his lofty perch high above the crowds.* And Bruno especially
delighted in the pronounced indignation wrought by the fact that the
man who had complete control of these fanatic fascists was an
American Negro from Detroit!

Fall Irmgard

The boy started turning handsprings on the left side of the stage and went all the way to its right, where he stopped cold and looked whimsically at the crowd. In the midst of raucous applause, he cocked his head back toward stage-left and flipped his thumb in that direction as if to ask, "Should I do it again?" The crowd's reaction was always humorous to young Mr. Brown. Their mouths open wide, their heads nodding feverishly. So, back across the stage he flipped, and then back the other way again, but this time when he approached center stage, he leapt high into the air and came crashing down hard into a full splits! The audience all gasped at once. His sparkling eyes were wide as saucers; his mouth formed a pink puckered *O!* Then he raised his palms skyward, flashed a pearly-white smile, and ever so slowly his legs began to draw themselves together, and he started rising magically to finally stand fully erect again as the band finished the last notes of the song.

Like every night he preformed, tonight the place erupted in pure bedlam.

"Little Blackie Brown, *meine Damen und Herren*," Enrico announced. "Little Blackie Brown!"

When things had settled down, Gep asked Rolf what he thought of Hans-Hubert's operation and especially of his nature, his professional devotion to the task.

"The man seems the flighty sort," Gep observed.

"I would say that's probably a fair assessment of my old friend. Hans-Hubert is of the tradesman class, Gep. His father owns a large plumbing or electrical company in Steglitz. One couldn't help but like him back at the university, but it was apparent to all that he was draining his family dry trying to keep up with the rest of us. I never really worked closely with him, but he always gave me the impression of being one who works quite intently at his play and plays intently at his work."

Gep chuckled. "Eloquent smugness." He fished through a plate on the table to create an impromptu hors d'oeuvre. "Should I trust him to give his all to this operation?"

"The fellow obviously has the admiral's ear. That has to be worth something. Still, I would have my reservations."

"Then my mind is made up." Gep spit an olive pit in his hand, dropped it on the plate, and swiped his palms together as he added, "The only way I stay is if you do as well."

"Then let's, shall we, devote ourselves to the Ritter investigation and have no more of my old friend Hans-Hubert. We'll

187

discuss it further in a few days." Rolf held his glass of Mirabelle up to Gep. "Agreed?"

"Yes. And prudent as always."

"So, who do I have here?" Suzi Rupp's childlike voice asked, her tiny fingers sliding around both their heads to hold them to her breasts like two pumpkins.

"Well, if it isn't the famous Sweet Suzi Rupp," Gep announced, smiling sinfully at her.

Suzi nestled herself in Rolf's lap. "You gents have me at a disadvantage. So, now who is"—she held up her dainty finger and popped it delicately on Gep's nose—"this."

"Oberleutnant Gephardt Fechter," Gep said, charmingly, giving the tiny woman an elegant seated bow, with his head and eyes.

"And you, sir?" She softly placed her finger on Rolf's nose, then let it drift down his lips to rest on his chin.

Rolf maintained what stoicism he could muster.

"Major von Gerz." A polite nod.

She wriggled her fleshy rump deeper into Rolf's lap.

"Oh, major," she cooed, furrowing her brow under an inverted question mark of black bangs. "Are you in there?" Again she squirmed, deeper. "I think not!"

Her inducements were, however, starting to have the intended affect.

"There you are!" she said, her face lighting up. "Oh, and aren't you, though!"

A cymbal crashed and the club went dark. Sabina appeared in the spotlight; dressed in a tight green sequined gown, a zebra-skin stole, and a safari hat. The song was "Nuages," and she floated through the audience tickling necks and chins with a braided riding crop. The familiar prop brought a wicked smile to Gep's rutty face.

As Sabina moved to Rolf's table, Suzi laid her cheek on Rolf's shoulder. Venomous malice swelled in Sabina's eyes. She snarled and seemed to nod slightly. *Just as I suspected!* With prima donna flair, she threw her head back and turned away, finishing the song.

Suzi reached up and whispered in Rolf's ear, her velvety lips never really leaving it. "So, major. Do you have a girl in Paris?"

"No, no I don't."

Again she squirmed in his lap and rocked slightly this time, heavy and deep.

"Feels to me like you could really use one."

28

Der Quartiermeister
Le quartier-maître
The Quartermaster

DAY FOUR—Paris—Tuesday, 8 April 41—10:34 PM
Quartermaster Arnold Felden had inquired first at the Soldatenheim in
the avenue de la Motte-Picquet where he knew Rutgers Heht had a
room. Arnold had until eight the next morning to return to the Port de
Brest. Between now and then, he had to find Rutgers Heht and find
out what had happened to his share in the Chesterfield cigarette
booty. At the Soldatenheim earlier this evening he discovered Ruti
had been ordered away and would not return for some time. The
dormitory's manager gave him a note left for a QM A. Felden. Heht
had told the manager to look for a man with dark hair and features
and a well-maintained Balbo beard. Arnold read the quickly scribbled
note from Ruti and exploded, startling the manager.
> *See Herr Ritter, today.*
> *The Ritz.*
> *Freundliche Grüsse, RH*

At the Ritz, the desk clerk's reaction should have been enough
to make Arnold wary. But, it wasn't. Arnold was due a large sum of
money. That was the only thing on his mind. It would ultimately be
his undoing.

"Your papers, please," the clerk asked.

Obviously, this man Ritter screened his calls, Arnold thought,
handing them over.

But the clerk was gone too long. Something was wrong. The
Ritz security manager appeared with Arnold's papers.

"You're evidently unaware, monsieur, but Herr Ritter was
murdered Sunday."

Arnold quickly grabbed his papers, thanked the man, and left.
He didn't see the manager dash to the phone and call the police.

The only other information Arnold had about the entire
Chesterfield affair was that of a "little fellow" who managed a Club
l'Heure Bleue in Saint-Germain. He was the one who was helping

Heht broker the deal. Having no time to waste, Quartermaster Felden hailed a taxi and made straight for the club.

The line at the club entrance was backed up all the way through the courtyard and into the street. Like a general, Arnold charged past the queue, excusing himself at each glare and blurted indignation. Once downstairs, he was held up at the crowded front foyer by some Negro boy who started tap-dancing, then turning amazing flips effortlessly through the air and on into the club. Arnold along with at least fifty others awaiting tables followed the boy, crowding their way on in to witness what they thought was an impromptu audition of some dishwasher gone berserk. Once inside Arnold slipped away from the crowd and squeezed himself in at the bar. He ordered a beer and asked to speak to the club's manager, the *little* man. The bartender, who himself was sandwiched behind the bar packed with cocktail waitresses, waiters, and other bartenders, raised his palms and rolled his eyes. *Look around? How would I ever find the manager?* A twenty-franc note was slapped in one of the raised palms, and the bartender tilted his head and gave a relenting nod. He then did his own dance, a sideways shuffle, palms still in the air, until he freed himself from behind the jammed bar and around the crowd to disappear in the swirling smoke and spotlights of the main club, a milky haze of green, pink, and blue shadows, where *oohs* and *ahhhs* and drum rolls and cymbals rose and fell like crashing Brittany surf.

Arnold sipped his beer and tried in vain to catch some of the Negro boy's performance, all to no avail. Some members of the crowd in the back were now standing on chairs; some of the women were on the backs of their Wehrmacht escorts.

"Little Blackie Brown, *meine Damen und Herren*," a sing-song voice announced. "Little Blackie Brown!"

Another beer and a cigarette, and the band started playing again. Arnold could see the distant stage now and then as people continued to file in. Violins and clarinets blew as a tropical breeze floating through a now green haze in the club, a xylophone dripped like rainwater, and a flute chirped like an island bird. A sultry woman in safari garb ducked under swaying palm branches decorating the stage. Then her deeply intimate voice purred the winsome lyrics to a tropical tune.

The stern quartermaster was briefly captivated. When he looked down at his watch, he was surprised by the tiny balding smile in a worn black suit who had slithered up next to him and was staring up at him intently.

"Twenty francs just to locate me, monsieur?" the little man said, sliding his pasty hand inside Arnold's arm and leaning the greasy bald dome on his shoulder. "Must be worth a hundred francs just to talk to me."

Arnold intentionally jerked his arm back hard to get to his wallet and shoo away the dwarf's cold little tentacle. He tossed the hundred-franc note at Xavier and watched the ugly little paws juggle it for a second, then swoop it out of the air and slide it into his inner jacket pocket. That nasty smile again.

"I am Xavier du Bois, and I am most humbly at your service, monsieur." He scooched his tiny rump up on the edge of the barstool next to Arnold, forcing the woman who already occupied most of it to share.

"I'm looking for a German officer. Leutnant Rutgers Heht."

"You and half of France, monsieur."

"He owes me money!"

"You and half of France, monsieur," Xavier quipped again. There was that nasty, yellow smile again. This time Arnold saw the fragments of baguette lodged between his hideous teeth.

"You were the one he used to move the cigarettes. I want my money."

"I'm quite sure you do. But you will have to get it from him." Again, that vexing smile.

"What if I cracked your little bald nut right here on this bar?"

Xavier's smile only grew wider, and he tilted his head and knocked on it twice with his knuckles. "Solid bone, monsieur. Why would you want to damage such a lovely bar?"

Arnold was coiled like a lion, ready to strike.

"Look around you, monsieur. You could do Xavier harm in front of all these very German witnesses?"

"You'll come outside one day and I'll be there."

"Oh, but monsieur, Xavier never leaves the Club l'Heure Bleue. You see, you are not alone. No, monsieur, the list of those who would do Xavier harm is a very long one, very long indeed. You would be wise to take special care, yes?" Again, the nasty little smile. "One of them could miss Xavier and hit you!"

Scorned and furious, Arnold Felden left the Club l'Heure Bleue and walked briskly down the boulevard Raspail. As he passed a shop portico, a man popped out from the darkness and joined him.

"Bonsoir, monsieur," he pleasantly said. "I am called Victor. I wonder if I might buy you a nice café on this chilly night?"

"Go away," Arnold said, picking up the pace. "I don't have time for you."

The man bore a new leather eyepatch and limped as he skipped somewhat to keep up. "Then perhaps just a cigarette, monsieur?" he added, as he slid a package of cigarettes into Arnold's tunic pocket.

Annoyed enough, Arnold stopped immediately and glared at the man, looking at his watch. He was about to warn the man he was breaking the curfew when a pack of Chesterfield cigarettes suddenly appeared in front of him.

"Where can we go?" Arnold asked.

"There's an alley," Victor said, pointing to the corner with a smile. "Just here."

"You see, monsieur, your colleague, this man Heht. He has done us a terrible injustice. Terrible, indeed. Not only has he stolen from us and run away like a thief in the night, but he has brutally murdered two people. Two good Frenchmen. One, a dear fellow, a family father, a trusted and highly regarded broker in the sale of stocks and bonds here in Paris. And the other man, a colleague of mine. A poor half-witted soul who had to find his way in life as a bare-fisted fighter in the most tawdry of quarters. Brutally murdered by a hundred stab wounds in Lyon on Palm Sunday. Why the poor, dumb fellow was even—how can I begin to say it?—mutilated like a butcher would a chicken." Victor shook his head and glanced to see if Arnold was impressed. "Appalling!" he added. "Your man, Heht, is nothing but a vicious beast!"

Arnold wasn't impressed.

"I could care less. I want my money!"

"I am sorry sir, but I cannot help you. This man Heht has your money. And ours. Until we find this comrade of yours, alas, we are both scorned."

Arnold grabbed Victor by the collar, pulling him close.

"I am sorry that you have been wronged, monsieur," Victor squealed, the German's tight grip choking him. "Maybe you could enlist the help of the police. Your own Gestapo, perhaps? I'm certain they would be happy to help you."

Fuming, Arnold felt bile in his throat as he shoved Victor against the wall.

"Help us, monsieur. Help us find this man who has cheated you. And cheated us. Find him for us, and you can have all the money from the sale of the cigarettes, your half and his. And a nice fee for your services. But first, we must find him, mustn't we?"

"Tell me what you know. I have a train to catch."

"I know only that he left town on Sunday with a lot of our money and, of course, with yours. I know that he was in Lyon that evening, where he killed that second man I told you about. Since then, monsieur, this murderous thief has"—he made a popping sound with his fingers on his open lips, then threw them up in the air—"disappeared."

"How do I get in touch with you?"

"The little mouse at the l'Heure Bleue. He can always find me."

"If no one kills the little cunt first," Arnold snipped.

Victor snickered. "He's quite well protected, monsieur. For now." Victor pulled his coat collar up to his chin as they left the alley. "But that day will surely come, no?"

29

Wednesday, 9 April 1941

Der Ochsenhorn Kämme
Les peignes de corne de boeuf
The Oxhorn Combs

DAY FIVE—Paris—Wednesday, 9 April 41—3:41 AM
Rolf threw the duvet off himself and rose quickly in the bed. A cold sweat covered his naked chest and shoulders and dripped from his hair. He switched on the lamp and looked at his watch. Sheerly by habit, he wound the watch and slowly shook his head. *The combs!* he thought. It was Tippi. Not his wife, but Tippi. That night in the Bristol in Warsaw. The second time they'd ever made love. It all came back to him. So fast it startled him. Woke him. Heitner! Kunsthorn Heitner! The combs! The man in Vienna Tippi had mentioned. Heitner! What had Tippi said? *The man was nothing but a hopeless and thoroughly brainwashed Bolshevik, but he had the most adorable eyes.* The combs? Why would she accept such a priceless gift from a Bolshevik? Tippi was a White Russian, a Czarist. She hated communists. Or did she? So many lies. Nothing but lies. Tippi was so good at lying. So good at so many things.

January in Warsaw. Major Rolf von Gerz stood proud and naked before the floor-to-ceiling windows of the second-floor suite at the Hotel Bristol. Huge flakes of snow fell straight down out of the dark Warsaw night, the heavier ones faster than the rest, piling up deep on the quiet, gaslit square below. Drunk, he stood there, the suite spinning somewhat behind him, proud and bold, a stag on the mountain, having repeatedly covered his doe. With sated nonchalance he blew smoke into the vastness of the dim room, lit only by a tiny lamp on the Biedermeier dresser where Tippi sat, naked herself, applying makeup and lipstick to a beautiful face that really never needed either.

Resolutely, the bottle of vodka emptied, he downed the last of a warm Żywiec and doused his cigarette in the glass. His rigid stand was now gone, but he was still big and swollen. He delighted in the way its sheer weight slammed and slapped against his thigh as he stumbled back over to Tippi.

Lamplight danced on the hourglass of creamy flesh perched before him. Drunken, lustful eyes caught hers in the mirror and in every beveled strip of mirror around it. Like a matador he quickly grabbed the oxhorn combs from either side of her hair, and the loosed blond locks cascaded and bounced on her naked shoulders. As though he'd finally slain the great bull, he held them high, between thumb and fingertip, pinkies erect, chin up. Then he quickly flipped them into distant parts of the room and swept Tippi up against his sweaty chest for another quick go.

"Rolfi, darling, you mustn't, those are hand-carved Heitner combs," Tippi shrieked, as he tossed her on the damp, wrinkled bed. Her arms and legs flailed, attempting to regain her feet before he could mount her. "They're very delicate, Rolfi! Very breakable!" In a dire haste, she quickly twisted the light switch and bright whiteness exploded from the crystal chandelier, blinding them both. Tippi held up one palm against the light and searched around the room. Rolf flopped onto his back and covered his eyes with the fold of his inner arm, his leg splayed out over the sides of the bed, his erection waning slowly.

Ultimately, finding them and seeing that the fiery passion had finally leaked out of her matador, she picked up the tortoiseshell comb case from the dresser, switched off the chandelier, and sat next to him on the bed.

"See, look at them. Aren't they lovely?"

Rolf moved his arm enough to glance at the brownish green box. She opened it and gingerly placed the oxhorn combs in the slot labeled *Ochsenhorn* among the other five sets with their own tiny silken-stitched designations: *Ivorie, Schildpatt, Nashorn, Ramshorn, and Kuhhorn.*

"They were a gift from a man I met in Vienna, some years ago. Quite full of himself, a revolutionary. He was far too old to still be a student, but evidently hung around the campus just to keep the villagers in torches. The man was nothing but a hopelessly and thoroughly brainwashed Bolshevik, but he had the most adorable eyes. His family owned Kunsthorn Heitner, renowned artisans throughout the world, handmade combs and jewelry, boxes and trinkets, even clock figurines and eyeglass frames. Werner Heitner. The poor fellow adored me. Just as all men do."

"So, I'm just another victim of your charms."

"Yes, darling. There have been many, many victims." She set the comb case gently on the nightstand and looked into his eyes. "But you, Rolfi. You made me the victim."

In Paris, Rolf rubbed his eyes hard and looked again at his watch, actually looking at the time. Kunsthorn Heitner. How could he have forgotten that? So, this Heitner fellow knew Ritter. Could Heitner have also been the one Tippi was sending information to or through?

That same night. The humorous analogy she had made.

Do you really think this Ribbentrop pact with the Soviets will last, Rolfi darling?

She was justified in asking. It was an impossible alliance. A pact between Hitler and Stalin? A pact that saw all the old Germanic lands of Poland fall back into Hitler's possession and Poland's ethnic Russian region claimed by Stalin. The rest of the crippled country becoming a de facto SS protectorate. What was it she said that had made him laugh so?

How long does the mad dog keep its pact with the alley cat?

It was all even more prophetic now. Now that Rolf knew about the upcoming invasion of the Soviet Union—Fall Barbarossa! But looking back, why would she ask the question in the first place? Hardly bedroom conversation. Wasn't it just one of many attempts at gleaning information from him? So many things were falling into place now. His love for Tippi was absolutely blinding. How could he let himself fall so deeply in love with a woman that he would miss such obvious signs?

Heitner! Mein Gott! He couldn't tell Gep. He couldn't tell him about Tippi and her probable connection to Heitner and possibly even to Ritter. One more way she'd betrayed him. *You should hate her, Rolf! Why can't you hate her?* Gep had stood by and taken up for him through the entire ugly ordeal. But Gep had seen enough. Rolf couldn't stand to see that look on his adjutant's face again. Was it just disappointment, or was it disgust? He'd have to find another way to lead Gep to Heitner. Hopefully, he could leave Tippi out of it entirely. God, he was such a damn fool!

He pulled a bottle of cognac from his drawer and poured a glass. Downing it, clammy hands ran through his sweaty hair. He flicked the wetness from his fingers and made his way into the bathroom to pee.

30

Anwesend ohne Urlaubnis
Absent sans permission
Absent without Leave

DAY FIVE—Paris—Wednesday, 9 April 41—8:12 AM
German admiral Wilhelm Canaris had an uncanny, unGerman way of commanding through delegation and trust. He chose most of his Abwehr intelligence officers from the ranks of Germany's titled elite. Many others were retirees from the grand old imperial days and heroes of the Great War. But all were simply nothing less than highly educated, well-bred, very rich, and not Nazi! And more than a few were Jews.

Money, to such men, was never thought about or fretted over, and was rarely discussed unless there were a considerable number of zeros involved. When it came to money, there was always plenty of it. No need for a fuss. Whenever the lord or lady of the villa needed something, they simply took it and left the dirty task of payment to butlers, chauffeurs, bankers, and accountants. *Do be a good fellow, won't you, Fritzi, and pay the man for me.*

So, as Abwehr and Foreign Office ranks expanded, with more and more of these men of privilege who were oblivious to money and viciously averse to thrift, it was only fitting that some special kitty or cookie jar be made available to them. Information, after all, cost money. Whether it was a fifty-franc note slipped in the suit pocket of a concierge who had an invaluable tip to impart, or a satchel full of American dollars intended for a German-American League office in Buffalo, New York, military intelligence was expensive and in most cases required cash, baskets of it. Kitties of it. Cookie jars of it!

For the wealthiest of these men, handling a great deal of cash was quite new, but not really that enticing. It was, after all, just money. But to others, especially the huge mass of men being recruited from law offices, business boards, and resort beaches all over the Reich to quickly fill administrative positions in occupied France, it was an irresistible seductress. For at this particular time in history, nowhere on earth did cash money flow more freely and inexhaustibly than in occupied France, and especially, in Paris.

So, the admiral's brilliance didn't stop at team building and intelligence gathering. He knew at least a small percentage of his clan would succumb to the temptations that freedom of movement, action, and deed—coupled with vast amounts of cash—would provide. Consequently, he put together a very secret staff of Abwehr Internal Affairs experts in a back corner of a second Abwehr building in Paris, on avenue Henri-Martin, whose operations arm consisted of two very effective weapons. The first was not really his creation, but that of the Reich Finance Ministry and Hermann Goering. It was the *Devisenschützkommando*. These units investigated people suspected of selling unregistered securities as well as illegal currency, diamonds, art, and gold. But as men who committed such crimes were usually enemies of the state, namely Jews and masons attempting to finance an escape, many of these offenders were not military perpetrators at all. So, a much larger and rapidly growing office of the Devisenschützkommando was established and run by the Gestapo from their bank of buildings in the avenue Foch. Soon, the military branch of this unit would be absorbed into the larger Gestapo unit, and thus the Gestapo would hand the Abwehr its first administrative corpse of the occupation. The first of many.

The second arm of Internal Affairs was indeed the admiral's creation and was devoted almost entirely to policing the Abwehr. It was the *Ablegekommando*. Or, literally, the removal or garbage squad. These men were not policemen, though their investigative talents were at or even above that par. Their talents were simply finding and eliminating deserters. These specialized units were under the direction of the admiral and his adjutants in Hamburg. Those Abwehr officers who decided to flee military service were tracked down and, if it suited the Reich and especially the admiral's beloved Abwehr, disposed of as the deserter garbage they were.

So now, fugitive German Leutnant Rutgers Heht's name appeared on a total of five official bureau lists in Paris that morning; the Paris Préfecture, the French National Police, and the German military police, along with the Gestapo and the Ablegekommando, or removal squad.

The hunt was on!

A deafening resonance like crashing bells rang off the stone walls with each slap of the blades. Sweat poured from both of them, their naked chests glistened, suspenders bounced at their sides as boots stomped and weary arms quivered. Rolf's silky parry countered

Gep's quick flèche. A sudden appel and a lunge ended in a coulé as Rolf's blade slid down to Gep's pommel and the two of them were suddenly *corps à corps*, body to body and eye to eye, smiling and gasping for breath. Gep gave him an ornery shove and swished the foil through the air with a randy gleam in his eye.

"Practice is paying off, Oberleutnant," Rolf exclaimed, his voice echoing in the vaulted, brick cavern of the hotel basement.

"I had a good teacher," Gep replied, saluting with the ancient *épée de terrain*, the only weapons the hotel could provide for Rolf's daily exercise sessions.

"Good teachers aren't usually bested by their students that quickly."

"You weren't bested." Blowing sweat from his lip, Gep stepped out of the chalk-lined piste. "Yet!" He went to the mirror and rubbed his hand over the red marks on his chest as the door to the basement flew open and slammed loudly against the wall.

In an unbecoming fluster, Hans-Hubert stormed in, fuming. "It's official," he bellowed as he stomped his boot viscously. "*Der Schweinhund ist weg!* Gone! One of my best men! Deserted!"

"Heht?" Rolf asked, knowing the answer.

"Of course, Heht! The criminal! Betray me? I want him found and shot!" Von Hirschbach briskly took Rolf's ancient épée and, sliding the sword into its ornately carved rack, continued his bombast. "He checked in at the Armistice Commission office in Marseilles on Monday but hasn't been seen since. The man has deserted, I'm certain of it."

"Perhaps something happened to him?" Gep interjected, handing his sword to Hans and unbuttoning his trousers, then stepping out of them.

"Happened to *him*?" Hans replied, following them both into the shower. "Highly unlikely. This is a man who makes things happen to others. The general staff kept him in their pocket for over a year now."

Once Rolf and Gep were stripped down, Hans tossed each a bar of soap.

"The man is a Brandenburger, like you were, Rolf. Assigned to me through von Oster and Beck. Gets his orders straight from them. He has special skills the general staff has enlisted on a number of occasions. They've kept him hidden, working at the Dienststelle on the rue du Faubourg Saint-Antoine, buying foodstuffs and livestock for the Army."

199

"What did he do in that role?" Rolf asked, wanting to see if Heht's duties tied him in with Ritter somehow.

"As you may or may not know," Hans-Hubert shouted, against the echoes of the falling water and splash from the shower, "in France there are two ways we procure Army goods. Say a boxcar load of wool. The official way would be to go through this French committee or that one. The shepherds' committee, the wool committee, the committee for the peasants that trim the wool, the one for the loaders, for the rail workers, and the general committee for agriculture and sheep shit! The whole process will take weeks, and your boxcar load of wool will arrive in the Reich sometime late next month."

Hans took two rolled towels from the stand and held them under one arm, throwing his loud voice over his shoulder into the shower.

"Or, you can work through the black market and a certain highly skilled French underworld racketeer, Hugo Sturekov, and your boxcar of wool will arrive on Monday! You pay a lot more, but like I told you, it's French money. So, what do we care? This was the world young Mr. Rutgers Heht found himself in. One of our best apples in a seedy barrel, and now he's rotten to the core. Probably skimmed a nice little nest egg for himself off of Sturekov over the past few months, then up and ran for the border. The lad's written his death sentence. If the Gestapo or the Ablegekommandos don't get him, Sturekov certainly will!"

"He's wanted by the French police as well, Hans," Rolf shouted into the shower stream, his eyes closed. "A French stockbroker was murdered the day before Ritter. Heht was at the scene, pummeled a gendarme and fled. He's on our list as a possible suspect in Ritter's murder, as well."

"Highly improbable, Rolf. This man is a loner. A rogue."

Barefoot, Rolf and Gep tread gingerly over the slick brick floor.

Hans tossed them each a towel, continuing, "I wouldn't see him in some conspiracy scheme. He's a man who does what he has to do and eliminates any possible witnesses. But I obviously didn't know him as well as I assumed, so who knows?"

Hans-Hubert shook his head and sighed.

"Heht was no different than all the other profligate Germans in Paris spending French money to buy French matériel for the Army. There are scores of such offices all over town, each with their own specific areas of trade expertise. But the most lucrative are those run by Sturekov."

Rolf donned a purple hotel robe. He could sense Hans' disappointment in Heht's betrayal. Heht was a man he had obviously put his faith in for some time. Rolf experienced the same sense of despair when he turned Tippi's tides on her and dealt with that embarrassing blow.

An orderly opened the basement door, stuck his head in, and motioned to Hans-Hubert.

"I have a meeting." As Hans walked toward the door, he added, "If Rutgers Heht has indeed bilked Sturekov somehow, you can be sure, Reich Internal Affairs will be the least of his worries."

31

Der Grillenwald
Bois de criquets
The Locust Wood

DAY FIVE—Paris—Wednesday, 9 April 41—9:09 AM
A crew of naval radio operators manned the bank of phones just off
the lobby at the Hotel Lutetia. Each Kriegsmarine operator was
naturally quick to grasp the operation of not only the hotel's phone
system but also the function and maintenance of the thirty-two tape-
recording machines stacked on four tables in the tiny office behind
the telephone bank. It was one sailor's job to watch the reel-to-reel
tapes and switch a recorder to its backup when a tape was in need of
replacement, after which he would add the stop time and date to the
spent tape, place it back in its white paperboard carton, and file it in
one of four rows of boxed tapes, separated by divider cards labeled 1
through 16 in a flat wooden crate. In this way every word of every
conversation that was patched through the hotel's sixteen phone lines
was recorded and categorized. Only to be, of course, reviewed,
rereviewed, and catalogued every day by another group of junior
Abwehr officers on the hotel's fourth floor, where another thirty
Kriegsmarine radio operators monitored and recorded hundreds more
tapped phone lines all over Paris.

"I am Inspector Luc-Henri Saint-Ruynon of the Paris
Préfecture. I call for Major von Gerz, s'il vous plaît."

"Moment, bitte." The Kriegsmarine communications officer
placed the caller on hold by pressing the button on the phone bank.
Unplugging the call, he ran his finger down the alphabetical list of
names assigned to the Abwehr operation at the Lutetia until he
located the extension of Major von Gerz's chargé d'affaires written in
pencil, obviously a temporary posting.

"No, inspector, the major is at the coroner's office," Gep's
voice echoed in the empty office. He and an Abwehr photographer
left early this morning to be sure we have every possible angle of the
corpse before they—"

"Forgive me, monsieur, but the murderers and the car were
discovered early this morning," Luc-Henri interrupted. "Please pick
up the major as quickly as possible and meet me at the *mairie* in

Limay. It's west of Paris on the north side of the Seine; you'll take the rue Nationale at Mantes-la-Jolie. Hurry. I don't know how long my people can keep the site undisturbed. We were, you see, notified of the discovery by the Gestapo."

DAY FIVE—Limay—Wednesday, 9 April 41—10:37 AM
Luc-Henri leaned against the trunk of his idling Renault Celtaquatre, smoking and continually looking at his watch. When the Voisin limousine pulled up beside him at the mairie, or town hall of Limay, Luc-Henri flipped his cigarette away, then dipped, hopped, and twisted his way around to the backseat of his car. The two vehicles headed northwest to where the Seine looped back to the north. The tiny caravan sped off the highway at the Bois de Criquets and followed narrow trails through the forest and down to the riverbank. They stopped behind six other automobiles that were already at the site.

Luc-Henri told them not to wait on him and to proceed straight on down to the clearing where the blue Matford with the shattered rear window sat in the bright midday sun.

"We didn't disturb your holiday, did we, major?" Kruder's smile was venomously snide. He stood by the car, his shirt sleeves rolled up, his tunic jacket folded over his forearm.

Rolf ignored Kruder and went straight to the body of the boy next to the car. Gep opened the Matford's back door with his handkerchief and looked inside, analyzing the glass fragments in the seat and pointing out the angles he needed to the photographer who had accompanied them.

"It seems your case is solved, von Gerz." Kruder twisted a cigarette out of its holder and pinched off the glowing ember. "Two French terrorist youths, probably communists, undertaking the clandestine assassination of a member of the Reich automotive industry. Two young heroes of de Gaulle's Free France!"

"Just how was it, Kruder, that the Gestapo made the discovery?" Rolf said as he knelt beside the boy, holding a handkerchief over his nose, shooing flies away while he touched the flesh of the boy's neck and cheek to determine how long he'd been dead.

"An informant telephoned us this morning. A Frenchman, no less."

"So, this good French citizen contacts the Gestapo. Not the French police, but the Gestapo?"

"Perhaps he felt it was a German matter. Looking for favor or payola."

Rolf shook his head and snorted as he put his pencil in the barrel of the pistol in the boy's left hand.

"I'm sure testing will prove it to be the murder weapon, von Gerz." Kruder leaned his palm on the fender of the Matford, then jerked away quickly from the hot metal. He set his tunic over the fender and, protected now, leaned against it again.

Lumbering arduously down the hill, Luc-Henri moved up beside Rolf.

"I have ordered a lorry to bring the automobile to Paris, as well as an ambulance. The other suspect is just over the bank there," he said, nodding toward the river. "Facedown in the mud with three bullets in his back."

Gep left the photographer at the car and made his way to the riverbank.

"I'm afraid you won't derive much out of that one." Kruder shouted over his shoulder, still smiling sardonically at Rolf. "It seems the turtles or bugs or some such creatures have eaten away most of the meat from that poor fellow's face. Pity, isn't it, von Gerz?"

"Yes, Kruder, quite," Rolf said as he stood up and looked into the car. "And perhaps quite convenient, as well."

"Why can't you accept the obvious, von Gerz? What would be gained by some SS conspiracy? Face it. This fellow here was shot at the scene by the grenadier. As he lay dying, begging the other chap to take him to get patched up, the two of them get into some sort of quarrel. That one bolts for the river. This one shoots him three times in the back! Case closed, major. We both have more important issues to address. I have been charged with locating and logging thousands of the less desirable French enemies of National Socialism. And you have to . . . well, do whatever it is you do."

"If you were truly an investigator, Kruder, instead of a simple headhunter, the last thing you'd ever do is accept the obvious!"

"I'm weary, von Gerz. My people and I have been out here since early this morning." Kruder started rolling his shirt sleeves down and buttoning his cuffs. "You and your French friends can knock yourselves out all afternoon. But if you'd move your automobiles, my team and I will take our leave. You can see we've left everything undisturbed for you."

Rolf looked at the tall grass, now crushed flat all around the site. He just smiled and shook his head.

"We'll gladly move out of your way." Rolf motioned to his driver and Luc-Henri's.

"And in an effort to demonstrate my cooperative spirit, major, I will send over a copy of my report in the morning."

"Thank you, Kruder." Rolf gave him a disingenuous smile, doubting he would see any report. "I will look forward to reading it."

While coroner aides removed the two bodies to Paris, Rolf, Gep, and Luc-Henri studied the evidence at the site. Gep filled out twelve file cards with notes. Six pages of Rolf's Moleskine were loaded with all sorts of "curiosities," as he like to put it.

Rolf moved over to the car and inspected the license plate and the shadow of dirty film around it. On the left side there was the smallest clean line. And the screws were just off-center enough to show a fingernail of clean paint at ten o'clock around each.

Gep was the first to pick up on the fact that the blood in the backseat was still damp in larger groupings. Holding up his bloodstained finger to them, he added, "It should have been dry and cracked throughout the car's interior if it had been three-day-old blood."

Rolf arose from behind the car, saying, "The plate has obviously been replaced."

"Isn't it interesting," Gep wondered, looking inquisitively at the string hanging from a capless fuel tank, "that an automobile could travel nearly a hundred kilometers on Palm Sunday with its front and back glass shot out, and no one would report seeing it?"

"The American woman," Luc pointed out, "and the grenadier both said the driver was an older fellow with a thick walrus mustache. The suspect in the river certainly wasn't an old man. Nor was the boy beside the car. And neither has, nor were they probably old enough, to grow a thick mustache."

"The entire scene is obviously a ruse," Rolf surmised, looking inside the car for possible papers from Ritter's empty file folder. "Say it is. How would it have been carried out?"

"I had my people check the area around the site, more than five hundred meters," Luc asserted. "There were no other signs of footprints or tire tracks. If anyone else had been here, he would have had to walk down to the site along the very tire tracks made in the tall grass by the boys' car. I didn't see any other tracks."

Gep conjured up the supposition.

"Two shooters, perhaps a third man, a driver who remained with an escape vehicle down at the road. One shooter had the actual murder weapon, the other a Mauser matching the grenadier's. The boys are given a matching Ford motorcar, told to meet on this spot for further instructions of some sort. Shoot one with the rifle. The other with the Luger. Place the pistol in the one boy's hand—"

"The pistol was in the boy's left hand," Rolf interjected. "We need to determine from his family if he was indeed left-handed. I'm certain that will turn out not to be the case."

"Still," Luc-Henri said, "we must ask why? To what end? Who gains from killing your man Ritter? Or killing any German in Paris? De Gaulle's Free French? The communists? Forgive me for suggesting it, but your own Gestapo?"

As they walked back to their cars, tunics and suit coats over their arms, Rolf chewed on Luc's conjecture but chose to limit his own opinion of Gestapo involvement—especially Kruder's—to himself and Gep.

"We can't rule out Leutnant Rutgers Heht and the dead stockbroker," he asserted.

"And what, if anything," Gep added, "would these boys have to do with Operation Irmgard? Whatever that is."

As they approached the cars, Luc-Henri removed his hat and wiped his sweaty brow on his shirt sleeve.

"Gentlemen," he said, dabbing his damp upper lip with his handkerchief, "I fear the discovery at the Bois de Criquets has dealt us far more questions than answers."

32

Lyon, Vichy France

Der herzliche Käse
Le fromage amical
The Cordial Cheese

DAY FIVE—Lyon—Wednesday, 9 April 41—11:40 AM
Abwehr Leutnant and Special Assignment Kommando Rutgers Heht
knew all too well the fragile nature of *the plans of mice and men*.
Wasting a full day to return to Lyon to meet with the frightened little
Lyonnais stockbroker was distressing to say the least. He didn't like
giving people *time*. Time could make cowards courageous. Bungling
policemen, brilliant. Ruti had lived—and stayed alive—by striking
hard and fast, and fleeing quickly. *Blitzkrieg!* So, now he had to
regain control of this situation, this second meeting with this little
stockbroker in Lyon. And of course, he would.

The man who stepped off the train from Marseilles this
morning in Lyon was not the same redheaded man who had been
there Sunday night. This man wore a classy black business suit, a
dark-navy necktie with an old-fashioned high scalloped collar, shiny
black dress shoes, a black top coat, and gray wool gloves. And he
carried a felt Homburg accented with black silk piping and a black
silk hatband.

And this man was completely bald. In his other hand, he toted
no tattered suitcase from his quick Paris departure, but a new black
leather Hermès satchel. So quite naturally, the little French broker,
seated again in the same mezzanine café, frantically looking down
and scanning every person moving from the platforms into the main
lobby of the Lyon station, missed the big, dangerous German
completely. Missed the hawk's eyes that stared at him like the
trembling prey he was. Missed the bald German standing in line for a
full four minutes at the ticket counter.

"Come with me!" Ruti softly beckoned from behind moments
later, startling the broker, who turned to see the German walking
away, toward the staircase.

"But we were . . . I have . . ." The man swooped up his
umbrella and his suitcase. Started to follow. Stopped. Returned and

plopped a two-franc coin on the table, grabbed up the hat he almost forgot, turned to leave, and gave a confused look and a shrug to his two colleagues seated at the table behind his. He looked up into the heavens—*Jesus, Mary, and Joseph*—genuflected, and scurried to catch up.

DAY FIVE—Avignon—Wednesday, 9 April 41—2:52 PM
The train ride to Avignon took two hours. A solid grip on a delicate shoulder invited the broker to take a window seat and be quiet. The businessman in the black suit then took a seat across the aisle, facing him. He leaned back and tilted the brim of the Homburg over his eyes. The unnerved broker could just see a single evil eye open under the hat, fixed on him.

A little park near the Avignon cathedral was a ten-minute walk from the station. Nothing was said, but the hawk's steely eyes could be seen darting keenly about, making sure they weren't followed. The sun was warm in a still, cloudless day. Finches and whippoorwills found shade in the newly leaved and flowered trees lining the broad sidewalks. Their chirps mixed with a cicada buzz menaced the butterflies and bees swirling about in thick patches of pansies and Gladiolus scattered perfectly throughout the park, an artful picture of French landscaping brilliance.

Seated at a bench on a lush, grassy knoll away from the sidewalk, Ruti smiled at the broker. "Where do we begin?" he asked.

"The man?" A hard swallow, then, "The dreadful assassin we saw that night?"

Ruti lit a cigarette and smiled. "Don't worry about that man. That fellow won't be harming you or anyone else, I assure you."

"They spoke of him in the newspapers. They called it *mutilation.*"

"We all pleasure ourselves in different ways, don't we?" Ruti's smile was more menacing than his words.

"Oui, monsieur." Another hard swallow. "I must peek in your bag," he said, nodding timidly at Ruti's satchel and forcing a weak smile.

Ruti lifted the heavy, thick satchel onto the bench between them and unlocked and unclasped it, pulling it open. On top of the colorful securities lay a stapled stack of typewritten lists, four columns per page. Listed were entries like 1900 Dassault, 2300 Lafarge, 600 Compagnie Suez, 1700 Total, 800 Lafarge, 500 Michelin.

The little man placed his fingers over his lips and muttered, *"Mon Dieu,"* as he shook his head and flipped through the lists and the crisp stacks of securities.

"It all seems to be quite in order." Another deep breath. "But your demand for Swiss francs is a very difficult one, monsieur. Very difficult indeed. Impossible in such huge numbers. I have—we have—been able to come up with a little over forty thousand francs in Swiss. And of course five and a half million French francs." He leaned forward and opened his suitcase to show the rubber-banded stacks of currency.

"We also have a collection of flawless diamonds with an appraised value of at least a hundred thousand French francs. Forgive me, monsieur. But that is the best we can do." He pulled a small coin purse from his inside jacket pocket. Ruti could see an envelope exposed as he did so. Pudgy hands unzipped the purse, squeezed its lips open, and dumped a few diamonds in Ruti's palm.

"Twenty-two. Classic Antwerp cut. Each nearly two karats."

The broker inhaled deeply and sighed. "I'm sorry, monsieur. It's the best we could do. We can't just dump these securities on the market tomorrow and deposit the proceeds. I'd be arrested before nightfall. You must surely understand that. It will take time. A few today. A few tomorrow. We will need time. Months."

The hawk's eyes grew shifty. He withdrew a folded piece of paper and handed it to the broker.

"You will open an account for me at your brokerage. Here is the name."

"This is you, monsieur?"

The look Ruti gave him said, *Ridiculous.*

"Of course it is not you, monsieur. But I must inform you, the days of completely private accounts in France are over. The German administration has required all accounts in the occupied zone be registered, and Vichy has acted in accordance. I will have to report the opening of this account within three days."

"That's fine. Just not a day before." Ruti scooted himself over closer to the broker. Uncomfortably close.

"I've dealt with your type before, my friend," he said to the broker, as he shooed away a bee from the shocked little man's pant leg. "Many times. You're not a coward. No, I don't think you're a coward at all. But just the same, you *are* a weak man, surely not so bold as to believe you can convince me that this is all the money you brought to this meeting."

The broker's lip trembled uncontrollably when he noticed the German was screwing a silencer on his very worn and scarred black pistol.

"You were told to sell me on this deal, weren't you? 'The German is desperate,' they told you. 'What more could he do?' But you brought more money with you. Of course you did. Just in case I was smarter than your colleagues gave me credit for. It's there, isn't it? In that envelope in your jacket? Maybe some more in your sock?"

Sweat dripped from the broker's brow as he nodded his wrinkled head.

"How much?"

"Five hundred thousand francs, monsieur. French."

Ruti smiled, proudly. "Where is it?"

"My socks."

Tears welled in the little man's eyes.

"And my shoes."

Weeping eyes, fixed on the cold silenced weapon.

"And in my pockets."

"And in my shirt."

"And in the lining of my hat."

Ruti smiled warmly and placed his arm around the trembling little coulisse broker from Lyon. He patted him on the shoulder and tugged on him, pulling him close.

"It's grown quite warm today, my friend, wouldn't you agree?"

The broker rubbed his snotty nose and started kicking off his shoes and removing his socks.

"Oui, monsieur."

One of his father's old sayings came to Ruti as he watched the frightened broker inconspicuously withdraw piles of francs from his clothing.

The cheese is always friendly to the rat!

DAY FIVE—Avignon—Wednesday, 9 April 41—3:16 PM
Twenty minutes after putting the broker on his train, Ruti rang up the Armistice Commission office in Marseilles. During the delay he thought of Mélina. Would she be strong enough? His heart told him yes. But his head? He had to prepare himself for the possibility that he would never see her again. She knew nothing of the plan beyond the Poseidon Hotel in Marseilles. If she didn't make it, Ruti would still be safe. But my god. How would he live without her? And what might they do to her? A crippling rush went through him as he

remembered the last time he'd seen his beautiful darling, quite possibly the last time he would ever see her; she was naked and warm and soft in his arms.

"Armistice Dienststelle Marseilles."

"Leutnant Rutgers Heht, security code 66289. Connect me with the Hotel Ritz in Paris."

Another delay, but shorter than expected. The crackling on the line dramatically worse than normal. *Someone was eavesdropping.*

"Hotel Ritz, *bonjour.*"

"Monsieur von Stendal, der Herr Ritter's chamber, s'il vous plaît."

"I am sorry, monsieur. I am afraid that is impossible."

"I'll leave a message."

"I'm very sorry, but you don't understand. Monsieur Ritter was . . . was tragically murdered this weekend."

No response.

"Hello? Monsieur?"

DAY FIVE—Paris—Wednesday, 9 April 41—3:28 PM

The Kriegsmarine communications specialist on the fourth floor of the Lutetia Hotel in Paris unclipped the cloth-covered wire from his headset and quickly finished scribbling his note on the yellow scrap of paper in front of him. He looked at his watch, jotted down the time, then headed out the door and down the staircase, headphones still on his head.

Major Hans-Hubert von Hirschbach was at his desk on the second floor when the sailor entered his office and handed him the note.

"The call originated in Avignon to the Ritz via the Armistice Commission office in Marseilles. Nine minutes ago. The man was asking for Herr Ritter. He seemed unaware of Ritter's murder."

Hans nodded and sent the radio operator on his way. He then picked up the phone on his desk and tapped the receiver hook a number of times until an operator answered. "Ring the avenue Henri-Martin address." His jaw clenched as he went over it in his mind. *Avignon? Heading to Switzerland, are we, young Leutnant Heht? Well, we'll just see. Why would you think you could do this? You were the best we had. It would have all been so very easy if . . .*

"Ach, yes, Internal Affairs, please, this is Major von Hirschbach." He coughed and snuffed out his cigarette. "Yes, I'll hold the line."

33

Identifizerung
Identification
Identification

DAY FIVE—Paris—Wednesday, 9 April 41—4:12 PM
Sheepishly, Gretl von Reinsdorf-Vilmer peeked around the corner of
the seventh-floor lobby at the Lutetia, a flour sack of booty in her
chubby hand and sweat beading on her upper lip. As quickly as she
quietly could, she lumbered to the end of the hallway and plopped
herself down on the floor beside the last door.

Fifi was barking before she could say, "Addie, can you hear
me?"

"Fifi! Bad dog. Yes, darling. Oh, yes, I hear you."

The portly Saxon girl tried to get her cheek onto the floor so she
could peek one eye under the door. It was useless. She then slid her
fingers under it as far as they could go.

"Can you see my fingers?"

"Oh, yes. You valiant, brave girl. Yes, I can!"

"The girls, we all put together some things for you. Things we
can slip under the door. First, here's some cheese." Gretl watched as
the slices of white, creamy cheese disappeared one by one.

"No, Fifi. Bring that back."

"I have bread too; we sliced it as thinly as we could, but it still
won't go under the door. I'll smash it." Gretl placed the slices of
bread on the dirty wooden floor and pressed each flat in her palm with
all her considerable weight. Still no luck. She then took the long
comb from the snake work of braids in her hair and used it to push
slivers and crumbs of the bread to Addie. Next from the flour sack
came a small stack of onionskin postage stamp envelopes.

"Each of these holds the tiniest portion of schmaltz. It will keep
your hair pretty."

"Do I put it in my hair?"

"No, silly girl. It's fat. You eat it!"

"Here, Fifi. We'll keep your hair pretty too. Don't eat the
paper."

"And finally, the pièce de résistance." More tiny envelopes
filled with honey and sugar.

"Oh, you extraordinary girl."

The feeding finished, Gretl put her cheek back on the floor.

"Addie, are you all right?"

"I am most certainly not all right. Did you contact the American consul?"

"It's quite impossible." Gretl rolled over on her back and turned her head to the door. "The Führer has closed the American embassy. It's on the radio. And we no longer have any time to ourselves. They forbid us from going to the club as well. It's like we're prisoners too."

"And it's all my fault. You must all just hate me to pieces."

"It's not you, Addie. Something has happened. Something bad. Everyone's so businesslike now. It's not any fun anymore. Don't say a word, but I think we lost a very large number of airplanes over England the last few nights. It's just terrible. All those poor boys."

"Sometimes we let ourselves forget about the war, don't we Gretl?"

"You're so right, Addie. We're hideous girls, aren't we?"

"I want to go home, Gretl. I'm so frightened, especially with the embassy closed. We could be at war any minute. I try to be strong, but . . ."

"You are strong, Addie. You're the strongest girl I know. I never knew you were frightened. I thought all American girls were just strong like you."

"I wish I was like everyone else. But I'm not. Ever since I was a little girl, I just was different. I had this burning desire to be someone my father could be proud of. The son he never had. But it's too much now. This is just a taste of what my life could be like if we go to war. I just don't know how long I could abide it."

"Oh, Scheisse!" Gretl rolled herself to her elbow. "Has it been five minutes yet? Hedy is flirting with the guard at the sixth-floor stairway. She wasn't sure she could keep up the small talk more than five minutes. I have to go. Is there anything else I can get for you?"

"A bath. I'm so filthy I can smell myself."

"I guess you'll just have to . . . No, wait. I know. Tell them it's your time! Men don't think about that. They'll do almost anything to make talk of that go away!"

"Gretl, you brilliant darling!"

"I'm sure it will work, Addie."

"Me too. Now go, quickly. Before they catch you."

"At least I hope it will work," Gretl said as she struggled to get to her feet. "They're all such dogs. They'll probably just send me up here with a bucket and a brush!"

DAY FIVE—Paris—Wednesday, 9 April 41—8:16 PM
The hot bath was like a luxurious day at the Ritz spa. The girls were even allowed to take the dirty clothes under Addie's cot to be laundered and pressed. And they returned with fresh sheets and crisp new pillow and duvet slips.

Fifi was already asleep, having had her bath after Addie's. Addie was dozing off when a knock came at the door. Fifi didn't bark anymore at the daily intrusions, she just growled as they both heard the lock being removed. The door opened.

It was Gep.

"Get dressed. Bring your coat and hat, maybe your gloves."

"Oh, Gep! Am I free?"

"No. We're just going on a short ride. Five minutes. I'll be waiting at the end of the hall. And leave the dog."

The Paris coroner moved some of the remaining pieces of Jean-Pierre Brisbois' face into some sort of correct position on his skull to make the victim at least somewhat identifiable.

"Gep, this is completely improper." Addie's voice and the clicks of her high heels could be heard down the hallway. "It's rude and frankly very disconcerting, not knowing where you're taking me and why I'm going there!"

In the main room of the morgue, Rolf jerked his head to the side, a silent command to the coroner to cover the bodies of the two boys.

Inspector Luc-Henri and Sturmbannführer Kruder watched as the frosted glass door opened and Addie entered the room. Everything hit her at once. The noxious smell, the men all staring at her, the two covered bodies on the gurneys.

"Oh, Lord Jesus." Her eyebrows dipped and her face contorted with fear. Unbuttoned at the wrist, her white cotton glove brought her wadded handkerchief up to face and she whimpered.

Gep gave Rolf a vexing glare then moved to her side and put his arm around her.

"They're Konni's murderers, aren't they?" she timidly asked.

"I have to ask you to make a positive identification, Miss Bridges," Rolf coldly remarked.

214

The coroner used a pair of tweezers to withdraw a piece of gauze from a glass beaker, then shook it out for a few seconds.

"Hold this up to your nose, mademoiselle, and take short, shallow breaths." The coroner handed the tweezers to her, and she tried to do as instructed, but jerked quickly away.

"It's hideous."

"Give yourself a few seconds to adjust. You need to try to use it. It will help you."

After a few brief attempts with the gauze, she finally was able to hold it close enough to her mouth to close her eyes and nod.

The coroner threw back the sheet.

"Oh, my god!" Gep's grip on her tightened, but she grabbed Rolf's sleeve.

"Is this the man you saw driving the car?" Rolf tilted his head back and stretched the stiffness out of his neck, ignoring the soft touch of her gloved hand.

She turned away. "I don't know. How could anyone tell? There's not a"—she burst into tears and squealed—"*face!*"

"You have to try." Gep's voice was at least consoling. "We need to hear you say, one way or the other. Now, look one more time."

She looked with a little more composure this time. Her head shook.

"Maybe, I don't know. Maybe. He had a mustache. There's no . . ."

"Shit!" Kruder exclaimed in German. "Get a damn mustache and stick it on the terrorist bastard and see if that helps her!"

"Enough, Kruder!" Addie couldn't understand what was being said, but it warmed her heart that Rolf stood up for her.

"I have had quite enough of this," Kruder grumbled, grabbing his leather overcoat. "I have more important business to attend to."

"Then you're dismissed, Alois!" Rolf barked.

The Gestapo officer fumed and snapped back around. He would remain where he was.

"So, Miss Bridges?" Rolf was as cold as ice again.

Nothing from her.

"Show her the other one," Rolf ordered.

When the sheet was off Vincent Brisbois, Addie shrieked.

"Noooo! He's just a baby!"

"He's sixteen. The other one was seventeen," Gep declared, remaining at her side, just in case.

215

She gently touched the boy's creamy cheek.

"So, is this the one you saw?" Kruder said in French.

She pondered and said nothing for a few moments. Her head moved slightly to one side, and a look of consternation grew on her face. Too much consternation for Rolf.

"Regardless of your answer, nothing changes." Rolf's steely stare told her regardless, she would remain locked up in her little attic dungeon.

But consternation was quickly evident on Kruder's face as well. This woman was obviously more to Major von Gerz than just a murder witness! And Gep noticed the epiphany. The man actually seemed to crouch a little, menace on his face, like a cat ready to pounce.

"No. What I saw was a man. A full-grown man. This is not him. These hapless little boys. What a waste."

Rolf jerked his head, and Gep led Addie out of the room. She tried to look up at Rolf as she left, but he ignored her.

"Exactly what the watchman on the bridge said, messieurs." Luc took his coat from the desk chair and started out the door.

Rolf followed him. "I am sure we can all agree, this whole thing was nothing but a ruse."

"If we'd have done like I said," Kruder interjected, "and put a mustache on the ugly one, they'd have both said it was the murderer. You got the answer you were looking for."

"Yes, Kruder, I did. The truth."

When everyone left Kruder remained with the coroner. He looked at the two boys and smiled. As he walked out of the room, he said, "Thank you, gentlemen."

The coroner looked around the empty room, then shrugged.

34

Thursday, 10 April 1941

Ach, ich vergaß
O, j'oubliais
Oh, I Forgot

DAY SIX—Paris—Thursday, 10 April 41—8:02 AM
The distinct sound of the key entering the lock, the lock being removed, and the hasp and hook sliding apart with a clank always sent a quiver of exhilaration through both Addie and Fifi, if usually short-lived. It was the stairway guard who tapped politely on her door. Addie was seated on the edge of her bed rereading Victor Hugo and waiting for her "breakfast gruel," as she lovingly referred to it.

"Fräulein Bridges," the tall thin orderly announced. "You free now to be."

His English was terrible. And wonderful! Addie was at the door in an instant and flung it open with wide-eyed wonder. The soldier stood frozen with one finger in the air and his eyes closed, obviously trying to remember the rest of what he was instructed to say.

"Only from lesson to learn musted."

She threw her arms around him and jumped up to kiss his cheek. Failing, she made him bend down to accomplish it on a second attempt. Fifi ran frantic circles around them both, yelping like some loosed toy. The soldier found Miss Bridges' appearance doll-like in a puffy white blouse with red lapel piping and a pair of high-waisted blue trousers with two strips of red sailor buttons running up her tummy. He wondered if all American women looked and smelled so delicate, like a crisp spring morning.

Fifi leapt into her arms as Addie motioned for the soldier to lead the way. He nodded, more of a bow, then added, "I *nehme* . . . I go *Hund im Hof.*" Embarrassed, he shook his head. "*Im Garten, Hund* I go."

"You'll take Fifi to the courtyard?" Addie remarked as the guard swallowed hard and simpered. "*Dankeschön*," Addie added, and curtseyed cutely, following him, capering down the hallway.

Thick pulp, three fingers of it, floated at the top of the chilled glass of freshly squeezed orange juice like the head on a cold beer. Puffs of steam rolled from the spout of the heavy silver coffee pot. Cigars of rolled slices of ham and salami were spread like a fan on half a plate, the other held warm croissants and *pain perdu* sprinkled with powdered sugar. Honey. Fresh blueberries. Whipped cream. Marmalade. Butter squares wrapped in parchment. In the center of a gold-rimmed Delft plate with a tiny clipper ship etched on top, a warm egg was held upright in a gold egg dish. Gold fork. Gold knife and spoon. And a white linen napkin folded like a swan around the egg.

Addie plopped herself down in front of the breakfast feast and almost cried. The tuxedo-clad French waiter popped the swan out of the napkin and placed it in her lap. Gep walked up and took a seat across from her in the sunny, glassed-in winter garden jutting out into the hotel courtyard.

"*Café*, mademoiselle?" the waiter asked.

"Oh." She closed her eyes and shook her head. "S'il vous plaît."

"Welcome back, Miss Bridges."

"Oh, Gep," she said, sensually chewing a quickly honey-dipped wedge of the toast. "I will be the best material witness you and Rolf have ever had."

"We'll see."

"Where is he?" she asked, covering her masticating mouth politely.

"He's busy. He won't be coming down."

"He hates me, doesn't he?"

"I rather believe he doesn't know what to think about you."

"Gep, why do you think he let me out?"

Gep took over for the waiter and sent him on his way.

"Frankly, Miss Bridges, I'm not sure I know. But I want to make certain you understand something. The major is a German officer of a different century, most definitely not of this last decade. A romantic. Not in the American moving-picture sense. Rather in a European way, like a knight. He is a modern soldier out of duty. But he has the heart of a poet, and the judgment of a nobleman. He plays the piano, beautifully. Beethoven and Schumann, the romantics. Were you aware of this?"

Addie spread some of the whipped cream on the remaining wedge of pain perdu, then spooned on some blueberries. She gazed up at Gep and shook her head, then closed her eyes and sighed as the glorious creamy sweetness melted on her palate.

"The major reads Herodotus, fences daily. He owns horses, trains and rides in classical dressage, as well as in hunts of wolf and fox. I would liken him to Friedrich der Grosse, Old Fritz, we call him. Do you know this Prussian king, Frederick the Great?"

"I'm sorry, no. Not really." She wiped cream from her lip with her napkin.

"He was the greatest king Germany or Europe has ever known." Gep leaned back in his chair, folded his arms, and crossed his legs. "A warrior, a great leader in the field, defeating my beloved Austria and laying claim to all of Silesia for Prussia. But he was also an artist, a painter. He was a philosopher, a close friend of Voltaire. Played many musical instruments and he even composed symphonies, works that are still played by orchestras today. He was also a tolerant king, opened all of Prussia to religious freedom, resulting in the immigration of thousands of Huguenots, Calvinists . . . even Jews to Germany. So, do you see this duplicity in the major?"

"Maybe, sort of."

"Karl-Rudolf von Gerz will be a good soldier for the Führer because it is his duty. But he would be a great and mighty knight for a true and worthy king! The knight struggles to do right, while the soldier struggles to do his duty."

"I knew he was a good and noble man, he gave me no reason whatsoever not to trust him. I was just a silly, frightened girl. I don't deserve his tolerance, do I, Gep?"

"Most certainly, you don't."

"I'm unsure how to say this without sounding precocious, but I think he fancies me."

Gep was silent. He looked down and sort of shrugged as Addie went on.

"And I think I have feelings for—"

"Don't flatter yourself, Fräulein. It's unbecoming and most certainly presumptuous indeed. I'm quite certain it's nothing more than some silly something you do that reminds him of his dead wife."

Gep fixed his stare on her with his stern eyes.

"The major lost her to a crippling disease six years ago. Theirs was evidently the rare pairing of two perfectly matched souls. He has never gotten over her and never will. Still, he seeks her out. And he finds her. Since I first started working with the man two years ago, there have been two such inamoratas. Both deceived and embarrassed him. It won't happen to him again. I assure you, Miss Bridges. American or not, if you betray the major in any way . . ." A chill ran through her as she watched Gep's warm blue eyes go cold and steely. "I will ensure that you simply disappear, my dear. And you will never be found. Trust me. We are very good at this sort of thing."

His warm smile and the pirouette of his acrimony was more chilling than his threat.

"So, now. That said. And understood. I am certain the two of us can become the most famous of friends!"

Gep took a newspaper he'd carried to the table and tossed it in front of her. It was folded to reveal a small headline that read:

Danish Steamer Sinks off Bordeaux.

Hits Mine. All Souls Lost.

"He saved your life, Miss Bridges. I guess he thinks his point's been made. And I suppose I concur."

Tears welled in Addie's eyes as they stayed transfixed on the article.

"Two crates full of my most treasured things are at the bottom of the sea."

She shook her head and held up her palm. "And I deserved it. I know I did. Thank you."

"Don't thank me. If you'd have pulled that stunt with me, you'd be in a parasitic cell across the street in the Cherche-Midi prison for at least a month." He smiled at her coyly. "I am not a romantic. I'm just a policeman and a soldier."

"Gep." She beckoned as he stood to leave. She put her hand on his tunic sleeve. "He's lucky to have you as a friend."

"The concierge at your building has the keys to your old apartment," he said as he topped off her coffee cup. "You paid rent through the end of the month, so you can move back in anytime. The girls here at the office have gathered some things to make the place bearable. When you finish your breakfast, I'll have some . . ." She started to leap from the chair and give him a hug. His firm grip on her shoulder settled her back into her seat. "I'll have some of my men take your things over. Now, do be a good girl and mind what I tell you. You are to inform your concierge or this office anytime you leave your building. You are not to be away for more than an hour. And if you do not abide by these terms . . ." Again, the sinister smile. "We'll do things my way. Is that clear to you, Miss Bridges?'

"Of course it is. Where is he, Gep? When will I see him again?"

"We'll be in touch. Bon appétit." A nod and a flick on the bill of his hat as he donned it, and he went on out into the garden to smoke.

DAY SIX—Paris—Thursday, 10 April 41—8:56 AM
Gep was on the second floor, about to enter Rolf's office, when Gretl and Hedy caught up to him.

"Oberleutnant! Oberleutnant, there was something we need to tell you." Gretl was out of breath as she continued. "Something we only this very minute remembered. A man . . ."

"A *mysterious* man, to be sure." Hedy was at her wide-eyed dramatic best.

"A man we saw Herr Ritter dine with the night before he was killed."

Gep held his hand out to invite them into Rolf's office. "Ladies."

Before agreeing to be interrupted, Rolf demanded to know if it was important. Gep was about to answer, but Hedy did it for him.

"Desperately so!"

Rolf closed the files on his desk and offered them seats.

Gep told them to start from the beginning.

"We took our dinner at Bistro Bruno's that evening. We saved up all week."

"*All* week." Guess who?

"And this strange man sat down at the table next to us," Gretl went on to say. "He was the most hideous creature. Sweating and very befuddled. His clothing, all wet and steamy. I couldn't help but take notice of him."

"I noticed him too, but I had my back to him." Dearest Hedy.

"I sat there talking to Hedy, trying to avoid his remarkable and quite frightening blue eyes for what seemed like an eternity. It was probably fifteen minutes."

"What time was this?" Rolf asked.

"Eight," Gretl said, looking at Hedy, then back at Gep and Rolf. " . . . *ish?*"

He jotted down the time. "Go on."

"Then Konni arrived. He was so agitated he didn't even notice us. I don't think he wanted to dine with the man. We didn't really think much about their conversation. It was mostly under breath anyway. But we were able to hear the man say something about a woman. He said, 'I don't think she is dead. I think she's alive and in Switzerland.'"

"Was a name mentioned?" Gep asked.

"The woman's name? I remember it exactly. It was Irmgard."

"*Ja*, Irmgard. Like in the operas." The nodding magpie.

"That was really all we got from the conversation. When the man left, Konni noticed us. He seemed put off that we had been eavesdropping. He told us the man was a colleague of his, from the Tirol in Austria, who wanted Konni to help him get Bakelite for his factory."

Gep looked at Rolf and chewed the inside of his mouth.

"Bakelite is used to make things for automobiles."

"All sorts of things. Konni told us that." Hedy, adding her mustard.

"Anyway, that was pretty much it. I felt just terrible today when Hedy and I thought of it. I don't know why we forgot to tell you the other day."

Then, as it seems the most muddled of minds are prone to sometimes do, adorable Hedy gave a goofy, charming simper as she looked up to the heavens and summed it all up quite perfectly: "*Ja*, sometimes my brains just have to catch up to me!"

35

Die Tätowierung
Le tatouage
The Tattoo

DAY SIX—Paris—Thursday, 10 April 41—10:12 AM
French gangster and black marketeer Guy de Forney dealt in anything
of value. Food, sex, and escape were the best-selling of his wares.
Unlike his adversary Hugo Sturekov, who dealt primarily with the
Germans through the Abwehr, overseeing several procurement
bureaus, Guy de Forney's markets were the masses. His Germans
were the tourist German soldiers and businessmen that poured out of
every arriving train at Gare du Nord and Gare de l'Est. It was a
common saying in Paris that the German Army took the city not with
a Mauser, but with a Leica camera!

Some of de Forney's most profitable items came from his
contacts in the Balkan quarter. Postcards. Many thousands of them
were distributed and sold each week. Not the sort of thing you'd send
home to *Mutti* though. These were lewd. Vile. Sordid scenes. The
Kama Sutra taken to its most base level. Young. Old. Fat. Thin.
Animal. Vegetable. Nothing was taboo. Most of the cards were
reproductions of bad reproductions. Terrible quality, but then? They
sold for five francs each, a hundred francs would get you twenty-five,
or even thirty if you haggled or played the Nazi conqueror card.

De Forney paid six hundred francs per thousand to the
warehouse print shop where they were produced and sold them to his
seedy distributors at two thousand francs a thousand. There were
more than a hundred distributors in Pigalle alone. He was greatly
disappointed when his take was less than a million francs a week. But
now de Forney was being pressured into becoming a Gestapo lackey.
This concerned him. These Nazi fanatics were less likely to accept the
practical business aspects of harmless vice. He and all of his people
would tread lightly.

Victor Roche limped into Guy de Forney's office, a dark den of
clutter, walls covered in plum silk above walnut boiseries. He carried
a fat envelope addressed to his boss, Monsieur de Forney. The
fanciful underworld chieftain was dressed in an emerald-green silk

robe and a yellow ruffled shirt. His unique haircut was a sort of haphazard *en brosse*, a style he chose from a portrait of Napoleon.

"It's posted from Lyon," Victor said as he took a seat.

Guy opened the letter and pulled an oily handkerchief from it. Startled, he dropped it on his desk and stepped back, daintily. With the tilt of his head, he motioned for Victor to unfold it for him. Victor tugged delicately on the kerchief until a rolled-up slice of what looked like bologna plopped onto the desk. He stabbed the meat with his knife and unfolded it on the desk.

"Ugh," Victor grunted, grimacing. A glare of suppressed exasperation filled his one good eye as he suddenly recognized what it was and to whom it belonged. He tried to conceal a tinge of terror that coursed through him.

"What is it?" de Forney asked, approaching the desk.

"It's flesh. From a man's arm or shoulder. And look. On the handkerchief. A message."

"What does it say?"

"Don't fuck with me."

"Who could this be?" This wasn't the first time someone had threatened Guy de Forney, and it wouldn't be the last. But this man may have sealed his fate, having written the message quite obviously in both German and French. *Ne baisez pas mit mir!*

De Forney noticed the tattoo.

"The tattoo, do you know it?" he asked.

Victor shook his head, then stopped. "It's not one of ours. But I have seen this tattoo before. The man it was sliced from was an assassin. Very thorough. I avoided him daily in prison. He was called Tournot. He worked for Hugo Sturekov sometimes."

"Then why was this sent to me?"

"Whoever did this is under the mistaken notion this Tournot fellow worked for you."

"Send it somehow, Victor, anonymously to my old friend Hugo Sturekov."

Victor turned to leave.

"Wait," de Forney quickly shouted. "Lyon, did you say?"

"Oui, Lyon."

"The stock exchange of Lyon? It still operates, does it not?"

"Oui, Monsieur de Forney. It is in Free France. It was never closed."

"Victor, my friend." De Forney gleamed at some obvious realization. "Did you hear of this broker's murder last week?"

"*Oui,* monsieur. Most tragic."

"Do you know who may be responsible?"

Victor held up the handkerchief. "Monsieur Sturekov, maybe? Wouldn't one think, by this?"

Victor could see that de Forney's mind was spinning. There was obviously nothing more he wanted to say. So Victor stuffed the handkerchief in his jacket pocket and left. In the alley, he found a fist-sized stone and dropped it in his pocket. He still limped from the knife wound he had suffered in his battle with the broker Lemay. The strap on the patch he wore over his eye still cut into his flesh above his ear. He would have to learn to live with it. For the rest of his life. But he was vindicated, wasn't he? The broker who caught him off guard and did this to him was now dead.

His trip to Hugo Sturekov's would take him across the Seine to the Right Bank and the fashionable 8th. He walked halfway across the Pont d'Austerlitz, stopped, and lit a cigarette, resting against the bridge railing. As he enjoyed the view of Notre Dame, "up the ass of the grand lady," he furtively pulled the handkerchief from his coat pocket. Then the stone. Checking to be sure he wasn't followed or being watched, he stopped, looked around. Sliding the stone into the handkerchief, he tied the four corners together tightly and nonchalantly dropped the greasy bundle into the river. When his cigarette was finished, he continued on into the Marias and took a coffee and a brandy at a remote café.

De Forney's dark-skinned errand girl was quickly sent out to follow Victor. A filthy little wretch in dungarees and a man's flat cap, kept snug over her curly orange hair by rags stuffed in the hat's rim, she had done just as Monsieur de Forney had instructed. Racing after Victor, then staying inconspicuous once she caught up, she found a shady tree trunk to hide behind as she watched him up on the bridge. When the handkerchief hit the water, she scurried to the corner, took the coin monsieur had given her, placed it into the slot on the payphone, and dialed the number. After a few buzzes, de Forney answered.

"Monsieur?" the girl announced. "He tossed it in the Seine."

36

Die Fälscher
Le faussaire
The Forger

DAY SIX—Paris—Thursday, 10 April 41—10:44 AM
An oversized office on the second floor of Gestapo headquarters at 84, avenue Foch had been made ready for SS Sturmbannführer Alois Kruder two days before his scheduled return to Paris. Kruder's reputation and special assignment orders had preceded his arrival. He and his staff were on the trail of a high-level communist leader and suspected Polish spy being operated by the Polish government in exile in Britain. During his intrusion into an Abwehr investigation of a White Russian woman, Tippi Rostikov, recently charged with espionage in Warsaw, Kruder had learned of the woman's possible accomplice somewhere in or around Innsbruck, Austria, a radical Marxist chum from her university days in Vienna.

He put Innsbruck-area Gestapo hounds on the hunt, and only yesterday he'd learned they had picked up a pair of old men who worked as artisans for a centuries-old company famous for carving combs and buttons from horn and bone. The suspects, Abner Karl, sixty-two years old, and his seventy-one-year-old colleague, fellow comb maker Robert Wilmer, still worked in the little horn and bone shop, Kunsthorn Heitner, in the tiny town of Telfs. Like most in the Gestapo, Kruder suspected all skilled artisans of possible document forgery. Learning that a spinoff of the company had moved into production of automobile and radio parts, Kruder's curiosity was piqued even further. It was operating in Innsbruck under the name Katz und Teller Kunsthorn Fabrik AG, and its owner was one Werner Heitner.

This morning Kruder sat back and stretched in his office chair, snidely peering across his desk at Obersturmbannführer Kurt Lischka, head of SD and Gestapo operations in Paris.

"So, can you enlighten me?" Lischka asked, his elbows on the desk, his long fingers intertwined, thumbs picking slowly at his lower lip.

"About Ritter's murder?" Kruder asked. He slid a mahogany box of Jägerlust cigars across his desk and offered one to Lischka with raised eyebrows. "I am sure of nothing yet, but I know I am getting very close."

Lighting his cigar, Lischka remarked between puffs, "It's important, Kruder . . . regardless of von Gerz's assignment to lead this murder investigation . . . it's important that it be the Gestapo . . . that you be the one to solve this crime. It's important to the SS and the future of the occupation."

"I'm doing all I can."

A knock came at the door, and a young SS orderly opened it and frantically announced, "Forgive me, mein Herrs. There's a call for you, Herr Sturmbannführer. Innsbruck Gestapo headquarters. A Gruppenführer Fein. Shall I put him through?"

"Indeed," Kruder said, smiling at Lischka. He let the telephone chime a few times before answering it.

"Kruder here."

"Heil Hitler, Herr Sturmbannführer. Gruppenführer Fein here, Innsbruck Gestapo office."

"You must have important news, Fein."

"Yes, sir, I think I do. We started our interrogation of the two old artisans who worked at Kunsthorn Heitner. It looks like you were—" In the background Kruder could hear bloodcurdling screaming, closer to the screams of a slaughtered pig than any mans. "Shut that old kike-lover up. What the fuck is wrong?"

The muffled retort was inaudible.

"Well, shut the fucking door! I'm on the phone!" Fein shouted, then back to the phone he said, "We love these artsy types. The bigger the imagination, the faster they crack. We worked on him for two minutes, and he spilled everything!"

"To the point, Fein!" Kruder scolded.

"Yes, sir. You were right. This one and the other old shit were forging documents and have been for quite a few years."

"And the owner of the company? This Werner Heitner?"

"The old fool is sure he's in Paris, with documents they created for him. Heitner is using an Ecuadorian passport and visas."

"And the Ritter connection I suspected?"

"The man knows him quite well and did most of his forgery work at Ritter's behest. Scores of identities over the past five years. But he seems to think Ritter and Werner Heitner had a falling-out. No recent contact that he knows of."

"Do you believe him?" Kruder winked at Lischka.

"Most certainly. This groveling piece of dog shit would give us his wife's beating heart if we asked for it!"

"What of any recent work?"

"Nothing in the last few months. A few Panamanian passports and some visas for Spain. Oddly, however, there is this. Forty printed paper bags, gold and green paper coffee bags, quarter-kilo size. He tried to remember the name they printed on the bags but couldn't. And I believe him. It cost him an extra fingernail."

"Very good, Fein. Congratulate your team on their expedient work. I will expect a full report teletyped to my office by sundown. Start on the other comb maker and see what he may have to add. See also if he can't be encouraged to remember the name on these coffee bags. And keep this one alive. I may want to call on him again. Start talking also to workers at this Katz und Teller Company. Keep me abreast of any information you uncover on Heitner."

"Jawohl, Herr Sturmbannführer."

"And Fein, if you ever use that vile, back-alley language with me again, I will have you shot!" Kruder's eyes smiled at Lischka as he went on. "Is that quite clear?"

"Yes, sir. Forgive me, Herr Sturmbannführer, very sorry."

"Yes, you shall be." He hung up. "Heitner is in Paris." Kruder gleamed.

"I could hear the conversation," Lischka said, leaning his forearm on the back of his chair and crossing his legs. "How did you know to suspect this man Heitner?"

"A hunch," Kruder bragged. But of course, it wasn't. The information was beaten from Tippi Rostikov during her private and excruciating interrogation back in Warsaw.

"If you're correct, you can be sure he is working for the Polish government in exile in England. And why wouldn't he then be suspected in Ritter's murder? The men were estranged."

"I wouldn't count that out. Heitner is an avid communist, as are a good number of Frenchmen. Putting together a team to do in old Ritter wouldn't be difficult. But to what end? What would be gained? A terror assassination? Bring down the wrath of Germany on the back of France over one silly old man?"

"That could be it exactly," Lischka announced, stern eyed. "Bring down the wrath of Germany." A wink at Kruder. "And thereby, shore up the weak spine of France."

Lischka stood to leave.

228

"Regardless, this places both men in Paris Sunday morning. You have to start with that." He stopped and asked, "Are you forwarding this information to Major von Gerz?"

Kruder chuckled and shook his head. "Excuse my vile, back-alley language, but . . . fuck von Gerz!"

37

Die Schauspiellehrer
Le répétiteur
The Acting Coach

DAY SIX—Paris—Thursday, 10 April 41—11:02 AM
With three young Wehrmacht orderlies in tow, Adelaide Bridges waltzed out of her Lutetia Hotel prison where she'd spent the last four days and headed joyfully down the boulevard Raspail toward her apartment building just around the corner and behind the hotel. The men carried virtually everything she owned in a Vuitton trunk and two suitcases, an overnight case, and eight hatboxes.

After the orderlies had set her things where she instructed and departed, a knock came at the door.

"Oh, Addie," Mélina said in desperation as she threw herself around her friend and sobbed. "I was certain you wouldn't get out in time. I'm so thankful I got to see you again before I left."

"Mélina? You're leaving?"

"*Oui,* it's all been arranged."

"You silly girl, you simply can't be serious."

"But it's true, Addie. It's true."

Addie closed the door and led her to the sofa, the only piece of furniture left in the room. Mélina told her of the plan Ruti had laid out. Originally, they were to rendezvous after the war in a certain port town, and from there, they would elope together. But when Ruti found out she was pregnant, he moved everything up. She would leave instead on the morning train.

"My father has a brother in Nîmes. Ruti drafted the letter and mailed it to me from Nîmes weeks ago. In it, my uncle asks that I come to his home and help him care for his dying wife. She is actually quite healthy, of course. Since then, Ruti pulled together all the necessary papers and laissez-passer. Before he left he sent everything to me by courier: train ticket, passport, money, everything."

Addie took her cold hand and kissed it. "You poor girl, you're trembling." She held it to her cheek.

"Addie, I'm overcome with fear. I can't stop shaking."

"Then don't go."

"I have to go. I love him. I love him more than anything on this earth. And I can't go back to my husband. I loathe the man. God forgive me, but, why didn't he just die, Addie? So, I'm going. I made up my mind. But look at me. I know I look frightened. How will I get across the border? I'll break down the minute they start to question me. I could be writing my own death sentence."

"No, you're not, you're going to be fine. I'll help you. You'll get to Ruti and you'll have a wonderful life together with a dandy story to tell your grandchildren. Right?"

Addie smiled and beckoned a halfhearted one from Mélina.

"You'll think of nothing but your uncle and his dear wife. Not of Ruti. Not of your husband or your mother. To make a lie plausible, you must turn the lie into the truth. In your head and in your heart. So, there is nothing but your uncle and his sick wife. Do you understand me? You'll think of how happy they'll be to see you. Think of their faces. Think of their home, everything you know about them. Think of the way you'll care for her. You'll keep fresh field flowers at her bedside. The meals you'll fix them. How, when she sleeps, you'll busy yourself cleaning and doing laundry."

Addie scooted over closer to her on the sofa and put her arm around Mélina.

"And when the border police ask you questions and you start to tremble and cry, you tell them you fear so for your aunt's health, and for your ability to care for her correctly, that you have never been out of Paris, much less crossed a military border to Free France. So it's only natural that you'd be wary. And frightened. You show them your documents and tell them how difficult they were to come by. Tell them you really didn't even want to go, but you felt an obligation to your family. To your dead war veteran father's brother."

Addie hugged her.

"Oh, Addie. I so wish that I was strong and shrewd like you."

Addie feigned a swoon and exhaled. "Spend a few days as the guest of the Wehrmacht, and you'll be shrewd too."

"I'm so selfish," Mélina whined. "You've gone through a terrible ordeal and look at me. I haven't once thought of anything but myself."

"Mine is behind me. We have to get you through yours."

"Oh, I forgot. My things. I left them in the hall." Mélina opened the door and retrieved her suitcase, an old faux-leather paperboard brand with dented brass corners and deep scratches and wear. She set the heavy suitcase down and then went back into the hallway to fetch one of her mother's laundry bags full of clothes. "I told *maman* about your losing all your things in the steamer accident and that I was returning the clothes you gave me because you were left without anything. That was the only way I could get all of my things out without raising her suspicions."

"I have plenty of things. I don't need the clothes back, Mélina."

"I have to give you these." She dragged the sack in front of the rest of Addie's things. "I only have the one suitcase. Ruti wrote that he would buy me all new things when we were together again in . . ."

"In where?" Addie inquired. "You simply must tell me."

"I can't, Addie. Ruti said I can't tell anyone, including *maman*. For their own safety as well as ours."

"You know I'd never divulge anything."

"Oh, Addie, please don't make me."

"Mélina," Addie implored with a dramatic tilt of her head. "You simply must tell me everything."

"Marseilles, Addie. We're meeting in Marseilles and then on to Spain. Ruti has everything set up. An associate of his has a small hotel in Marseilles. He'll be there waiting for me."

"Where will you go in Spain?"

"I don't know."

"What if he is not . . ." Addie thought better of finishing the question, not wanting to add to Mélina's apprehension, but with the cat loose, she went ahead and turned it quickly into a statement. "Mélina, if you get there and Ruti isn't there yet, you just stay in your room and wait. Don't wander out and don't go looking for him at the train station. He will show up. Just wait."

Mélina's face melted into horror.

"I'm sorry to even bring this up, darling. But I must. He could get detained and be late. But we both know him. If he says he'll be there, he will. Won't he?"

The frightened girl was nodding but not convincingly.

"You know he will, Mélina. Has he ever let you down?"

Her nod ended. She paused, contemplated, then shook her head. "He'll come for me. I know he will."

"Good. Now do you have everything you need?"

"I don't have a cosmetics bag. Luggage is next to impossible to buy today. And I wouldn't have the means anyway."

Like bicycle tires and coal, luggage was at a premium in occupied Paris. Most of it had left with the fleeing multitudes when the Germans arrived the previous June, and very little of it ever returned. With leather scarce as well, Parisian cobblers were not only building expensive carpetbags, but many had become carpenters, building square suitcases from plywood and stretching fabric over the finished form.

"Sabina has an old one. She's letting me have it."

"Good. Now, let's play a little game, shall we?" Addie determinedly suggested, pushing the sleeves of her blouse up her arms. "I'll play the part of a border policeman and will ask you questions. You simply answer as I told you. Forget everything but your dear uncle and his poor wife. Are you ready?"

Addie began.

"So, what is your name, mademoiselle, and your purpose for leaving the occupied zone?"

DAY SIX—Paris—Thursday, 10 April 41—1:24 PM
Suzi Rupp cracked her door open when she heard the voices in the hallway. She watched the tiny blond French girl standing in front of Sabina's room. She had learned the girl was the AWOL German Rutgers Heht's girlfriend. Nibbling a loose cuticle, she stealthily watched the blonde take a boxy makeup bag from Sabina and thank her repeatedly. When the French girl left and Sabina's door was closed, Suzi lifted the receiver on her phone and dialed five times, the dialing cylinder clicking loudly with each return.

"SS Sturmbannführer Alois Kruder, *bitte*. I'll hold."

233

38

Good Friday, 11 April 1941

Verbunden an der Hüftentasche
S'est joint a' la hanche poche
Joined at the Hip Pocket

DAY SEVEN—Paris—Friday, 11 April 41—10:04 AM
Houston lawyer Bentley Henderson took the call from his sitting
room and agreed to meet the German military investigators in the
lobby in ten minutes. He was the only remaining member of the team
of American attorneys who had met with Konni Ritter at the Ritz the
day before his murder. The rest of them had already moved to their
offices in Zurich. Bentley was to join them tomorrow.

A group of four chambermaids were half-finished with the
arduous task of packing his luggage for him. All spoke English, but
only one was adept enough to have a complete understanding of the
nuances and absurdities of south Texas English. So the entire morning
had been spent with Monsieur Henderson barking out orders and the
maid with the gifted ear translating them from Texas English to
normal English, which, after a trio of aha nods, smiles, and snickers,
were confirmed in French and cheerfully carried out.

Before he left for the meeting with the Germans, he asked his
translator to take down a list of instructions with pencil and paper in
order to ensure their work went on without interruption. As he started
each topic, he numbered it, keeping track with a different finger touch
to his right thumb. An absurd amount of time was then wasted
arguing with her that even though he had returned to using his index
finger in the count, the list had only reached number five and not
number six as she was insisting. He explained his use of multiples of
four, not five, in that he had never actually used his thumb as a
placeholder. The maid was quite certain he was wrong and equally
certain that she had omitted a task. But the monsieur was the
monsieur, and therefore he was right and she would deal with his
wrath for having forgotten one of his commands with her normal
grace and deference.

Fall Irmgard

A woman's sweet voice singing "Si Petite" floated throughout the Ritz lobby accompanied by a three man salon ensamble.

"Gentlemen," Bentley barked intrusively in boisterous English as he sashayed up to Rolf and Gep. "Bentley Henderson, Houston, Texas, attorney at law. Pleased to make your acquaintance." Then to a lobby waiter he commanded, "Coffee and a Bloody Mary. Couple extra sticks a celery too."

Rolf and Gep rose to greet him. Palms pressed, greeting cards exchanged, they took their seats and Rolf posed his first question, with typical German pointedness and sangfroid.

"What was your relationship with Herr Ritter?"

"And why would he even have one with an American attorney?" Gep quickly interjected. Rolf glanced at him and he realized his impertinence, settling back in his chair.

"Well, before we get started, gentlemen, I want to point out that it is like a breath a fresh air to hear a couple Germans speak such good English. Probably pay off someday for you boys. Probably land some good jobs in international sales or something once all this war shit runs its course."

"And I'm sure it will quite soon, sir," Gep quipped, taking an immediate dislike for this abrasive fellow from Texas and saying so, regardless of the major's browbeating. "I'm not sure I can speak for the major here, but I for one expect to be posted to occupied London when we've won the war in a few months!"

Henderson was taken aback for a second, then bellowed a loud Texas guffaw, "I like that! You're a pretty quick-witted old boy. I like that, yes sir, I do."

A smug glance at Gep, and Rolf continued. "Again, please explain your relationship with Herr Ritter."

"Of course." Henderson stirred both his coffee and his drink with a stick of celery, then sucked off the remnants. He frowned slightly as he watched a worn Moleskine and a stack of index cards be withdrawn from tunics. Legs crossed. Pencils licked. Henderson puckered his lips and settled in for a longer time than he had planned.

"I am the de facto leader of a group of American attorneys who represent American businesses with holdings in Europe, especially, lately, in German-occupied Europe. I am sure you can understand the corporate boards and company presidents of these American businesses have really got their shorts in a wad over fears of what could happen to their investments should Germany suddenly take a notion to nationalize their businesses. Just as America did to your

Bayer Company in the Great War. Hell, it's still under American ownership. So it's our job to find ways to protect all of the licensees, patents, trademarks, and the like in case that should happen here, or of course in case America was to ever enter the war. Which is another big old ball of beeswax, ain't it?"

Bentley expected to have to explain the beeswax statement. When the pause proved it unnecessary, he continued.

"The invasion of Poland shocked the business world. Even the most naïve could see it coming. Still, it was an awakening. Foreign companies suddenly had to assess where they stood. With both sides. And, most important, where they might end up. Preparing for a German victory was usually just the status quo. But a German loss could be catastrophic if a company threw in completely with your Herr Hitler. Especially an American company."

"How does that have anything to do with Ritter?" Rolf blared, becoming put off by the man's rambling. "Get to the point, Mr. Henderson."

"I'm getting there. You boys need to learn to appreciate a fella who's good at spinning a yarn. Our friend Mr. Ritter, he was attached to your German automotive parts commission. I guess that's what you'd call it. And as such, he had taken up the task of trying to get all auto parts makers in Germany to standardize their products. A generator from an Opel, for instance, would work on a Ford or Mercedes. A monumental undertaking, I assure you. And quite frankly, an impossible one. You see, one of the biggest manufacturers of parts in Germany is Delco, owned by General Motors. And I assure you those boys wasn't interested in matching up with Bosch or that other German company—what was it? Eh, hell. You get my drift. But old Ritter, God rest his soul. He was persistent. The man was . . ." Bentley took a nasty, open-mouth gulp of the Bloody Mary. He wasn't as much fat as just big, with large jowls that rippled as he swallowed. His mouth did some skewing and chewing and he went on.

"Stubborn. So stubborn, so single-minded. You know, at first you laugh at a silly goat like that. You poke fun at them, you tell stupid stories about them in bars. But after a while, a fella starts to admire them. And it gives you this warm feeling that God sees fit to put a few creatures on this earth that just refuse to accept hopelessness! That, gentlemen, was your man Ritter. A stubborn old goat."

"Interesting," Rolf said. The folksy wisdom was lost on him. "When was the last time you saw Herr Ritter?"

"I ran into him a number of times. Like me, he always stayed here at the Ritz when he was in town. But the last time I saw him, let me see. That would've been Saturday last. We were holding a meeting upstairs, the other lawyers and me. Our last here in Paris. We're moving things to Switzerland, you see. All this Roosevelt Lend-Lease business, don't you know. Anyway, I asked Ritter to drop by the meeting so we could all tell him good-bye. Every one of us, to a man, hold—or held—him in the highest regard."

"Any idea who would want to kill him?" Rolf asked.

There were yellow roses in the table vase, just buds really. Henderson plucked one and sniffed it. Then threaded it into his lapel.

"Can't imagine anyone would, frankly. He was quite an affable fella. Might start with his wife. Old Ritter liked the company of young women and was pretty light on his feet. Loved to go out in the evening. What do the Frenchies call it, *swarm-ayes*? I tell you, if I was to carry on like that and somebody put a bullet in my melon, gentlemen, about the first and only person you'd need to talk to would be my missus . . ." Seeing confusion on Rolf's face, Henderson added, "My wife."

Happy with his new boutonniere, he smiled and went on. "So, boys. If that's all, I'm gonna have to ask to be excused. My train leaves this afternoon, and I have some chambermaids upstairs trying to pack for me. No telling where that's going with me being down here."

"Herr Henderson," Rolf interjected. "You never told us what business Ritter had with you and your associates."

"Well, sure I did. That silly auto parts standardization windmill old Ritter kept chasing."

"How did he expect you to help?" Gep liked the direction Rolf was leading the conversation.

"Guess he thought we might have some influence on Delco and them."

"How did he help you?" Gep added.

Henderson snorted and smiled. "You boys is a couple a damn Mickey Spillaines, ain't you? It was during the race for the Volkswagen contract. He sorta kept us abreast of what was going on with Dr. Porsche, DKW, and Daimler and the like. We was on the outside, looking in through that deal. Not so much Ford; they dropped out pretty damn quick. But Opel—that's General Motors, of course—

they stayed after it. But c'mon, gentlemen. Produce a family-size car for under an eight hundred marks retail? Four hundred dollars? And make a profit? I think the Opel boys finally told them they could produce the car, but it would come with a horse hitch instead of an engine."

"How often did you see Herr Ritter?" Rolf felt there was a worm in this apple, and he was going to find it.

Henderson was becoming upset. "As often as he might wish! You boys is just sucking up a bunch a wind now. If you think that I, or any of my associates, had anything to do with or are somehow withholding information about that sweet old man's murder, you're both full a some real stinky shit. We—all of us to a man—admired Ritter, and we tried to help him any way we could. Now, you have my number in Zurich on my card there. If you think of anything else, don't hesitate to call. I hope you get the sack a shit that done this. And I know you boys will. You're good at this sort a thing. I know the sombitch'll get his due."

"Mr. Henderson," Rolf interjected, before the sizeable Texan could stand up to leave. "I'm still not satisfied with your explanation about such a large number of American attorneys in the occupied Reich. I need you to further explain your presence."

Henderson sighed resolutely.

"Gentlemen, no two countries on earth are as closely connected from a business standpoint as America and Germany. Joined at the hip pocket. You have American companies like DuPont and Ford, Standard Oil and IBM. Shit, even Coca-Cola. The list goes on. All of them have holdings in Germany and have had them long before your Mr. Hitler took over. Hell, General Motors owns the biggest automobile manufacturer in Germany, the Opel car company. That big new Opel factory they just built in Brandenburg is putting out a hundred thousand four-ton Blitz trucks for your army every year! That's quite an achievement. Why, Hitler gave Henry Ford—Ford's got that big auto plant in Cologne—Mr. Hitler gave him the highest medal any non-German can receive just a few years ago. Hell, I understand Opel's Rüsselsheim factory is gearing up to produce parts for Junker bombers, I believe."

Rolf was fuming over Henderson's loose talk about such important war production information. "How is it, Mr. Henderson," he sternly asked, ready to grab this American bumpkin by his neck and haul him off to the Cherche-Midi. "How is it that an American attorney from Houston, Texas, is privy to such sensitive intelligence on the German industrial composition and production figures? I demand you produce your source! Who is it?"

"That's easy, sir," Bentley said, biting off a piece of the celery and chomping indignantly on it. He smiled and leaned forward as though to impart a guarded secret.

"*The Wall Street Journal!*"

As Rolf and Gep were leaving, the hotel concierge stopped them and pulled them to the side. He told them of a lobby waiter who'd seen Ritter and another man quarreling the night before he died. The concierge handed them the man's business card. He had left it with the waiter when he told him he was waiting on Ritter's arrival.

Rolf took it and asked when they could talk to the waiter.

"He's already been summoned, monsieur. He'll be here in a few moments."

Rolf looked at the card.

Willy von Kanderstein,
Lodei Vergaser Gmbh, The Lodei Carburetor Company
Berlin-Köpenick

39

Mittagessen
Déjeuner
Lunch

DAY SEVEN—Paris—Friday, 11 April 41—12:38 PM

The concierge's wife had volunteered to pick up a few essentials at the market for Addie. When a knock came at the door Addie opened it holding a ten-franc note and ration vouchers in her hand. But, it was Rolf.

"Have you had lunch?" he asked, with a warm smile.

Rolf waited a few minutes while she changed. When she presented herself, he was stunned. Her shapely form bloomed under a thin blue forty-button alpaca sweater, light and snug, the top ten tiny mother-of-pearl buttons loosed to display a pronounced décolletage. She grabbed up her jacket and scarf, tossed them at him, and pinned a blue wedge hat in place as she bounced like a schoolgirl down the stairs.

Blue sky, a breathless day. Chilly in the shade, hot in the sun. Had spring finally arrived? They followed the rue du Cherche-Midi toward the Saint-Germain-des-Prés. The streets were full of people. The lack of motorcars made bicycles and carriages the new mode of transportation, and side streets became joyous neighborhood gatherings on bright, sunny days. And today's bright sunshine had stirred even the most embittered of Paris' *citoyens occupeés*. Old men walked three and four abreast, smoking and smiling. Women strolled arm in arm and children frolicked. Remnants of the days of old, the belle époque, had settled back in, or rather had been forced down the throat of Paris. As the resilient French say, "One must flower where one is planted." And no people on earth flowered more warmly than Parisians.

"So, tell me about your relationship with Herr Ritter," Rolf said before he realized such a question required some groundwork before being sown.

"So, this isn't a date then." The hot sunshine made her unwrap her scarf. "Just a pleasant interrogation."

"Forgive me. I'm not very adept at small talk. It's just the only thing we have in common and thus, first to mind."

"Okay." She tucked the scarf in her jacket sleeve. Rolf motioned with an outstretched palm to let him carry them. She accepted.

"Konni was a dear man. One of those few blessed souls the lord gives us who somehow is able to make it all a little easier. He always led the most entertaining and erudite badinage. He was the consummate raconteur. His stories just twisted us in knots. And it was not so much the tales themselves as his telling of them. Those absurd front teeth and sparkly eyes. The man loved to be seen with us. He showed us off at every possible turn."

They passed a French couple, and Addie felt the woman's hateful glare—*another pretty French girl out with a Boche officer*. She considered switching quickly to English, to mask her assumed complicity and guard against those thousand scornful eyes all around her. But she didn't. She parlayed on.

"I was introduced to him at the club." She stopped Rolf and placed her hand on his shoulder. "That would have been in '36." Crossing her leg, she reached down to adjust a fold in the throat of her shoe. "I was twenty-two and was taking some classes at the university." In the process the strap of her brassiere slid down her shoulder. Reaching inside her sweater, she made the necessary adjustment, rolling her shoulder, then squashed a bug with her shoe until it felt comfortable on her foot, and on they preceded.

"I met him through Bruno, the big scary fellow that owns the l'Heure Bleue. He had a club in Berlin before Mr. Hitler's time, and Konni was a regular there. Dear Konni was the most affable creature. Big, gaping-mouthed guffaws and jelly-belly chuckles. He could get cleanly away with the most indignant deeds. Two other American girls, students as well, we were the closest of chums, along with Yvette and Sabina. He called us the 'Clique of Quack,' the way our heels would make riotous noise as we dallied about, sashaying down the boulevards. Said the noise was reminiscent of the quacking of ducks, and so we became his 'Little Duckies.'"

They found sunny seats at Les Deux Magots. Rolf held her chair for her as he ordered fois gras and settled on a '37 Chassagne-Montrachet. She preened her skirt with a few flaps. Sunglasses came out and went on, him in his Carl Zeiss nickel-rims and her in white cellulose pantos. And they were soon caught up in the contagious cheer of the beautiful day.

"We would make all the cafés and quays, the parks and cemeteries. He read us Maurice Dekobra. 'Lurid and exotic stuff, this,' he would say, and his bushy little brows would dance about so spectacularly." She mimicked the face, cutely.

"*Madonna of the Sleeping Cars; Macao, l'enfer du jeu.* The kind of pulp romance young girls just adore. Terribly naughty. And he never tired of it. It was all quite beneath him, I assure you. But on he would read. Smiling with those Cupid 's bow lips and that big wild-hare grin. Pursing his little mouth into the most lurid of shapes when he'd come to something profoundly sordid or juicy. He made each paragraph a pure delight. We were all like children at the fire. 'Read us more, Konni, darling. You simply must.' We know the man had grandchildren. They must have relished every moment at his knee."

She pulled her scarf from the sleeve of her jacket and dabbed a tear from the corner of her eye. Then she draped it around her neck and tied it at her throat as a fetching blue gorget.

"Then came the war in '39, and we didn't see him anymore. We were all terribly saddened. The silly war that really wasn't. But last June, the German invasion. Like most, the other two American girls left France immediately. But I stayed. I wanted to show my father . . . I stayed."

Cigarettes were offered up and lit. Rolf was finding her completely enchanting. He was hearing her story, but was captivated by her beautiful face, her cant, her glow. He let himself be reminded of his wife. She always told such engaging stories herself.

"I volunteered as a nurse's assistant for Anne Morgan's American ambulance service. I wasn't in Paris when your soldiers marched in. Those few weeks I was with the service were the most frightening days of my life. I learned what war truly is, and does to people. They make it all sound like such adventurous sport. But it's really just base and frightfully disgusting. Day in and day out, living with such morose fear. That's the terror of war. I was so glad to get back to Paris. I wanted to go immediately home. I even booked passage. But my friend at the embassy convinced me to stay. The worst was over. None of the rumors about the Germans had come true. Your army didn't come swashbuckling into Paris, having their way with everything and everyone, he told me, but rather as gentlemen. How long that would last, no one knew. But Germany didn't want a war with America; on that point, he convinced me. And so I stayed. And I am glad I did. At least until last winter. I never knew that a person could cry from being cold. I never knew a person could get that cold. That was the second time in my short, white, and very privileged life that I confronted true hardship. And all in a matter of a few months. We'd all been such an insouciant breed before the war, naïve, insulated from the deprivation of the lesser classes. So, last winter, when we'd had our dose, I assure you, Rolf, darling, we wanted little more of it."

She snuffed out her cigarette in a green brushed-aluminum ashtray and pushed its spinning top plunger to flush the butt away. A quick breath caught, and she leaned forward and stuffed her hands under her legs. Somewhere across the boulevard, an accordion was playing "La Chapelle au Clair de Lune." Sandwiches, berries, and walnuts appeared in front of them somehow.

"Within a few weeks of the German takeover, Konni was back! The German girls, Gretl and Hedy, took the place of my American friends, and there we were again. The Clique of Quack was back, he would declare. But of course, it really wasn't. The war had changed everyone. Yvette was never the same. And who would be? Her husband was a prisoner in Germany. Her brother was killed by the English in the sinking of the French fleet at Mers-el-Kébir? So she really hated both sides, didn't she? Said she wished the two sides could just keep fighting until they killed each other off. But her opinion of Konni certainly changed that winter. He became our guardian angel. We would have all frozen to death, three little frosty girls in my tiny apartment; me, Yvette, and her little daughter. I assure you, we truly would have if Konni hadn't been able to procure a ration of coal for my building. Then a steady flow of letters started between Yvette and her husband, Claude. And soon she came around, pulled her chin up, and made do, the way all of France has."

She set down her drink and dabbed her red lips with her napkin.

"So, there you have it. Dear Konni and me in a nutshell. Now it's your turn," she added, picking up her sandwich and ducking down to take a bite, looking over her sunglasses at him. "Tell me about Major Rolf von Gerz."

He told her of his military career and very quickly moved to the loss of his wife. Gep was right. The man was truly overcome with grief. She stopped eating for a few moments and placed her elbows on the table, twined her fingers together, and held them against her cheek. Listening intently. He spoke of his daughter in the past tense. Addie felt it rude to try to confirm if the child was even still alive. But she gathered from his overall demeanor there had been some sort of falling-out, the details of which he chose not to disclose.

They left the café, half-eaten sandwiches, and an empty bottle of wine, and wandered toward the Pont Neuf. She was so happy she nearly capered as she moved ahead of him now and then. Conversation moved to silly things. Favorite movies. Books. Music was thoroughly discussed. She marveled at his love of American jazz. An epiphany hit her. Count Basie had been playing in her room when they first set eyes on each other across their courtyard a week ago. She told him she was sure Django Reinhardt was playing somewhere in Paris. An absolute must for him. Perhaps she would accompany him? Delighted.

Their next stop was the DuPont-Bastille bar in the Opéra district. They took al fresco seats and ordered coffees and more sunshine. A little girl of perhaps five stood at the street corner holding her mother's hand and sniffing a dandelion floret. She stared at Rolf, at his crisp gray uniform while she swung one stiff leg back and forth. Taking note, her mother suddenly jerked the tiny thing up on to her hip and turned her view away from Rolf. But one little eye peeped around *maman*, still transfixed on this gallant German chevalier. Rolf smiled and waved his index finger at her. The mother sternly gave up her wait to cross the street and stormed down the sidewalk to cross at another corner, the girl peering around her at the handsome soldier.

They had barely finished their coffees when a wind came blustering up, whipping the sidewalk umbrellas and stirring up dust and trash.

"It's going to shower," Rolf declared. "And we're caught without umbrellas."

"Not to fear, darling." She untied her scarf from her neck and wrapped it around her head. "This is Paris in the spring. Showers rarely last. And besides. There are cafés and bars on every corner. It's called the old duck-in!" She batted her long eyelashes at him dramatically, and added, "Duckie!"

The shower flushed the city stench away and songbirds gave up praises. With her on his arm, they continued their stroll on shiny sidewalks that sparkled when the sun returned.

"I need to try to visit an old friend," he said. His invitation was warm. "Would you care to join me, Addie?"

"I'd be delighted."

Rolf hailed a fiacre taxi and gave the driver an address in the 16th. The slight breeze in the open carriage gave her a chill.

Gallantly, he pulled the wool blanket from behind them and wrapped it around her as she shivered and cooed and smiled at him. The carriage made its way through the 1st and the 8th, twisting along quiet, shady side streets, through shafts of twinkling sunbeams. It rounded the place d'Iéna and the place de Mexico.

"I was raised here in Paris," he added, jutting his strong chin as he admired the sea of detailed relief on the beautiful buildings as they passed by. "Spent the first twelve years of my life here."

"In the 16th? You *poor* soul."

He smiled. "It was my mother's villa. Her family's, actually."

"Is she still alive?"

"No, she died years ago. And the house was sold. But the Polish woman who raised me and her husband were allowed to live in the apartment above the garage as long as they drew breath. That was my stipulation. The woman died three years ago. She was my governess, my daughter's governess as well for a few years after my wife died. But her husband, our gardener and chauffeur, he may still be alive. Only way to find out is to go and see. He'd have to be ninety now."

They wound through the cream-frosted and caramel-iced lanes of the luxurious 16th arrondissement until they came to the rue de la Faisanderie. Rolf explained his parents' decision to separate with true Prussian dignity. His father in Berlin, his mother in Paris. How Rolf had lived with his mother until his confirmation, then spent the rest of his younger life under his father's command. He explained that he really didn't even know his mother, spending most of his time in boarding schools. For Prussian aristocracy, child-rearing was best left to domestics. So, he was very close to his governess.

"For every night I spent in my mother's villa, I spent at least ten in the little apartment above the garage. And we spoke nothing but Polish in that friendly home. Which, of course, is why I am fluent and spent the last six months in Warsaw, and am . . ." He was about to say "returning," then caught himself, remembering how easily he had let his plans flow in conversations he had had with Tippi only a few weeks before.

Addie sat listening attentively with the blanket tugged up around her chin.

"I'm such a selfish ninny. You must be cold. You want to share, love?"

He smiled at her, shaking his head. "I'm fine."

Rolf tapped loudly on the door to the magnificent villa. The woman who opened the door was aghast to see a German officer on her stoop. She called out immediately to her husband, who rushed to her side.

"I'm Major von Gerz. This is Mademoiselle Bridges. I have come to inquire about an old man who may still live above your garage."

"Well thanks be to heaven," the man said, stepping out onto the stoop. "It's about time someone did something about these beggar Jews."

"So, he's still alive?"

"Oh, yes. He's quite alive. Up there above my garage, dithering about the way they do. Filthy, disgusting. Truly, a rat's nest. Well, good riddance, I say!" He stepped off the stoop.

"Come. Follow me. I am more than happy to point him out to you."

"That won't be necessary." Rolf stopped him and turned him around abruptly, a menacing look in his eye. "I don't need your help."

"Forgive me, but what did you say your name was?"

Rolf snapped around and through clenched teeth spat, "Von Gerz!"

"Why, I bought this house from a von . . ."

Rolf took Addie's hand as they climbed the rickety stairway, long in need of paint, up to the apartment. He tapped on the glass of the door, and they could see a figure squirming, trying to free himself from his rocking chair. He stopped, took something from the side table, and put it in his mouth, then continued the arduous process of gaining his feet. As he shuffled toward the door, he kept moving his mouth around. When the old man opened the door he squinted in the sunlight. His yellowing white hair was uncombed, his beard was only partly shaved, and one of his baby-blue eyes displayed a tiny yellow worm of a cataract. And his teeth still weren't completely in.

"No speak French no more," he mumbled, motioning with the sideways wave of his hand for them to inquire at the villa's front door.

"Dziadunio?" Rolf said.

The old man kept slapping the air at them, trying to get them to understand they needed to go to the villa. Then, he suddenly stopped.

"Who calls me *grandpa*?" he asked in Polish. Gasping suddenly for breath, he started crying. *"Synek? Synek,* is that you at my door?"

Addie teared up as the old man hugged Rolf, shook him, looked at him, then hugged him again.

Old Jakub invited them in and threw papers, magazines, and books off the sofa to make room for them. He sat in his rocker, rocked it, and tugged on the floor with his feet until it walked its way over to be right in front of Rolf.

"This is your woman?" He spoke Polish. Addie just watched and smiled every now and then, but knew she was being talked about.

"Just a friend."

"You should make her your woman." He looked Addie over and gleamed. "I would certainly make her my woman!"

Rolf chuckled.

"She has a good frame. Bountiful body. Many strong sons could suckle such a woman."

"I'll keep that in mind."

"She French?" Jakub went on to ask.

"American."

"Yankee dandy!" the old man shouted proudly at Addie in the only English he probably knew.

Addie smiled and curtseyed with a dip of her head.

"Are you well, *Dziadunio*?" Rolf asked, grabbing the old man's hands and tenderly shaking them.

"Sorry I lost myself when I saw you."

"Me as well," Rolf admitted, smiling.

"You're still a good boy, *Synek*. You take time to come see an old man."

"I'm forty years old now. You still call me *sonny*."

"I'm twice your age. It's my privilege."

Rolf nodded and patted his knee. "So, are you all right?"

He shrugged and trumpeted his lips. "I'm old. I'm lonely. I miss things. No wine anymore. They tell me the Boches took it all. So I miss that."

Addie watched the hair at the front of Rolf's ears stand up as he clenched his jaw.

"And I miss my wife's pierogi, *Synek*." He smiled sweetly at Rolf. *Yes, Synek. I miss my wife too.* "They let me live here. It's added years to my life. Is that good? Some days. Some days, yes. I didn't like your mother, *Synek*. But she left us this house, me and mama. So I take flowers to her grave now and then. Nice days mostly. Sunny, warm days. Hers and mamas. I take them flowers I grow in the garden. Something to do, isn't it?" The whites of his eyes turned suddenly pink. His lip quivered as he added, "I still smell mama in this house."

Addie could see tears welling in Rolf's eyes. She placed her hand on his arm. She had no idea what was being said, but she was fighting tears as well.

"I still hear you running and playing. I don't hear things too well anymore. So I hear that. That's added years to my life. So I take the flowers. Now and then. But I do miss the wine."

Rolf quickly asked him to be excused for just a moment and told Addie to find some glasses, that he'd be right back. She tapped the old man on the hand and motioned toward the kitchen.

"Oh, yes. Most certainly," he said in Polish. He threw up a shaky thumb and index finger, adding, "You will need to flush twice. Most times it doesn't go down."

Addie switched on the light to find the dingy kitchen the most cluttered and filthy collection of dirty dishes, rancid glasses, and crusty pans and utensils she had ever seen—weeks, possibly months' worth. She snooped around for soap. Finding none she went into the bedroom to find it just as disorderly as the kitchen. Finally, in the fetid bathroom where the disgusting toilet was about to overflow, she was able to locate some tooth powder. She kicked the toilet lid down with her toe and cleaned the bathroom sink, running hot water in it as long as possible. With her fingertips, she took three of the least sickening glasses, scrubbed them with the tooth powder and her fingers, rinsed them in the now scalding water, and dried them with her skirt.

When she returned she watched Rolf come in the door, its dusty lace curtains emitting a faint cloud as he kicked it to with his heel, two bottles of wine in his arms and one in each hand. He took them to the dining table and pulled a beautiful brass and crystal corkscrew from his tunic pocket. The table was draped with a soiled and rusting square lace tablecloth juxtaposed so that corners of the tablecloth hung down at the sides of the table while its corners remained bare. Addie rubbed her fingers over one of the corners, where obvious teeth marks scarred its edge. She looked at Rolf. *Yours?* her eyes asked. He smiled and nodded as he popped the cork and held it under the elated old man's nose.

Addie watched the two of them, for nearly two hours, drink and laugh at each other's stories. Then suddenly, Rolf's eyes grew wide as he said. *"Mam samochód?"*

248

Rolf was like a little boy when he turned and translated for Addie.

"He still has the car!"

Jakub's glee needed no translation. Smiling eyes wide open, he held up one finger and shoved it at them many times while he tried to think of where he put something. Sliding the chair back he quickly shuffled into the bedroom. When he returned in a few minutes, he had donned his chauffeur's hat and a wrinkled and stained white shirt. His black servant's jacket with frayed sleeves was over his arm as he struggled futilely with a plain black tie.

"Here," Addie said. "Let me do that."

The old man threw his head back and jutted his stubby chin off to one side. Straining, he looked down at her, then over at Rolf. "So, she's not your woman?" he snapped out of one corner of his mouth.

Smiling, Rolf shook his head.

"Then leave her for me."

"You'll spoil her!"

"That's what they're for, *Synek*!"

Old Jakub, former chauffeur of Madame von Kleisen-Rudolph und Gerz, motioned for Rolf to go to the other side of the car as he held the door open for Addie. Save a slight tinge of dust, the black Hispano-Suiza Berlina Kellner limousine was in mint condition.

"Mademoiselle," he said. Tipping his hat to her, he took her hand and nestled her into the car. Like a giddy kid, he then shuffled rapidly behind the car and raised the garage door. Next, it was on to Rolf's side of the car, Jakub's frail little hands dangling, feet shuffling ever faster. He stopped, clicked his heels, and bowed to Rolf, opened the door, and gave his *Synek* a pat on the butt as he jumped in. In another minute Jakub was in the driver's seat straightening the mirror until he could see them both.

"Where to, master?" Jakub asked in Polish.

"Where to?" Rolf asked Addie in French.

She quickly grasped the game. "But darling, the opera, of course."

"So then, to the opera, driver. And make it snappy." Rolf's Polish command was accentuated with a haughty gesture of his index finger. And the grandest smile on his happy face.

The car actually started with just a few turns of the starter. Jakub put it in gear, and it crept slowly out of the garage. Rolf and

Addie glared at each other, his eyes wide, her teeth clenched and neck cinched up. This part of the game wasn't expected!

With a twinkle in his eye, the old man stomped on the accelerator and the huge limousine lunged backward into the courtyard drive. Addie screamed. Rolf made for the separating glass to try to help him. Then suddenly, the chauffeur slammed on the brakes and everyone lunged back in their seats. Both passengers gave their chauffeur a vexing glare in the rearview mirror. But they could see his squinting blue eyes laughing back at them.

"So, that one is the brake!" he glibly remarked in French.

Addie smartly turned to Rolf and quipped, "Oh, look, darling. We're already here!"

Dusk was settling in when Jakub told Rolf he was growing weary. Rolf asked Addie if she wouldn't mind terribly running along to the waiting carriage. He wanted give his good-byes in private. She understood and bid the old man au revoir with a kiss on his scratchy cheek and a sweet smile.

Out in the fiacre, wrapped in the blanket, Addie waited for what seemed like an eternity. Her patience exhausted, she walked back toward the apartment, but stopped in the porte cochère as she heard a crashing sound and shouting coming from inside the villa. She ran around to the front stoop. Shouting persisted. The door started to open, then stopped as Rolf added, "And I want clean linens and towels every three days. I want his clothes washed weekly and his dishes washed and returned to their proper places daily." A muffled retort. "That's of little consequence. You receive ample funds to care for him from the monthly trust. If you can't afford to have it done, then do it yourselves." The door was slowly swinging completely open. "And he eats what and when you eat. If you have wine, then he has wine. You can't get wine? Here." Rolf pulled a ration booklet from his tunic and tossed it at the frightened shadows huddling in the dark foyer. He took a wad of hundred-franc bills and threw them on the floor. "You are to see he has all the wine he wants! I will be checking on him, and if I find that even the slightest of my orders have not been followed, you will see your next sunrise in a labor camp in Germany! Is that all quite clear?"

Rolf turned to leave and was startled to see Addie standing before him on the stoop. He glared at her.

But she glared right back at him. "And fix the toilet," she barked.

He fumed and snapped back around.
"And fix the fucking toilet!"

40

Die Grenze
La frontière
The Border

DAY SEVEN—Vichy France—Friday, 11 April 41—2:36 PM
The train slowed to a bucking halt at the border separating the
German Occupied Zone from the Free Zone of France. Passengers
were forced to disembark with all their baggage and form three lines
at the border office to await their turn at transit interviews.

Twice Mélina was within a few people of her turn, but feigned
this excuse or that to move back in the line. She needed more time to
summon her courage. This didn't go unnoticed. Her bolstered
confidence evaporated when she saw the German soldiers standing
beside each line, feet apart, hands folded squarely behind their backs,
watching the procession the way eagles watch a wary prey.

Finally, she mustered her nerves and took her turn.

"Papiers."

She handed her passport and laissez-passer to the young border
guard.

"Purpose?" he barked.

Her hands shook as she took out the letter from her 'dear
uncle.'

"I don't have time to read letters. What's your purpose for
leaving the Zone Occupée?"

"My father has a brother. He is a veteran. Not the brother, but
my father. He died in the Great War. My uncle, my dead father's
brother, he has my aunt, his wife, and she is ill and . . ."

"Enough!" The guard snapped his fingers a few times and
pointed at the ditzy girl in front of him.

"Go with him." A man in a dark suit appeared out of nowhere
and grabbed up Mélina's papers, motioning for her to follow him into
one of the interrogation rooms. Mélina was trembling uncontrollably.
It was all she could do to keep from crying as she entered the room,
lugging her heavy bags, bouncing them against her trembling knees.
The man took her suitcase and handbag and motioned for another
man in street clothes to take them, no doubt to rummage through
them.

Fall Irmgard

As the interrogator took his seat, he lit a cigarette and picked tobacco from his tongue as he flipped through her papers.

"Why are you so nervous, mademoiselle?"

Now tears did start to flow. She tried to speak, but couldn't for her sobbing. The man scooted the chair legs back on the linoleum floor loudly and tilted himself into the tiny toilet room. His hairy hand appeared under her nose with wad of toilet paper rolled around it.

"Why are you so nervous?"

Mélina struggled to turn her fear into anger at herself for acting so suspiciously. She blew her nose and went through the entire explanation just as she had rehearsed it with Addie, as well as for hours on the train.

The man looked at her and shook his head. "I don't buy it. You're up to something. Do you know how many sick aunts and mothers and such there are in Free Zone nowadays? I've been doing this for years. I know a play-acting performance when I see one."

Just as Mélina was about the go through the routine again, the door opened and a tall, thin man in a crisp German officer's uniform entered the room. She had to squeeze her legs together to keep from peeing. The interrogator jumped to his feet.

"What seems to be the holdup here?" the officer asked. It was obviously a rhetorical question, for as the interrogator started to speak, the officer held up his hand to stop him. He glanced through Mélina's papers and quickly over the letter. Then he folded them and handed them to Mélina.

"Yes, everything seems to be in order here. Let's not make the child miss her train, shall we?" He opened the door for her, and she snapped up her quickly rifled bags and scurried back to the train. She was about to explode with relief, but held it together until the redcap helped her with her luggage and held her hand as her trembling ankles took her up the iron steps.

Through the glass, along with the border guard, Gestapo Sturmbannführer Alois Kruder watched the cute blonde board the train. He nodded to a man in a green corduroy jacket, who flipped his cigarette onto the tracks and boarded the train himself.

Kruder left the border office and walked swiftly to his waiting car, where his driver held the door open for him. "The bait is in the water," he told the driver. "Let's see what we catch."

Mélina would arrive in Marseilles at half past two the next morning. She would sleep in the train station that night, where she would get some sleep, mostly just whimpering. The next morning she would go straight to the Poseidon Hotel, where the clerk would tell her she had one of the best rooms overlooking the old port far down below. He would promise all her needs would be met, that he would be personally delivering all her meals to her room. Should there be anything she required, she only needed to twist the knob above her bed and ring the desk.

Heartsick, Mélina would enter her drab room and lay on the bed and cry herself to sleep. She would awaken at midnight and cry until she fell back to sleep at four. She would spend the next three days, including Easter Sunday, alone in Marseilles and would not take Holy Communion. So, she would cry a great deal more while she prayed for forgiveness, feeling alone and forgotten, much as her Lord Jesus Christ must have so long ago.

41

Dulce et Decorum est pro Patria Mori
Süß und ehrenvoll für das Vaterland zu sterben
Sweet and Proper to Die for the Fatherland

DAY SEVEN—Paris—Friday, 11 April 41—6:23 PM
Rolf rose from the stool at the salon piano where he had been playing
Schumann's "Des Abends" and what he remembered of Beethoven's
"Andante favori." The bar was crowded and smoky. He took his
aperitif into the lobby and found a seat next to the small Greek
fountain. Gep followed an orderly into the velvety room and watched
him click his heels and hand Rolf a telegram on a silver tray.

"Good evening, major," Gep said, taking his seat. He withdrew
a pack of Chesterfields, ripped the red stringer from the cellophane,
and tore the foil wrap away, shaking out a cigarette.

"That's evidence, Oberleutnant." Rolf shook the morning
edition of Le Petit Journal and feigned ignorance of the display.

"I'm conducting my own investigation! There's nine more
packs up in my room." He offered one to Rolf as he lit his own.

Rolf shook his head and folded the paper. He looked at the
cigarette pack briefly then tossed it back on the table and opened the
telegram.

"It's been eight years since I had an American cigarette," Gep
reported. "I forgot how smooth they were. You sure you wouldn't like
to try one? No? You prefer, then, that camel-shit-grown North
African dust we smoke?"

Rolf smirked and shook his head, unfolding the telegram.

"Looks like we're going to spend Easter in Cologne, Gep, my
friend."

"I love Cologne. I have an old friend there."

Rolf ignored his reply and went on. "We'll be taking Herr
Ritter along with us."

"The corpse?"

"The ashes. The telegram is from Herr Ritter's wife, the
Baroness von Lindenbach. She sent instructions to the mortician
yesterday to the have the body cremated and the ashes placed in the
finest urn to be found." Rolf read the telegram to Gep. "I shall mourn
my husband's passing through the coming Good Friday, and shall

take audience with you on Saturday, 12 April at precisely three o'clock."

"And so." Rolf leaned forward in his chair and looked at Gep. "She'll meet with us Saturday afternoon. I think we'll stay the night for Easter, Gep. You can see your friend."

"I'll get our man to book us on the morning train to Cologne, major," Gep said, standing to leave.

"One last thing." Rolf lifted his finger. "Here, at the last minute, she has requested we have an inscription engraved on the urn. The one from the Horace Odes."

Gep knew this much-treasured verse as did most Wehrmacht soldiers. He recited it from memory. "*Dulce et decorum est pro patria mori.*" He nodded his approval. "One could hardly ask for better epitaph in such a situation." *Sweet and Proper to Die for the Fatherland.*

"Have our man see to her wishes. It will need to be done tonight," Rolf said, handing the telegram to him. "Make him understand, Gep. I am not to be disappointed."

When Gep returned, he sat on the edge of his chair and rested his elbow on his knee as he drew Rolf's attention.

"I heard from Richter in Berlin," Gep said. "He has been tailing the von Kanderstein man. I should probably continue on to Berlin from Cologne to talk to him."

"Yes, Gep. Quite. I'd also like for you to look up an old professor of mine from my university days. He was an expert in Norse mythology. See what sort of light he might shed on the Irmgard name as it relates to old Germanic myth. That too could give us further insight into this 'Operation Irmgard.' He's retired now and has an apartment somewhere off the Potsdamer Platz. Professor Doktor Klepp."

"Easter in Cologne." Gep was contemplative. "I wonder if it still is. Easter. Doesn't seem to be anywhere else in Germany."

Rolf took the paper back up and answered into it, "We'll see, won't we, Gep?"

"What about the girl, Miss Bridges? Do you think you can trust her to be here when we return?"

"No, Gep, not sure I do!" Rolf folded his paper and rose to leave, adding with an amazing parenthetical nonchalance, "That's why she'll be going with us."

"Ach," Gep snorted. "That's the reason, is it?"

42

Saturday, 12 April 1941

Cologne, National Socialist Germany

Die Hitlerjugend
Jeunesses hitlériennes
The Hitler Youth

DAY EIGHT—Cologne, Germany—Saturday, 12 April 41—1:44
PM
Konni Ritter's wife, the Baroness von Lindenbach, was young Adair
Schneider's neighbor. His parents owned the villa two doors down
from hers. Thirteen years old, a tall, lean boy, Adair struck an almost
comical pose in his outgrown mustard-tan khaki Hitler Youth uniform
as he stood on the landing in the Cologne train station, awaiting the
arrival of the train from Paris. He had grown a full hand taller since
the uniform's first donning, and his pant legs exposed the entirety of
his skinny ankles. In his hand he held a letter addressed to a Major
von Gerz from the baroness. It was his very proud duty to serve as
messenger and deliver her news to a Wehrmacht officer. The
baroness' butler had rewarded the boy with one mark for the task's
expedient completion, but Adair would have done it most certainly
for free. A Wehrmacht major! After all!

He heard the shrill train whistle, a long cadence then short
blasts, even before he could see the train. Soon, the great black
mammoth of iron gadgetry slowly chugged around the bend of tracks
heading toward the station entrance, plumes of charcoal smoke
pumping from its stovepipe and blasts of white steam spitting from its
gills. It crept to a near standstill, then suddenly reversed its steel
wheels on the track and raced the great engine, bringing itself to a
sudden stop, slamming the trailing cars together with a series of
clanks and bangs. A giant cloud of steam was released onto the
platform as the train's cabin doors started flying open.

The boy approached the first car, chanting his announcement
over and over: "I call for Major von Gerz!" He raised the letter high
above his head. "I call for Major von Gerz! Call for Major von Gerz!"
A flood of people poured from the train's doors. Many of them, many

more than Adair expected, were German soldiers. "Call for Major von Gerz! I call for Major . . ."

"Here, lad!" a voice called out from the doorstep just behind Adair. "I am Major von Gerz."

The young Hitler Youth rushed to stand in front of the compartment's steps and jumped to attention, jerking his right arm high into the air. "Heil Hitler, Herr Major! And I welcome you to Cologne!"

Rolf stepped onto the platform, clicked his heels, and saluted the boy. "Heil Hitler, my young comrade."

"I have for you, sir, a letter from the Baroness von Lindenbach." The boy took Rolf's bag. "The baroness has fallen ill. She regrets that she must ask you to wait until Monday to call on her." Adair smiled, handing Rolf the letter. "Two rooms have been reserved for you and your adjutant at the Hotel Dom for tonight and tomorrow night." The boy grabbed up Gep's bag as well, gave him a hasty Hitlergrüß, and turned to leave, expecting to be followed. "Follow me, Herr Major. I will take you there."

After a few steps he turned and stopped suddenly, watching the major take the hand of a beautiful lady as she descended the coach steps. Then he noticed the major's adjutant, he was an Oberleutnant the boy discerned by his chevrons, who was pointing out a number of luggage pieces to a baggage porter.

"I'm afraid, comrade, we will need three rooms," Rolf quipped as he helped the lady straighten her fur.

"Three rooms. But of course." The boy choked and coughed a little. "Yes. Three rooms. It is Easter weekend. But yes, I am sure that can be arranged." The boy dropped the bags he was toting and stood before Addie. He clicked his heels and started to give the Hitlergrüß again, then thought suddenly better of it and bowed elegantly instead. She was no doubt French, after all. "I kiss the hand, mademoiselle." Again Adair clicked his heels, folded his left arm squarely behind his back, and took Addie's hand with his right and kissed it. Then very quickly, he snapped back to attention and moved over to the old gray-haired porter.

"I command you to deliver mademoiselle's luggage to the Hotel Dom." Adair displayed imperious, inbred airs he no doubt used in all dealings with the servant class. "And you will do so with all due care and haste. Is that quite clear?"

"Ja," the sweet-faced old fellow said, removing his flat cap and bowing. "*Alles klar*, young master."

Adair then turned to his charges as the porter snugged his cap in place and started loading Addie's luggage. The boy tossed his head to the side and politely announced, "And now, if you will follow me."

Addie and Rolf did as they were asked, while Gep turned to the porter. Handing him a one-mark coin, he widened his eyes at the old man and smiled. The porter knowingly smiled back, cocked his head, and just shrugged, adding, "The luggage will arrive at the hotel by horse cart within the quarter hour."

They proceeded down the stairs, and once inside the station, Addie was struck by the sight that opened up on display before her. The beige tile walls, the squeaky-clean glass, and the silver steel trimmings all sparkled like pearl and crystal and chrome. The station teemed with life. At least a thousand people were rushing and bustling this way and that, but in such an orderly, quiet fashion, with such a grace of motion, it was unlike anything she had ever seen. And the exorbitant abundance of everything that could possibly be edible in the world struck her as almost vulgar. The station was a cornucopia of feeding possibilities. As they passed each set of stairs leading back up to the trains, small passages led to her right and left, and in each were pairs of shops and stands and kiosks selling anything and everything. She couldn't help but lag behind the men as she continued down the station's wide grand hall. Her head spun back and forth. She never thought there would ever be this kind of abundance in the wartime world again!

There were baker stands selling black, brown, and caramel-colored breads with shiny turtle shell, knotted, or seeded tops. Pretzel carts displayed their twisted and looped wares—some of which were shaped like swastikas—stacked high on rods or hung over clothesline strings. Pastry stands sold sugar-dusted marzipan tortes, prasselkuchen and flaky filo oxen ears with a thick sugar glaze. She passed smoldering grills where sausages sizzled and pig knuckles and chestnuts crackled and popped. There were spits roasting hens and ducks and shoat hocks. A pyramid of oranges was stacked on a tabletop where fat, rosy-cheeked women were squeezing them into thick, pulpy juice. Buxom tobacco girls were selling cigars, exotic tobaccos, and scores of different brands of cigarettes from trays strung from their shoulders. There were stands where men stood smoking and drinking beer in the tiniest of glasses.

Just the combination of aromas—the bread, the tobacco, the grilled meats—was in itself the most intoxicating thing she'd witnessed in almost a year. But her euphoria suddenly melted into disgust as she remembered how Parisians, especially of the lesser classes, were nearly starving to death. And just look at this revolting display!

"Are you coming?" Gep quipped, holding his hand out for Addie to catch up. "Makes you hungry, doesn't it?"

"I've been hungry for a year, Gep. This just makes me . . . mad."

"We'll get settled in the hotel and take some lunch. But you have to keep up. You don't have papers, remember? I assure you, you don't want to be caught in Germany without papers!"

"Yes, I'm quite certain I don't. I'm coming."

Throughout the station red banners with white circles emblazoned with bold, black swastikas hung from every possible and visible wall or window. One huge banner above the entrance of the station's grand foyer displayed the rune-lettered words *Deutschland siegt an allen Fronten*. Addie knew the translation of these words. A much grander banner displaying those words had hung from the Eiffel Tower in Paris for months after the occupation began. The exclamation translated as *Germany is victorious on all fronts*!

Around the foyer's perimeter there were long draped tables with all sorts of Nazi trinketry and regalia on display. Boys dressed like Adair in their cross-belted Nazi scouting uniforms with red swastika armbands manned the displays as did girls in pleated navy skirts and white peasant blouses with more subtle swastika collar patches. On the tables lay every sort of possible swastika-laden thing. There were thimbles, pins, broaches. Shaving cups, shaving brushes, pillboxes. Silverware, tea sets, dishes. Pocketknives, hunting knives, flashlights. Combs, brushes, scissors. Toy trucks, toy tanks, toy Wehrmacht soldiers. Board games, playing cards, even collectable bubble gum cards that displayed Nazi Party or Wehrmacht heroes the way baseball and movie stars appeared on bubble gum cards collected by kids in America!

Gep held the door for her. As she walked out into the bright morning sun, she continued looking over her shoulder at the spellbinding displays. When she turned around, her whole body snapped in a start. Her knees actually went weak.

"Holy sh . . . Mother of Jesus!" She said it in English. Heads snapped around to gawk at her. Rolf smiled as he went back to where she was frozen looking upward into the heavens.

"It's overwhelming, isn't it?" he said in English as he approached her.

"Oh, my word! It's as though I walked out of the train station and I'm suddenly standing in the very presence of God!"

"I think that was probably the idea when they built it."

Before them stood the gigantic gothic cathedral of Cologne. Its prickly twin spires, streaked in blacks and grays with shadowy patches of green moss, rose up perfectly plumb against the powder-blue sky. When she had composed herself, Addie rushed ahead up the steps of the promontory where at least a section of the cathedral had stood for more than six hundred years. When Rolf and Gep caught up to her, she spun around and quipped, "Oh, darlings, this is what it feels like to be an ant!"

"It holds the relics of the three magi," Gep boasted.

"You mean, 'We three kings'?"

He nodded.

"It is extraordinary, major. It seems more like a dream, more a vision than a reality."

"Come," Adair interjected. "The hotel is just across the square. You'll be able to enjoy the cathedral from your very rooms."

"But you must understand, it is Easter weekend," the mustached desk clerk of the Dom Hotel pleaded. "All I have are the two rooms. One of them is a large two-room suite. If the officers would not mind, I could have a bed added to the suite's sitting room?"

"That most certainly will not do!" young Adair scolded. "I will have immediate words with the manager! You will summon him forthwith!"

"Your hospitality is greatly appreciated, young Sturmführer," Rolf said, placing his hand on Adair's shoulder. "But the Oberleutnant and I will be perfectly comfortable sharing the suite."

"Are you quite certain, major?" The boy's eyes were wide with fervor. "For I am more than happy to intercede."

"You've done more than either of us could have ever expected." Gep stepped up and clicked his heels. "Young Adair, I salute you. You shall make a fine Junker quite soon!"

Adair snapped to attention. No greater praise had ever been bestowed upon him. *Junker. A cadet. Someday . . . an officer!* He couldn't have been more proud of himself.

"It is my honor and privilege to be of some service to officers in our great German army, fighting in our struggle to restore purity and honor to Aryan Europe." He saluted Gep and then did the same to Rolf. The gushing continued. "I will take my leave now as I am certain you are both tired from your long journey and have many important war-related matters to discuss. I add only that the Baroness von Lindenbach has instructed me to inform you that she will have her driver fetch you at nine sharp on Monday morning."

He took a perfunctory step backward.

"With that, I bid you both auf Wiedersehen and"—he snapped his arm straight into the air—"Heil Hitler!" He then turned to Addie and bowed politely, adding, "Mademoiselle, adieu." And one of Adolf Hitler's most true-blue youths turned and vanished out into the warm spring day.

"Well," Addie said in French, "I didn't comprehend a single word of that, but I can tell you if that lad would have stayed around another two minutes, I believe that poor thing might very well have spotted himself!"

Rolf, Gep, the hotel clerk, and even the bellman burst into raucous laughter. When they had composed themselves, the desk clerk handed a key to the bellman.

He too switched to French. "The officers will be in suite 203, and for the lady, 202. No wait, you're French, aren't you?"

"I'm from Paris and I speak French. Will that do?"

"But of course it will. I have just the room for you. Mademoiselle will take room 206." He raised his eyebrows and smiled.

Addie gave him a puzzled look.

The clerk summoned her closer with his finger, then whispered. "It's the Mata Hari room!"

43

Easter Sunday, 13 April 1941

Die Passion
La passion
The Passion

DAY NINE—Cologne—Sunday, 13 April 41—10:53 AM
With glorious indifference, the bells of the monolithic cathedral of
Cologne tolled on as they had on the quarter hour since eight that
morning. A bright Easter sun had risen in the cobalt skies over the
Rhine and cast a brilliant sheen on the whitewashed, half-timbered
city of slate gray and red tile roofs. In the shadows of buildings,
patches of nighttime frost awaited their inevitable doom as the sunlit
warmth of the new day crept closer with each passing minute. In the
vast cobblestone square between the cathedral and the Dom Hotel,
groups of people strolled slowly along toward the Easter Mass
celebration, many in their *trachtenkleider*, traditional clothes;
lederhosen and smart wool waistcoats for the men, and intricately
embroidered dirndl skirts and wool capes for the women. Members of
the military in their dress uniforms, with smartly shined shoes and
sparkling buttons, escorted finely furred women in new spring hats.
And it seemed each passing little girl's bouncy locks were adorned
with more brilliant fresh flowers than the last.

"Guten Morgen," Gep declared, as he came from the parade's
midst and made his way through the crowded outdoor café attached to
the hotel. He snaked his way over to where Rolf and Addie sat in the
bright sun, as a waiter was pouring bubbly Sekt into strawberry-laden
Villeroy & Boch flutes. "Have you ever seen such a fine morning?"
Gep added, in French.

"So, there you are, Gep, my man." Rolf pulled his sunglasses
down on his nose and peered at him under the bill of his hat. "Where
on earth have you been?"

"Ambling along the Rheinufer, enjoying the morning. The early
bird gets the sunshine!" Gep said as he took his seat, nodding at the
waiter's polite bow and unspoken offer of champagne. "Some of us,
you see, get up in the morning."

"A real bed." Rolf took his glass and held it up to Addie's and Gep's. "Truly, the best night's sleep in two weeks." Glasses were clinked and sips were taken. Rolf smiled coyly as he added, "The one at the Lutetia is so tiny."

Addie raised the floppy bill of her big spring hat, slid her own sunglasses down her nose, and leered dramatically at him. *Don't try to tell me about a little bed!* She could see Rolf's eyes smiling behind his dark lenses.

"I am astonished at the parade of people making off for mass," Addie remarked, realigning her napkin in her lap as she scooted her chair closer to the table. The waiter hastened to her in order to assist, but did so too late. "I guess I didn't think church was allowed in the New Germany."

"This is Cologne, Addie," Gep interjected. "The very heart of Catholic Germany. The Party has found it less attracted to National Socialist enlightenment."

"Still, I find it shocking and, I guess, delightful," Addie confessed.

"It's Easter, my friends. And the end of the self-deprivations of Lent." Rolf looked at the gray-haired waiter. "We'll take one of everything." The waiter simply nodded and smiled.

"Well, Lent certainly isn't over for France," Addie remarked, coldly remembering the misfortunes of her friends in Paris. "And shan't be for some time, I am quite sure."

"And, it seems not for Germany either, my dear." Gep took the Saturday edition of *Kölner Stadt-Anzeiger* from under his arm and read the front-page headline: *"A Call for Wartime Self-Discipline! Führer Commands, We Follow!"* Gep took his cigarette lighter from his pocket and held it up to Rolf, before the major had taken his cigarette completely from its case. Cigarette lit, Gep sat back in his chair and held the paper out to the sunlight, translating into French as he read:

> *"As the mighty armies of the Reich progress to victory in the deserts of North Africa, in the burning skies over England and now in the Balkans, I call on all Germans to continue and, yes, even to elevate your attitude of conservation and self-denial. As families and comrades throughout our vast German Reich take part this weekend in this great Feast of Spring . . ."*

Gep stopped and looked at Addie and Rolf. "That of course would mean Easter." He tilted his head back, shook the paper, and read on.

> "...*remember our brave lads in the field and in the skies and on the ships. Think of their hardships! Do you really need that second slice of bread? Those new shoes? Are you donating every week to Winter Relief? Do you cook Eintopf only once a week, or many times?*"

Addie furrowed her brow. *Eintopf?*

"A single this-and-that leftover stew rather than set meals," Rolf interjected.

"So." Gep folded his paper and took another sip of the Sekt. "You can clearly see, as war expands, belts must tighten."

"I hardly think giving up a slice of bread compares to what the French are dealing with," Addie scolded. "And no doubt, the Poles and God only knows who else."

"I appreciate your concerns, Adelaide." Gep turned his coffee cup upright as the white-gloved, oblivious waiter poured a steamy cup of coffee for Addie from a heavy silver pot. "But my dear, to the victors go the spoils. I am afraid it's been that way for centuries and will continue for centuries to come. Think your British friends aren't occupiers? India, China, Palestine, Egypt?"

"Let's, shall we, move on to other topics of conversation," Rolf interjected, the smoke from his cigarette swirling gently as it drifted above him. "How was your night's rest, Miss. Bridges?"

"Quite extraordinary," she answered. "This note was slipped under my door when I returned from my bath. It was from the manager. In it, he explains the history of my room, room 206. The very room where the devilish seductress Mata Hari would rendezvous with her German officer during the Great War, feeding him information from the French front."

"Poppycock," Gep said. "Such rumors are spread by hoteliers to fill up rooms. The woman was little more than a courtesan to many officers—French, British, and German—and would have been shot by us if the British hadn't spared us the bullet!"

"Gep, why must you take all the fun out of everything?" Addie asked, pronounced chagrin in her eyes. "I think it's just swell, and I will believe it true just to spite you!"

"Regardless, you slept well," Rolf interjected.

"Seldom have I slept better."

"So, how shall we spend this perfectly marvelous Easter day in beautiful Cologne?" Rolf went on to ask.

"Well, I simply must see the cathedral at some point," Addie implored, dropping a lump of sugar into her coffee and stirring it with the polished silver spoon.

"And see it you shall." Gep took a cautious sip of his coffee, his eyes squinting as he did. He licked his lips and continued. "As I have arranged for us to attend the Choral Evening tonight at the cathedral. Selections from the *Matthäus-Passion*. The Passion of St. Matthew."

"Oh, Rolf, I love Bach." She placed her hand on his forearm. "What on earth shall I wear?"

"Thank you, Oberleutnant." Had Rolf's gratitude been sincere, it would have been, "Thank you, Gep."

"Surely, major."

"And until then?" Rolf took a puff and skewed his lips to blow the smoke up and away from them.

"Well, I absolutely must take a quick jaunt up there!" Addie pointed up at the great bridge across the Rhine, visible above the rooftops.

"Yes, you should," Gep interjected, looking at the menu. "And the two of you should also take a stroll along the Rheinüfer."

"You're not coming, Gep? But you must."

"I am going to call on an old friend of mine here in Cologne."

"Are you now?" Rolf's head tilted toward him, jaw clenched tightly.

"With your permission, major." A playful gleam grew in Gep's eyes. "And yours, of course, Miss. Bridges. An old friend I haven't seen in years."

"But of course, Gep, darling. I insist that you do just that." She looked down at the menu, then glanced back up at Gep and winked. "I know the major will be more than happy to squire me around Cologne this wonderful day."

"And who exactly is this 'friend?'" Rolf's eyes never left him. Gep looked into the sky.

"A name, Oberleutnant. Spit it out."

"I plan to be gone all day, sir."

"What?" Rolf frowned, puzzled.

"It's a woman, silly," Addie scolded, clenching Rolf's forearm with both her hands and shaking him. "And you're supposed to be the detective."

DAY NINE—Cologne—Sunday, 13 April 41—3:09 PM
The sunny calm of the afternoon made even sweaters and jackets uncomfortably warm. Rolf escorted Addie along the wide boardwalk over the magnificent Hohenzollern Bridge across the Rhine. The great web work of reddish steel girders and beams creaked and swayed as trains now and then crept slowly across from Deutz on the east bank of the river to Cologne. Each time Addie would clench Rolf's arm and close her eyes until the roaring and shaking stopped. From the bridge Addie noticed the huge red sign of the Ford-Werke, the manufacturing offices of the German division of Ford Motor Company. She thought of Konni and the many times he must have called on them. As they returned from the Deutz side of the bridge, both secretly wished for another train that unfortunately never showed.

The stroll along the banks of the Rhine, the Rheinufer, was "just delicious," as Addie put it. The promenade was packed with old people, children, couples lazily enjoying the sunshine and soothing rustle of the great gray river's rush. They took seats at one of the cheery, flower-bedecked outdoor cafés along the river front. Boughs of thick purple clematis dripped from overhead latticework, and dark-yellow, blue-throated pansies and red Gladiolus spilled over planters around the shady perimeter. They ordered drinks, coffee for him, a Coca-Cola for her. Rolf removed his hat and hung it on a small hook located at each corner under the table.

"I have to confess something," Rolf said, opening his cigarette tin and offering Addie an Ernst Udet. He lit hers with his gold-plated lighter, then his own as he continued.

"I've never really known an American. Are they all as unfettered and direct as you?"

"No, I think I am probably just about the worst."

He laughed.

"What brought you to Paris?"

"After two academically unremarkable, yet socially quite satisfying years at Pembroke in New England, I convinced my daddy to let me study in Paris for a year."

Rolf was captivated by her supple complexion and the girlish web of frayed, very faint red tracks in her rosy cheeks. The soft breeze made her hair gravitate to the corner of her mouth, forcing her to remove it with her dainty little finger. Then there was the subtle

bounce of her button nose and the tossing of a word now and then
with the dip of her head and a shoulder as she spoke.

"So, in the fall of '36, I came to Paris, a completely naïve,
lonely, and childishly frightened girl. I attended university, perfected
my French, studied French art, literature, and especially French food.
That's when I took the apartment in the rue du Cherche-Midi and first
visited the Club l'Heure Bleue. When my year was up, I bought
another six months doing 'character-building' work (as I
convincingly put it to daddy) at the American Hospital.
Intercontinental communication with my dear daddy was
accomplished with ten-word *economy* telegrams, if you can believe
that. Daddy is a disgustingly rich business and industry banker who
could probably buy Western Union, yet he finds a way to say all he
has to say to his only daughter in ten short words.

"So, when I was within a week of sailing home, after a solid
score of ten-word pleas and denials, I wired him demanding that I be
allowed to remain in Paris. He wired back his own demand, telling
me to return home at once. I taxied immediately to the post office and
wired him right back!"

She sat forward in her chair and used her pointer finger to tap
out each word on an imaginary blackboard above her head:

"FATHER STOP
STAYING PARIS STOP TOOK COCKTAIL WAITRESS
JOB STOP
GOOD PAY PEOPLE FULL STOP
ADELAIDE"

"So, late that night, a knock at my door, another wire."
"SISSYPIE STOP
SEE M-MORESTEAD FIRST AMERICAN BANK CHAMPS
ELYEES STOP JOB STOP CONVINCED MUM FULL STOP
DADDY DEAR"

As they were talking, Addie noticed over Rolf's shoulder a tiny
woman approaching, pushing a tattered baby carriage. The woman
never looked up, moving just quickly enough to propel herself on
down the quay, obviously trying not to draw attention to herself. A
rush ran through Addie when she then noticed the woman's yellow
bandana around her head, a practice dating back centuries, requiring
Jews to wear distinguishing headwear, still being followed more as a
custom, especially by the Jewish peasantry in much of Catholic
Europe. *Absurd*, she thought.

268

"What's wrong?" Rolf asked, not looking over his shoulder but dipping his eyebrow, aware that something had disturbed her.

"Just another aspect of Germany I find it difficult to come to terms with."

Now he did look around but failed to see the woman, overlooking her.

"I'm sorry, I don't see the—"

Suddenly, Addie shrieked, "My god, Rolf! They're going to kill her!"

Two SS soldiers stood in the Jewish woman's path. One held her up by the throat and slugged her as forcefully as he would any man. The little woman fell limp into a flower bed of tulips and daffodils.

"You shit-Jew! This is a sidewalk for Germans! And on Easter, no less," the soldier said as he kicked her, hard, his boot finding bone in her rump.

"I'm German!" the dazed woman shrieked. "My husband died in the war for Germany!"

"Good," the other soldier said, pulling the woman up by her hair. "That's one less Jew dog in the world!" Then he kicked the baby carriage, sending it hurling into the café's entrance.

Addie's second shriek was joined by gasps and groans from other women sitting in the café. Rolf quickly donned his hat and was on top of the carriage, righting it. Everyone sighed to see it was only full of soiled clothes and sundry personal possessions, not a baby! He rushed to stand over the woman and barked at the SS men. He pointed toward the café as he shouted more reprimands at the pair. The Jewish woman took this interlude as an opportunity to escape. Reeling, barely able to walk, the entire side of her face already red and swollen, she gathered her things and hurried away from the quay along an alleyway to disappear into the city.

Addie slowly stood. She wanted to do something but knew she was powerless. She watched in shock as the two SS men argued with Rolf. She couldn't understand what was being said, but she could see Rolf's rage, could tell he was having to defend himself, pointing to the café. There was a fire in his eyes unlike anything she had ever seen. Then he pulled out his Moleskine and pen, obviously demanding the names of the pair. Immediately, they both were transformed from drunken Nazi thugs into SS gentlemen soldiers. Satisfied with their newfound demeanor, Rolf ordered them on their way with an indignant jerk of his head and stormed back into the café to a remarkable display of disinterest from everyone seated at their tables. Addie was sickened at how the whole affair was discounted by everyone as quickly as it had occurred.

"I'm sorry you had to see that," Rolf said intentionally in English, taking his seat and wiping beads of sweat from his upper lip. "Let's not let it ruin a perfect afternoon."

"How do you coexist with such displays, Rolf? I know you're a better man than that. How do you, how does everyone just ignore it?"

Rolf's nostrils flared. "I didn't ignore it!"

"No, but you didn't stop them because it was wrong. You stopped them because it was unsightly!"

The look on her face made his chest ache. He didn't say anything, just stared at her. And stewed.

"Rolf, I don't speak German, but I can read body language. You had no intention of—"

"Don't tell me of my intentions." The rage in him was frightening. "This is the new Germany. The Jew should know her place. Walking the streets of Cologne on Easter Sunday is not the place for the smart Jew. My intention was to stop the woman's flogging, and I stopped it. Whether my methods met your approval or not is entirely inconsequential to me."

"Oh, Rolf, darling, please forgive me my naïve nature. This sort of thing happens in America too—with Jews, Negroes, God knows who else. And I'm as guilty as anyone else when it comes to the snide jokes. I grew up in a home that preached the separation of the classes and races, and for the most part I probably concur. I know these things happen. But here, they're policy." She tilted her head down and looked under the bill of his hat.

"Rolf, darling, beastly behavior like that to anyone, to any of God's creatures, should never be acceptable to any modern-day Christian, American or German."

She reached across and softly placed her hand on his.

"Please, Rolf, I know you did what you could, and I am proud of you. You were the only one in this entire café who did anything at all. I'm sure I have no idea the courage and valor it took to step up like that. It was all just such a disgusting shock to me. You're right. Let's not let it ruin this beautiful day."

Still looking down, he nodded a few times, his jaw still clenched. Then, finally calmed, he raised his head and smiled at her.

"Yes, we should get back to the hotel," he said. "The St. Matthew Passion could be quite lengthy."

"I have a hair dresser scheduled at 4:00." Addie looked at her Bulova. "God knows what on earth I'll wear."

The waiter brought Addie her third Coca-Cola, ordered before all the chaos ensued. He said something in German to Rolf, then shrugged his shoulders and gave a snarl and a weary-eyed pout.

"He says," Rolf translated for her, "it seems this is the last bottle of Coca-Cola in the restaurant, possibly in all the Reich. His supplier tells him the American embargo has cut off syrup shipments from . . . 'Atlantis.'" Rolf hesitated briefly for effect and smiled at the waiter's misunderstanding of the city's name, then went on. "Germany's supply of syrup has been exhausted. He says to tell you, if you order another bottle, it will have to be a brand known as Fanta!"

With a pleasant smile, the waiter set a clean branded glass in front of her, turning it so the Coca-Cola label was directed at her. He cradled the precious bottle and displayed it before each of them as though it were the finest Bordeaux.

Addie looked up at him, pleadingly.

"Oh, darling. Could you put it in a Dixie?"

Oblivious to English, the waiter looked at Rolf, puzzled.

Rolf smiled.

"*Mitnehmen.*"

DAY NINE—Cologne—Sunday, 13 April 41—6:00 PM

Adelaide Bridges was the most stunning creature as Rolf watched her enter the foyer before the second-floor stairwell where they had agreed to meet. *How is such a beautiful woman able take her appearance to the next level?* he thought. He stood up, then froze for a moment so he could take her in. Her black dress—satin and lace— embraced her shapely form and flowed down to a heap of trailing foam at her high heels. Its winged collar toyed with her peachy cheek and a movie-star perfection blossomed in her beautiful face as her red lips smiled at him. Her updo was draped perfectly over her left eye and around her head, held in place by a small black hat with blue and purple feathers and a dark-blue lace half veil. Lancel leather evening gloves ran to her elbows, and a mink stole and diamond necklace and earbobs completed the picture of enchanting glamour like nothing Rolf had seen since the death of his wife. The thought of wearing this dazzling woman on his arm tonight made him glow.

Clouds had moved in, and a chill had returned to the early afternoon air as they left the Dom Hotel and joined the gathering procession of Choral Evening attendees strolling to the cathedral. She rested her gloved hand inside Rolf's arm and he laid his hand over it, touching the long, elegant fingers under the soft leather. As they made their way into the cathedral, she delighted in his freshly shaved, very manly scent. Smiling discretely, she thought, *This is, after all, Cologne!*

They entered the cathedral and made their way to the front, where Gep and his attractive lady friend were holding places for them. There was something about having Addie at Rolf's side that somehow, this night, filled an empty hunger within him. He missed touching a woman's evening-gloved hand. Holding it, the way the tiny bones moved soft and fragile under the warm kid leather. Like holding a swallow.

They took their seats as the huge chorale assembly and orchestra started the poignant, beautiful Easter cantata. Rolf reluctantly released her hand and sat in erect and stoic German propriety in the pew. But by the start of the "O Haupt voll Blut und Wunden," Addie's hand had wormed its way back under his arm. Her cheek found his shoulder. With undetectable guile, he turned his head until his cheek barely touched her hat. Everything about her always smelled the glorious same. He didn't know the name of the soft, sweet scent, but he would not soon forget it. It reminded him of one of his mother's garden parties. Discreetly, he looked down and watched the hypnotic fall and the rise of her breasts under the black lace and satin. He turned his head away and took a deep breath and let it out.

Addie could feel his eyes on her. She squirmed and nestled herself closer to him, realizing she wasn't just being ogled. She was being adored.

Back at the Dom Hotel starlight turned everything blue in the Mata Hari room. It was silent and dark in the huge suite. The silhouette of the massive cathedral shone against the starry sky through the room's four giant windows. Rolf's first touch was the faint stroke of his knuckle down the side of Addie's neck. Slow. Relaxed. She smiled with wonder and approval. Reaching up, she slowly ran her fingers over the shortly cropped hair above his ears, then down his solid neck and around to his cheek.

He kissed her.

She threw her arms around him.

"We'll never have this again, Rolf, darling," she groaned as she nibbled his neck. "All these explosions in us. This anticipation. Make it last, my love, last as long as we can." Her lips toyed playfully with his ear as she went on. "This night's going to take all night. I'm going to make you wait until we both ache with longing for each other."

That magic knuckle pressed against her lips, then slid them this way and that as he spoke.

"You talk too much," he said in French.

"Speak English to me, Rolf. When I make love to the man I love, I want it to be in English. I want to tell you how I feel. I want to use words like 'cherish.' Like 'desire.' And 'luscious.'"

He his eyes smiled as he said, "But those are French words, Addie!"

They laughed and hugged each other.

He held her away from him.

"English. All right then, English." Rolf made a small circular motion with his finger and continued, "Turn around. My beautiful darling. I'm going to undress you now."

She smiled widely. Closed her eyes. Inhaled deeply. And did as commanded.

Her zipper seemed to creep one tooth at a time. And there was the tender touch of that knuckle, following the zipper slowly down her spine. The tiny blond hairs on her bare back went erect under her goose bumps. As he skimmed the gown away with the sides of his hands, she unpinned her hat and threw it off somewhere, then snapped off her earrings and tossed them somewhere else.

Like ten feathers, his fingertips moved slowly across her shoulders until the gown was loosed, first on one side, then on both, and plunged to a heap at her ankles. His fingers then slipped down her soft, warm belly into her slip and panties, then slid around to her hips and downward. The lingerie came finally free at her knees and joined the dress on the floor. In nothing but her silk hosiery, she turned to him, naked, and looked into his eyes.

In the fireplace an ember avalanche brought a brief glow of flame. The golden flickering light danced in her huge, sassy brown eyes.

"I am very fortunate to have won your heart, Adelaide." He pulled her to him and kissed her bare shoulder.

"You didn't just win my heart, Rolf, my love. You laid siege to it the moment my eyes met yours across that courtyard that morning."

44

Marseilles, Vichy France

Monday, 14 April 1941

Der Milchmann
Le laitier
The Milkman

DAY TEN—Marseilles—Monday, 14 April 41—6:06 AM
Henri Jordan had helped his father on the dairy farm and on the
delivery wagon for seven years now. He was fifteen. He had always
followed his father's instructions and had even run the milk route by
himself when his father had taken ill last year. But this last command
his father had issued yesterday made no sense to him at all. Why
would he be told to ruin five perfectly good wooden milk cases?
Sawing out the center wooden dividers that kept the one-liter glass
bottles from hitting each other. And the bottoms as well. They would
all be ruined! This certainly made no sense to Henri, no, not all!

The canvas-covered milk wagon and team had stopped at the
side of the Poseidon Hotel as it did every morning around six thirty.
The sun was just clearing the mountain and gulls could be heard
barking down at the old port of Marseilles. Henri's father had taken
the first stack of milk cases into the hotel and was returning with the
empties stacked on his two-wheel dolly. At the sound of his father's
whistle, Henri scampered down the wooden gangplank and bent down
to help his father back up the ramp, Henri pushing the stack from the
bottom. Once inside, the old man inspected the stacks of full milk
cases. There was indeed a cavity in the front right corner of the
wagon as he had commanded, but Henri had left no way to access it.
Explaining this to his son, the boy lifted one of the heavy Hussar
sacks full of ice from the damp stacks and pulled out a few so the
cavity could indeed be accessed.

The second stack of milk the farmer wheeled into the Poseidon
Hotel was one filled with five empty, bottomless cases. Within
minutes he returned. Again he whistled at Henri, and the boy bounced
down the ramp and helped his father run quickly back up and into the

wagon. The rear flap flopped down. The only light was from an isinglass slit in the curtain flap.

Inside, like a circus magic act Henri had once seen, his father removed the wooden cases one at a time and a tiny, very beautiful, shivering blond woman suddenly appeared, wrapped in a wool blanket. She quickly hid in the cavity Henri had created as he moved the stacks of milk back in place. Strapping them tightly to the sides of the wagon, he covered her milk-wagon burrow with a bag of ice.

Frightened, Henri looked down from where he had lunged himself onto the stacks of milk to settle the ice sack over the woman, imploring of his father, "Why, papa?"

Papa pulled his son down from the stacks and took him by the shoulder, looked into his confused eyes, and said, "You shall know only this. On the street in front of the hotel there is a blue Peugeot. The man in that motorcar is a German. This woman is French." With that, Papa put the side of his index finger to his lips and twisted his hand, hard. Henri smiled and did the same. Enough was said. Lips were sealed.

The milk wagon rounded the corner and passed in front of the hotel. The matched team of huge Belgian horses high-stepped, their front hooves smashing their heavy iron shoes on the stone. Steadying themselves to descend the perilous hill, their dinner-plate hooves stomped and clicked loudly on the quiet street. Soon, they came to the blue Peugeot where a bald man with a few days' stubble on his stern face wearing a green corduroy jacket watched them intently. But he seemed to be anxious for the wagon to clear his sight line so he could once again keep his eye on both the front and side doors of the hotel.

The clanking of jostling milk bottles was deafening as the heavy wagon jerked and swayed over the cobblestone and started down the hill. Henri's father sat atop the wagon with the reins and worked the front brake while Henri held fast to the rear brake handle from behind, the wagon pulling him down the street as if he were skating on ice. As it passed the Peugeot, water dripping from every crack and seam in the wagon's heavy oaken floor, Henri looked over his bouncing shoulder at the man in the car, tipped his cap, and said, "Bonjour, monsieur."

The man flopped his hand in acknowledgement and tilted his head to once again cast his gaze and the hotel's entrance. Satisfied, he flapped his newspaper open, drew heavily on his cigarette, and blew thick smoke into the morning breeze floating in off the sea.

Henri now smiled proudly as he skated on down the bumpy hill toward the old port of Marseille.

DAY TEN—Marseilles, Vieux Port—Monday, 14 April 41—6:58 AM

In the whitewashed Hotel Côte d'Azur on the old port, the window to Rutgers Heht's room was open to the back street. For some time he heard the clinking of milk bottles growing louder in the salty morning breeze. When the milk wagon came into view, Ruti's heart fluttered. A few minutes later a knock came at his door.

"Ménagère. Housekeeper," a sweet voice announced.

Ruti threw the door open, and the tiny blonde in a powder-gray chambermaid uniform froze for a second and glared at the totally bald man in front of her. Then she ran and jumped on him, sobbing uncontrollably. She locked her ankles behind him and her arms around his neck, kissing him and wailing. He scooped his arm under her firm rump, waddled to the door, and closed it with his foot. Then, laughing joyously, he stumbled backward into the room and fell onto the springy bed.

45

Cologne

Die Baronin
La baronne
The Baroness

DAY TEN—Cologne—Monday, 14 April 41—10:03 AM
The tires of the gun-barrel-blue Maybach W5SG crunched acorns and
pine cones as it pulled onto the damp brick drive of the von
Lindenbach villa in a quiet, affluent suburb of Cologne. A soft, gray
drizzle swirled through the chilly spring air. The driver opened the
motorcar's rear door and watched the crisply uniformed Wehrmacht
major and his adjutant stride through the foggy morning to the stone
villa's black oaken door. A lonesome lark's call echoed through the
tops of the estate's budding larches as the major tapped on the door
with his cane. It opened, and a tiny old woman continued some
previously initiated conversation with herself.
 "Who could it be at this time of day? *Ja, ja, ja.* How may I help
you?"
 "Guten Tag," Rolf said, bowing and clicking his heels. "Major
von Gerz. The baroness is expecting me."
 To his astonishment, the door suddenly closed in his face.
"Some young major, this one," she yelled. "You are expecting him?"
Rolf heard a muffled voice, then from the old woman, *"Ja, ja. Ja, ja.*
Already a fire in the study. *Ja, ja. Alles klar."* She reopened the door
and abruptly barked, "Come in. You will await the baroness in the
study. A good, warm fire there." Rolf and Gep followed the little
dwarf of a woman into a high-ceilinged cherrywood-choked study full
of ancient volumes, tapestries, and a huge mahogany mantel clock
that tick-tocked regally. Once inside, the little woman suddenly
stopped and spun around to face them. "Kaffee, schnapps, oder
brandy?"
 "A coffee will do me nicely, thank you," a startled Gep
answered.
 "For me as well," Rolf added.
 One finger at a time, Rolf removed his brown leather gloves
and seated himself in a royal maroon Biedermeier chair. Folding the

gloves over the end of his cane, he rested his naked wrist over them, crossed his legs, raised his chin, and stoically glanced around the room, waiting for the wife of Konni Ritter.

In a few moments, the baroness floated into the room like an aberration, dressed to the hilt, with long sections of her gown floating behind her. Her wrinkled face was caked in makeup and thick lipstick. Her hair was an obvious brunette wig.

"*Guten Morgen,* gentlemen."

As Rolf and Gep arose from their chairs, she took a set of tortoiseshell lorgnettes, held the opera glasses up to her nose with the long handle, and came straight up to both of them.

"Let me look at you." She studied them both for an uncomfortable few moments, then went to Rolf and said, "I make my decision on how I feel toward a person within the first minute of meeting them, major. I assess you as being a nobleman, probably Prussian, and I think I like you." She then cocked her head toward Gep and added, "But this other fellow. Not so much."

Rolf tried to suppress a smile.

"He seems quite the snippety sort," she added.

"Oh, but he is, baroness. He is the most snippety of sorts."

Suddenly, the old woman burst out into laughter, slapping a bewildered Gep on the shoulder. "I get this sort of playful fervor from my dear husband, God rest his lovely soul." She stepped back and looked at them both. "So now, who do we have here?"

Rolf clicked his heels. "I am Major Karl-Rudolf von Gerz. And this is my adjutant, Oberleutnant Gephardt Fechter." Gep nodded, bowed, and clicked as well. "As you know, we have been placed in charge of the investigation into your husband's murder, Baroness von Lindenbach."

"Please be seated, gentlemen," the ghost-like woman said as the little dwarf entered the study, pushing the coffee service. Gep placed the urn containing Herr Ritter's ashes on the coffee table, completely unnoticed or ignored by the baroness.

"I like military men. Good hard crust, those. Typically an intelligent and cultured breed. My father held the rank of lieutenant colonel under Otto von Bismarck, you know." She pointed at the table next to the armchair by the fireplace, instructing the dwarf where to place her coffee. "Now, I am a seventy-three-year-old, newly widowed Baroness, aren't I?"

"Please accept our most heartfelt condolences, baroness," Rolf interjected formally.

278

"Accepted and thank you." She handed the sweet-faced dwarf her lorgnettes. Preening her gown across her lap, she settled back in her chair.

"So, you're after my dear husband's murderer, are you? Well, gentlemen. You need look no further than myself! I am quite certain I am the guilty party. Having done all but pull the trigger."

Rolf and Gep could not hide their bewilderment.

"Where do I begin? Yes, of course. My husband. His mother was a Bavarian, you know. A Bavarian, *Gott im Himmel*, such was my curse. Every gene the woman had ended up buried in my poor Konrad's chromosomes, or whatever those little bugs are called. My father nearly disowned me before we were wed. At least the man came from the privileged class, my husband, very well educated and a veteran as well, don't you see. Also, a knight, if you didn't know. With a linage dating back to the Reformation. But he was still always a Bavarian at heart: the life of every party, ever the last dog to die, as they say."

She dropped sugar cubes in her coffee and stirred as Rolf glanced at Gep and suppressed a smile.

"You must understand, gentlemen, young ladies who bloomed of my day and especially of my social layer were quite delicate by today's standards. As you should be able to therefore imagine, my wedding night came as a completely unexpected and quite appalling epiphany to me. It was on that very night my dear husband informed me, very profound insight on his part, I might add, looking back. He told me that he could tell I was overcome with shock at the realization that the act of making love required that one remove one's clothes!"

Her grandiloquence stopped suddenly, and she made a silent offer of cake to go along with their coffee. Rolf politely refused and she jumped right back into her story.

"So, I am sorry to say that I have probably performed the bedchamber duties of my marriage as just that—an obligatory and most disgusting chore. Moreover, my real joy in the whole base and unkempt process was derived each night only from its expedient completion."

Again, she suddenly paused and looked at Gep.

"Forgive me for saying so, young man, but you look as though you've just seen your grandmother naked!" the baroness interjected. "Are you quite all right? Am I being too direct for your tastes?"

"No, of course not," Gep replied, looking at Rolf with an incredulous glare. "Please, Baroness von Lindenbach, proceed."

"So, I suppose I am really responsible for my husband's flirtatiousness and philandering. Frankly though, after the first year or so of our marriage, I found his little trysts almost liberating, if you can believe that. A man, after all, must tame the beast one way or other, mustn't he? Look who I am talking to, two strapping bucks. And though prone as he therefore was to relieving his carnal demons under the skirts of many a silly trollop through the years, I truly believe they all, and I mean all of them, gentlemen, meant little more to him than the toilets into which he peed."

Again she changed gears and out of the blue, asked, "I wonder, major. Do you think they removed the bullet before they cremated him?" She tilted her head and studied her husband's urn intently. "Or is it here somewhere, perhaps in the bottom?"

Rolf knew very well that both bullets had gone straight through the delicate old man and torn huge chunks of flesh and bone out of his back. "I'm quite certain they removed it, Gnädige Frau."

"Hmm." She sat back and took another sip of her coffee. "There were nights when I was consumed by the thoughts of his folly, I will admit. But I knew that my husband loved me. That he relished spending time with me and was devoted to me in every sense of the word." She almost chuckled as she then added, "Well, except of course for that one thing. Perhaps unfaithful, but never disloyal!" Her expression then quickly melted into anger. "Then we grew old, my Konrad and I. And with his flaccid loss of mustard he stopped seeking out the attractive and the willing in favor of the interesting and the compelling. My husband's need to simply pop his cork became a need for companionship. And this hurt me, gentlemen. To no end, this hurt me. And none more so than this last creature he's been larking about with. Because after I found out about *her*, I truly wished that someone *would* put a bullet in him. And I didn't want him hurt, don't you know, I didn't want him to suffer." She gestured with her finger, moving it straight ahead. "I dreamed that the bullet would be true and go straight through his heart so that he would die immediately. Which, I understand, is exactly how he died. So, now that's yet another thing I must put out of my mind, isn't it?" She looked at Rolf with her old, long teeth clenched tightly and visibly, her little hand making a fist. Then she looked down and shook her head. "Be careful what you pray for, young man. Because"—she nodded, eyes wide and transfixed—"God's answer quite possibly will be, 'Someday.'"

Rolf had to interject. "Pardon me, but you said, 'Especially after you found out about *her*.' What did you mean?"

"You rush me, young man. I was getting to her." She looked at her husband's urn. "That villainous tramp. His beloved Irmgard!"

Rolf wet his lips and tried not to look excited.

"The thought of my husband rooting some dirndl-clad beer maid in the back room of a village *Kneipe* has always sickened me. But I kept my composure by putting such thoughts out of my head. A woman in my position must do that, mustn't she? *Noblesse oblige* and all. The burden of privilege. Then of course there's all that Catholic rigmarole, isn't there? Because the humiliation, the disgrace of a divorce was a choice I simply could not, would not abide. Never, not in my position."

She shook her head as she touched the urn.

"Nothing ruins a woman's spirit and youth like bitterness. I didn't want my husband dead. I wanted him back. I wanted him to pine for me when he laid his head down at night, the way he used to when we were young. The way he lay in bed these last years, oblivious to me, pining for his dear Irmgard. Said her name in his sleep. More than once. When I confronted him about it, he said he was probably referring to his sister, Irmgard—that's her name as well, you see. But one doesn't pine for one's sister! Does one? I'm a fool, gentleman, but I'm an old fool. There's wisdom that comes with age. And nearly fifty years of marriage."

"Can you tell me anything else about this woman? This Irmgard?" Rolf interjected, setting his coffee on the table and shifting forward in his chair. "Where we might start our search to locate her."

"Well, I suppose I would start in Berlin. Can't tell you your business, but he traveled there fortnightly for years and spent multiple days doing some sort of motorcar business or other. Always stayed at the Adlon. I'd start there. But then, you're the investigators. Aren't you?"

Rolf looked to Gep.

"So there you have it," she went on. "I prayed for my husband's murder. He was murdered. So, I suppose it's off to the hangman with me, boys!"

She gave a thoughtful stare, then added, "Are you quite certain you wouldn't like cake?"

As they returned to Cologne, Rolf directed Gep to indeed continue on to Berlin.

"Look up this Willy von Kanderstein fellow. And put some of your people on this Irmgard woman, see if she showed up at the

Adlon during any of Ritter's visits. Ritter's Fall Irmgard file and this Irmgard woman can't just be a coincidence."

Gep agreed, then looked at Rolf and snickered. "I was quite lonely last night, you know."

Rolf was staring out the window, his mind far away. He frowned and turned to Gep.

"All alone in that big suite. I worried frightfully about you."

A sinister smile came to Rolf's face and he turned back away.

"Supposed you had passed out on some cold park bench. Hope you didn't catch something."

Rolf turned back to him. "Are you quite finished, Oberleutnant?"

Gep quickly became serious. "Do you love her, Rolf?"

"I'm not sure." He shook his head. "No. I am sure. Yes, Gep, I'm in love with her."

"I have to admit, I think she suits you." Gep ducked his head and rubbed the back of his sore neck. "Far more than the Rostikov woman in Warsaw. But I have to say, that little Normandy stunt she pulled. That concerns me."

Rolf just stared again out the window.

"Your career can't take another close call, major," Gep continued. "You know that. I have nothing but the highest regard for you and will stand by you right up to the end. But I won't lie for you, Rolf. Not again."

46

Berlin

Tuesday, 15 April 1941

Abwehrzentrale
Siège de l'Abwehr
Abwehr Headquarters

DAY ELEVEN—Berlin—Tuesday, 15 April 41—8:05 AM
Willy von Kanderstein had learned only a few days ago about Ritter's death in Paris. The memorial service in Cologne this afternoon had been thrown together so fast by Ritter's wife that only a few hundred people were expected to be in attendance. Willy would have probably tried to attend, had there been time, but there would have been talk. The entire auto industry knew of his falling-out with Konni Ritter. The pressure would have been too great for him. Best that it worked out the way it did. Willy's floral arrangement would no doubt be one of the service's finest.

Then yesterday, a Wehrmacht courier delivered an informal summons requesting that Willy present himself at the Tirpitzufer office of one Oberleutnant Gephardt Fechter at eight o'clock sharp. Willy's concern about this meeting was evident on his sour face. This summons was no doubt in regard to Ritter's death and probably pertained to events surrounding Willy's conversation with Konni in the lobby of the Ritz Hotel in Paris Saturday before last. More than a few people heard Willy's tirade that afternoon. But surely these officers didn't think Willy von Kanderstein would have anything to do with his old friend's murder. Friends have disputes. Friends work things out. He'd tell them that.

Willy entered the Tirpitzufer building and shrugged the gray wool cape off his shoulders. It fell off his back, then stopped suddenly, held in place like a backpack by two plaid suspenders. He handed the guard his identity papers and the official summons issued by an Oberleutnant Fechter. The guard nodded and motioned for a uniformed woman, who led Willy, hat in hand, upstairs and had him wait in a fauteuil at the start of a long hallway.

Gep had instructed some of the Abwehr *Forschers*, researchers in his unit, to visit the Adlon Hotel and nine of the other best hotels in Berlin: the Esplanade, the Bristol, the Königshof, and the like. They were to requisition guest registry records for a period of two years, 1939 through the end of 1940. He further instructed them in logging all of Ritter's stays at the Adlon, checking to see if any patterns developed for women staying alone during the same times at any of the hotels and being especially cognizant of any woman named Irmgard.

His meeting with these research investigator interns concluded, and each on his way to his respective hotels, Gep strolled out to the vast marbled hallway where Willy von Kanderstein waited patiently, if not a bit distraught.

"Herr von Kanderstein, I am Oberleutnant Fechter. Very nice to meet you."

Willy shook the crisply dressed officer's hand and was impressed with his finely pressed tunic and pants, his boots shined to a sharp military gloss. Gep led Willy into his office and invited him to take a seat in an armchair in front of the desk. Willy was a bit taken aback when the officer sat not at his desk but in the opposing armchair.

"You're no doubt aware of the death of Herr Ritter," Gep said as he lit a Juno cigarette and offered one to Willy, the remaining Chesterfields hidden safely in his grip.

"Yes, Herr Oberleutnant. I learned only Thursday. Very disturbing news."

"I know you and Herr Ritter were business partners—"

"Yes, sir," Willy interjected, nervously. "And we became estranged and had a quarrel last week in Paris, but I had no hand in the poor man's murder, I assure you!"

"Explain this business partnership dispute," Gep directed, looking coldly into Willy's eyes.

"We'd been successful since the end of the Great War. Ritter was a silent partner with twenty-five percent ownership. Throughout the Depression he was able to find contracts for us when they were next to impossible to locate. He had immeasurable influence in the industry and with the army. Then." Willy paused, deciding how much of the Göring story he would impart. One had to be careful in disparaging the Reichsführer or his dealings. He warmly remembered an anecdote Konni had used a number of times: "One must use great tact, Willy, my friend, when telling a man his children are ugly!"

Fall Irmgard

"Then, last year, Konni sold his percentage to the Hermann Göring Konzern. And in doing so, we became estranged."

"How so?"

Willy swallowed. It was going farther than he had hoped.

"He . . . I . . . We had intended to each give up a percentage to HGK, but he . . . but I backed out. So now I have a new partner."

"And how is that working out for you?"

Willy almost gleefully answered, "We are doing triple the volume we were before!"

"I fail to see reason for this dispute," Gep interjected.

"Young man, Ritter and I were partners and friends for twenty years. And then, suddenly, he just walks away. I'm an old man, Oberleutnant. When you are my age, you will understand."

That seemed to be enough.

"Tell me about others in the industry who may have had disputes with Ritter."

Willy sighed under his breath and became a wealth of information.

"Konni had regular visits to all the major motorcar factories and auto parts manufacturers. He was especially reviled by a number of small independent parts producers who had balked on the Führer's standardization requirements, usually due to little more than a lack of capital. Ritter threatened to withdraw raw materials when his demands were ignored, and some of them became very upset with him. One in particular."

Willy took another of Gep's cigarettes and gushed.

"A man from Innsbruck with a contract for steering wheels or sun visors or something. His plastics company was a spinoff of the famous combmaker Kunsthorn Heitner. As a matter of fact, Ritter had mentioned on a number of occasions his disdain for this Heitner fellow. Werner was his name."

Willy's attempt to deflect suspicion off himself was working. The army investigator seemed intent on knowing more.

"Explain this disdain," Gep requested, jotting notes on index cards. Not looking up at Willy at all.

"According to my good friend Konni Ritter, this Werner Heitner was responsible for murdering his own brothers. The official report concluded the automobile had defective brakes and sped off a mountain road. But Ritter didn't buy it. Werner Heitner became head of the family business overnight. But nothing could be proven."

285

"I'm Austrian, Herr von Kanderstein," Gep asserted. "I have heard of this comb and button maker. An ancient little shop outside Innsbruck, I believe. But not of this plastics company. Do you know the name?"

"Most certainly, Herr Oberleutnant. Katz und Teller!" Willy smiled; his time, his reputation, and his neck would be saved. Delightful with relief, he added, "Yes indeed, the Cat and Plate Plastics Company of Innsbruck."

"Thank you, Herr Kanderstein." Gep rose and extended his hand, then held onto Willy's overtly and added, "You will consider yourself under a material witness warrant. You are not to leave the city for any reason. I will be in touch with you again. I will have further questions for you, especially in regard to your dispute with Herr Ritter."

Then Gep smiled. One of his most intimidating tactics.

"Good day, sir."

Willy was able to hold his tears in check, but not the smallest portion of pee.

DAY ELEVEN—Berlin—Tuesday, 15 April 41—1:05 PM

A staff car delivered Gep to the Bayernhof Bierstube in the Potsdamer Platz just ahead of the appointed time. An orderly had rung up Rolf's old retired professor who was able to coax Gep into meeting with him at the ancient beer hall, where the educator was "very much a regular."

Retired Professor Doktor Gottfried Klepp entered the famous Stübbe bent almost halfway over, his spine rounded like a wilted tulip stem. An affliction from his many years at a desk studiously pouring over volumes of old text, Gep assumed. His jacket of hodgepodge tweed and patched elbows, baggy wool trousers, and old scuffed shoes all told of the crippled little man's inadequate pension under the Nazis, owing to the regime's official disdain for the intelligentsia. The professor looked sideways up at Oberleutnant Fechter and smiled, shook Gep's hand, then took his seat at one of the long tables in the friendly beer hall.

"A pleasure to meet you, my young friend," the professor said, smiling with squinting eyes. "Rudolph is doing well?"

"Yes, quite, he sends his greetings from Paris," Gep answered, looking at his watch and wanting to get to the point. "Forgive me, Herr Doktor Klepp, but I have an appointment after this. If we might proceed?"

"But of course. Your invitation mentioned a name?" A silver van Dyke beard fluttered with each word he spoke. "Irmgard, I believe it was?"

"Yes, Irmgard," Gep answered, looking around for a waitress. "The major said if anyone could shed light on its origins and possible connotations, it would be you."

Immediately, Gep realized the educator was one of those characters who annoyingly communicated by asking questions and answering them for you.

"It's an interesting old name, isn't it? Irmgard." Even seated, the old university professor was hunched over and had to look at Gep above his smudged glasses. "So, let us look at it. It is, of course, what? Of what origin? Germanic origin? But of course, old high German. Derived from what? From the old German *Irmengard*? Or *Armingart* in Dutch? Yes?"

Gep held up a thumb and forefinger to a beer maid who stopped behind the little man, ordering two beers. The professor popped around to survey the situation and wore an appreciative smile on his sweet face when he turned back to Gep.

"The name can mean what? Shall we break it down? Irmen? What? The protected one? The one who protects? Gard? Gart? What? The enclosure? The wall? The gate?" He doubled his fists and bounced them on the table a few times smiling gleefully; he was back in the classroom and loved it. "So, what do we get then? The one who what? The one who protects us all? So, in one word, what? The guardian?"

"Like a Valkyrie?" Gep asked, lighting a cigarette and offering one to Professor Doktor Klepp, holding the pack out to him and shaking it until a few were extended.

"No, less like a Valkyrie. More like what?" The professor happily accepted two, then three. But when Gep reached out to light one for the old man, he was surprised to see them all go in the tattered jacket pocket.

"More like a what? A sentry?"

The beer arrived. Professor Doktor Klepp could hardly wait for the waitress to set the serviette on the table and place his beer. He took it immediately from her and swilled a few luscious gulps, a pile of foam building on his smiling lip and total contentment in his happy eyes. Another swig and he looked through the sudsy glass at Gep.

"A guard? A sentry?" he continued. "At the gates of Walhalla?"

He set the heavy beer glass down and moved his finger up the outside of it, catching a few golden drips. Then, touching the finger to his lips, he watched the Oberleutnant raise an eyebrow as he pondered what he had been told.

Another quick sip and Klepp closed his eyes and emitted a slight sigh.

"So. From a mythological standpoint, who do we find Irmgard to be? From the old German myths? Whose daughter was she? Was she not Wotan's daughter? But beyond that, what? Very little is known about her. She's mentioned only in passing in regard to what? Her wedding? You see, Oberleutnant, unlike with the Greeks, legends handed down from the ancient Norse and old Germanic tribes were never really written down. There was no German Homer or Horace in ancient times, was there? No two tribes told these stories the same way, did they? So, when did it all come together? Wasn't it the transcription of the Neidlingen poems? Wasn't that when all the legends found a congruent path? And that was when? The eleventh, the twelfth century?"

He took another sip of beer and shrugged.

"It's a code name, isn't it?" he then asked of Gep, a twinkle in his eye. "That's it, isn't it? A code name?"

"Perhaps." Gep leaned back, turned sideways in his seat, and rested his elbow on the back of his chair. He cocked his head to the side, pointing at the professor and asking, "If it were, what would such a name conjure up in that studious head of yours?"

"Apparently not one of our code names. It must be British." Klepp's wry smile was met by stern eyes from Gep. The little professor proceeded with his conjecture.

"If Irmgard is a code name, Oberleutnant, significant of anything at all . . ." Another quick sip. "I would think it would have to do with what? Defending someone? Or what? Something? Something of great significance? A king? A treasure? A whole way of life, perhaps?"

Again, Gep paused and considered what Klepp had said. A king. A treasure. A whole way of life. Treasure. The word kept turning over in Gep's mind. What about this broker who was killed just before Ritter? Was there a connection? Did they know each other, the broker and Ritter? A treasure? Millions of francs in unregistered securities?

Jesus! The old scheisskerl had Gep doing it now!

288

Fall Irmgard

"Anything else?" Gep asked, looking grimly at his watch. Hoping, frankly, the etymology lesson was over.

"Good beer," Klepp answered, smiling again.

Gep thanked him, placed a ten-mark note under his own barely touched glass of beer, bowed to the professor, clicked his heels, and took his leave, owing to another appointment.

Professor Doktor Klepp watched Gep leave. Looking awkwardly around he poured the remainder of Gep's beer into his own, stuffed the ten marks in his jacket as well as the cigarette pack that had been intentionally left behind. The hunched-over professor squirmed around this way and that in his seat to try to catch sight of the waitress. Finally doing so, he raised his hand, slurped, and chirped, "Oh, Fräulein!"

DAY ELEVEN—Berlin/Kudamm—Tuesday, 15 April 41—2:00 PM
At the Café Kranzler on the Kurfürstendamm, Gep met a woman who served on the secretarial staff of General Beck. She was tall and blond with eyes the color of an Austrian mountain lake. Dressed in a beige cotton suit with a navy Alpine fedora, more brim in front than anywhere else, with a plume of feathery color, she carried a black and brown briefcase that matched her saddle-throated shoes.

They chose a table in the corner with a view though the lindens of the Kaiser Wilhelm Memorial Church. Cheeks were kissed, and Gep placed his hand on the side of her face tenderly and held it there.

"Have you been well, little sister?" he asked with a tilt of his head and a loving smile.

"Quite well, Gep," she answered as they took their seats next to each other, her a full hand taller than him. She held his hand.

"General Beck is a good man, Gep. A very good man. I want you to get to know him. I really do."

"I promise, I will." He nodded and blinked reassuringly.

Kathe Fechter had always been adorably chatty. The type who could chortle on about nothing for hours. And now, while she did just that, telling him about her latest boyfriend and having visited their mother only last month, Gep set the briefcase in his lap and withdrew a file.

HEHT, RUTGERS
It was a thick file. Many of the words were blacked out. There would be no way for Gep to read through it in the hour or so they had. But his efficient little Kathe had ensured there would be no need. Nearly every page had a dictation scratchpad note paper-clipped to

289

it—a short synopsis of the document. While she chatted on, Gep unclipped them, read them, and put each note and each paper clip in his tunic pocket. Every moment possible he kept his eyes on his sister, smiling and nodding now and then, oblivious to whatever it was she was saying.

Rutgers Heht was a skilled and prolific assassin. There were no names. No dates or places. They'd all been blacked out. But there were scores of hits. Most obviously political. Many foreign. Heht was an army covert operations specialist. He'd been trained as a Brandenburger. A paratrooper. Brandenburgers in Polish uniforms had staged the so-called Polish attack against Germans in Danzig that had been used as the political pretext for the German invasion of Poland. Brandenburgers had been dropped into Maastricht before the invasion of Holland and France to seize the bridge over the Meuse. They'd driven Citroens and Renaults deep into France and Belgium dressed in plain clothes to cut enemy communications. And Rutgers Heht had been with them.

But not all Brandenburgers were assassins; they were just highly trained soldiers. Heht was more. Much more. Heht worked not just for the Abwehr, but also for the High Command. Heht was in General Beck's back pocket. And certainly those who knew it and shouldn't were soon deceased.

Kathe stopped for a breath. She looked at her brother and breathed deeply.

"Well?" she asked. "What you expected?"

Gep shrugged with his eyes.

"Like I said, general Beck's a very good man, with a circle of officers around him, very good men as well. Patriots. True patriots, Gep. Even some of the army hawks." She nodded at the file in his lap. "And Rutgers Heht is on their leash."

"I worry about you, Kathe," he remarked, concern in his eyes. "This circle of patriots, their kind of patriotism can be very dangerous. Are you safe?"

"You don't have to protect me, big brother." A spontaneous chuckle burst from her, and again she nodded at the file, smiling. "I have him!"

47

Tangier, French Morocco

Das Ablegekommando
L'équipe d'enlèvement
The Removal Squad

DAY ELEVEN—Tangier—Tuesday, 15 April 41—1:08 PM
A crashing turquoise surf broke into thinning foam on the stony Moroccan shore. As each plunging wave withdrew, it jostled and tossed the piles of smooth stones on the sand-stripped beach, creating a deep roar of rumbling clunks and clinks under the weight of the frothy surf. Nestled in a shady grove of coconut and date palms, German Abwehr Kapitan Kaspar Koch sat in a woven wicker chair under a loosely flopping Courvoisier table umbrella that popped and tossed with each fish-scented gust off the Mediterranean. Kaspar wore a white straw hat and beige linen suit. He sipped and chewed his banana rum tonic loaded with heaps of shaved coconut. He loved the syrupy bite of the rum infused in the chewy chips of sweet Moroccan coconut. Smoking a Week End cigarette, he read the French Morocco news as the breeze off the Mediterranean whipped the ends of the canvas cover that protected the beach bar from the blazing sun.

Kaspar's Ablege squad had just tracked down a Frankfurt attorney attached to the German embassy in Madrid who, over five short months, had bilked scores of hopeful emigrant Jews out of nearly a million francs, posing as their clandestine contact en route to Lisbon and ultimate freedom in Argentina. The sum came to 873,605 francs to be exact. His planned escape route to Saint Martin in the French West Indies was all set. The only man aware of his plans was the one man he could trust, a Moroccan freight handler in Tangier who was well paid for his part in the odyssey. But the thieving Frankfurt lawyer's Spanish girlfriend had not been so tight-lipped. Her boast to friends of her new life in the Caribbean was quick to land on official ears, so that within a few days and a few thousand pesetas, Kapitan Kaspar Koch was informed and his team, out of Barcelona, set in motion.

Kaspar's Ablegekommando IV, Refuse Squad IV, was made up of two Germans, both small but sensuous sorts and one Sardinian bull of a man. All were fluent in French and Spanish, but the latter was also quite skilled in Arabic and Portuguese. Two nights earlier, Kaspar's three-man team abducted the Frankfurt attorney as well as (this time) his very feisty Spanish tart in a shabby Tangier hotel just off the medina. They drugged them both with phenol, hog-tied them, and tossed their sweaty, naked bodies into the backseat of a waiting Abadal-Buick sedan. After turning over the loot to Kaspar—as the squad commander, it was his job to count and record the totals—they drove to a secluded Moroccan beach where the attorney was cuffed to the camel-toe trunk of a date palm. When the German members of the crew had fallen asleep, the gagged woman was awakened and dragged by her bound wrists and her hair down the beach, where the huge Sardinian beast with dark drunken eyes and protruding black moles spat questions at her, slugging her when he didn't like the answers. When she proved to be penniless and quite common with little ransom value, she was repeatedly raped and beaten and left for dead on a rocky atoll fifty meters out in the swells.

Then last night, the three Removal Squad team members carried the dazed, condemned Frankfurt lawyer onto a Junkers 52 transport plane along with the suitcase full of loot and Kaspar's receipt for 863,605 francs, to fly to Germany with a fourteenth captured AWOL German officer or Abwehr official, who within a matter of weeks would hang as a deserter at the military prison in Ruhleben or Berlin.

But fifteen minutes into the flight, the kidnapped lawyer threatened to expose his abductors as rapists and murderers, having witnessed last night's hedonistic tarantella with his Spanish girlfriend. A minute later, one of Kaspar's men opened the door to the Junkers flight cabin, poked his head in, and told the pilot they needed to return to Tangier. Their abductee had somehow freed himself and jumped to his death over the Mediterranean.

A waiter in billowing white linen and a blue kepi approached Kaspar from the bar. He pulled the domed wicker cover off his silver tray, and Kaspar took the small envelope, plopping a copper coin in its place. Looking over his shoulder to be sure the waiter was gone, he tossed down the last of his rum, and as he chewed the syrupy coconut, he read instructions about what would soon be his fifteenth target.

PROCEED BARCELONA STOP AWAIT INSTRUCTIONS FULL STOP

Fall Irmgard

Kaspar held his tortoiseshell sunglasses up to the sun to reveal the location of a vexing smudge. He breathed moisture on the emerald-tinted lens and cleaned it with his napkin. As he gained his feet to leave, he rubbed the other lens for good measure, then snugged up his loosed tie, dropped a few coins in the dish, gathered up his wicker-throated shoes stuffed with sheer silk stockings, and smashed his way barefoot through the thick, dry sand back to the breezy hotel lobby.

48

Wednesday, 16 April 1941

Totenkopf
Tête de mort
SS Death's Head
(Skull & Crossbones)

DAY TWELVE—Paris—Wednesday, 16 April 41—2:10 PM
The gold and onyx continental phone in SS Sturmbannführer Alois
Kruder's suite jingled loudly in sets of three short blasts. He flushed
the toilet and buttoned his trousers and made his way over to it.
"Kruder here."
"Herr Sturmbannführer, Suzi Rupp. I received a message to
come see you?"
"Yes, of course, my dear. Third floor. Suite at the end of the
hall. Come right up."
Kruder took Suzi's coat in the foyer and showed her into the
sitting room. When she turned around, he was standing within inches
of her with an unsettling look on his face.
"So, what can you to tell me about our Abwehr friends?" he
asked, menace on his stern face.
"I'm working on the von Gerz man, the major. But that whole
breed. They're so aloof. Difficult to get close to."
"You're not trying hard enough. Or else, you've lost the will."
"Never, Sturmbannführer."
"I wonder."
"You needn't, I assure you."
"We'll get to that. But first, the reason I asked you over was
because I want a command performance, want to see you dance and
sing. Just for me."
"But that's very queer, Herr Sturmbannführer. I'd feel most
uncomfortable; there's no music."
"Let me make the music for you."
He grabbed her and threw her on the sofa.
"There's no need to be so rough. I submit willingly."
The sinister look on his face frightened her as he tore open her
blouse and peeled it off her. He flipped her over and tried to unhook

her brassiere, she even reached back to help, only to have him take her hand away as he jerked on it, dragging her off the sofa. When the bra lodged under her arms, he grabbed her by the hair and pulled her across the floor, finally ripping the stubborn thing off over her head. She gained her feet and tried to run, but he tackled her, falling hard on top of her, slamming her head on the floor. Quickly, he cuffed her hands behind her, stripped the rest of her things from her trembling body, and stuffed her bloody mouth with her panties.

Then he beat her with his open palm. He beat and slapped her on the back and buttocks and legs. Flailing at her, hitting her in the face. For a brief moment as he straddled her, sitting backward on her neck and shoulders, he stopped to catch his breath, unbutton his tunic, and wipe sweat from his brow and lip.

Then he jumped up and dragged the naked girl through the suite, from one room to the other, by her hair or by an ankle or by her shackled wrists. Dragging her, tossing her, spinning her like a top on the cold waxed parquet for no purpose other than defamation, delighting in her muffled, snotty screams. He unclipped the Sam Browne belt running diagonally across his chest and used it to whip her rump. By the time her bruised and blistered cheeks started bleeding, the tiny girl had lost consciousness. He plopped down hard in a silk armchair, lit a cigarette, and stared at her. Composed, the cigarette finished, he lifted her by one thigh and around the waist and carried her on his hip back to the sofa.

Grabbing his officer's hat from the foyer stand, he seated himself beside her. Splayed out on the sofa, wearing nothing but a now-crooked gray satin ribbon gorget that held a peach rosette tightly against her throat. Kruder crossed his legs at the knee and leaned over to rest his elbow on her bruised, naked hip, his SS officer's hat on his lap.

"I believe I am mostly finished with you, my dear. I am fairly certain you have now come to understand that I do not accept halfhearted compliance with any command I put forth. You will do what I require and will do so with complete conviction. You do understand that now, don't you, Sweet Suzi?"

Not hearing a reply, he grabbed the poor girl by the hair and jerked her up to him. "I need to hear you say it! Do you understand?"

Half-conscious, unable to focus her eyes, she nodded.

"Good girl," Kruder said, as he reached into his inside tunic pocket and withdrew a black leather manicure kit. With his luxuriously manicured fingers, he delicately removed the tweezers from the kit.

"You see, Suzi. There was just something about you that reeked. This darling little Austrian diva, a slight Hungarian accent, quite understandable, I suppose. But that beautiful olive skin. Those stunning and very dark eyes. What's the word? Exotic. Yes, exactly. Exotic eyes. More Mediterranean than Germanic or Magyar, I would think. Anyway, it all got me to thinking. Must be something amiss here with Sweet Suzi Rupp. So, I had some of my colleagues in Vienna, very adept fellows, do some research into your past. Hoped to at least find some Jew in the family closet. Turns out it's almost as interesting as that, isn't it, my dear?"

He smiled. "You're Romany. Aren't you, Suzi Rupp? Not a Jew, but lowly subhuman vermin all the same. A dirty gypsy. Suzi Rupp, indeed. So, this fat, pig-faced Herr Rupp. He's your uncle, is he? I think not, my dear. An opportunistic Party pipsqueak, that's all he is. He sees a talented gypsy slut and promotes her as his homespun Alpine ingénue. Selling this dreadful lie all over the Reich."

As he continued, he unsnapped the metal SS death's head pin from the front of his hat.

"So, Sweet Suzi.. Perhaps I got carried away. Went a little too far. But the fact is that you come from nothing but lying, thieving gypsy vermin. Therefore, of course, the two of us can either make life difficult for each other, or we can simply move forward in our little game. Which do you think it should be, my dear?"

He slid another Trommler in his tortoiseshell cigarette holder, lit it and took a long, dramatic drag, forcing the smoke out through his perfect white teeth.

"Of course, for my part I would no doubt get an official tongue-lashing followed by a few slaps on the back and chuckles for having knocked a gypsy slut around. You, on the other hand, would be shipped off to Ostmark, where we will be concentrating some of our less desirable types in new labor camps."

The cigarette holder clamped in his sinister smile, Kruder clicked the lighter again, took the tweezers, picked up the Death's Head hatpin with them, and held the emblem to the flame.

"I will take your silence as our being in agreement. But before I leave for the evening and give you a chance to pull yourself back together, I'd like to give you a little memento."

Fall Irmgard

He quickly threw himself on her and stabbed the white-hot emblem into her flesh, burning the SS skull and crossbones on her groin just above the hairline.

"Sweet Suzi," he barked as she groaned and squealed, far too weak to scream. He laughed as she flailed her arms and legs about in excruciating pain, her knee catching him with a few blows to his shoulder and back. He was unfazed. His sinister laugh just grew louder as he realized, "Sweet Suzi! My little SS bitch!"

49

Port of Barcelona

Herr Schmidt
Señor Schmidt
Mr. Schmidt

DAY TWELVE—Barcelona—Wednesday, 16 April 41—4:05 PM
Mélina was a giddy girl, having spent the entire day shopping along
the ritzy lanes around the Plaça de Catalunya, still being rebuilt after
the Spanish Civil War bombings two years before.

Just as Addie and her crowd had done before the war, Mélina
didn't give a second thought to the cost of anything. She wore a
brightly colored floral dress with a new hat that flopped its huge brim
in the Mediterranean breeze. Ruti enjoyed the spree as much as
Mélina, but now and then he would look over his shoulder at shady
characters who seemed to loom everywhere. There were four of them
who turned up more than once, a few two or three times, seated on a
bench near them, at their same café, or at the tabac just down from a
shop Mélina had chosen. He made mental notes about each, naming
them so he could keep them straight: Melendes, Martines, Morales,
and Schmidt. The latter simply because he looked like a Schmidt, and
therefore, the most troublesome of the bunch. Schmidt wore a white
linen suit, with a matching Italian parabuntal fedora and horn-rimmed
sunglasses. His boutonniere was a red carnation, and he read the same
folded page of the newspaper all day long. As a matter of fact, the
only aspect of Señor Schmidt's actions that led Ruti to believe he was
anything but a Gestapo or Abwehr snoop was his complete and utter
ineptitude.

The ferry would depart at five thirty. They took sunny seats at a
sidewalk café on shady Les Rambles. A cold beer and a soda, *por
favor*. Ruti's Mexican-accented Spanish was compliments of his
close-combat drill instructor in Hamburg. Mélina moved her wedding
ring around on her finger and smiled contentedly at Ruti. She was
such a wondrous vision to him, dark sunglasses and white teeth
framed in blond hair under the big floppy hat.

"Ruti, my love. Tell me again about our new home?" she said
in French.

He frowned and pointed his finger at her forcefully.

"Rodrigo, my love. Relate to me one more on our new home?" She stumbled through this time in Spanish.

From now on they were Señor Rodrigo Guerrero and his lovely new bride, Señora Lalania Maria. Son and daughter-in-law of the famous Marcus-Antonio Guerrero, world-renowned coffee plantation magnate from Panama. *Most surely, you've heard of us!* If not, why, the young Guerrero could quickly produce a sample of their fine produce by taking any one of forty beautifully printed gold-and-green paper bags he kept in his possession, filling it with whatever coffee happened to be available, and spinning the bag's top around in his fingers until it tightly closed. Like the bags, their passports were perfect, some of the best work of Europe's finest artisans. Their Spanish visas were accompanied by a letter of welcome from the Spanish minister of agriculture, wishing the young Señor Guerrero and his lovely new wife a glorious life in their new home in Spain.

Ruti wanted to force Señors Melendes, Martines, Morales, and Schmidt, especially Schmidt, into some act that would expose their true intent. He whispered to Mélina, kissed her, and she headed into the café, apparently to powder her nose. Ruti rose and walked across the street to the broad tree-lined boulevard where hundreds of hawker tables formed two rows that ran the entire shady block. The grassy boulevard was teeming with shoppers and gawkers, and Ruti was quickly swallowed up in the shadowy thicket. He never took his eye off the four men. Martines scowled and looked down the street to Melendes. So, they were a team. Two down, two to go.

Ruti moved down a couple of tables, his menacing blue eyes darting back and forth, watching the sunlit spots on his suit coat and shifting around until they disappeared. Morales never moved. He didn't seem the least bit interested in the empty table at the café or the stack of shopping sacks and hatboxes beside it. However, when Schmidt, who was seated at the far end of the same café, looked up from his newspaper, there was immediate panic on his chiseled face. His neck seemed to grow twice its length as his head swiveled back and forth; he stood up searching the other tables in the café. Then Mélina came out of the café and returned to her seat. Señor Schmidt seemed to let out a sigh as he retook his seat and read the paper.

Satisfied with his flushing operation, Ruti looked over the display of intricately painted porcelain ring and trinket boxes on the table in front of him. One leapt out at him. It was about the size of his fist, yellow and pink roses on brilliant alabaster porcelain with a brass-banded lid sporting rhinestones all the way around it. Even with his Spartan sense of style, he found it atrocious. But it would be one of those cherished, albeit hideous mementos women graciously accept from their men, never to be parted with, though kept in the back of some bottom drawer.

The lovely couple boarded the ship twenty minutes before embarkation and settled into deck chairs on the middle deck of the ferry. Señor Schmidt, whose real name of course was Kapitan Kaspar Koch, had followed the two newly Spanish lovebirds since earlier that morning. What troubled Kaspar most was that although they were both lugging sacks and boxes of shopping booty, there was really no luggage, nowhere for the man to be hiding his criminal takings. Oh, well. Kaspar had always felt that things worked out eventually. These deserters weren't brilliant criminal minds. They were dreamers, idealists who wanted to escape the turmoil of wartime life. Men who thought they had everything worked out. And they never really did. This one would be no different. He had the money somewhere.

Sure that the young Panamanian coffee heir and his lovely bride were settled in on their second-deck chairs, Kaspar Koch flipped his cigarette into the water and scurried up the plaza at the ferry dock to a small telegraph office to send off a cable to his squad. He tore off a wire form and licked his pencil, quickly jotting:
PALMA DE MALLORCA 22:00 STOP
CAFE D'ORCA KK FULL STOP

50

Berlin

Irmgard

DAY TWELVE—Berlin—Wednesday, 16 April 41—8:08 PM
At Tirpitzufer, Gep had seven Abwehr secretaries at work identifying names coincident to the dates that Ritter stayed at the Adlon. Within an hour a name was handed to him, much to his surprise. At the Kaiserhof one woman was registered eight times from June 1939 to January 1940. There were another three times throughout that same time period at the Bristol. Gep looked at the name and tried to swallow his astonishment. He immediately sent everyone home and instructed all the agents to return the registries to their respective hotels the next morning.

Gep then went to a local kneipe to drink. To think.

Firstly, it was so farfetched, it was ludicrous. He'd probably be a laughingstock for even suggesting it. Coincidence. That's all it was. Nonetheless, this was indeed the woman. Registered with a Swiss passport. Easy movement between Switzerland and the Reich. Eleven times in seven months? And most damning of all, no other registries showed this woman at any other time in any of the ten Berlin hotels. This was Irmgard! And the name Irmgard was indeed a code name.

But now what? A call to Rolf? It was his duty. Or would it be best to simply board the night train to Paris and tell him face to face? That was most assuredly the best plan. But no, he decided, it had to be a phone call. This couldn't wait. But he wanted to be sure first. He'd need to research the name with data offices in the police and Gestapo files first, and he would start that process the minute he returned to the office this evening. But he owed his commanding officer the intel as soon as he discovered it. Even if it was disturbing news. Especially if it was disturbing news.

DAY TWELVE—Berlin—Wednesday, 16 April 41—10:10 PM
Back at his office, Gep phoned the Lutetia. It was late. He was almost relieved when Rolf didn't answer the phone in his room. The switchboard operator broke in and told Gep he would check in the lounge. As moments passed, he convinced himself it was good that

he'd phoned tonight, he'd let fate determine whether Rolf heard the news tonight or in the morning. It was doubtful Rolf was even in. He was probably at the l'Heure Bleue with Addie. An eternity passed. Gep tried to conjure up logical explanations for the troubling name. Most assuredly, this was all just a coincidence. The name was, after all, at least a stretch of translational and auditory similarity. Still, it was also a viable possibility. And very damaging to Rolf if it was in fact . . .

"Major von Gerz here."

"Rolf, it's Gep. From Berlin."

"Gep, old man, of course you're in Berlin. I sent you there. This better be good, I left an extraordinary Napoleon brandy to take this call."

"I think I've identified the woman, Irmgard."

"Good show, Gep. Who is it?"

"Please don't overreact. It's very preliminary. I have a great deal of verification to do before—"

"Gep. That's quite enough. Out with it, my man. Who is it?"

"Major, eight of the eighteen times between June '39 and January '40 when Herr Ritter was at the Adlon Hotel, a woman with mostly the same dates of arrival stayed at the Kaiserhof. On three other occasions, she was at the Bristol. If this turns out to be the woman, she is Swiss and Irmgard was indeed a code name."

"If, if, if! My god, Oberleutnant. I'll have no more of it. Out with it!"

Gep wanted to pronounce the woman's name in English. Avoid the obvious correlation. But he didn't.

"The woman's name is . . . Brückner. Edith Brückner." But he used the German pronunciation of the name Edith: Ay-deet.

Ay-deet Brückner!

The phone line went dead.

"Major? Major von Gerz? Rolf?"

Buch Drei

III

Die Entdeckung
La découverte
Discovery

16 Months Earlier
Samstag, 23 Dezember, 1939
7:56 PM
Berlin-Charlottenburg

Frost laden and eerily dark against the new wartime blackout, the S-Bahn train pulled to a stop at the deserted Grunewald Station with the deafening shrieks and groans of iron on iron. A single passenger disembarked and made her way out the paved entrance and up the hill into the quiet wooded neighborhood. Her heels clicking on the frosty sidewalk were the only sounds knifing through the thinly snow-blanketed night. The bitterly cold day had given way to a still and somehow warmer evening, not uncommon for winter nights in Berlin. Crystals of ice floated in the crisp, moonlit air, and now and then bald limbs in the very tops of larches tossed by a slight breeze would resound and echo through the dark like stag antlers in a fairy-tale wood.

The small woman's cold, rosy cheeks and the long foxtail fur of her full-length coat danced with each determined step she took. As she moved deeper into this affluent quarter of Berlin, with its centuries-old villas guarded by tall brick walls and thick iron gates, the voices of children raised in carols of Christmas pealed in the distant darkness. Four months into this new war and Germany had known nothing but victories. Spirits were high. Yet, for many even their fashionable Nazi euphoria was overshadowed this night by the sweet voices of the children, by the Christ Child season, and the *Entsprungen Rose* the little ones sang loving praises to.

As she climbed the steps into the church, lit only by flickering candlelight, she removed her fur hat revealing dark hair, tightly pulled back into a bun, and a steely businesslike glare as she surveyed the crowded church. Not twenty pews back, on the aisle to her right she spotted him, waving his embroidered kerchief at her. As she seated herself, she gave both cheeks and her hand to him. He kissed all three and smiled warmly at her.

"I'm cold, Konni!" She pouted.

He slid his arm around her and snuggled her closer to him.

"Not to fear, Irmgard, my love. I'll warm you up." From seemingly nowhere he handed her a capful of Christmassy

305

peppermint schnapps from his pocket flask. As she stealthily threw it back, he whispered to her, "The Father, the Son, and the Holy Ghost."

A gleaming smile broke through her icy glare.

"Am I too late?" she asked, shaking the empty cap, a request for another.

"It just started," Konni answered, pouring her another tiny shot.

"Where is she?" She strained to see the stage and altar.

"She's an angel. They'll come down from above." He watched her toss down the second shot of schnapps and shiver slightly, then he asked her, "Are you at the Bristol?"

She nodded, inhaling deeply, then turned her frightened eyes to him.

"I don't want to sleep alone tonight, Konni." He pulled her to him and kissed her cheek. He loved her distinct Swiss-accented German. "My nerves just can't take it."

"You'll stay with me tonight, Irmy."

"I want out, Konni."

"I know you do. I do too. I'm working on it, my love."

The children's voices swelled into the sweet strains of "Ihr Kinderlein kommet," and all the tiny children in the church who weren't a part of the performance made their way to the stage and to the manger crib where each, the well-practiced demonstrating for the tiniest of them, knew to withdraw one piece of candy from around the baby doll portraying the Christ Child as voices sang out, "Your little children are coming." Then from above the stage, descending from the high darkness into the flickering glow, six little angels dropped slowly down from ropes held by proud fathers in the wings. Five of them joined in the singing. The sixth only kicked, screamed, and wailed, frightened beyond consoling by both the darkness and the heights.

Laughter rose from the crowd, and the Swiss woman Edith Brückner, code named Irmgard, asked Konni Ritter, "Is that her?"

"No. Elsa is the one to the right of her. The true angel. That child is possessed!"

"She's adorable, Konni."

"Of course she is." He smiled proudly and seemed to wag his tail in his pew as he continued, "She takes after her grandfather."

"What of your daughter? Don't you fear I'll be seen?"

"That's her up front, directing little Elsa from below. She doesn't even know I'm here." He handed Irmgard a final shot of schnapps and, once downed, returned the cap to the flask and

306

commanded, "I'll move to the doorway and make my exit. You come a few moments behind me. Go to your left when you leave the church. You'll find my carriage at the curb." With that, he kissed the back of her glove and waddled his way along the wall of the church as a thunder of applause filled the sanctuary. A brief prayer followed from the pastor, and immediately thereafter the crowd began to stir. Edith Brückner was just ahead of it as she hurried down the steps and out to the waiting carriage and into a wool blanket, warmed by three hot rocks left in the velour seat. Konni held the blanket out as she climbed in the carriage and wrapped it around her. He kissed her, then pulled her cheek to his chest, leaning his on top of her fur hat.

The third-floor corner suite of the Adlon Hotel looked out on the Brandenburg Gate and the four-horse chariot of victory. Edith Brückner stood at the tall window, her arms folded and one hand up to her chin, looking down at the historic symbol of Berlin. More dry-air crystalline snow swirled like fireflies in the moonlight, and the golden laurels of Victoria riding triumphantly atop the gate in the quadriga chariot glowed magically.

Konni had ordered dinner in his suite's sitting chamber for him and his dear Irmgard. They dined in quite repose. She talked of her trip that day from Bern and how weary she was. Twice she asserted her desire to bring their "dangerous little game" to a quick end. He repeated his plan to accomplish just that, but told her he preferred to keep its details from her, for her safety as well as that of any other participants."

As she stood at the window, Konni gazed upon her. She was so beautiful in a crisp, Swiss way. Her form was slim, curved, and full. Her horn-rimmed glasses and schoolteacher hairstyle made her look much older than she probably was. The beige crepe blouse and hound's-tooth jacket and skirt only added to the picture of sleek businesswoman perfection. She played the part of the banking policy transcriber to perfection. Down to the mechanical pencil pinned to her jacket—where other women might wear a virgin pin—and the linked tortoiseshell chain around the back of her neck, clipped to her glasses.

"I'm exhausted, Konni, dear." She took her champagne glass and downed it, then lifted the folded stack of sheets and blankets from the sofa and started preparing her bed for the night.

"You're welcome to sleep in my bedchamber, Irmy."

"I would almost do that just to watch you try to get all of that"—she pointed to his round, well-extended belly—"in there." She pointed to the sofa.

Her things back at the Bristol, she later came out of the bathroom in only her full slip with a black Adlon robe sporting gold detail. Once settled in the cozy cocoon she'd made for herself, she pulled the crisply pressed sheets up to her chin and closed her eyes. Konni twisted the light switch off and went over to her in the moonlit suite. Clumsily, he started the arduous process of taking one knee beside her. Once accomplished, he stroked her hair away from her ear and kissed her soft cheek.

"Get me out of this, Konni. Please."

"I shall, my love. Not to worry your pretty little head." Another kiss. "I shall."

51

Wednesday, 16 April 1941

Alles in einem Namen
Tout dans un nom
All in a Name

DAY TWELVE—Paris—Wednesday, 16 April 41—10:15 PM
"Oh, ducklinks, is der anything qvite as funderful as an urgent pee?" Addie bellowed in a deep, German-accented voice, mimicking her sorely missed friend Konni Ritter. A forced smile suppressed a tear as she reseated herself at the usual banquet at the rear of the Club l'Heure Bleue.

"That sounded exactly like him," Hedy quipped, looking at Gretl and Sabina and smiling as well.

"And that's when Sabina would say . . ." Gretl held her palm out toward Sabina, giving her her cue.

Sabina tossed her hair and turned her shoulder to them and said, "Konni, darling." She raised her eyebrow and continued, "Then either I don't know how to pee, or you, mijnheer, don't know how to fuck!"

They all laughed with tears in their eyes, and Addie added in her Konni Ritter voice, "Sabina, my love. I've been married fifty years. I'm quite happy to get even . . ." They all joined in: "The good pee!"

More laughter ensued. Addie put her hands between her knees and pulled her shoulders up, adding, "We mustn't, any of us, ever let him be forgotten. Do promise me, all of you, that you will remember him 'til the day you die?"

Cheeks glistened as they all nodded and smiled their agreement.

Addie picked up the small pile of change in the center of the table and let it slide through her fingers. Konni was the one who suggested they keep it there throughout the night for any and all urgent pees that might arise. *Pinkelklink*, he called it, toilet change, kept on the table for just that probability and purpose.

"And all of us," Addie continued, reaching out to join hands with them, "all of us, without exception, will agree to meet at this table exactly one year after the war ends."

Heads nodded as the portly bartender took the stage in his Winston Churchill persona only to have Xavier enter in a British uniform three times his size. He stomped his feet twice and tried to salute, ultimately having to roll up the long sleeve to even see his hand.

"Terribly sorry, sir," Xavier's whiny character said.

"Yes, Babcock."

"But now that the Germans and the French are allies, how will we tell them apart?"

"Why that's easy, Babsy, old fellow. The Germans will be fighting us."

"And the French, sir?"

"The French will be fighting with each other!"

The lights grew dim as the band played "Der Glocken Ruf." No one saw Rolf storm in. When he appeared suddenly out of the darkness, the look on his face immediately troubled them all. Addie tried to lighten the mood.

"Well," she quipped. "Aren't you the dreary bug!"

He grabbed her forcefully and jerked her out of her seat.

"Come with me," he demanded.

Shrugging, feigning a smile to the others, she scooted out of the booth, trying not to show her trepidation against his tightly clenched grip.

He led her upstairs through the courtyard and down the boulevard Raspail. When they were far enough away from the club, he threw her up against the stucco wall and demanded: "Tell me about Operation Irmgard, Fräulein Brückner!"

"Rolf, darling, you're frightening me." A confused frown extolled her possible innocence. "What in heaven's name are you talking about?"

"Ritter's contact in Germany was a woman named Brückner. Edith Brückner!" He used a harshly distinct German pronunciation of Edith, *Ay-deet*.

"How on earth would that have anything to do with me?"

"So, you're still holding to this charade of not speaking German? You don't see the obvious correlation between the two names: *Ay-deet*, Addie, *Brückner*, Bridges?"

"My god, Rolf. You're not suggesting I had something to do with Konni's murder? That's insane! I loved that dear old man."

"Your dear old man was involved in some sort conspiracy with US automakers, and you were his partner."

"Darling, do you hear yourself?"

"I knew there was more to you and Ritter than you let on. I just didn't know you were accomplices in espionage!"

"Rolf, I don't know what you're talking about. And I don't think you do either. You must be grasping at some vague notion and trying to judge from my reaction if it is true. That has to be it. Otherwise, how could you be so harsh and unreasonable, over a ridiculous name?"

"So, you're telling me you know nothing of this Brückner identity?"

"Rolf, I have no idea what you're talking about."

"Go to your apartment. Do not leave it for any reason. Consider yourself under house arrest."

"Rolf, please don't scare me like this. I told you when you released me last week I would never lie to you again. I'm telling the truth. Please, darling, you must believe me."

He grabbed her arm again and led her around the corner to her building. She tiptoed the last few meters to keep from breaking a heel. As she pulled the key out of her purse and handed it to him, he snarled and unlocked the door, saying, "Not a foot outside this door!"

52

Bois de Boulogne

Die Ausgegraben
Le déterré
Unearthed

DAY TWELVE—Paris—Wednesday, 16 April 41—11:46 PM
Scores of flashlight beams danced in the darkness. Headlamps from
as many cars and trucks lit the woods of Boulogne in a white glow.
Shadows of gendarmes and French National Police moved about in
the beams of light that danced on trees like forest ghosts.

A winch truck was backed up to a huge oak tree. Its long steel
cable was suspended from a pulley attached to a high limb in the
sturdy tree, giving it the necessary leverage to dislodge the heavy
automobile from its wedged position in the deep ravine, where it had
been buried under thick brush. Inspector Luc-Henri pulled up just as
the blue Matford automobile jerked free of a large stone embedded in
the slope of the ravine. The car thrust suddenly back toward everyone,
causing workmen to jump and dash out of its way as it came to rest on
its side in the soft, torn earth.

Luc stepped out of his car and limped over to the muddy, topsy-
turvy automobile. His flashlight joined scores of others searching out
the bloody interior. Blood in both the backseat and the front.

"Good evening, inspector," Rolf said, coming up from behind
him. "Maybe this is the real one."

"Seems your grenadier's shots did ring true, major," Luc
responded, his flashlight held out through the dashed front glass to
examine at the bloodstains in the front seat. "Hitting both assailants."

A few of the younger policemen and workers pushed the car
over. It righted itself on its flat tires with hard jerks one way and the
other. White-coated women wearing red rubber gloves opened the
doors and started retrieving tiny pieces of anything evidentiary,
stuffing the items in numbered cellophane bags they took from their
pockets. When one picked a matchbook out of a backseat ashtray and
held it up to the jostling flashlight beams, she was touched on the
shoulder and ordered to give the book to Inspector Luc-Henri. He
held it by its edges delicately, avoiding the face and rear of the book,

not wanting to contaminate it with fingerprints. Inspecting it against his flashlight, he nodded, showing it to Rolf.

Rolf shined his own Pertrix canister pocket flashlight at the matchbook. On its front was an advertisement for a Mediterranean restaurant in London. The perfect clue. Left behind by the perfect murderers. And not a single spot of blood anywhere to be found on it.

"Planted?" Rolf suggested.

"Probably," the inspector answered.

"But why?" Rolf dropped it in the woman's bag and she moved away. "To misdirect us further, of course. But to what end?"

"To put the hounds on the wrong scent," Luc offered.

"But suppose it truly was a British team. Bungle it all with an obvious plant and send us scurrying down the wrong path. Dumb like a fox."

"Then let's say it is." Luc started limping toward his car. "I still must ask. What would your man Ritter have to do with the British, or what would they gain from his association? I, of course, am not as close as you to this man, but what I do know of him prevents me from believing Monsieur Ritter could be up to this sort of intrigue."

"Well taken," Rolf said, keeping his real opinion to himself. If the British were going to assassinate someone in Paris, wouldn't it be more logical to kill a high-ranking German officer instead of a sweet old businessman?

Luc's driver held the car door for him, and Luc gyrated himself into the backseat.

"May I offer you a ride?"

"Thank you, no," Rolf said. "I have a driver."

"You are correct though, major. We must keep our eyes open in even the silliest and darkest corners of this drama."

Rolf truly admired this man. He nodded graciously and smiled.

"You're a good sort, major." Luc put his palm out the car door to shake Rolf's hand. "It's almost as if you were part French." Another twinkle appeared in his droopy gray eyes. "Only the best parts, of course."

Rolf placed his forearm on the roof of the inspector's car and shook the man's soft hand, smiling warmly.

"*Bonsoir*, inspector."

53

Palma de Mallorca

In einem Augenblick
En un clin d'œil
In the Blink of an Eye

DAY TWELVE—Palma—Wednesday, 16 April 41—11:54 PM
Señor Melendes, as Ruti had named him, was pointing at the light on
the top floor of the tiny apartment house off the Sant Magi in Palma
de Mallorca, a vacant apartment in a new building. Ruti had broken in
and commandeered it for the night. From a slit in the curtains he
watched Señor Melendes and his dark-skinned partner, Señor
Morales, down below. The hapless team moved quickly with a
practiced, yet foolish confidence, entering the building and climbing
the stairs with skilled stealth. They barged into the apartment ready to
go straight to work, a cellophane bag of ether-laden cotton wads at the
ready. And in *einen Augenblick*, as was his trademark saying, in the
blink of an eye, both men lay dying on the apartment floor with two
small seven-millimeter bullet holes in each of them.

"Two hundred pesetas just to stand here with you and 'look
interested'?" the prostitute quipped, cuddling herself up to the quite
fashionable German businessman. "Why, I'm yours for the entire
night, señor."
The man Ruti had named Señor Schmidt watched the apartment
building from below. Known to the rest of the world as Kaspar Koch,
leader of Abwehr Ablegekommando IV, he took his newly purchased
whore in his arms and hugged her to him, kissing her and nuzzling
her neck. But his eyes never left the apartment building. He had
watched the two Gestapo operatives as they scrambled from their car
and followed Ruti from the hotel where he left Mélina, then onward
the apartment building. Kaspar waited for the perfunctory gunshots.
Like awaiting the last ticks of an alarm clock, a smile of vindication
crossed his stern face as he saw three quick flashes of white light in a
top-floor window, followed presently by a fourth. He was certain the
two Gestapo agents who had no doubt barged in on Heht, expecting to

take him by surprise, were now dead or dying on that apartment floor, suffering from one head and one chest shot each.

Kaspar kept the prostitute turned such that his left eye could watch the side door to the building. Ruti walked out and headed up the sidewalk toward Kaspar and his newly purchased lover. When he was certain of young Herr Heht's course, Kaspar took the woman's arm in his and softly touched her cheek, urged her head onto his shoulder as they proceeded up the sidewalk themselves, and into the park well ahead of Ruti.

"Tell me you love me," Kaspar whispered to her in Spanish. "I am Claudio."

"I love you, don Claudio," the nameless woman cooed.

"A little louder." He staggered with her, forcing her to catch him from falling into her.

"I love you so much, my sweet don Claudio," she repeated just as Ruti Heht rushed past them, these two oblivious lovers on their midnight stroll.

Kaspar kissed the top of his trollop's scented hair as he watched Ruti Heht bound up the steps into the Santa Catalina quarter. When Ruti was out of sight, Kaspar grabbed the girl by the hand and they ran up the steps themselves just in time to watch Ruti enter the Bellevue Hotel. It was only then the prostitute came to realize this German's intent. She'd been used as part of some stakeout drama. She smooched up her lips and pouted, stomping her foot and staring childishly at her new lover. Lighting two Week End cigarettes, Kaspar just smiled back and handed her one as he walked away.

"Was it good for you?" were his parting words.

54

Thursday, 17 April 1941

In Namen des Herrn
Pour faire l'œuvre du Seigneur
Doing the Lord's Work

DAY THIRTEEN—Palma—Thursday, 17 April 41—3:08 AM
Three hours had passed since Kaspar watched young Rutgers Heht
enter the hotel. Kaspar had collected his crew on the dock outside the
Café d'Orca and together they went over his plan. The Sardinian was
to pose as a vagrant, sleeping in a palm cluster just off the square with
a view of the hotel's front door. One of the Germans was to duck
down in a rented car parked at the back of the hotel with a view of the
service entrance, as well as the parking garage under the hotel. The
third was to take the motorbike and find a nearby vital crossroad to
stake out in case the targets escaped the others.

Kaspar had slithered his way into the garage and was moving
his tiny flashlight from one automobile to the next, slowly examining
each of the four vehicles parked there. One stood out above the rest, a
like-new Peugeot 202 Cabriolet midnight blue with its headlights
cloaked behind the sloped grill. Unlike every other car in the garage,
this one had absolutely nothing inside. No maps, no papers on the
dashboard, no umbrella or scarf tossed in the backseat, and the
ashtray was clean and had never been used.

Kaspar reached in his suit coat pocket and pulled out a thick
leather wallet, elongate and black with a full zipper and scores of tiny
clusters of stitching on the outside. Once unzipped, a single
carpenter's finishing nail was propped up in the tire tread such that
backing out of the parking space would puncture the right front tire.
With the wallet returned to his jacket, he strolled into the hotel from
the garage entrance.

The silence of the empty lobby was broken by Kaspar's
footsteps on the marble floor. The boy working as night clerk was
obviously sound asleep when Kaspar rang the front desk bell. When
he rounded the doorway from a back office, Kaspar saw a serrated red
line across his rosy cheek where he'd slept on a braided cord of some
sort that no doubt served as the seam trim to some throw pillow. The

boy's hair stood straight up on the left side of his head, and the skillfully trained Abwehr assassin Kapitan Kaspar Koch was able to deduce that this sweet-faced, honest young fellow actually had three jobs. This one, the one he slept at a few hours a night, a day job involving hard physical labor that embedded grime in the creases and prints of his fingers and under his fingernails. And his third, most important job, evidenced by his new gold wedding band, was caring immensely for and servicing regularly his brand-new and very sexually active young wife.

"How may I help you, señor?" he asked, rubbing his eyes.

"My young friend," Kaspar said, pulling out his other wallet stuffed with folded money from his right inside coat pocket. "Today is the luckiest day of your life."

Kaspar started lining six fifty-peseta notes on the front desk for the boy to gawk at. Picking one up and folding it, then moving it back and forth in his fingers, Kaspar smiled and said, "A German, posing as some other nationality, checked in last night with his wife, requiring a room that looked out onto the square."

The boy nodded, never taking his eye off the bill. Kaspar stuffed it in the boy's shirt pocket, then picked up another.

"Good," Kaspar said. "We understand each other. Now, this man left his wife in the hotel café at about ten thirty this evening. He returned thirty minutes later."

The boy nodded.

"And when he returned, he gave you some money and told you to ring his room if anyone should inquire about him, did he not?"

"Si, señor."

Another fifty-peseta note was slipped into the boy's pocket.

"How much did he give you?"

"Twenty pesetas."

Fifty more went into the pocket.

"You have a room directly across the hall from his, do you not?"

Another nod. Kaspar's new lapdog was now aptly trained. Another fifty.

"Is it occupied?"

The boy looked to the key slots behind him. "The man is in 506. So that would be 505." Seeing the key hanging in that key slot, he snapped it up and turned eagerly to Kaspar. "It is unoccupied, señor." He gleamed.

Another fifty.

"Now, how much for the room?"

"Seventy-five pesetas. But for you, señor, since it's so late—"

"Let me guess," Kaspar interjected, throwing up his hand and smiling. "Fifty?"

"Si, señor."

"And you'll fill out all the silly registration nonsense for me, won't you, my friend?"

The final fifty was left on the desk under the boy's sappy nod.

"One last thing. Can't have you thinking there is something nefarious going on, so I am going to tell you the truth about this whole business. I am an international policeman, a part of the Swiss Guard. You've heard of us, I'm sure. I work for the church, for the pope. And for God. I am simply following this man because I have reason to believe he has stolen from the Vatican treasury. I mean him no harm. When he leaves in the morning, I will simply slip away and follow him. That's the whole extent of all this intrigue. There is nothing for you to be alarmed about. Nothing for you to report. Not to your manager, not to the police. This is all just between us. Anything you would say could very well cost you your three hundred pesetas. Couldn't it, my friend?"

The boy nodded a number of times in coming to complete agreement with this officer of God.

Kaspar smiled back and shook his hand, but held tightly to the boy's grimy mitt and placed his left hand over it, adding, "It's so good when we do the Lord's work!"

The elevator was avoided. One could never trust them not to be noisy. The stairway was on the opposite side of the hallway from Leutnant Heht's room. Kaspar opened the hallway door to the fifth floor just enough to take inventory of its layout and decor. White ceiling. Beige papyrus wallpaper. Cream-painted doors and trim. He closed the door and returned down half a flight of stairs, sat there, and took out the thick leather service wallet again. This time when he unfolded it he laid it open to reveal its contents. Sundry tools of a skilled investigative assassin were secured neatly in tiny elastic loops sewn into the inside of the wallet. Five nine-millimeter hollow point bullets lined one side. There were two glass syringes. A surgeon's scalpel. Two glass vials of phenol. A tiny glass perfume atomizer filled with linseed oil. A wine cork was stabbed with thumbtacks, carpenter's finishing nails, sewing needles, straight pins, safety pins, and two hypodermic needles. There were four glass vials of sodium cyanide, a straight razor, a spool of white thread, one black spool, and six double-edge razor blades enclosed in cardboard. There were small rolled-up donuts of string and cord and wire, and a garrote made from a length of piano wire tied to two sticks of hickory was wound up nice and flat along the bottom of the wallet.

Kaspar Koch was a brilliant assassin with more than a decade of experience in the field. This young upstart Rutgers Heht was no match for him. A part of him even reveled in the sport of it all. His crew would have simply been used for this abduction were it not for the fact that young Herr Heht had demonstrated such cunning and prowess in eliminating the two Gestapo assailants. In doing so, Heht had cast down the gauntlet, so to speak, and no doubt the end of his miserable and very short life.

Kaspar withdrew the perfume atomizer filled with linseed oil, the spool of white thread, and a single thumbtack from his task wallet and quietly set to work. He made a small knot on the end of the thread, looped it over the tack point, and cinched it tight. With his shoes tied together and strung around his neck, he crept up barefoot to the door of room 506, Heht's room. Slowly, he embedded the thumbtack in the upper outside corner on the doorknob side of the door, then strung the thread across the hall to his own room, 505, where he popped the spool in his mouth and very quickly sprayed the atomizer of oil in the keyhole and on the hinges of the door. Like a surgeon, he slipped the key in and slowly twisted until the latch quietly snapped. He stepped inside, strung the thread over the top of his door, and quietly closed it. Switching on the bedside lamp, he took a teacup and a tiny tin spoon from the tea service on the desk and tied them both to the thread about midway down the door. Now, when Herr Heht or his poor wife opened their door to escape, the cup would ring like a bell and Kaspar would know.

Satisfied the trap was set and inescapable, he stretched out in the bed, still in his jacket, just in case. The lamp switched off and Kaspar Koch was soundly and carelessly asleep in ten minutes.

DAY THIRTEEN—Palma—Thursday, 17 April 41—5:44 AM
The ornate brass door handle to room 506 slowly moved downward. The door, however, didn't open immediately, but did so very slowly, centimeter by centimeter. Across the hall in Kaspar Koch's room the cup and spoon inched slowly, silently, down the inside of his door. With the door to 506 barely open, two fingers and a thumb pinched the thread tightly. A sharp knife cut the thread while it remained taut

between Ruti's fingers. He opened the door and pried the thumbtack from it, popped it in his mouth, and tiptoed across the hall. Stabbing the tack in the lintel of room 505, he made a tiny sheepshank, keeping pressure on the thread at all times, then cinched it around the tack, wrapped it a few times for good measure, and snickered.

Ruti and Mélina were quickly in the parking garage. He opened the trunk and stuffed her night bag on top of all the shopping sacks and suitcases. While she got in, he raised the hood and checked the coil and plug wires and the fuel line. Quickly, he slid under the car, checking the brake lines, the rest of the fuel line, and the tires. Smiling, he shook his head as he flipped the finishing nail out from under the front tire with his middle finger.

Ablegekommando team member number two was upset with himself that he hadn't noticed the garage door opening. But he was primed and ready when the blue Peugeot 202 passed him, heading up the hill and out of town. He quickly flipped his cigarette in the street and pushed the starter button. The car started, but died immediately. Again he tried. It started, but died. Cursing, he jumped out and opened the hood. Everything looked fine. All the wires were in place and intact. He slid under the car and saw nothing out of order.

It wasn't ten minutes later that the man formerly known as Wehrmacht Leutnant Rutgers Heht, now known as Señor Rodrigo Guerrero, and his lovely wife were winding their way out of town in their midnight-blue Peugeot, purchased only last week by Rodrigo himself, and driving through the calm, juniper-scented morning to disappear forever into the remote Mallorcan mountains.

DAY THIRTEEN—Palma—Thursday, 17 April 41—6:48 AM
The door to room 505 flew open. The spoon slammed against the wall. The cup shattered. Kaspar dashed across the hallway, through the open door of room 506, and rifled Ruti's room, finding nothing. He ran down the stairs and across the lobby to the garage exit. The Peugeot was gone. The garage door was wide open. And at his own car with its hood raised stood the Sardinian and the perplexed driver.

"How did he do it?" Kaspar scolded them. "Why aren't you in pursuit?"

"He must have come sometime in the night and sabotaged the car. It starts then immediately dies." The hood still raised, Kaspar checked the cables, the fuel line. Nothing out of order. He quickly slid under the car.

"You imbeciles!" his muffled voice exclaimed. He scurried back out from under the car and demanded they look at what he had found. Both men surveyed the car's undercarriage. Neither saw anything at first, then the Sardinian noticed the problem. In three places along the fuel line, Ruti had pinched the brass tubing shut with a pair of pliers.

"Verdammt!" Kaspar cried. "We lost him now for good."

"No we have not," the Sardinian said, jumping up from under the car and pointing down the street. There came team member number three on his white moped, smiling and nodding proudly.

His position for the stakeout had been the only fork in the street leading from the hotel. He had been hiding there all night, watching, waiting. If Ruti had been more attentive, he could have seen the glow of the man's cigarette in the dark shadows of a small park nestled in the street's fork, where traveling right and downhill led to the southern coast of the island, and taking the left fork uphill sent one ultimately into the foothills of the Mallorcan mountains.

"You have his location marked?" Kaspar asked, before the man could come to a stop.

"Not exactly," the man said, quickly continuing in order to stifle Kaspar's rage. "But I stayed with him until he headed up into a remote area where there will be only three possible roads to stake out." He then smiled. "Won't that do?"

After Kaspar accepted his own shortcomings, he had no recourse but to smile at his crew member and reply, "Yes, it will have to."

DAY THIRTEEN—Bunyola—Thursday, 17 April 41—8:17 AM
The car stopped at the fork in the northbound Mallorcan highway. All four men got out, and the third member of the team, with his moped stuffed in the trunk, explained he had lost Leutnant Heht in this area along the road to Sóller.

"There are a number of small roads leading up into the mountains. If I were him, I'd be back in these mountains, away from everyone," he surmised.

"Couldn't he have just continued over the mountain on into Sóller?" Kaspar asked.

"Impossible," the man answered. "If he'd stayed on the highway, I'd have been able to see from my vantage point. Besides, there's a German submarine base at Sóller. No, he turned off on one of these roads. There are only three ways he could have gone."

"Good, then you amble around on them today and see what you can find. Be discreet. What's the name of that village over there?" Kaspar asked pointing through the trees.

"Bunyola."

Team member number two was assigned to Bunyola for the next few days. He was to especially watch the local bank and the post office. The Sardinian was to find a vantage point high above the highway and watch it. Kaspar would take the car and meet up with each of them throughout the next day or so.

"None of you are new to this," he said. "He will make a mistake. And we will find him. Be vigilant."

55

Ein Winter voller Unzufriedenheit
Un hiver du mécontentement
A Winter of Discontent

DAY THIRTEEN—Paris—Thursday, 17 April 41—10:14 AM
An unusual feeling settled over Rolf when he walked into the First
American Bank. No one looked up. No one seemed the least bit
concerned that a German major was in the bank. It was as if his
presence, or that of any German officer, was just a normal part of the
bank's regular day. He announced himself to the woman at the central
desk and told her a member of his staff had set up an appointment
with a manager.

The bank official's name was Williams. He was quick to
announce he was set to return to New York in six days and was very
happy to get out of Europe before it all "turned ugly." Rolf showed
him Addie's passport.

"I was sure I would know Miss Bridges if I saw her, but I have
to say, major, I don't remember her. You must understand. Paris was
full of 'Miss Bridges' in the thirties. So many young, rich girls
chasing the 'movable feast' and getting daddy dearest to fund it with
a so-called 'job' at an American bank or at the American Hospital, or
some English-language bookstore or other. But I did talk by telephone
to a young woman at our branch in Châtel-Guyon who did indeed
know of her."

Rolf had concerns that he was being brushed aside by this head
teller and was about to request a meeting with the bank's general
manager or president when this man, Williams, explained further.

"You see, major, most of our American staff left Paris ahead
the German invasion. Many went home. A few moved to our branch
in London. And a handful to Châtel-Guyon. The Paris branch is now
operated almost entirely by French staff."

"When did Miss Bridges start working at the bank?"

"Again, with the German army bearing down on Paris, while
most of the deposit records and deposits themselves moved to Vichy,
employee's files and nonessential records were simply destroyed. So,
all I'm really able to offer you is general information about all our
American staff and the few details I could garner from the former

employee who is now in unoccupied France. So, to answer your question, Miss Bridges started somewhere around 1936 or '37."

"What were her duties?"

"I was told that she really did little more than odd jobs for the first few years she was here. I believe a position was basically invented for her as a favor to her father, who is also a bank executive in the states."

"Would she have had set hours and been expected to work each day of the week?"

"Well, again, most of these girls had never done a day's work in their lives. So, I'm sure tardiness and absenteeism would have been common. But I have to say, for a lot of them, I really think they accepted their jobs as a commitment to a path toward independence and adulthood."

"What about since the war started?"

"I do know she took a leave of absence after the invasion of France. She and a number of nonessentials volunteered for Anne Morgan's ambulance service. That would have been since May of last year. Before that, she probably would have just worked in the filing room, done errands and courier runs locally now and then, like most of the Scott and Zelda set employed at the bank."

"Would there have been occasion before the war for her to have been a courier to either Germany or Switzerland?" Rolf asked, oblivious to the Scott and Zelda reference. He had brought her passport with him and in the ride over had checked all her visas. No Swiss or German visas were found on the passport. Nothing but French. The latest was to expire in January of 1942.

"Germany would be very doubtful," Williams answered while the whole bank lit up radiantly as the sun broke through outside.

"Switzerland? Perhaps, but running to Switzerland would more than likely be handled by regular and more managerial employees, rather than these *femmes de favor*. I'm sure her courier efforts were mostly within Paris or maybe to Lille or Reims at best."

F. Scott Fitzgerald! Rolf thought. The American novelist who obviously worked from Paris. The Scott and Zelda set. Of course, his wife was Zelda. *The Winter of our Discontent.*

"What does an American bank do in foreign cities like Paris?"

"Really, the same as Credit Suisse or the Reichsbank. Handle the needs of countrymen or their business concerns in France, in Paris. Before the war, you know, there were over fifty thousand

Americans living or working in France. More than half of them right here in Paris."

"I may wish to talk to the young lady in Châtel-Guyon. Could you arrange that?"

"I'm sure I could. If we could coordinate a time."

"Does the name Edith Brückner mean anything to you, Mr. Williams?"

"I'm sorry, no. It doesn't. Did she work here too?"

56

Die Sterbenden und die Toten
Près de morts et les morts
The Near-dead and the Dead

DAY THIRTEEN—Paris—Thursday, 17 April 41—11:10 AM
With Sabina at his back, whipping the belt cords of her silk robe back
and forth on her hips, Bruno slid the key in the door, turned it twice,
and opened it. Suzi's room was dark and smelled foul. Sabina threw
the drapes open and daylight exploded. Nothing in the room looked
like it had been touched in days. Bruno slowly lifted the duvet from
Suzi. She was on her side in the bed, turned toward the wall, wearing
only cotton panties, terribly soiled with urine. And her tiny body was
covered in bruises—black, green, violet, purple, the colors of a
sadistic rainbow. He feared her dead at first. But when he touched her
shoulder, she moaned.

Gently and very slowly, he rolled her over to her back, stopping
briefly each time her whimper became a weak scream. Sabina stood
back and watched, in shock. She had been the one to suggest to Bruno
they break in to her room. Suzi had missed three nights'
performances, much to Sabina's delight who ultimately grew
concerned and told Bruno she feared the girl's possible rotting corpse
might create problems for the club. When Bruno softly turned Suzi's
head toward them, Sabina groaned. Suzi's head was swollen
freakishly. Both her eyes were swollen shut. There were rings of dried
brown blood around her nose and ears.

"Why the hell didn't you say something before now, Sabina?"
Bruno bellowed, looking over his shoulder, glaring at her. But his
sour face melted immediately when he saw Sabina with her kerchief
to her gaping mouth and tears in her eyes. She moved to the bed and
pushed Bruno aside.

"You poor darling," she said, sitting down next to Suzi. She
rolled up the slinky sleeves of her robe and folded them over tightly
above her elbows. Then, turning to Bruno, she commanded, "Bring
me some towels and soap and water. Some witch hazel and some ice
too. I'll take care of her."

Bruno turned to leave, then stopped short and spun back
around.

"What does that mean, exactly, Sabina? 'You'll take care of her,'" Bruno remarked, snidely. "You're going to push her out the window?"

"Go," was all she said.

Bruno looked around the room before he left, searching for evidence that Suzi's beating had happened here, perhaps some drunken customer. A customer he would find and beat like a dog. But the room was neat as a pin.

"How did this happen?" he barked. "Who did this to her?"

"How does it always happen, Bruno?" Sabina snapped back. "Who always does it?" She turned back to Suzi and sweetly touched her cracked, swollen lips.

"Fucking Nazis."

DAY THIRTEEN—Paris—Thursday, 17 April 41—1:54 PM

"Kruder here," Sturmbannführer Alois Kruder announced as he picked the phone in his office.

"Kruder!" the voice at the other end of the line screamed. "I am Obersturmführer Reiner in Madrid."

"Heil Hitler, Herr Obersturmführer."

"Yes, of course, Heil Hitler! Now Kruder." The voice grunted and cleared its throat. "Are you the one who put my Spanish adjutant and his sergeant on the trail of one Leutnant Rutgers Heht from Paris?"

"I am indeed. Do you have news of this man, Heht?"

"Yes, I do have news of your man Heht, you self-serving piece of pig shit. I do 'have news.' My adjutant and his sergeant were both murdered—executed—in a Palma apartment last night. What do you have to say about that?"

"Sir, I would say your men are very inept, or very foolish, or both."

"Under what authority do you assume the right to dictate orders to my men?"

"Under my own, sir. I am investigating the murder of a high-level German businessman here in Paris, and I asked your people to catch up to this man Heht and follow him. Report his movements back to me. If they tried to arrest the man, then they are fools. I warned them he was dangerous. They failed to take heed."

"These men weren't desk jockeys. They were trained and highly skilled investigators working for the Gestapo, for me, Kruder.

Men who have performed some very specialized services for me for years."

"And who obviously lack an understanding of the word 'dangerous,' sir."

"You listen to me, Kruder. You flippant back-office golden pheasant. I'll have you busted to Sturmführer before you can count to ten, young man. Do you hear what I'm saying to you?"

"Quiet regrettable, sir. But you're cutting out dreadfully. I can hardly catch every few words."

"Don't you hang up on me, Kruder, you—"

Kruder slammed the phone on its hook and snarled. Incompetent fools! He'd lost Heht now, for sure. Verdammt!

57

Friday, 18 April 1941

Dummköpfe
Les imbéciles
The Nitwits

DAY FOURTEEN—Paris—Friday, 18 April 41—7:10 AM
Two Frenchmen bounded briskly up the steps leading from the Métro, one in a felt beret and charcoal work dungarees. The other had the brim of a brown trilby pulled down to his eyes. He wore a corduroy day jacket and chewed continually on a toothpick. Their step was lively and their course well-traveled. After three blocks of gawking at every remotely attractive woman they passed, and patting or pinching a few rumps, they entered a tenement apartment in the 18th and made their way up to the top floor. They argued loudly about the merits or lack thereof of two popular French football teams, Excelsior de Roubaix or Club Français. Their rumbling voices left a wake of screaming babies and barking dogs behind them as they stomped up each flight of worn wooden stairs. A few taps at the door and they heard footsteps on a creaky floor. Identities verified, the door opened and the men were let into the squalid, tiny attic room.

"Did you bring food?" the man in the room with a Kaiser mustache implored. A ripped stretch of shirt was tied around his head with a glob of dried blood where his right ear might still be. The top third of his right suspender was blood soaked and dried as well.

"I haven't eaten in days, you dogs."

"We're supposed to move you," the man in the beret said. "You'll have food there." He looked over at the bed where a huge man lay soaked in sweat, his face ashen, his mouth wide open. A pillow, brown and black with blood, was tied to his side by a belt around his waist.

"The bullet went through his kidney," the trilby with the toothpick mumbled. "How is he still alive?""

"He's given off the stench of death for two days now," the man with the bandaged ear remarked.

"So do you."

"What took you so long? I have been starving. And you bring me no food?"

The man in the trilby took a pillow from the worn-out sofa and pressed it firmly over the face of the man in the bed, Konni Ritter's true shooter. He moved the toothpick from one side of his mouth to the other with his tongue, fighting off the weak, flailing arms of his victim. The smothered man's partner simply watched eagerly for death to take his fellow conspirator, so he could be moved to some other hideout and finally get something to eat.

When the flailing arms went limp, the trilby with the pillow kept pressure on his face for five more minutes. Certainty was, after all, important. When he regained his feet, he withdrew a glass capsule from his pocket and smiled. Suddenly, the man in the beret grabbed Konni Ritter's second murderer from behind, tearing the makeshift bandage from his head and strangling him with it. The man with the capsule quickly tossed it in his gaping mouth and forced his jaw shut several times until the glass broke. With the poison doing their work for them now, the assassins released him and let him squirm, kicking and flailing in desperation on the floor while one of them tugged the pants off the dead man in the bed and the other slipped something into a tweed jacket hanging on the back of the tenement door. A pair of underwear was pulled up on the legs of the dead man in the bed. With a twinkle in his eye, the man in the beret glanced down at the poisoned man on the floor, then tossed his head toward the bed as he winked and smiled at his partner. Together, they fought and fumbled with the choking, wheezing man on the floor until they had him completely naked. They lifted him on top of the man in the bed, laughing and joking while the poison took its final effect. Once accomplished, a pair of wire-rimmed glasses were placed clumsily on his now lifeless face.

Out in the hallway and all the way down the six flights of stairs the two of them poked and jabbed each other as they lit cigarettes and chuckled at the funny prank they had pulled. Wouldn't the police be entertained!

58

Das Ergebnis
Les résultats
The Findings

DAY FOURTEEN—Paris—Friday, 18 April 41—8:18 AM
"Berlin calling for you, sir." Rolf looked at his watch and wound it as he followed the orderly to a booth in the telephone bank and the call was put through.

"Major? Gep here. I have further information regarding this Brückner woman."

"Let's hear it, Gep," Rolf said, glancing again at his wristwatch and making a mental note of the time.

"The woman Edith Brückner was arrested in Berlin on the twenty-eighth of December, 1939, for possession of false documents. On January fourth, she was sent to Ravensbrück, where she apparently died of pneumonia ten weeks later on March nineteenth."

"Are you quite sure of this?" Rolf asked.

"I'm holding her cancelled passport, her *Sterbeurkunde* showing death from pneumonia at 3:41 on 19-03-40, as well as her *Häftlings-Personal-Karte* right here in front of me. Under the Special Characteristics section on the prisoner's ID card, the administrator jotted only 'infirm.' The woman was evidently ill when she was admitted to the camp."

"Bring photographs of each with you, won't you, Gep?" Rolf looked at his watch again. "When do you return?"

"I'm catching the ten AM, but I wish to route back through Cologne, with your permission, major. I want to check on my friend."

"Completely acceptable, Gep. I just myself heard about the British bombing of Cologne last night. I would expect no less of you."

"So that should put me back in Paris first thing in the morning."

"Good, I'll see you then."

"Rolf, there's something more. Have you talked to Kruder?"

"No, not at all."

"I received a call this morning from my man in Innsbruck informing me that a pair of Kunsthorn Heitner artisans were arrested by the Gestapo. It seems they have given up information

331

incriminating Herr Ritter in a smuggling and possible espionage operation. Rolf, that information was given to Kruder two days ago. Has he shared any of this with you?" Gep asked.

"No," Rolf replied, fuming. "It seems he has chosen not to do so. I'll confront him immediately."

DAY FOURTEEN—Paris—Friday, 18 April 41—8:22 AM
Sturmbannführer Alois Kruder had joined the SS in 1934. A former Nuremburg criminal prosecutor, his talents were quickly noticed and acquired by the Gestapo. He was attached to Reich's security sub office IV E-3—Security and Counterintelligence. He was the kind of man who trusted nothing and no one. Every remark, every statement, every question posed by anyone was subject to his suspicious scrutiny. His immediate excuse for coming to Paris was, of course, the Jew. Though secondary, if important at all, to the military administration, the registration and location of French Jews and especially foreign Jews who had immigrated ahead of the German invasion was paramount to the Party and to the SS. And the French police and Vichy administration were more than happy to help.

Kruder looked over the list of names he had just been handed. Excitement swelled in him as he rifled through the pages, nearly a hundred of them, checking the *Rasse und Politik* columns to see that nearly four thousand foreign Jews with questionable papers would be rounded up by the local French authorities in the next few days.

The wonderful morning was made even brighter when Kruder snapped up the ringing telephone.

"Kruder here."

"Kruder," Rolf bellowed. "Von Gerz here. I'm phoning you so I might listen to some contrived excuse as to why I was not informed of the interrogation of some Kunsthorn Heitner artisans by the Gestapo in Innsbruck. All quite relative to the Ritter murder. I'm told you have had the transcript in your possession since Wednesday."

"Regrettable. I had truly forgotten to send that information to you the other day. Planned to get that to you first thing this morning, but it must have slipped my mind. I'll be more than happy to meet you somewhere with it, if you'd like."

"I'll send one of my people for it."

With a gleeful, almost orgasmic glow, Kruder smiled as the line went sorrowfully dead.

59

Versöhnung
Réconciliation
Reconciliation

DAY FOURTEEN—Paris—Friday, 18 April 41—9:26 AM
The knock on her door startled Addie. She prayed it would be Rolf
and she could get to the bottom of last night's ridiculous accusation.
When the door was opened, a tinge of anger grew in her as Rolf was
just standing there, smiling.

"Have you had breakfast?" he said with a glib smile.

She stared grimly at him before answering.

"Yes, as a matter of fact I did," she pouted indignantly. "I found
a moldy cracker behind the stove and I gorged myself on it!"

"Pity," Rolf declared, inhaling deeply and biting the inside of
his cheek as he quietly added, "Lunch, then?"

"I love you, Rolf, darling. But it's official. You've gone quite
mad, haven't you?"

He nodded, snorted, and rolled his eyes.

"Twenty minutes, then?" he added.

"More like an hour. I'm not even dressed."

More nodding, then Rolf flipped his head to the left and said,
"I'll be on the Alphonse-Deville."

"Then I shall meet you on the Alphonse-Deville."

While he waited, Rolf ordered an espresso on the shady little
square. He sat smoking and reading the newspaper as a warm and
very pleasant breeze made florets of sunbeams dance over the pages.
The outdoor seating area of Bistro Bruno covered in the sparse shade
of sycamores and a few Bitburger Pils umbrellas was full of
Wehrmacht officers enjoying the warm spring day. The German ban
on all unnecessary automobile traffic was a blessing on such a lovely
day. An eerie quiet prevailed throughout, especially where any
number of German officers gathered. Conversations were barely
above whispers.

A remnant of last night's fierce rainstorm ran as a wide brown
puddle across the boulevard Raspail. Cyclists quickly splayed their
legs straight out as they suddenly found themselves about to wheel

through the deep water. In an effort to keep themselves dry, female cyclists would not only raise and spread their legs, but would simultaneously draw their dress skirts hurriedly upward with one hand. Many times the process revealed their white, pink, and black lace and cotton panties to the rows of appreciative officers seated along the street. Occasionally, very gentile fingertip applause would run through the tables as the men politely demonstrated their gratitude.

During one such display, a speckled farm horse drawing a bulky wagon clopped her way along the rue d'Assas and stopped on the other side of the small delta-shaped square. Perfunctorily, a family of Eastern Europeans set immediately to work as the huge horse snorted and shook his unkempt mane. Papa drove a section of rusty pipe into the ground with a sledgehammer while mama set up a tall chrome and Naugahyde chair in a shady spot at the base of a tree trunk. The couple's teenaged daughter unfolded a wooden table and set up a display of colorfully embroidered handkerchiefs and doilies. A red-and-white-striped pole was slid into the pipe section by papa and a matching cross member with ropes sporting red bows strung from both ends was set over the top of the pole. This was followed by the untying of two tiny Welsh ponies that were led to the makeshift carrousel and tied each in his place, a Bedouin merry-go-round. Two French children ran to the tiny horses. The gypsy daughter lifted them on the backs of the ponies, taking a few sous from their au pair.

While papa donned his accordion and started playing "L'accordéoniste" mama set her array of scissors, mirrors, and clippers on a long table next to the barber chair. Before she could get the chair completely wiped down with a scented cloth, one of the officers removed his hat and set it down on the table, then quickly sat smiling in the woman's chair for a haircut. A second officer arose and set his hat next to the first man's, then returned to his seat. Seeing how the procedure was played out, Rolf set his hat in the line, making him third for a haircut.

When it was Rolf's turn, he took his seat and the gruff woman flopped the white barber's apron over him, cinching it around his neck. She came around in front of him and, seeing his curly brown locks, gave him an anxious look. Tilting her head, her face slumped in sadness, she seemed to ask, "Are you sure you want me to butcher these lovely curls?"

Smiling, Rolf closed his eyes resolutely and nodded. The woman shrugged, snapped the scissors a few times, and moved back behind him, muddling her doubtless displeasure in this disagreeable task in her native tongue.

"Having your ears lowered, I see," Hans-Hubert quipped as he moved up beside Rolf from behind. "Don't let her overcharge you. She'll ask salon prices—ten, twenty francs—but she'll take five. A Frenchman pays two."

"How do I make it through life without your direction, Hans?"

"Just protecting you from yourself, Rolf, old chum." Hans-Hubert snapped up a parchment-wrapped sugar cube soaked in lemon juice from the woman's bowl and dropped a coin in its place. "You're far too pleasant for a German officer, Rolf. We need to work on your demeanor. Especially if you're determined to return to dreadful Warsaw."

"My mind's made up, Hans. However, I am serious about leaving Gep here, if he is so inclined. I really think he can be of genuine value to you. And a . . . Old Shatterhand."

"We can speak freely, Rolf. This woman's just a Balkan peasant. She barely speaks French, much less German." Hans-Hubert pulled a chair up backward in front of Rolf and sat astraddle it with his arms folded on its back.

"I'm afraid," he said, the sugar cube bouncing around against his straight white teeth, "our friends in Hamburg didn't share my vigor for the 'Shatterhand' name. They're coming up with something 'less conspicuous.' But the operation is proceeding, nonetheless. That's something to be pleased about, I guess. I'm traveling to Monaco to interview another American recruit next week. Oh, yes. Something else. I have two American recruits flying in for explosives and radio training with von Gröning at La Bretonnière, our training facility in Brittany. They arrive from Lisbon on the twenty-sixth, a week from tomorrow. You're welcome to use the return flight to get Addie to Lisbon for her steamer back to America. I hear your investigation is winding up. A British terror plot?"

"Not sure. It's all too convenient, Hans."

"By the way, Rolf, my man Heht, the deserter. He turned up in Barcelona. An Ablegekommando has tracked him to Mallorca. But he somehow gave them the slip. They'll find him though. Those boys are good at their job."

"I know this is your man, Hans. And I'm sure this is all very unsettling for you. But I want to be kept abreast of any developments in his regard. I'm convinced this is all somehow tied to Herr Ritter's murder."

"You could be right, Rolf. But I'm convinced he's nothing more than a simple thief and a traitor." Hans shook his head and slapped the chair back.

"By the way, old man, while I'm gone, you and Addie are welcome to use my villa in Saint-Germain-en-Laye." He smiled coyly at Rolf and added, "And my convertible!"

His haircut almost finished, the Balkan barberess withdrew a length of twisted wire with a handle at one end and a hairpin curve at the other. She skewered a large ball of cotton at that end and dipped it in alcohol. Her rough fingers softly touched Rolf's chin and turned his head to one side. She lit the cotton ball afire and dolloped it against and about his ear a few times.

"That's quite nice of you, Hans. I'll consider it."

The woman turned his head the other way, and the blue flame singed ear hair away on that side.

"Do you have a suit of clothes, or just your uniforms?" Hans-Hubert asked as he lit a Luxor and let the smoke crawl upward from his mouth, only to suck it back in through his nose. "There's a number of good suits and sport jackets in my closet. Feel free to wear any that suit you."

The barberess slipped a comb through Rolf's hair and handed him a mirror.

"When will you return from Monaco?" Rolf asked, looking at his new haircut and showing his complete satisfaction with smiling eyes, a nod, and an antithetical frown.

"I depart on Tuesday and should return by Friday. I would have left tomorrow, but I'm told I can't miss the Führer's birthday party. Otto Abetz is planning some gala at the embassy. Everyone will be there. I'll put your name on the guest list. Addie's too."

"We'll see, Hans, my friend."

"So. When do you leave, Rolf?" Hans asked in return. "For Warsaw."

"I leave Sunday morning the twenty-seventh on the Paris-Berlin Express," Rolf said, handing the barberess twenty francs.

"I should be back by then," Hans-Hubert said, shaking his head at Rolf's generosity.

"Good," Rolf added, grabbing his hat from the table.

"I'd hate to miss seeing you off."

Addie was radiant in a white summer dress with red Swiss dots, a red belt, and matching gloves and bag. Cocked to one side on her head sat a Tyrolean tasseled perch. Only took a few steps down the rue du Cherche-Midi before Rolf stopped her and asked if this wasn't the dress she had covered herself with the first time he saw her across the courtyard that day. It pleased her immensely that he had remembered.

"You very well know, Rolf," Addie said, tucking her hand in the fold of his arm. "I refuse to let you take another step without explaining to me what on earth you were talking about the other day. This mysterious woman I'm supposed to be."

"It was as you mentioned," he confessed. "A coincidence."

"Really," she quipped, polishing possible lipstick off the front of her teeth with her tongue.

"The Brückner woman, it turns out, died March before last. Gep is returning with documentation."

"So, I went through another drilling and, I might add, a de facto arrest! And all over a mere coincidence? You're completely insane, darling!"

Rolf tightened his lips. "I'll give you that. I deserve it." He shot her a frightening look and added, "But I wouldn't take it any further."

"Rolf, I told you. I will never lie to you again. I learned my lesson. I'm not angry with you. I was hurt. Deeply. I love you, Rolf, darling. And earning your trust again is the most important thing in my life right now. Please believe me."

He stopped and turned to her, touching her pretty cheek with that magical knuckle of his.

"I have to ask your forbearance, Addie. I'm telling you this only to explain the overt distrust I may display now and then. I was . . ." He searched for the right word, discarded a few, and came up with, " . . . betrayed by the last woman in my life. I won't allow it to happen again."

She looked up at him and gave him a reassuring smile.

"I promise, it won't, darling. I never will."

As they strolled along the fruit and flower market on the Seine promenade, Rolf stopped suddenly and pulled Addie back to a stand selling homemade jams and preserves. He lifted one from a wooden divider box. The words *Confiture Fraises Cerises—50 de fruit / 50 de sucre* were handwritten on a paper sticker pasted to the jar's lid. Rolf

held it up to the daylight and tilted it this way and that. A smile
gleamed in his face. Its black contents turned to streaks of ruby red as
it slid down the sides of the glass jar. He quickly overpaid the sweet
old woman and removed the lid's ring and popped off the lid. With
his knife he cut away half of the thick layer of paraffin with *08-39*
scratched into the wax that covered the sweet nectar. The strawberry-
cherry jam had been in someone's cellar since the war had started, a
few jars no doubt brought out every so often to supplement the
family's existence.

A brief stop at a bakery, and they headed to the rose garden
behind Notre Dame, Addie on one of Rolf's arms, a baguette under
the other, a bottle of Vichy water in his hand. They splayed
themselves out in the sunny grass. Rolf drizzled the wonderful goo
over chunks of bread and fed it to the both of them. Noticing a dab on
her cheek, he pulled her to him by her sticky chin and licked it off.

Breakfast finished, faces and fingers washed in the fountain, the
stroll across the Seine to the Right Bank was delightful. Springtime
was budding along the crowded Quai d'Orsay as Rolf and Addie
ambled past art, sculpture, and used-book displays. Their path was
littered here and there with mounds of various types of anti-Semitic
tracts that had no doubt been stacked on a number of book stands by
members of the PPF, the French pro-Nazi militia, then mysteriously
knocked off onto the sidewalk—accidentally. The smudged and
crumpled leaflets underfoot displayed all sorts of caricatures, one
depicting a hooked-nosed Jewish villain raping the grand dame
Liberté of France. They reminded Addie of Rolf's defense of the little
Jewish woman in Cologne.

"Disgusting," she said, kicking a small pile to the side as they
moved along. "How does one cope with such vile displays?"

"You become accustomed to it," Rolf exclaimed, to himself as
much as to her. He was reminded of an incident in Warsaw, where he
and Gep watched through a frosty café window as an old Jew sneezed
on the sleeve of a passing SS colonel. The Jew was shot on the spot.
He and Gep and every other witness to the execution simply sipped
and chatted on in the warm café while the little Jew lay dead on the
frozen sidewalk.

"In time one's spirit must toughen to stone in that regard," he
coldly added.

"Well, I can tell you this," Addie quickly interjected. "You
weren't being tough in Cologne, Rolf, darling. You were being

strong!" She squeezed his arm and leaned her cheek against his shoulder, smiling proudly.

Rolf could only clench his jaw and wonder.

They hadn't walked far before they noticed Sabina hurrying toward them. Deeply absorbed in some purpose or other, she walked right past them.

"Sabina!" Addie shouted, breaking the singer's determined stride.

Sabina snapped around, startled the see them and also a bit annoyed. The Dutch bunny fur on the collar of her urban cape danced in the breeze. She was made up beautifully and dressed in a very conservative ensemble, for her. Still, she was an incongruent vision against the bright sunshine. And Addie was quick to point it out.

"Sabina, dear," she chortled, smiling sweetly. "You're such a beautiful, but queer sight away from the club. An owl in the daylight!"

Or a bat, Rolf thought, chuckling to himself.

"Where are you off to in such blur?" Addie added.

"Having lunch with an old friend, ma chère," Sabina said, giving them each three Dutch cheeks and glancing quickly at her diamond watch. "And I'll never get there on time. Sorry, but I simply must hurry along. Ciao, darlings!" And off she strode, her muscular calves balancing bouncing fur and wriggling flesh on teetering high heels as she maneuvered the uneven cobblestones.

Rolf and Addie continued their stroll through Paris, working their way around le Marais, Montmartre, and by late that afternoon down past the Palais Royal and through its budding gardens to the restaurant le Grand Véfour, where, owing to Rolf's uniform, they were seated immediately. Under the beautiful stained-glass ceiling, they partook of duck terrine, lamb with truffles, and quince tortes. Remarkable fares that this ancient kitchen of Napoleon and Josephine was somehow still able to produce quite handsomely. This was paired with a '35 Cheval Blanc, ubiquitous toasts to the war's expedient end, and abundant banter and smiles.

Later, a leisurely evening walk ended at a cinema off the Champs-Élysées, where they somehow found room to quickly dispose of a shared pasteboard cone of sugared popcorn and beer in paper cups. Rolf had questioned why the lights were left on in the gilded theater during the newsreels. Doing so, she explained, kept sneezes and coughs at bay while the newsreels proclaimed the week's victorious exploits of the juggernaut German army. After a few advertisements, one of which starred Maurice Chevalier touting Week End brand cigarettes, and a cute cartoon, they purely and thoroughly enjoyed the motion picture.

The story was an hilarious French comedic farce set in the 19th century about the slapstick antics of a bungling, cross-eyed French barber, summoned to cut the hair of the "Occupying Military Eminence," whose original barber had been handily dispatched for a "bad haircut." Avoiding *flics et faucons* (highbrow acrimony for that century's German occupiers), a madcap chase throughout Paris ensued, ending with the cockeyed barber's capture and delivery to "his Eminence" at his palace, who turns out, as it were, to be almost entirely bald!

Addie and Rolf both fought for breath and wiped tears from their eyes as they laughed unfettered throughout the entire glorious tale.

Sabina entered the seedy café in the Marais and took a table, ordering an espresso and a poire William. It wasn't long before a thin Chinese woman in a purple wool coat and dark green cloche hat joined her at the table. She was from the Paris Indochine quarter, comprised for a century of Siamese, Indonesian, and Chinese immigrants from French Indo-China.

"Where is man, Ritter?" the Chinese woman asked. She remembered Sabina, but had concerns about meeting her without Konni's presence.

"He's gone home," was Sabina's response.

"What is real name?" the woman asked, as Sabina handed her the passport and an envelope full of one hundred franc notes.

"She'll answer to the name on the passport," Sabina said, sipping the sweet schnapps and peering at the belligerent woman.

"Have her here tonight, alley behind café, just before curfew. Look for truck. *Ville de Chine—Service de blanchisserie* painted on doors."

"I know the drill," Sabina retorted. "You just make sure she gets through."

"Have we ever let you down?" Then the woman chuckled, adding, "Of course, how you know?"

"Now and then," Sabina told her, indignantly, "I receive a visit from an old friend of mine who oversees the border control at the Vichy frontier. A man your people also know and rely upon. I assure you, if I'm betrayed in this at all, I will know." Sabina lit a Panter

Mignon, blew smoke above the unfazed statue of a woman before her, and went on.

"And I will be allowed to watch while they hang you and the rest of your lot by the neck like chickens in your Chinese storefronts."

Sabina crossed her legs and one of her arms under her breasts to support her other elbow. She flipped an ash in her empty glass, held the cigarette high with her chin jutted imperiously.

"Don't fuck with me, bitch!"

It was chilly and dusk loomed when Rolf and Addie left the movie theater. A wind was up. Inadequately dressed, they snuggled up to each other and plodded their way along from one cozy bar to the next oasis of warmth, eating up all of the evening and most of the night as they drank, laughed, and toasted their way back to her apartment. Being free of curfew restrictions was liberating to Addie. Shamefully so, she admitted to herself. With Rolf at her side, she was able to enjoy a side of Paris none of her friends had seen in almost a year.

By the time they reached her apartment, both of them were drunk, more so than they had ever been together. Before the church bells of the Église de Saint-Germain-des-Prés struck midnight, they staggered and stumbled out of their clothes, then crawled and climbed and fell into her icy bed, bumping into and clambering and cuddling up to each other for a wanton night of unfettered, unsober lust.

Rolf rolled himself on top of her and struggled to focus on the vacant glare in her half-mast eyes. Gazing in his direction, if not really at him, she smiled sweetly and, just before passing out, was able to say in English, "Oh, Rolf, darling. I'm snockered!"

60

Saturday, 19 April 1941

Abzüge
Déductions
Deductions

DAY FIFTEEN—Paris—Saturday, 19 April 41—8:03 AM
Gep's return from Berlin was announced to Rolf in his office by an orderly. Their orderly. *Gep should get this man's name,* Rolf thought. *He could serve him well in the American operation.* When the young corporal opened the door further, Gep appeared before him. Heels clicked, hands shaken, Gep tossed his overcoat on a chair, opened his briefcase, and withdrew some files.

"How's your friend in Cologne?"

"She's quite well, thank you, major. But parts of the city were devastated in the bombing. Trains delayed for hours." He withdrew a gray *Confidential—Foreign Office Matters* envelope and handed it to Rolf. "Photos of the identity card and such from the deceased Brückner woman."

Gep surveyed Rolf for a second and then asked, "I can only assume you . . . shared the news of the Brückner woman with Miss Bridges. Poor girl wasn't executed, was she?" Gep quipped, smiling.

Rolf chuckled. "I must admit. News of the Brückner woman's demise was most timely."

Gep withdrew his own *F. Irmgard* file and from it pulled a transcript of the interrogation of the Kunsthorn Heitner artisan.

"Have you read this?" he asked of Rolf.

"Yes," Rolf replied. "Seems Ritter was into a great deal more intrigue than I was willing to give him credit for." Rolf wound his watch. "We must now consider, Gep, how producing identities for emigrants would be cause for the man's murder."

Gep nodded, crossed his legs, and lit a Chesterfield, ready to move on to his Berlin investigation.

"Herr von Kanderstein, this carburetor manufacturer from Köpenick, was a business partner with Ritter. I assure you, he's no conspirator. More apt to commit suicide than murder, I would say.

Ritter sold his shares in their partnership to the Göring people and the little man was left working for the SS. Much to his delight."

Rolf snickered and shrugged with his eyebrow, then lit his own cigarette.

"He brought up Heitner. I contacted my people in Innsbruck. That led to discovery of the Gestapo arrest of the two artisans. As you now know, Friedrich Heitner, it seems, and these two craftsmen at Kunsthorn Heitner had been producing false papers for émigrés as early as 1936. It appears Friedrich and Ritter helped scores of people, no doubt their Jewish friends, escape Germany. Like me, Friedrich Heitner was a staunch Austrian imperialist and hated no group more than the communists. And his brother was a pink-skinned card carrier. Then Friedrich was killed along with his other brother in the automobile accident. Werner discovered Ritter's smuggling operation with the Brückner woman, code named 'Irmgard,' and demanded his help of some sort, perhaps to get some of his Marxist colleagues or information of some sort out of Germany as well."

Rolf pulled a bottle of La Grande Marque from his credenza and poured a measure for each of them.

"Werner's presence in Paris during Ritter's murder would seem to vault him to the front of our suspect list, wouldn't you think, Gep?" He sat Gep's drink down and leaned against his desk, a heavy piece of sixteenth-century oaken history.

"Perhaps, Marxist circles are tight. Putting together a team of assassins in Paris wouldn't be difficult in some of the workers' quarters of the city."

Gep sipped his cognac.

"Your former professor was an interesting fellow." Eyes rolled.

"He is a character. But brilliant in his field." Rolf took a seat and placed his elbow on the desk. "What was his assessment of the Irmgard name?"

"A sentry. The 'protector of us all.' A guard at the gates of Walhalla."

"I was unaware it was also a male name."

"It isn't." Gep pointed out after a dramatic pause.

"So then," Rolf summoned, "the operation of this Brückner woman was indeed Operation Irmgard. The 'protector of us all.' Smuggling enemies of the state out of the Reich."

"Smuggling, or perhaps something else," Gep interjected. "What about Werner Heitner? Could this Operation Irmgard be related to him as well?"

"That association can't be overlooked," Rolf added.

Gep slipped his note cards into his tunic. "Anything new on your end?"

"Inspector Saint-Ruynon and I retraced Ritter's steps the last few days of his life. We interviewed managers at a number of automotive concerns around Paris, including the new Ford plant in Poissy and the Renault factory at Boulogne-Billancourt. Apparently, the Renault people are just now able to start producing trucks for the Reich. The manager was quick to express to me that his company's delay in starting production had been entirely dependent upon working out resupply of components and raw materials, and not at all due to any sort of passive resistance to the occupation."

Gep smiled and shook his head.

"In visiting with the inspector afterward," Rolf went on to say, "he holds forth very well on his opinion that none of these French parts or vehicle manufacturers would have anything to gain in Ritter's murder. He believes, as I was starting to myself until your news about this Werner Heitner fellow, this murder was about the securities swindle and our Leutnant Rutgers Heht. We must find this man Heht."

Gep went on to talk about his research on Heht and the man's sordid past, serving the Reich and especially the general staff in many clandestine operations. He did not mention his sister to Rolf, convinced it would serve no purpose. Gep had great respect for the major, but family was family.

"So then," Rolf summarized, as he stood and marched around the room, "a seventy-two-year-old wealthy Frankish aristocrat working for the economics ministry as liaison to the Wehrmacht for automotive parts production is in Paris regularly. And regularly haunts the Club l'Heure Bleue. But on this one particular occasion, he decides to take one last walk with an American woman he has befriended over his many years in the club. And in doing so, he is murdered on the Alexandre III Bridge on Palm Sunday morning by two assassins in a blue Matford."

"Assassins who knew the old man would be on the bridge," Gep added.

"They no doubt followed him."

"Ritter came from the Left Bank," Gep pointed out. "They came from the Right."

"So, someone slipped out and made a call, telling the assassins of Ritter's plan to go to the bridge." Consternation on Rolf's face was

344

expressed in his wrinkled forehead. He looked at Gep, watched his adjutant's head nod once and his eyes grow wide.

"Don't even suggest it to me, Gep." Rolf grew defensive.

"She said she left, major," Gep stated, withdrawing his index cards again and fumbling through them. "What was it she said? She had to run home and change her shoes. The walk to the bridge would have been impossible in heels. Why not make a phone call, as well?"

"I'll have none of it, Gep. The woman held old Ritter in the highest regard. Besides, Oberleutnant, she was leaving Paris forever. She told us her telephone was removed from her apartment at the end of March."

"Still, major. We can't allow ourselves to discount—"

"I tell you, I'll have none of it!" Rolf was perplexed. He would check with the telephone company first thing in the morning. "What about you, Gep? You and Hans were both there after I left. Am I to suspect you as well? Are you the murderer? Is Hans-Hubert?"

Gep knew better than to take the supposition any further.

"Still," Rolf concluded, "we know there had to be someone in the club who made the call about Ritter's plans to walk to the bridge."

"There's a pay phone at the coat check," Gep interjected.

"Kruder, Gep!" Rolf set his drink down. "The very day of his return to Paris."

"My god," Gep answered. "He was there that night, at the club."

They both said it at the same time.

"With Guy de Forney!"

"An SS conspiracy . . ." Gep had to stop himself.

"Just as you said, Oberleutnant," Rolf answered. "We can't let ourselves discount it."

"We've been down this road. It's insane. Don't you agree, major?"

"Gep, Hans-Hubert went on and on about how closely the military administration is connected with the gangster Hugo Sturekov in purchasing goods for the army. What if the SS were to make the similar arrangement with de Forney and his bandits?"

"The broker, Lemay," Gep interjected. "Who was murdered the day before Ritter. The Dolchstoss dagger found stuffed in the man's body. It had SS markings."

"A ridiculously obvious plant, Gep?" Rolf suggested. "Or a divergence? A double cross?"

"Major, we must consider that this could at the very least tie both murders together."

"As well as lead us down a very dangerous path."

61

Das Walross
Le morse
The Walrus

DAY FIFTEEN—Paris—Saturday, 19 April 41—11:40 AM
"They were found . . . just as you see them now," Inspector Luc-Henri
explained to Rolf and Gep as they entered the tepid attic apartment in
an old run-down quarter of the 18th arrondissement. They studied the
pair of dead assassins, Konni Ritter's murderers, cuddled up together,
lying naked on a single mattress on the rotting wooden floor.
   "The one . . . festering with gangrene . . . had unsoiled
underwear at his knees. British brand. Yet the bedding . . . is . . . crisp
with old urine." Luc took pauses in his statement to catch his breath
from the agonizing climb up seven flights of stairs five minutes
earlier. "Just once . . . I'd like to see these . . . murders . . . happen on
the fucking ground floor!" A painfully embarrassed look was cast
toward Rolf, and he gritted his jaw and added, "Forgive me,
monsieur."
   Rolf did so with a smile and a wink.
   Oblivious, Gep looked at the corpse on top, froth of saliva
around his mouth. "Cyanide," he said.
   "Yes," Luc agreed. "But he died here." He pointed to a ring of
dried, frothy saliva on the floor.
   "It's all very clumsily engineered for us, isn't it?" Rolf said,
looking into the eyes of the corpse on the bottom. A pristine pair of
spectacles was cockeyed on the corpse's nose. Gep removed them
with his tweezers and checked the tiny logo on the inside temple of
the earpiece.
   "Algha brand," he said, handing them up to Rolf.
   "British," Rolf added, familiar with the brand from his youth in
England.
   The bottom man's nose was clogged with blood, and in his
beard were traces of orange cotton fuzz. Rolf took the sharpened end
of his pencil and pulled the victim's lip to one side, revealing a tiny
feather plastered to his dry gums. A brief look around the room
revealed a filthy orange throw pillow. Turning it over with his toe, he

nodded at a gnarled knot in its center where teeth had frantically bitten it, pulling apart a tiny rip.

"The murder weapon," Gep interjected.

Luc held up a cellophane bag. It contained a laundry receipt he found in a jacket hanging on the wall. "A Soho address."

"London, again."

"Whether this is all contrived or not," Rolf said. "We are dealing with absolute buffoons. First, they try to convince us two rosy-cheeked boys were the assassins. And tip us off about the pair with an anonymous phone call, not to the Paris police, but to the Gestapo. Now they attempt to convince us these two men, who obviously are indeed the true assassins, are working for the British."

Rolf looked at the inspector.

"How were you notified?"

"A phone call, monsieur," Luc answered. "The smell."

"No one is this stupid." Rolf waved his hand over the half-missing ear of the man on top, disturbing a swarm of fruit flies. "Even those hapless goons . . ." Abruptly, he stopped himself short of saying, "at the Gestapo" and cursed himself for his weak-mindedness in thinking out loud. He just added, "Most unclever."

"This I know for sure," Luc added. "This fellow here, the one on top, is Pepe Duroc. Small-time pickpocket and purse snatcher. I don't recognize the other man, the walrus. But I am sure he will turn out to be just as insignificant."

"Would he have ties to the black market?" Gep asked, looking up at Rolf.

"I'm afraid there would be no part of the Paris criminal element who would not have ties of some sort to the black market. But if this one did, it would be *crushed dogs,* insignificant stuff. The sort neither of our black-market kingpins, Hugo Sturekov or Guy de Forney, would waste their time with."

"I will want a positive ID on the walrus from Miss Bridges and the grenadier," Rolf commanded.

"That shouldn't take long," Gep replied, rising to his feet.

"If I may, major?" Luc asked, looking out the window to see what these two killers had seen these past weeks, jammed in their attic tomb. "I am not privy to German military matters, but I must ask you if you both have pondered how the English would benefit from the elimination of Monsieur Ritter? I'm quite sure it can't be discussed in my presence, but I must be sure even the remote possibility is not overlooked."

348

"Well put, inspector," Rolf said. "I can tell you there is no political or military reason we know of that the British would want Ritter assassinated."

"Then I must conclude the obvious," Luc declared. "A murdered broker. Missing securities. A cover-up, designed to look like a political assassination. A German lieutenant disappears just after the crimes are committed. How do we not conclude that we have our murderer and his name is Heht?"

"It's the word 'obvious' that concerns me, inspector," Gep replied.

"Criminals are not clever," Luc stated as they snaked their way through the coroner's people and out to the stairway. "They are most times just simple, stupid men, being simple and stupid."

62

Der gefährliche Pfau
Le paon dangereux
The Dangerous Dandy

DAY FIFTEEN—Paris—Saturday, 19 April 41—2:12 PM
Guy de Forney wore a gray seersucker suit, purple Sulla shirt, and
yellow silk tie. His sunglasses were blue-lensed Mont Richards. His
tasseled loafers, white patent leather. Diamonds and jewels sparkled
from every manicured finger on his hands. On his head sat an absurd
Berteil porkpie with a wide paisley band. He dabbed his lips with his
chartreuse lace hanky as he rose out of the backseat of his Rolls-
Royce Phantom limousine, telling his driver to "return in an hour and
a half and circle until I need you." Guy de Forney was fast becoming
the most dangerous underworld dandy in Paris. He knew it, and he
liked it. And he wanted to be sure this new SS man, this Kruder
fellow, knew it as well.

Whistling, he waltzed down a shady, sun-speckled alleyway to
the stone-arched gate of his favorite little al fresco bistro in the 8th.
And there he stood, momentarily annoyed, until two waiters, the
maître d', the owner, and one of the chefs all rushed up to greet him.

"Your corner table awaits you, monsieur," the portly owner
announced, his hands clasped timidly under a sappy smile. De Forney
was led to a shady back corner along the bistro's waist-high, rock
walled veranda, heels clicking on brick tile laid in a hound's-tooth
pattern. Other waiters were lugging in two redwood shrubbery
planters to improve the table's privacy. Another was setting up a
silver champagne stand as a waitress fluffed up a centerpiece of
freshly cut tulips; red and orange and yellow. As the entourage passed
an occupied table close enough to be within earshot of his own, de
Forney forcefully snapped his fingers twice at the occupants and
flipped his thumb out to one side.

The owner set immediately to work, offering the astonished
couple a bottle of wine and a "more suitable spot elsewhere" as
waiters swooped up plates and glasses in the very middle of the
woman slicing off a bite.

De Forney took his usual seat. Suddenly, swarms of fingers and
hands were popping folds out of napkins, popping caps from bottles

of mineral water, and snapping fingers until the man's favorite aperitif was plopped down before him.

Like startled hares, they all froze.

German Sturmbannführer Alois Kruder stood in the opening between the two privacy planters. The owner stumbled slightly as he hurried to greet the menacing Occupier. The maître d' already had the German's chair pulled out and a courteous bow started. As de Forney stood and offered his hand to Kruder, a quick-acting waiter caught the gangster's napkin before it could slide off his lap to the ground.

"Welcome to one of my favorite hideouts, Monsieur Kruder," de Forney said, shaking hands with the stern-faced Gestapo officer. "I pray you will forgive my use of the 'Monsieur' title, as I am unable to pronounce your official one, the *Sturm*-something-or-other title. Exactly what rank would that be, if I may ask?"

"Major," Kruder answered as both of them graciously had chairs slid under them and napkins laid over their laps. "Please, Monsieur de Forney, feel free to call me major." A snide smile followed. The only smile the man obviously ever used, de Forney surmised.

"I'm in the mood for lamb," Kruder continued, looking up pensively at the proprietor. "I trust I won't be disappointed?"

"Lamb it is, monsieur," the owner nodded. He nonchalantly raised an eyebrow at one of the waiters. If either of these important customers had cared to observe, they would have noticed the waiter running around the corner of the bistro to no doubt procure a portion of lamb from a neighboring restaurant.

"I was glad to take your call," Kruder said, sipping his aperitif. "I expected to hear back from you much sooner however."

"Important decisions should be made only after . . ." De Forney hesitated to sniff a tulip, steal it from the vase, and stick it proudly in his lapel. A few flips of his fingers and all the waiters disappeared. "After much consternation."

"So then," Kruder continued. "You've decided to team up with the SS?"

His own snide smile, then de Forney answered. "We'll see."

Kruder's upper lip curled slightly.

"Monsieur, or major, I have a story to tell you. I trust you have the patience to hear me out?" He lifted his empty champagne flute and tapped it a few times with his fingernail. The sharp ringing brought a waiter. The chilled champagne was uncorked and glasses poured.

"I have all day," Kruder responded, sipping and nodding his approval of the vintage as the waiter displayed the bottle to them both. When they were alone again, Guy de Forney went on.

"There is a man who works . . . or, should I say, worked for me. One of my most loyal. Or so I thought. A man who seems, however, to have questioned my leadership. This man has chosen to strike out on his own, to hang his own shingle, as it were. Consequently, it seems he has taken a terrible fall. I have him on ice in hopes of preventing his wounds from being fatal. His name is Victor. You met him that night at the l'Heure Bleue."

Kruder nodded and shrugged with a scowl of his chin.

"Over these past few days, this man, my old friend Victor, has imparted a great deal. Not everything . . . not yet. But a great deal nonetheless. And I have seen an opportunity arise from what I have learned so far. Information that can benefit us both."

He adjusted himself in his chair to settle in for an interesting afternoon.

"Where do I begin?"

Kruder lit a Trommler and cocked his head to one side, his interest finally piqued.

"It all started with the American cigarettes you were so bold to display at our first meeting that night."

"That isn't news," Kruder interjected, prematurely, with his usual German impertinence. "We arrested a German quartermaster who told us they were being sold on the black market through you and your people."

"You are . . . almost correct. Some of the people I associate with did sell some twenty-four cases. Victor handled the deal. Told me it was compliments of some rogue German officer. Guaranteed security. He makes a few piddly thousand francs. What harm could there be in it?" He bent forward, leaned on the table, and clasped his fingers.

"But, it turns out, there were actually hundreds of cases!"

"I want to talk to this Victor fellow myself," Kruder demanded.

"Your people can dig him up out of the trash dump in the morning."

A bell rang from the entrance of the café. De Forney held up a finger at Kruder.

"Yes," he said aloud.

Fall Irmgard

The waiter soon rounded the planter, well aware he should never approach the monsieur's conversation unannounced and without permission. He quickly took their orders as other waiters rushed in bringing bread, assorted onions and olives in oil, and a half-kilo block of butter. Then, like Kruder's smoke in a sudden breeze, they disappeared.

"Hundreds of cases," Guy continued. "With the help of the little Alsatian who manages the Club l'Heure Bleue and a beast of a man, a Basque assassin who roams some of my city's darker quarters, Victor went out on his own and quite successfully, I must add. He made a small fortune for each of them, selling the cigarettes in the provinces. For this alone, I would be profoundly interested in seeing all three learn the intricacies of swimming hog-tied. But this was only their first taste. From it came the pièce de résistance."

Throughout the relaxed *déjeuner*, de Forney dished out just enough of the information he had tortured out of Victor to entreat Kruder to at least listen to the Paris gangster's plan. He told the stern Gestapo major that Victor had uncovered a conspiracy between old man Ritter and a local stockbroker whose clientele were mostly desperate Jews.

Guy de Forney actually saw Kruder's ears rise somewhat on the side of his head.

"Ritter and a number of investors, including Hugo Sturekov, had funded the purchase of a large cache of securities and planned to profit from their sale on the Lyon Exchange. Then Victor was contacted by an anonymous German and told of this plan. Conspired with him to intercept the securities before they were sold. They would eliminate Ritter and the broker and make it look like a clandestine assassination plot, to the discredit of the occupying authorities."

"Victor thought the German was the owner of the Club l'Heure Bleue at first, Bruno Kestler. Then, after he met you—forgive me—he was certain you were the conniving German conspirator."

Kruder frowned. De Forney simply shrugged, then continued.

"Then the little cocksucker Jew, Xavier, at the l'Heure Bleue overheard an apparently quite vexing German arguing with Ritter at the bistro attached to the club the day before he was killed. He rang up Victor and the German was tailed. He discovered the man was being hidden by a local group of Marxists who, like all good communists, are intent on anarchy. But when Victor's less-than-adept goons invaded the hideout, they found this man and his partners had flown the coop."

De Forney pushed a bite of his pheasant on his fork with his knife. As he masticated, he smiled and went on.

"Victor did some research on this Marxist German. It turns out he isn't German at all, but Austrian. His name was—"

"His name is Heitner," Kruder again interrupted. "We've been on his trail for some time. The lamb is dry, Monsieur de Forney. I would suggest you give me some other reason I should remain here wasting my time listening to you disclose details of which I am already aware."

"So then, you have already arrested this man, Heitner?"

"His whereabouts are still a mystery," Kruder confessed. "We're of the opinion he has escaped to Vichy."

"But these whereabouts are not a mystery to me," de Forney gloated.

"So, where is Heitner hiding?"

"Major Kruder, is the virtue of patience lost on all Germans?"

"I don't have time for this. What's your price, then?"

"I don't want money." The underworld peacock shook his head, disappointed that his lunch guest would think him so base. "Not even the money from the sale of the securities. I'm quite certain those funds are to become property of the Reich anyway." A sinister grin. "Including my friend Hugo Sturekov's share. Nor am I after Victor's cigarette booty. Furthermore, I could care less about this champion of communism, this Heitner fellow. What I do want, major"—he held up his finger—"is the status quo. I don't want our apple cart upset by the fact that Ritter's murder, while ordered by a German, was carried out by Frenchmen. Imbecilic Frenchmen, but Frenchmen nonetheless. I also want to be completely sure that you are the one to arrest this Heitner fellow. I want him to give you his full confession. I am certain you are a very persuasive man. I am quite sure you will be able to get him to say the things we would both want him to say."

De Forney took a deep breath.

"Then, as the lone man to solve the murder of one of Germany's most beloved businessmen, I want the occupying powers to give you a nice promotion. And with your newly acquired status in the German administration, and me serving as your special police force captain, I want you to award me with a good deal of the contracts Hugo Sturekov currently enjoys with the army! Give me these few paltry things I request, and I'll lead you to your criminal Heitner."

Fall Irmgard

With his diamond-ring-enhanced pinky held high, Guy de Forney raised his wineglass.

"Vive la paix?" he toasted. Long live the Peace?

That devilish smile was back on Kruder's menacing puss as he accepted the toast.

"You may be useful to the Reich after all, Sonderführer de Forney."

"You didn't ask me to work for you because I'm a snappy dresser."

Kruder snickered wine into his nose and had to turn to cough it free.

63

Die Wurst-Mühle
Le hachoir à saucisse
The Sausage Grinder

DAY FIFTEEN—Paris—Saturday, 19 April 41—11:51 PM
Werner Heitner indeed never left Paris. He was followed for most of
that day he first met with Konni Ritter and was only able to steal
away undetected to a safe house in the 20th by dogged determination
and sheer luck. And there he stayed. For a week. Nearly two. Then he
was moved to a second-floor apartment in the 9th that was leased by a
French Canadian woman who had been among the first to leave Paris
the minute talk of the French collapse found solid ground. The
subletee, it turned out, was the most famous house of prostitution in
all of Paris, One-Two-Two, presiding at that address in the rue du
Provence. Its current occupant, due to the building's elevator, was an
olive-eyed beauty from Azerbaijan who had lost her left leg in a tram
accident. This resulted in any number of sexually exotic machinations
and an unbridled if not horribly unnatural popularity.

And the one-legged girl from Azerbaijan was a viciously
devout communist!

Her duties and demand at house One-Two-Two required her
absence from the apartment for all but a few hours a day. So, offering
it for use by the most ardent and determined of Paris Marxist
partisans was only to be expected. At the present time, there were
four souls flopping on the floors of the tiny apartment. Besides
Werner, there was an Algerian, a Spaniard, and a Danish Jewess.

French resistance to the German occupation at the time was
mostly nonexistent. Lacking organization and true conviction, what
there was fell mostly to students and youths and consisted of little
more than hastily printed poison placards, obscene anti-German
graffiti, and adolescent stunts like drawing Hitler mustaches on
images of Pétain or blotting out letters on German signs like *Rauchen
Verboten* (Smoking Forbidden) changing it to *Ra c e Ver t* (the Green
Race).

Slowly, however, serious organized resistance was developing
and was doing so almost entirely from the many diverse camps of the
socialists and communists. The apartment in the 9th played host to

three such resistants. And when Werner Heitner arrived, with his distinctive German accent, each of them was wary.

In his many years at the University of Vienna, one of the hottest melting pots for European communism at the time, Werner had learned from some of the best how to incite passion in the leftist heart. He was quick to show the other three his conviction and acumen. As well as his adoration for the Dane. Her white hair and barely visible eyebrows stirred something deep in Werner's gut. And lower.

"Don't believe for a second, comrades, this pact the Nazis have made with Stalin," Werner preached, his distrust of the Germans becoming apparent enough to the others to disprove their first thought that he was a plant. "Hitler hates us as much as he does the Jews. German prisons and labor camps are teeming with every level of our brothers—social democrats, socialists, and Marxists alike. I have seen many of my friends taken from their homes and jobs."

"I'm sure I can get us all to Britain, comrades," Werner exclaimed, his enchanting eyes glued to the beautiful Dane's. "We can make our way to the edge of the city before curfew, then slip into the countryside and move toward the coast at night. Once in Britain we can join up with our comrades in London and take up arms against the fascists."

Werner's last words were lost against an explosion at the apartment's front door. A man the size of a small bear hit the door with his shoulder, taking hinges, latch, bolt, and even the door itself with him all the way through the apartment and into the kitchen. He was followed into the apartment immediately by two other caped gendarmes as well as two leather-jacketed Gestapo agents. The Spaniard lunged, stumbling, for the window, a three-story drop that would have no doubt done him in. Werner and his Danish darling headed for the bedroom. The Algerian was frozen at the table, in a comatose shock. A single, deafening shot from a Gestapo agent's pistol concussed in the tiny room and stopped everyone in their tracks.

A half-hour later, the four of them were at the newly acquired Gestapo jailhouse in the "rue des Saussaies," the sausage grinder, the Germans would mistakenly call it, as would the French after a while. For good reason. And to his accursed discredit by the other three, Werner Heitner was removed immediately. They all were now certain he had been the one to do them in.

357

A black sack over his head, Werner was taken to Gestapo headquarters in avenue Foch by police van. He sat in the rear of the van, his shackled wrists and ankles chained to iron rings. When the door opened, he could feel the rush of springtime air hit his shirt, damp with sweat, but could see nothing in the darkness of the hood.

"So nice to finally make your acquaintance, Herr Heitner."

The voice was high pitched, but pleasant, like that of a hotel concierge, Werner thought.

"We've put together a little welcoming affair for you. Just a short ride outside of town. Once you arrive, I would ask that you excuse the clamor. Some of our other guests are undergoing treatments. It could be some time before we can work you in."

Heitner jumped slightly as a cold hand softly patted the top of his own.

"Forgive my improper manners. My name is Kruder. And I shall see you quite soon."

64

Sunday, 20 April 1941

Geburtstag des Führers
Anniversaire du Führer
The Führer's Birthday

Der Vorschlaghammer
Le marteau
The Sledgehammer

DAY SIXTEEN—Paris—Sunday, 20 April 41- 3:23 PM
Rolf was in the smoking lounge of the Lutetia talking to Hans-Hubert
and Oberst Oskar Rheile as he sat at the piano playing Fritz Kreisler's
"Liebeslied." Their orderly drew his attention and held his fist to his
ear in front of him, pointing at the doorway. A phone call. Rolf took
the call on the hallway phone. He ducked into an arched oaken
cubbyhole under the staircase and backed into the velvet-covered
seat. Switching on the lamp with the pull of a silk tassel, he lifted the
receiver on the new, elegant ebony and brass continental phone. The
operator transferred the call to him there. It was Kruder.
"Didn't wake you, did I, major?"
"What is it, Alois?"
"I captured the Heitner man, Werner Heitner. Slithering about
Paris yesterday morning like the alley rat he is. I have him downstairs
here at Romainville, doing the dance. I think he's about to crack. Why
don't you and that *Katzenjammer* kid of yours hurry over here. I'll
demonstrate how a real murder interrogation is handled."

SS Sturmbannführer Alois Kruder could have passed for a
butcher, in only his shirtsleeves, rolled up above his elbows, and
wearing a leather apron, turned a greasy black in its center from old
blood.
"Kruder, you look like a man in the throes of afterglow!" Rolf
quipped.
An evil smile, and Kruder agreed, "Perhaps I am!" He held his
palm out toward the basement door. "Shall we, gentlemen?"

As they walked down the pale-green tiled hallway, Kruder leaned back and asked Rolf, "You sure you have the stomach for this, major?"

"I have the stomach for it, Kruder. I just don't delight in it the way you do. That's the difference between us, isn't it?"

"No, von Gerz, that's just one weakness of your many."

They came to the stairway door, and as Kruder opened it, he smiled and told Rolf, "I do so love our little game, von Gerz!"

When they were led down to the basement of the ancient prison, Werner's ear-piercing screams startled Rolf and Gep. Their driver pulled wads of cotton from his pocket and tore off a portion for each of them.

"We used to start on a man at his testicles," Kruder shouted, gleefully, above the mortifying peal of Werner's agony. "Bind rubber bands above them, bash them about awhile, then hit them with a few bolts of electricity. It was effective, but men generally passed out too deeply and too often. So, we discovered smashing fingers with a sledgehammer to be vastly more effective. Fingers and toes are the second most sensitive appendage on a man, you know. Three. Four fingers spaced out through a day. Day three we might revisit a few of them, but this time a little higher up at the knuckle. We used to pull out the fingernails, but found doing so only relieved the pressure and therefore the pain of the smashed finger. So, now, of course"—he wrinkled up his long, thin nose with a sinister smile—"we leave the nails on."

"Most fellows don't last past the first day. Frankly, most don't even get as far as the hammer. Our reputation, I would assume?" Another proud smile, then, "Unfortunately, however, some are like this fellow. Tough nuts. Especially the fucking communists. Some Bolshevik esprit de corps or something. So we have to work a little harder at cracking them. But they do ultimately crack!"

A fat French guard opened the steel door to the cellar hallway, and Werner's unfettered screams seemed to pound against them all like a terrible wind. "Toes are generally day three," Kruder continued, shouting even louder. "Hate to get to toes with someone. Then we have to carry them back and forth to the interrogation room. Don't like wearing out our people like that."

Werner sat naked, securely strapped to a makeshift stool made from a metal toilet seat welded to four lengths of rusty pipe embedded in the concrete floor. His left hand was tightly cuffed and cinched to a steel table made of thick plate pig iron with four braced pipe legs welded into two skids of channel iron. The table squealed and shrieked as it was dragged around on the wet slab floor, earning it its torture-chamber moniker, *der Schreienschlitten*, the screaming sleigh.

The jailer was a sweaty, musclebound beast of a man with a pile of greasy black hair and a deeply recessed widow's peak that gave his face the oddest heart shape. He moved about shirtless in rubber boots and a rubber slaughterhouse apron, his hairy shoulders bristling with beads of sweat. The beast swung the hammer again, intentionally missing any fingers, just pounding the iron table in an explosion of steel on steel that Rolf could hear in his stomach.

Werner screamed just as loudly, as if the jailer's shot had been true. He jerked frantically, again and again on the steel sled table until he slammed one of the channel iron skids into his ankle. More screams were followed by a rapid series of deep, wide-eyed, opened-mouth moans that brought up a pair of convulsing dry heaves.

Kruder showed tortured Werner pictures of the two dead assassins found in the 18th.

"This one, with the walrus mustache," Kruder screamed at Heitner. "Recognize him? One of your Bolshevik comrades, is he?"

"Maybe." Heitner was delirious. Near passing out.

"Maybe? Sounds like he's still confused. Let's find another finger!"

"No! No!" Heitner shouted. "Yes, he was. Comrade. British . . . comrade. Communist. Ritter refused to get information out. British team in Paris. We killed him."

Rolf was appalled. He looked at Gep in disbelief. It was as if Werner Heitner was being scripted in what to say. This wasn't a man, it was a trained dog. It was all just a show Kruder was putting on for them. The man was playing them for fools.

"Yes! Yes!" Werner screamed. "We had information to get out to Switzerland, and he refused to get it out. So we killed him. I had them kill him."

"But why would you kill the man?" Kruder coaxed. "What good would that do you? Weren't you really trying to make his assassination look like a French terror plot? Weren't you and your conspirators really trying to force the Reich to react to Ritter's assassination with such brutality it would start a groundswell of French Marxist patriotism? Weren't you hopeful that a whole revolution might start and we hideous German occupiers would be driven out of France? Wasn't that your real purpose?"

"Yes! Yes! So that hundreds of thousands of Frenchmen would rise up and slit the throats of all you German pigs!" Werner spat at Kruder. His bloody spittle ran down the shoulder of Kruder's white shirt.

Kruder slugged Werner. Then raised his arms high in the air and very dramatically boasted.

"There you have it! There's your killer, von Gerz. That's how a murder investigation is properly conducted." Kruder was enraptured, having fed on the screams and blood for almost an hour. With pride that bristled from every fiber of the man, he continued. "Hopefully, your lesson is now learned, von Gerz!"

He slapped his crop against his leg and made victory circles around the bloody mess of humanity that had once been Werner Heitner. The young stenographer folded up his notebook and tucked his pencil in his pocket.

"Your investigation is completed, von Gerz. You are dismissed."

"Doubtful," was all Rolf said.

"Take this pile of rat shit to his cell," Kruder told two relieved guards as he made toward the door to leave.

"I'd like to ask him a few questions, if I may," Rolf interjected with a quiet aura of sanity.

The stenographer turned around to return. Kruder stopped him and sent him on his way.

"But of course you would, von Gerz." Kruder's turgid words echoed off the damp stone walls. "I solved your murder investigation for you, but I guess you must find some morsel or other to lay claim to it, mustn't you?" Kruder brought himself back up to Rolf's face and snapped his fingers at the sweaty jailer, who was now washing down the bloody floor and sledgehammer with icy water from a hose. The man shut off the water, dried his hands, and left the room.

"Have your lapdog here take notes," Kruder continued, motioning toward Gep. "See to it that I get a copy on the odd and quite improbable occasion that you should produce anything of value."

Gep's venom turned his blue eyes to steel. Kruder snorted a victorious smile and strutted as he left the room.

Rolf took the blond oak desk chair the stenographer had used and placed it in front of Werner, who was still panting viciously, moaning and now and then letting out a wail. His unshackled wrists were folded on top of his head in an attempt to keep his massive, dripping fingers elevated to alleviate some of the throbbing pain.

"Would you like some water?" Rolf asked.

Heitner looked up at Rolf and smiled through bloody teeth. "If you mean the fucking hose again, no! I don't think I would!"

Even with all the man had been through, there was still a spitefulness about him that made the charade of dispassion on Rolf's part much easier.

"No one is going to hurt you any longer," Rolf calmly told him. "But I don't think I believe your story about Ritter's murder. I, frankly, don't believe you had a thing to do with it."

"Tell that to that mad dog! What does it matter, anyway? I'm hanging regardless. It saved a couple fingers, didn't it?" Another toothy, bloody smile.

Werner went through some well-practiced soliloquy explaining how he wanted to get back at Konni Ritter, whom he blamed for everything going sour. He explained his practice of using phonograph records to, with the help of a fellow conspirator somewhere in Warsaw, send information on German troop movements in Poland through Ritter's *Irmgard* to a handler in Switzerland.

"And the name of that Warsaw conspirator?" Gep immediately inquired.

Heitner shook his head. "For his safety and my own, I was never told."

You mean for her safety, Gep thought.

Heitner went on to tell them he had one last communiqué to deliver. His most important since his Warsaw contact had been arrested or killed. He had to get this info out. Now that the Irmgard woman was dead, he felt the only way was to come to Paris and find Konni Ritter. Force him to get the info to his contacts in Switzerland. He went on to explain his letters posted from Warsaw contained only sheet music, with no return address. He didn't know what the music meant. Only that it was important. The sheet music was delivered to him, this last with two words, *Most Important*, scribbled at the top. He played it on the piano and recorded it at the end of a regular rerecording of Schubert's Eighth. Evidently each series of six notes represented a word and a page number in some book. Only the Warsaw contact and the recipient somewhere in Switzerland or London had the book that could break the code. He said the last vital recording had been delivered to Konni the night before he was killed, but that Konni refused to deliver it.

Rolf remembered the worn place at the bottom of the F. Irmgard file in Konni's briefcase. Gep's eyes told him he remembered it too.

Gep ordered the jailer to tend to the prisoner's wounds, that the major would return in the morning to question the man further. With his heart pounding in his chest, Rolf took a deep breath and bit his lip. The Warsaw contact was undoubtedly Tippi Rostikov. And the book . . . *War and Peace!*

"Why would any woman want to read War and Peace?" he had asked of her.

"I'm Russian, Rolfi darling," she answered. *"It's expected. Of course I've had the silly thing for over a year, and I'm barely halfway through it."*

Rolf glanced at Gep. His stare was excruciating.

DAY SIXTEEN—Paris—Sunday, 20 April 41—5:45 PM
Once in the limousine en route back to Paris, Gep closed the glass chauffeur window, looked at Rolf, and fumed.

"I like you, major. I've learned a great deal at your side over these last two years. But it is now completely apparent you were pitifully if not criminally culpable in the Tippi Rostikov affair, and I can't let you take me under with you. I am very proud of my work and my career. I have to protect myself from your dangerous nature."

"That will be quite enough, Gep. I'll have no more of it!" Rolf stared through his adjutant. "You're a brilliant man, Oberleutnant," he continued. "But your most brilliant quality seems to be your hindsight! Help me remember, if you will, those evidently numerous times when you came to me during the entire time I was sleeping with Tippi, or when we were both dining or having drinks with her. Tell me about those times that you came to me with even the slightest concerns about the woman's credibility. I admit, I must come to terms with the fact that I let myself be duped by the woman because I had my head up her skirt. What exactly was your excuse, Oberleutnant Fechter?"

Gep could only brood.

"You think," Rolf continued, "simply because I was sleeping with this woman I should therefore somehow have a leg up on her espionage activities."

A twinkle returned to Gep's stern eyes.

"You did indeed have a leg up on her."

Rolf spat a spontaneous snicker. Then they both laughed.

"Gep, my friend, you're correct. I do have to be more wary and discerning. And I am trying to be. That must surely be vividly apparent to you in my dealings with Addie. I'm certain I have been most unfair with her. But just as you point out, I can't take the chance of falling down that slippery slope again."

Gep removed his hat and ran his fingers through his hair, adding, "The hot pot burns twice only the fool."

"And believe me, I know; being made the fool was most disgraceful, Gep."

"For a German officer, it's also dangerous, major."

65

Zucker und Gewürz
Sucre et épices
Sugar and Spice

DAY SIXTEEN—Paris—Sunday, 20 April 41—8:52 PM

Otto Abetz was Germany's ambassador to France. It was a post he assumed with great joy, taking over for Count Wenzl when the Germans marched into Paris. For Abetz was a self-pronounced Francophile. The man loved the French, their language, history, culture, and art, and as much as anything else, their social soirées. He and his wife never missed an opportunity to throw a dinner party and loved the flow of gentile conversation, of stringed instruments and cold champagne. The very best in all of Paris. His parties at the German embassy were de rigueur for the high-society Frenchmen of Paris and were required for German business and military leaders. While many of his parties were hastily thrown together under just about any pretense, Führer Adolf Hitler's birthday celebration, the first such the city of Paris had ever known, had to be the grandest party ever.

And Otto Abetz knew exactly who to put in charge of such an important affair. Zucki von Platzow-und-Wiesenfeld was her name. Berlin's grand dame of any and all of the best elite soirées. Her given name was actually Elsbeth, but her father's childhood moniker was the one that stuck throughout her long, glorious life. *Zucki,* or Sugar, had been flown in to Le Bourget on a Lufthansa charter in the last week of March and had worked tirelessly planning and organizing the affair every day since, bringing the rest of the embassy staff to near collapse. And Zucki was every bit of seventy years young.

Zucki made her entrance into the embassy ballroom escorted by her young, sweet *sugar* boy, who would take immediate refuge in a corner of the vast room, as close as possible to the bar and service exit. Her trained lapdog dispensed with, she was as a springtime breeze floating back and forth in the crowded room. She wore a diamond butterfly broach on the front of a feathery white beret, just a little lighter than the wisps of hair that leaked out here and there from under it. A childlike face was betrayed only by sagging jowls and deep creases radiating from her mouth. White greasepaint adorned her eyelids as well as the fleshy skin up to her artistically painted, highly arched eyebrows. Her green gown was taffeta over satin, and her earlobes, her delicate décolletage, her wrists, and her fingers all sparkled with probably twenty karats of diamonds. There was an urbane charm in Zucki as she danced around ensuring conversation never waned, bandying her finger about, part matchmaker, part madame. "Come, my dear, you really must meet Colonel so-and-so. Him from the Tirol and you, the Allgäu. Mountain folk, the pair of you. The man will simply adore you."

Major Hans-Hubert von Hirschbach usually escorted some of the most beautiful and famous of Paris' social set to such gatherings. But now, lately, the finer set was losing its luster for Hans-Hubert. He had spent his entire life struggling to fit in with these pretentious melon heads, and now it all seemed such a waste of his valuable time.

Still, he had accepted the invitation and therefore had to attend. So, he decided tonight he would escort two ladies to the party. Two ecstatic young women, this being their first chance to test the social waters of occupied Paris' fine life: Gretl von Reinsdorf-Vilmer and Hedy von Rohrbach.

"I'm just so glad you're both here," Addie exclaimed. "Who on earth would I have to talk to, while the men are all huddled up telling their little war secrets?"

"We're happy as well," Gretl professed. "Though not so much with the sparkling water. They all still consider us children."

Rolf joined them and handed Addie her vermouth cassis.

Not very far away stood Zucki with Pierre Laval and his entourage. Her fingertips suddenly touched her heart, the wrist of her other hand went to her forehead, and she dramatically tossed her head back, no doubt overtly awestruck by the brilliance of the collaborationist minister's discourse. Then soon, as the conversation floated way above her head, Zucki breaststroked her way through the crowd searching for better aire. Suddenly, her attention drifted to Rolf. She froze, aghast. Her head fobbed to the right. Her shoulders wilted as she feigned a pout of astonishment.

She wagged her green taffeta tail as she hurried over and wrapped herself like a boa around Rolf's arm.

"My sweet Rolfi!" she exclaimed, batting her eyes. "I was certain you were your father when I first noticed you. By the way, he's not doing well, darling. You're quite aware, are you not?"

"Good evening, Zucki," Rolf said politely, if with a bit of resignation. "Yes, I saw him a fortnight ago and he is failing, I agree."

"Well, he has lived a good, full life, my dear, and you should—" She directed a polite gasp Addie's way.

"And who do we have here?" she asked in German.

Introductions were made around and Zucki beamed.

"An American?" she quipped, changing to French. "Why, you must be the last of your clan in all of Paris, my dear!" Addie looked Zucki over. Her tissue-paper skin hung on her tall frame like thin drapery. Her tiny, pale eyes had once been blue, and her eyelids sagged like a bloodhound's.

"Of course, Ernst Achenbach's wife is American," Zucki added. "If I see her, I'll point her out to you."

Zucki nervously bantered her long finger at Addie's nose, saying, "You must tell me everything about yourself, my sweet."

Addie explained her coming to Paris five years earlier, her work at the bank and her brief experience in the ambulance service during the German invasion. She voiced her concerns about Roosevelt's Lend-Lease pact bringing America into the war, which set Zucki off like a cannon.

"This man, your president, is quite ill, isn't he, my dear?" Zucki's questions rarely needed answers. She was usually eager to supply them. "But of course he is. Otherwise, why on earth would he antagonize the Führer so unkindly? All this lending and leasing and such!" She slumped over and gazed at Rolf and Addie. "Do you think it's the polio, darlings?"

"Oh, no," Addie shot back, coyly. "Not at all. He's just a democrat!"

Zucki quickly caught up with everyone else's laughter, but obviously never truly understood the joke.

"You're a most charming girl, and you speak French eloquently, young lady," Zucki complimented.

"My father preached to me from an early age," Addie said, proudly. "Whether in English or in French, it will be a strong vocabulary and not a strong arm that wins the most battles in one's lifetime!"

"How profound!" Zucki cupped her blue-veined hands and clasped them at her cheek. "Rolf, darling. You must immediately set the date! I'll handle all the arrangements. You leave everything to Zucki." She cupped her tender palms about Addie's face. "What an utter delight you are, my child."

Rolf cleared his throat with a cough into the side of his fist.

"Zucki," he said, smiling halfheartedly. "Is there even a shred of decorum left in that pretty head of yours?" Rolf kissed her clammy temple and whispered, "Isn't that Dolly de Castellane and Queen Amélie of Portugal over there?"

In a jolt, the silver-haired bloodhound brought the opera glasses up to her baggy eyes, saying, "Where, darling?" Once discovered, she snapped back around to Rolf. "Why, yes. I believe it is."

Her icy fingers softly brushed Addie's arm and she started to slip away. "Back in a jiffy, my dear." And off she pranced, adding, "When I run into Margaret Achenbach, I'll send her your way."

"Who on earth was that?" Addie asked.

There was obviously a confession coming that came none too easily for Rolf.

"Zucki was almost my stepmother." He swirled his glass and looked into the icy light of the brightly chandeliered ceiling. Returning her stunned look with one of resolve, he added, "She and my father were an item for some score of years. The talk of Berlin society and the bane of my first decade as a young man back in Berlin."

"Well, she certainly fits the role of ghost-from-one's-past, I would say!" Addie's eyes toyed with his as she sipped her vermouth through a cute smile.

Gep made his way to a gaggle of junior officers, where Hans-Hubert was holding court.

"I firmly believe," a young Leutnant was saying, "America has no stomach for war right now. I don't think they ever did."

"You have to admit," another interjected, "they were the saving grace for the Allies in the last war."

"They were fat, fearful, poorly trained, and weakly commanded," a third interjected. "The only advantage they brought to the war was their sheer numbers and plentiful equipment."

"It will be the British, gentlemen," Hans-Hubert barked. "The British will bring America into the war. Just as they did in the Great War."

"But this time, we will crush them," the first added. "Their mongrel ranks are filled with nothing but pinkos, Jews, fairies, and zoot-suit boys. They'll scatter like field mice at the first sight of our tanks and armor."

"Be that as it may," Hans quipped. "Their women are quite delicious!" He nodded and gazed across the room at Addie standing next to Rolf. They all turned.

Since their first meeting, Gep found Hans to grow distasteful. He watched him gesticulate gleefully as he boasted further of his female exploits since being stationed in Paris last September.

"A man, especially an officer, must establish himself in the same manner as a noble lion might claim his territory and his pride." Hans' eloquence impressed no one more than himself.

"Believe me, I've left my mark in every quarter of this wonderful city and under the most diverse of skirts. Unlike von Gerz over there." He directed everyone's attention again to where Rolf and Addie stood laughing and talking across the room. "The man has always been the most hopeless romantic. Falling deeply in love with the first woman that shows even the slightest hint of interest in him. Pathetic, gentlemen. A Wehrmacht officer must be ravenous and unrelenting in his dealings with the tender sex, just as he is with his enemy, consume of her fruit while it is at its sweetest, its ripest, then toss it to the earth and let the romantic scavengers, like my poor friend von Gerz, nursemaid the sour remains."

"I could only add, Hans-Hubert," Gep interjected through clenched teeth, "Major von Gerz may indeed lack your cavalier consumption of female delights, but then, he has the integrity you lack, doesn't he? He would never undermine a friend behind his back and in front of a gathering of junior officers!"

"Oh, you've wounded me, Oberleutnant," Hans retorted, holding his head high in an attempt to bolster a degree of dignity. "I do admit, I've crossed the line, haven't I? Been a bit unfair." He placed his hand on Gep's shoulder. "You are indeed a true friend to him."

"How would you know?" Gep's dangerous eyes grew even more menacing. "Major," he spat, indignantly adding, "Sir."

Rolf's hand slipped slyly into the slit in the back of Addie's evening gown, and a tingle ran the length of her spine. "Let's sneak away," he whispered.

"I thought you were obligated to be here."

"Obligated to make an appearance. I've done that." His whisper became a gentle kiss behind her ear. "I want to go back to your apartment and ravage you."

"You're making me blush."

370

"I live to make you blush." A subtle nibble, then, "I know where those buttons are!"

Gep was pleased at how easy it was to convince Rolf and Addie to escape this menagerie before the festivities reached a point where doing so would become impossible. They would dine at a tiny Italian place in Montparnasse and then hit Harry's New York for a few rounds of Soixante-Quinze cocktails, French 75s, named for the great artillery piece. Next, they would catch the last metro and dash off to the Quartier Latin to see the dance of Scheherazade at the Cabaret El Djazaïr in rue de la Huchette. It was the other Abwehr club in Paris particularly popular for its exotic Old Algiers atmosphere and Ali Baba motif. Finally, they would end up in the comfortable bosom of the cozy Club l'Heure Bleue. Sabina would join them every moment she wasn't performing on stage and would once again play host to Gep up in her room after the club had closed for the night. Rolf and Addie would retire to her apartment and engage to the crack of dawn in the finding and pushing of buttons.

Seeing him standing alone, Zucki sashayed over to Hans-Hubert and cocked her head to one side.

"I see you there, young man," she said, wiggling her long finger in his face. "A hawk on the henhouse, aren't you now? Surveying all these tender young chicks. You're the von Hirschbach boy, aren't you? I remember you. Your family lost it all in the crash, didn't they? Of course they did. But just look at you. You look as though you've done quite handsomely for yourself, don't you, my dear?"

"Zucki, Zucki," Hans-Hubert snapped, his head held high and arm folded behind his back as he bounced back and forth on his toes. "You don't forget a thing, do you?"

"Doing my job, darling. Tell Zucki, won't you?" She peered around the room. "Which one do you fancy tonight?" Again the finger darted about. "I know your game. I see those beautiful dark eyes of yours bouncing about from bosom to bum." She stood next to him, pointing around the room.

Hans nodded toward the green-eyed blonde in the ivory evening gown with matching wimple.

"Oh my, no, Hans-Hubert darling. Not her. That's Nika! She's not for you, not Nika."

"And why not?" he asked, frowning.

"Princess Nika? Surely, you've heard of her. Veronika von Forsthaus? Daughter of Count von Forsthaus? You listen to your *tante* Zucki, young man. She should be avoided at all costs by your ilk. She's the thirteenth of fourteen children, darling." Zucki's silver head dipped, and she looked at him over her onyx lorgnettes.

"Hers," she went on to say, "is the most fertile earth in all of Germany." Her penciled-on eyebrows crawled up her delicate forehead. "If I were you, lad, I wouldn't even stand too close to princess Nika." Zucki noticed a conversation dragging across the room, and she was off to the rescue, her cigarette holder held high, throwing her final words back over her shoulder to Hans.

"Else we'll have little counts and countesses popping out from under that gown like candy from a dashed gumdrop machine!"

66

Monday, 21 April 1941

Der Verrat
La trahison
The Jilt

DAY SEVENTEEN—Paris—Monday, 21 April 41—7:03 AM.
The call from General von Stülpnagel's office had been taken at the
Lutetia switchboard for Major von Gerz at just before seven. Their
orderly and driver hurried upstairs, woke an extremely hungover
Oberleutnant Fechter, and notified him of the call, saying he would
have the motorcar ready in less than ten minutes. Gep quickly
washed, dressed himself, and dashed over to Addie's apartment.
Rolf finished dressing in the waiting car.

DAY SEVENTEEN—Paris—Monday, 21 April 41—7:46 AM
When Rolf and Gep entered the office in the Majestic Hotel, the
general exploded.

"Why was I not told of the arrest and confession of Ritter's
murderer, von Gerz?" he shouted, slamming his fist on the desk. "I
instead receive word from Berlin? From the SD office in Berlin, no
less!"

Rolf gritted his teeth and stared blankly, standing at attention,
letting some steam escape from Stülpnagel before he started stirring
the pot. Gep stood next to Rolf. He wasn't about to say anything. As
the general blared on, Rolf could think of nothing but Kruder.

"I'm told of the glorious birthday present Gestapo operatives in
Paris were able to give to the Führer. The capture and confession of
some Austrian Bolshevik spy who had Ritter murdered in hopes of
creating German reprisals upon the French that would incite a wave
of terrorism by Gaullist resistants."

Rolf had had enough of the general's tirade. He answered with
solid purpose and fire in his eyes.

"I didn't tell you, sir, because I am convinced it is not true."
Rolf was livid about being undercut by Kruder and with himself that
he hadn't seen the general yesterday afternoon, immediately after the
trumped-up confession. "I was at the embassy affair last night and

fully expected to see you there; I intended to update you then. When you didn't show, I planned to interrogate the accused again this morning and report to you afterward. This is all news to me as well. It's Kruder, general. The man is doing all he can to establish himself and elevate the presence of the SS in Paris."

"And it would seem he's done a rather decisive job of it, wouldn't it, von Gerz?" Stülpnagel leered at Gep. Gep didn't move a muscle.

"The last thing you told me was to find the truth, general. This is not the truth. Allow me to interrogate the prisoner one more time under much less draconian circumstances, and I'll know—"

"That won't be possible." The tall, slim infantry general walked to the window overlooking the avenue Kléber and shook his head. "He died in his cell last night."

"And that ties up all the loose ends, general."

Rolf started walking around the room with one fist on his hip.

"Kruder coaxed the man into every word of his confession. I witnessed it myself. It was pathetic. While this man Heitner was indeed sending information out to British or Soviet Marxist contacts somewhere in Switzerland, he and his cohorts did *not* conspire to kill Ritter."

He walked over to the general and looked into his eyes.

"It was just as I suspected in my report to you last week. Old Ritter was being coerced somehow into helping a Swiss woman, one Edith Brückner, deliver information of some kind for Heitner. I don't think for an instant that Heitner had any part in Ritter's murder. I believe it may instead have more to do with the AWOL Wehrmacht officer I told you about, Leutnant Rutgers Heht. And the cache of bearer securities that have gone missing along with him. I really think, general, this all has little to do with political intrigue and everything to do with grand larceny. I am quite certain the assassination was simply a charade to cover it all up."

"I'm afraid, von Gerz, that unless you can come up with something very soon, I'm going to have to let this travesty stand. It's an appalling feather in the cap of the SS. But I must admit, it maintains the peace and harmony of the occupation. And right now, with the developments in the East, that's the only thing that's important."

"You asked me to find the truth, general. I will do just that."

"Then carry on," Stülpnagel said. "With urgency." His eyes tightened, "And with discretion."

67

Ein Herz, unbefleckt
Un cœur pur
A Heart Untainted

DAY SEVENTEEN—Paris—Monday, 21 April 41—12:55 PM
For nearly two weeks, the Lyon préfect's office and the French National Police had been investigating the murder of one Marcel Tournot. Not only had the man been brutally murdered on Palm Sunday in Lyon, but a patch of skin on his arm, obviously where a tattoo had once been, had been mysteriously cut away. The investigation led to a witness, a waitress in the train station café, who saw two shady characters discussing something sinister on that very night. One of the men looked familiar. The witness had seen this man before, but couldn't place him at the time. A phone call this morning to the préfect's office brought the police back to the train station. The girl now remembered the man to be a local Lyon stockbroker. And the man with him, to have red hair.

Inspector Luc-Henri had phoned Rolf from the Paris Préfecture and asked that he meet with him at Luc's regular lunch spot on the Île-de-la-Cité. A small café tucked away in an alley, it was far enough from his office to avoid any run-ins with colleagues, yet close enough not to wear him out getting there.

After a half hour, he noticed Rolf on the street corner, obviously having trouble finding the place. With a few waves of his hand, he tried to draw Rolf's attention, but to no avail. So he placed his finger and thumb in the corners of his mouth and made a shrill whistle. Rolf found him immediately and joined him at one of the café's sidewalk tables.

"I was certain I was on the wrong island." Rolf sat his upended hat in the unoccupied seat next to Luc and settled into a third bamboo and wicker chair, ordering a beer from a somewhat taken-aback waitress. He frowned at the waitress, then to Luc added, "Sorry I'm late."

"You'll have to forgive her rudeness, major. We don't get many Germans in our more remote little streets. Your colleagues tend to stay on the beaten path, if you will."

"I don't consider it rude. It's just 'French.'" Rolf smiled and offered Luc an Ernst Udet.

Taking the smoke and tapping its end on the table while Rolf snapped his lighter lit, Luc bent forward, cupping his hand against the pleasant breeze as the cigarette finally glowed red and crackled.

"I have information"—Luc stopped midsentence to cup his hands around Rolf's cigarette, until it was finally lit as well—"that will no doubt be pertinent to the Ritter case."

The arrival and just short of indignant serving of Rolf's beer brought another brief hesitation.

"The French National Police were investigating a murder in the city of Lyon. It seems a prominent Paris gangster was basically mutilated. This happened Sunday before last."

Luc picked up his croque monsieur with one hand, his cigarette still in the other, and raised his eyebrows, asking, "May I offer you a sandwich, major?"

Rolf shook his head and took a sip of beer.

"So, it seems the investigation into this man's murder has uncovered a possible connection to our broker friend, Monsieur Lemay, who was murdered here in Paris the day before Monsieur Ritter. There is a Lyonnais stockbroker who was approached by a German trying to enlist his help in moving a number of stolen securities. A redheaded German."

"And this broker in Lyon, of course, wanted no part in it?" Rolf interjected.

"This he has told us, but we remain watchful. According to this broker, the German was a dangerous, very sinister type, but then . . ." Luc took a drag on Rolf's Ernst Udet. As he exhaled through smiling teeth, he added, "Aren't you all?"

Rolf smiled back. "Yes, aren't we?"

"This man claims the German had demanded Swiss francs as payment."

"Could these stocks be sold there?" Rolf said.

"Possibly." Luc added, sipping his eau-de-vie d'Alsace. "But, more than likely, the majority of these securities were of smaller French companies. Much easier to move them undetected in France. Vichy France. For it, you see, is the last bastion for the sale of anonymous unregistered French securities. With the Paris Exchange closed, moving a large cache of stolen stocks and bonds on an open market could occur in only three places, major." Luc used a cocktail napkin as though it were a map of unoccupied France, pointing to each location. "Lyon." His finger touched one corner, then it slid across the napkin as he chewed a bite of sandwich, his cigarette bouncing in his lips. "Bordeaux, and"—the finger moved to the bottom and tapped a number of times on "Marseilles." Again, he smiled. "Period."

"If not Lyon, Marseilles would seem the most logical, to me." Rolf asserted. "Collect the preceeds, then board a slow boat to Spain and overland to Portugal."

"*Oui*, but I'm told it would depend on the type of securities. If all the instruments are of local or French companies, then moving them in any of these cities is possible. But if any of them are international companies, then only in Lyon could they be sold. Next to Paris, Lyon is the largest exchange in France. Since we are fairly certain there were a number of international stocks involved in this case, Lyon is the city, monsieur."

"And this broker in Lyon is lying."

"*Oui*, monsieur." Luc took the last bite of his sandwich, swished his palms back and forth together over the plate, and chewed.

"I will need to talk to this man, inspector," Rolf demanded. "You will arrange it?"

"As you wish, major." Luc dabbed his lips with his napkin. "The man is being followed every minute of his life. And he knows it. He is a very nervous sort, and I am told he is on the verge of cracking at any time now."

"Being interrogated by a German major might just send him over the edge, mightn't it?"

"Yes, it very well could. It certainly would me!" Luc's charming smile caught Rolf off guard. "As a matter of fact, major, I'm told under the terms of the armistice you actually have the power to have this man brought to Paris for questioning. Then we could both talk to him."

"What do I have to do?" Rolf asked.

Luc pulled a trifolded set of documents from his inner pocket and offered Rolf his fountain pen. "Just sign these extradition papers."

"Inspector?" Rolf started signing in the places where tiny check marks appeared. "You are a delight."

The waitress appeared and coldly asked Luc if there would be anything else. Luc shook his head and she tossed her head sideways and quipped, "What about this one?"

Supplying the woman with a brief lesson in courtesy, Luc asked Rolf in French, "Would you like another beer, major?"

Rolf smiled at the woman and answered Luc in unaccented perfect French, "No, I'm afraid I am going to have to get back to my office, but thank you for asking, madame."

The woman curled her nose, tossed it in the air, and wandered off.

"Please forgive her, major. She could very well have a husband or son held prisoner in Germany or, heaven forbid, killed in the battle."

"Inspector." Rolf stood, and the inspector grabbed his cane to do the same. "I think you and I have proven these past two weeks that we can be honest and candid with each other."

"I wholeheartedly agree, monsieur."

"Then tell me. Does everyone feel the way that woman does? Because if so, we don't really see it. My people tell me, from a German perspective they are almost amazed at the cordial cooperation we have received since the occupation started last year. Sure, your countrymen seem to avoid and ignore us; we sense their disregard. But when we ask a question or engage in some dealing or other, we mostly see only affable consideration at every turn."

Luc snickered and started his tarantella, swaying back and forth as he shuffled himself on down the sidewalk.

"Yes, major. I think we can be candid. So, I will tell you this. I believe the whores who loiter about the place Pigalle say it best."

"What do they say?" Rolf asked, cocking his head inquisitively and flipping his spent cigarette to the gutter.

"They say." Luc stopped and looked at Rolf with twinkling eyes. "They say, 'While my pussy may have a little German in it, I assure you, my heart is completely French!'"

68

Überwachung
La surveillance
The Stakeout

DAY SEVENTEEN—Mallorca—Monday, 21 April 41—1:34 PM
Kaspar Koch had spent the last two days moving back and forth from
Palma to Bunyola, checking banks, grocers, apothecaries—anywhere
he might run into Rutgers Heht or Heht's wife or any lingering sign of
either. He made rounds to each of his crew members' positions,
keeping them fed and hydrated and asking them ad nauseam if they'd
seen anything at all of the car or the two fugitives. None had.
Nothing. The man had simply disappeared. A fart in the Mallorcan
wind. Kaspar feared, despite assurances from his operatives, that Ruti
had actually gone on over the mountain into or past Sóller, maybe
even to the remote northern coast of the island. But the German navy
still operated a Spanish Civil War–era submarine base in the port of
Sòller, so more than just a shred of doubt, or rather, optimism
persisted in Kaspar's mind.

    Earlier he was driving on the outskirts of Palma, heading back
into the city, when he passed a large truck. The letters on the canvas
front of the cargo bed spelled *Muebles*. A furniture truck!

    Kaspar whipped the car around and followed it from a distance,
staying back far enough to be inconspicuous, but never losing sight of
the truck. Sure enough, beyond the road that led off to Bunyola,
perhaps ten kilometers past, the truck pulled off on a remote gravel
road heading up the mountain. Ecstatic, Kaspar pulled over and
watched it climb slowly up the steep grade, whining in a rolling
cadence as the truck lunged and sunk its way up the hill. When the
road's switchbacks led the truck around the mountain and out of his
sight, Kaspar jumped in his car and followed it. Within five minutes
he caught sight of it again. Across a deep and very wide ravine he
could see it, still climbing and whining and lunging. He pulled over
again at a clearing, got out of the car, and lit a cigarette, patiently
watching the creeping vehicle far across on the other side of the
ravine.

    Then it stopped.

Through his binoculars, Kaspar watched a man get out and walk back to an overgrown set of tracks leading off the road. The man then went back to the truck, looked around a few times, and peed. A shiver and a quick shake, and he jumped back in the truck and slowly backed it up until he could turn off the road and head almost straight up the mountain along the overgrown path. The huge truck swayed and tipped almost over on its side a few times as its tires dug in and climbed one kicked-up rock or chunk of turf at a time up the steep grade.

Kaspar flipped his cigarette over the edge of the cliff where he had stopped, got back in the car, and headed to Bunyola to round up his crew members.

DAY SEVENTEEN—Mallorca—Monday, 21 April 41—3:52 PM
Mélina had never been so happy. She lived in a beautiful little bungalow with a view through the pine trees and junipers of a huge green valley with a river running through it. Her husband, whom she loved above all else in the world and who loved her, was so happy and so at peace, living in a tranquility he'd never known before. She skipped out the front door of the mountain cabin with a basket of clothes on her hip. A mockingbird sang from somewhere in the trees. She whistled at it and delighted in its attempt to mock her whistle. The crescendo continued as she carried the basket of clothes out to the clothesline. The hectic past few days had left Ruti exhausted, and he was still fast asleep, snoring away in the brand-new bed she had made him buy for their tiny stone bungalow, their new nest.

As she hung up his undershorts, a flicker of light caught her eye, then two more flashes from the same direction made her turn around and search for its source. It had come from somewhere on the next hill. It was surely nothing. The sun was low now in the sky, and it must have reflected off something in the trees. She discounted it. Still, with all that had happened, she would mention it to Ruti later. When he woke up. If he woke up. The poor man was absolutely exhausted.

Kaspar jerked his binoculars down and twisted himself as flat as he could on the tree limb. As he had watched Heht's wife at the clothesline, he noticed her suddenly turn in his direction and realized he was looking directly into the sun. She had seen the reflection off the lenses. He cursed himself as he quickly climbed down the backside of the tree and slid down the grassy ridge, then gained his

380

feet and hurried off to the road. He uncovered the camouflaged moped and walked it down the mountain road for a few hundred meters before hopping on it and coasting down the steepest part of the hill, ultimately engaging the clutch and starting the machine with a wobbly, sideways, and sudden jerk. He sped on down the road and back toward Palma. There he would check his men into a nice hotel, feed them a huge feast of every tapas the place would have to offer, and they would drink into the night and plan tomorrow's assault. This time they would plan carefully, thoroughly, and this time they would follow the plan.

But his first stop was at a post office, where he would make a call to the Madrid Abwehr office. A call that would be patched through to Paris.

DAY SEVENTEEN—Paris—Monday, 21 April 41—4:48 PM
The telephone rang. Two jingles. Then two more.

"Major von Hirschbach here." The call was patched from the Hotel Edward III and Madrid. Kaspar Koch was on the line from Palma de Mallorca. Hans quickly shooed the grey-aproned girl away and closed his office door behind her.

"We have located the man, Heht," Kaspar told him. "I plan an assault in the morning. When it's over, how should I proceed?"

"If you find the money, then the Reich has no further use for this fellow. If you don't, you are to use the girl to force him to disclose its whereabouts. But we must have the location of the money."

"And then?"

"I plan to be in Monaco on Thursday morning," Hans informed him. "I could meet you in Marseilles. Can you get there by then?"

"Yes, most definitely," Kaspar said, then paused and added, "Meet me in the warehouse in the freight port. Eight o'clock sharp. And major?"

"Yes, Koch."

"If I do get the money or its whereabouts, then what?"

"Then see that both of them are—how was it you so perfectly put it before?" Hans' dark eyes grinned. "Oh, yes. Never to soon be seen again!"

381

69

Tuesday, 22 April 1941

Der Angriff
L'assaut
The Assault

DAY EIGHTEEN—Mallorca—Tuesday, 22 April 41—4:02 AM
"Both must be taken alive!" Kaspar reminded his crew as dawn
revealed a gray day blooming behind the rocky crags and blanket of
blue-green pine covering the mountains. He could see a hangover in
all three pairs of eyes straining to focus on him. *They can all be such
buffoons sometimes,* he thought. No doubt, the drink they told him
they were going to finish after he turned in last night became another
bottle. But he'd been in this very position many times before, and
they had all always proved their mettle.

The plan was simple. A plan they had used frequently. The
primary assault would be the first two team members. They would
dash straight into the bedroom, gain immediate control of Heht's
arms, and then whistle. The Sardinian would stay at the front door
and Kaspar at the rear entrance to the cabin to cut off any escape.
When Heht was under control, Kaspar would hear the whistle, come
running with the syringe, and it would all be over in less than a
minute.

Everyone was at the ready. A nod from Kaspar. And the two
lead assailants rushed stealthily into the bungalow.

With two intruders dead or dying in the cabin's bedroom floor,
and echoes of three gunshots as well as Mélina's piercing screams
still reverberating on the cabin's stucco walls, Ruti and a cloud of gun
smoke burst through the living-room doorway. Suddenly, he was
pointing his Dreyse pocket pistol in the nose of a man who was doing
the same to Ruti. In two swift moves, Ruti reached out and clamped
down on the man's pistol and twisted it backward, breaking the
intruder's trigger finger and sending one round into the bungalow's
ceiling.

"Run, Mélina!" Ruti shouted. "Run for the car!"

That she did, running into the stone-hard chest of a fourth intruder at the front door.

Ruti grabbed the third man by his broken finger and wedged his seven-millimeter Dreyse in his ear as he forced him toward the door where the fourth man, a huge southern Mediterranean, held Mélina around the neck, his left hand clenching her right breast, his right holding a Luger to her temple.

"Ruti!" Mélina screamed. "God, Ruti!"

"Stop hurting her!" Ruti shouted, pushing his captive even closer to the man who had Mélina pinned to him. The giant jutted his whiskered chin and smiled at Ruti, squeezing Mélina's breast even harder, forcing a deafening shriek from her.

"Stop hurting her, or you'll never see any money." Ruti watched the man he was holding motion for the giant to release his grip on Mélina. This man, Ruti quickly deduced, was the leader of this team of Abwehr assassins.

The Mediterranean did as instructed, reluctantly. He tucked Mélina's head in the cleft of his arm and held it to his ribs like it was a rugby football, his huge arm under her neck. Never taking his eyes off Ruti, he gave a sinister smile as he bent down and sniffed her hair, then jutted his nasty tongue. A yellowish stain ran down its center. He ran it around in her hair, laughing and tugging on clumps of her blond locks with his thick blue lips.

"Take that weapon away from her head," Ruti demanded. "Tell your moron to take that weapon away from her head, or I kill all four of us right now and no one sees my money."

Ruti bent the broken finger forcefully, and Kaspar Koch screamed for his best operative to do as Ruti commanded. As soon as the gun barrel moved inches away from Mélina's temple, Ruti fired two shots, one into the huge man's elbow, the other into his knee. The Luger went flying through the air, and the giant crashed to the floor screaming in pain.

Mélina ran to Ruti as he released Kaspar and pushed him far enough away that he could fire a shot into him without a chance of hitting Mélina. As he was about to release a round, Mélina screamed and pushed Ruti's arm up into the air. The shot went astray.

"No, Ruti! No more killing!" She pleaded as she clung to him.

He hugged her to him and leveled the Dreyse again at Kaspar Koch.

"Please, Ruti. Please. I can't run anymore. We must turn ourselves in. No more killing. I can't take any more killing."

"These men are part of an Ablegekommando, Mélina. Assassins. They are not here to arrest us. Once they get their hands on the money, they will eliminate both of us. And they will torture you until I turn the money over to them."

"We can't keep running, Ruti. We have nowhere else to run. You must think of our child."

"She's right, Heht," Kaspar said. "I've reported your position. Kill us if you will, but you, your woman, and your unborn child will never leave Mallorca alive. You're a dead man either way. But she and the baby could live. Give up and I'll see that your woman and child go free. You can trust me."

"Trust the man who broke in and tried to shanghai us? Never! There's not a single German on earth I would ever trust again."

Mélina hugged herself to Ruti, kissed him, and whispered in his ear. Kaspar couldn't hear what was being said, but he took reasonable joy in the fact whatever it was, Ruti seemed in agreement. Finally, Ruti nodded, nostrils flaring as he panted forcefully in an attempt to regain his composure.

"What's your name?" he asked, but couldn't be heard for the vulgar filth coming from the giant on the floor, screaming details in some dialect of what he planned to do to Mélina once he had the chance.

Ruti fired off another shot into the man's other knee.

"Order that dog to shut up. I can keep doing this all day!"

The Sardinian bit down hard and rolled back and forth on the floor.

"What's your name?" Ruti asked again, now that he could be heard.

"Koch," Kaspar said, slowly regaining his feet, showing Ruti his empty palms all the while. "Kapitan Koch."

"I will surrender, Kapitan Koch." Ruti glanced at Mélina, and she nodded her approval. "And these," he added, "are my terms."

DAY EIGHTEEN—Paris—Tuesday, 22 April 41—9:27 AM
"Major von Gerz here."

"Bonjour, major," Luc said. "I have news about our friend, the broker in Lyon."

"He's in Paris?"

"There was no need to bring him to Paris. It seems your reputation was enough to force the man's hand. At the mention of being extradited by a German major, the little man evidently gave up the ghost. Figures, names, dates. The man literally gushed information. His ability to keep a secret is matched only by my dear wife's."

Rolf buttoned his top tunic button as the levity caught up with him and he snickered.

"More than a thousand separate securities, mostly of French companies, were delivered to our broker friend in Lyon by a German officer *en* disguise, no doubt your Lieutenant Rutgers Heht. Each separate block of securities was valued at between two and sixteen thousand francs at the time the Paris Exchange was closed. Our economic department suggests they would have appreciated at least eight percent in the current economic climate. They were sold in Lyon for a mere six million francs, and our little friend collected the investors and handled the sale. Your man Heht demanded Swiss francs at the last minute, but the broker and his clients were only able to round up forty thousand or so. This Heht fellow was traveling under a Swiss identity. His next step was obviously to move the funds to a numbered Swiss account."

"And the broker? He is under arrest?" Rolf asked.

"He has been charged with dealing in stolen securities. But his lawyers are contending that there are documented bills of sale for each. So, the little man keeps his head. At least for now."

70

Die Postlauf
L'envoi par la poste
The Mail Run

DAY EIGHTEEN—Paris—Tuesday, 22 April 41—5:40 PM
"No, Rolf, old comrade!" Hans-Hubert exclaimed, tossing him the car keys. "You drive."

An orderly was still loading heavy suitcases in the trunk of the motorcar as Rolf and Addie followed Hans down the steps of the villa's rear portico to the courtyard driveway. Rolf's driver was peeling back the black rooftop on the Hotchkiss 680 Cabriolet convertible. The car was a dazzling spectacle shining in the sunlight; cream-yellow exterior with wide white walls, a regal red-leather interior with polished tortoiseshell and chrome dash and appointments.

"What a pip of an automobile!" Addie exclaimed as she wedged herself in the tiny afterthought of a backseat. "If you'd have mentioned this car, I might have been persuaded to date you, Hans."

"Now you tell me." Hans and Addie helped the driver snap the canvas cover on the folded-down rooftop.

"I thought these Hotchkiss people just made machine guns and tanks," Rolf said as he climbed in the driver's seat and examined the classy interior.

"It's solid as a tank, Rolf, old sport, and purrs like a machine gun." Hans-Hubert hopped in the passenger seat and looked coyly at Rolf. Pointing his finger toward the arched doorway that separated the courtyard and driveway from the street, he smiled and told Rolf, "Fire at will!"

Rolf grinned gleefully as he switched on the key, pressed the starter button, and threw the car into gear while the orderly and the driver opened the wooden doorway out of the villa. The sparkling yellow machine crept through the tight opening and turned onto the street. Rolf suddenly gunned it, and the powerful car fishtailed and screeched over the bumpy cobblestone.

Addie barely had time to get her scarf tied around her head before the wind started whipping hair about her face.

"Can you tell me where you're going, Hans?" she asked, sitting sideways behind the men and looking over her shoulder at them. "Or is it guarded information? You're all just so secretive. It's absolutely impossible to even have a conversation with any of you sometimes."

"Forgive me Addie, but no, I can't tell you." He turned and rested his chin on his forearm stretched over the back of the seat. "However"—his head moved up and down on his chin with each word he spoke—"I promise to return in time to see you and Rolf off."

Her lips gave a pout of disappointment at being reminded of their doomed affair. She struggled against the wind to keep her skirt cinched up around her legs with one hand while she used the other to poke strands of her windswept, misbehaving hair under the scarf. Then she gave up on the latter, ripped the scarf off, and shook her hair with carefree abandon.

"I hoped to surprise you, but it's time you knew, Addie," Rolf interjected, looking at her through the rearview mirror. "We have some good news. Hans has been nice enough to arrange transportation to Lisbon for you."

Hans looked back to Addie, smiling rakishly.

"You'll be leaving Saturday night on a daily Lufthansa airmail flight that runs between Lisbon and Paris." He of course couldn't give her the real reason for the flight, couldn't let her know it was bringing two of Hans' recruits to Paris to train for his American operation.

"You mean I'm really going home!" she exclaimed, squirming herself over with her heels and rump and throwing her arms around Rolf from behind, kissing his taut cheek. She moved over to do the same to Hans.

"Oh, Hans, what a wonderful gesture. It makes me almost want to take back everything I've ever said about you."

"I have also given Rolf the use of a quite impressive country estate I've taken in Haute-Normandie. It's compliments of a British duke. Beautiful, overlooks the Seine valley. I'm certain it will suit you. My gift to you both on your last night together."

"Well, that settles it then, doesn't it?" Addie quipped. "I take it all back. Every morsel. You're truly a swell darling, Hans."

She stretched out to give him a kiss as he pointed sweetly at his extended cheek. Then, just as she was about to kiss it, he turned to her and planted his wet mouth on her lips.

"Hans, you're incorrigible and salacious." She grabbed his shoulder and shook it. "And wonderful."

The car purred like a sleek yellow cat as it sped down the deserted avenues and out on the highway toward Le Bourget and the airport. Addie had to squint her eyes and clasp her hair in a knot behind her head to keep Rolf in her sight. He looked so happy and so completely out of place racing the sporty car along the empty highway in the full dress uniform of a German officer, grinning like some feisty schoolboy. His short hair rustled in the wind. He had his left wrist resting on the top frame of the windshield; his watch crystal caught the setting sunlight in random flashes of light. She pictured him in America, on some Midwestern country road in one of her daddy's sports cars with her sitting proudly at his side. Then a dose of reality slapped her in the face like the blasts of wind whipping over the windshield. *There she went again,* she thought. The dreamy, silly girl. What made her think he would ever go to America? He was a German. An aristocrat and an officer. With a daughter and a career in the army. Did he love her so much that he would abandon everything to run off with her, probably to work in the bank for her daddy? She knew the answer. Of course he wouldn't. Not a strong, independent soul like this. And what about her? Could she abandon her home and live the rest of her life in Europe with him? She did truly love this man, though. Far more than any she had ever known. And the thought of them being separated, even for a few months until the war ended, was almost more than she could abide. The war. There hadn't been a night's prayer that didn't end with a plea that she would awaken the next morning to headlines declaring the its end. How wonderful would that be? Their affair could slow to a normal pace, could progress with a liberating transparency impossible to imagine right now. But the war, if anything, was escalating rather than winding down. So, all she could do now was stare with wind-burned eyes through the annoying swarm of her windswept hair at this handsome, gallant man. And dream of, or hope for, a future. Any future. America, Paris, Berlin. Any future with her gallant German officer, her Rolf.

At the airport Rolf pulled the car right up to the chain link gate. A French flic in cape and kepi was standing guard. His smile at the sight of the car evaporated when he saw the German officer driving it, realizing it had probably been commandeered from some countryman. With credentials checked, the gendarme snidely opened the gate and Rolf drove the convertible right up to the Fokker Trimotor awaiting Hans-Hubert's arrival. The engine on the far wing was already running on the Brussels-Paris-Marseilles mail plane, and the nose engine was working laboriously to start. Before the yellow Hotchkiss beauty came to a full stop, Hans stood up in the car and motioned for a member of the flight crew to assist him with his luggage.

While he took two heavy suitcases from the car's trunk and set them on the tarmac for the man to lug to the plane for him, Addie came over to Hans-Hubert and put her arms around him.

"Thank you, Hans."

"I still don't understand, Addie, my dear." Hans-Hubert hugged her to him and tossed a pained look at Rolf. "What on earth it is you see in my friend Rolf here that isn't abundantly visible in me?"

"Let me see," she responded, smiling proudly at Rolf. "Integrity, honesty, humility, class—"

"What about generosity?" Hans-Hubert interjected, with a pronounced frown. "Surely, you can give me that?"

"Yes, Hans, love, you're the most generous scoundrel I've ever known."

He clutched his wounded heart and staggered pretentiously.

"Really, Hans, darling. Thank you so much for everything." She kissed his cheek again.

"I'm rather happy to do it for you." Hans pulled a third bag from the trunk and shook Rolf's hand. "Take care of things while I'm gone, old friend."

"I shall, Hans." Rolf looked at the bag. "You sure you'll be just gone two days?"

"You've caught me, old boy, haven't you though?" Hans gave a sheepish grin. "Doing a little smuggling, aren't I? A couple cases of champagne for a lady friend of mine."

"How gallant of you," Addie interjected.

"Believe me," Hans quipped. "She's quite worth the trouble." He winked and added, "I'll see you both on Friday," as he turned and headed for the airplane. "I promise. We'll give you a send-off not to soon be seen again."

71

Wednesday, 23 April 1941

Das Missverständnis
Le malentendu
The Misunderstanding

DAY NINETEEN—Paris—Wednesday, 23 April 41—8:08 AM
A leaden sky covered Paris and the Hotel Lutetia. Rolf and Gep took
a private breakfast in the peaceful courtyard garden surrounded by
thickets of manicured topiaries and statuettes shadowed in faint wisps
of brown winter mold. The only sounds were the occasional turning
of pages, the clinking of cups on saucers, and the rants of a
quarrelsome rascal of a songbird somewhere overhead. A stack of
German newspapers newly arrived on last night's train were being
quietly perused by Rolf. Gep read through single pages of intelligence
wires from a thick gray file folder.

"Have you kept up on some of the war reports?" Gep asked, not
looking up, pushing his reading glasses up on his roman nose. His
deep voice sliced through the quiet like a sharp knife.

Rolf frowned for a second. "What?" His train of thought
derailed, he shook his head and smiled. "Sorry, Gep." He held up the
Monday edition of the *Berliner Morgenpost*. "I was just taking in
some of the accolades Goebbels showered on the Führer in his
birthday speech Sunday. Listen to this. 'We are, all of us, witness to
the greatest miracle in history. That of a genius who is building us all
a new world!'"

Rolf's smile grew sinister as he peeled a recently very rare and
obviously pithy orange. A quick tip of his head and he added, "I'm
certain a great deal of it is indeed going to need rebuilding."

Gep put down the boiled egg he'd been gently breaking,
dropping and turning it on the table. He fumbled through the stack of
reports he'd already read. "Yes, here it is," he said, finding what he
was after.

"It seems our Führer's birthday gifts are unending." Gep
smiled. "Sunday, April 20 (the Führer's birthday). Albania. The
Greek army evidently waited until this very day to surrender. And of
course, to whom do they surrender? None other than SS Panzer

Division Leibstandarte *Adolf Hitler*. How do these people breathe with their noses wedged up there so deeply?" Gep quipped, peppering his egg and biting off nearly half of it.

"It's disconcerting, Gep." Rolf folded his newspaper and placed it on the stack in the chair next to him.

"It's a necessary evil, major. An evil of which we should be mindful. There are already too many of us in the Abwehr who have run afoul of the Nazis for this reason or that. Far too much independent thinking in our circles, not enough cajoling."

The house wren's rants echoed intrusively against the courtyard's walls and windows.

"You know, Gep," Rolf said, breaking the orange apart and tossing a wedge in his mouth. "we make light of these SS peasants, but they grow more firmly entrenched as a formidable arm of the German military with each passing day."

"We need their numbers," Gep responded, turning the top of the rest of his egg brown with pepper. "As the war escalates and Wehrmacht ranks are spread thin over the four corners of Europe and North Africa, SS divisions become more important and necessary."

"It's not their soldiers," Rolf explained. "They're just cannon fodder." Rolf tapped his middle finger on the beveled glass top over the wrought-iron table. "It's the SS officer corps that will be the Reich's curse. Their lack of breeding and training, their base, Bierstube language and draconian tactics diminish us all. Mark my words, Gep. One day we shall all wear their stain."

Rolf relished the last bites of his priceless orange as he went on.

"You saw what happened to that little Jew in Warsaw, Gep. That SS colonel gave the man's summary execution little more thought than he would the swatting of a fly. And we all sat there. Watching through that café window." The emphasis he applied in his next words displayed his disgust in himself. "We finished our fucking lunch! While that little man lay dying on that frozen sidewalk. Finished our lunch, Gep, until the meat wagon came to retrieve him."

"It was an isolated incident, Rolf." Gep was finding Rolf's discontent worrisome. "I'm sure I heard that colonel was reprimanded for the incident."

"What for?" Rolf quipped. "Littering?"

He shooed a hovering bee from the table and took a sip of his coffee.

"Still, it haunts me, Gep. And not just that I witnessed it. But because it compels me to pose a question. Could this become the norm? The accepted scene as we conquer our way through the rest of Europe. Will we be walking the sidewalks of a city, stepping over a dead Jew here, then round a corner only to do it again?"

"I do share your contempt for the SS, Rolf, but not your love of the Jew." Gep was not just an Austrian, he was an Austro-Hungarian imperialist with no qualms about what could befall a Jew. "The Jew has no business in our circle or our day-to-day lives, and most definitely not in our beds. They are enemies of the Reich, Rolf."

"An enemy without a weapon. A defenseless enemy. A nonbelligerent. Perhaps I'm being too visceral, but that's not the war I'm fighting, Gep. I'm fighting the war that raises the economic and social tides of Europe and thereby all of her ships. The war of retaliation against the rape of Germany at Versailles and Trianon. And I'm fighting the war against communism, Gep. Truly, the enemy of the entire civilized world. What I'm *not* fighting is the war that wastes manpower and priceless effort herding Jews into ghettos and then trying to keep them there."

Rolf sat back in his chair in a fluster and let his terse words soak in with both Gep and himself.

"No, Gep. I'm not a lover of the Jew. But nor do I hate him. I frankly regard them all in the same fashion as the other lower races or classes. And I too firmly believe in Germany's destiny of preeminence." Rolf leaned forward and tapped two fingers on the table, adding, "But its cost doesn't have to be the enslavement of the other races, and certainly not their summary execution."

"The Führer disagrees with you," Gep declared as he swished egg crumbs and pepper from his fingers over his plate.

"Then I respectfully decline to agree with him," Rolf retorted, proudly.

As a figure appeared in the many beveled frames of the glass door leading from the hotel, Gep frowned slightly and nodded toward the hotel.

"Let's, then, keep that between the two of us," Gep said with a worrisome smile.

That single vexing songbird scolded the courtyard's new intruder with unceasing chirps and whistles, as the door opened and an orderly entered the garden stringing an olive-colored, cloth-wrapped phone wire along with him. He set the candlestick telephone on the wrought-iron table in front of Rolf and handed him the receiver.

"An urgent call for you, Herr Major," he said, bowing his head and clicking his heels. "Forgive the static, sir. The call originates in Barcelona, patched through Madrid. It is, however, a secure line," the orderly added, then urbanely disappeared.

"Major von Gerz here," Rolf said, looking over his shoulder and watching the orderly close the door behind him as he reentered the hotel.

"Major, this is Kapitan Kaspar Koch. I lead an Ablegekommando unit based out of Madrid. Yesterday I accepted the surrender terms of one Leutnant Rutgers Heht. A Paris deserter."

"Superb, captain," Rolf said. He quickly put the handheld microphone piece to his chest and told Gep, "They have the man, Heht."

"Major," the caller went on to say, "the condition of his surrender is that he will only do so to you. And to no one else. I can have him and his wife in Marseilles in the morning."

"His wife? Did you say wife?" Rolf's brow furrowed. "Talk louder, I can barely hear you."

Gep looked at Rolf, his own lips silently asking, "Wife?"

"Yes, his wife," Kaspar Koch shouted. "Which brings me to Heht's final demand. You must also bring some American woman along with you, the . . ." Kaspar's pause was obviously to acquire the woman's name again. "Yes, Bridges, the Bridges woman. She must accompany you as well."

"That's quite impossible," Rolf retorted. "I'll have none of it."

"Major, if you don't, it's going to cost the Reich six million francs!" Kaspar replied.

"Koch? Was that your name?" Fury was displayed in Rolf's clenched jaw. He once again held the mic piece to his chest, quickly looked over to Gep, and barked, "Get rid of that fucking bird, Gep. I can't hear anything against that infernal racket!"

"So Koch," Rolf shouted back into the phone. "You'll know this, my man. I'll be the one making the demands, Koch! Do you understand me?"

Gep flicked his napkin at the bird and watched it circle the courtyard as Rolf went on.

"You are to put this man, Heht, in chains. His wife as well. And you are to deliver them both to me in my office here in Paris by tomorrow night. Is that quite clear?"

"I'm afraid you're the one who doesn't understand, major. Heht has killed two of my operatives and left the third in a mountain cabin in Mallorca with bullet wounds to both his knees. You should also know, he currently has a silenced Dreyse seven-millimeter stabbing me in my right kidney!"

72

Nachtzug nach Marseilles
Train de nuit à Marseilles
Night Train to Marseilles

DAY NINETEEN—Vichy Frontier—Wednesday, 23 April 41—8:08 PM

At Rolf's command, Gep had taken three Pullman cabins on the night train to Marseilles. He found the third cabin an unnecessary frivolity, fully aware Rolf would end up in Addie's, and he went so far as to tell him so. Rolf had only smiled at him with twinkling eyes, saying, "For the sake of propriety, humor me, won't you, Gep?"

After duck à l'orange and two bottles of Châteauneuf-du-Pape in the dining car, Gep excused himself and retired to the smoking car while Rolf and Addie shared digestives. Dinner conversation had danced around the subject of Rutgers Heht and his possible involvement in the Ritter murder, and with Gep gone, their conversation sashayed directly into it.

"Addie, I'm of the opinion Leutnant Rutgers Heht is involved indeed in Herr Ritter's murder in some way." Rolf swirled his Courvoisier. "I haven't felt comfortable sharing this with you."

"Even someone who shares your bed?" Addie replied, making thoughtful folds in her napkin on her lap.

"Yes, Adelaide. Especially, if that someone is a gadabout I must chase down all over Normandy!"

She could only swallow hard and smile.

"How well do you know this man, Heht?" Rolf went on.

"He came in the club with Hans-Hubert and some of the others a few times. Rolf, he was the most painfully quiet species. Of course, bandying about with Hans-Hubert, wouldn't anyone seem the subtle sort, though? Then sometime before Christmas, I felt the queer impulse to introduce him to my sweet friend, Mélina, she being the insufferable wallflower herself. I was certain they were kindred spirits, and I was proved correct. They became inseparable."

"You were, then, aware of her slipping off into Vichy France and joining him?"

Addie's eyes would have betrayed her if she'd have lied and said no. She cast them downward and just nodded.

"Why did you feel compelled to keep this woman's rendezvous plans with Heht from me?"

"Rolf, darling. You said yourself, you never gave me any clue that Ruti was a suspect and you couldn't expect me to just volunteer information that would very well get poor Mélina arrested." Addie steadied herself as the train jerked, slowing to a stop. "I assure you, had you even once told me any of this about Ruti before now, I would have told you about Mélina in an instant."

"They're married now, you know. Heht and this friend of yours."

Addie's eyes smiled, then the rest of her beautiful face caught up.

"I didn't, but I won't deny the fact that I hoped they would tie the knot."

"Why do women delight so in all that business?"

"It's our nature. Our duty to the war effort itself, *mon* major." Her sweet eyes grew impish. "Men make war. Women make war romantic."

"Then I salute you," Rolf told her as he snuffed out his cigarette in the tiny chrome ashtray under the dining car window. The train crept slowly down the three hundred meters from the German checkpoint in the occupied zone across the demarcation line to the French checkpoint at the Vichy frontier. Free France.

"Why do you suppose Heht would demand to surrender only to me?"

Addie looked down again and bit her lower lip.

"And why did he require your presence?" he inquired, bending his head somewhat to look into her deflected eyes.

"I'm sorry, Rolf, darling, but to be bluntly honest, I told Mélina you were neither a cad nor callous like the other Germans we've all grown accustomed to this past year. I told her you were a truly decent sort, a man who could be trusted to keep his word. I know any other German would have seen me locked up in the Cherche-Midi after my little Normandy escapade. I told her as well I was quite certain I was falling in love with you and was pretty sure you fancied me. And do forgive me for this, Rolf, darling, but I told her that if she got into any sort of trouble, she should mention your name." She bit her lip again, then answered his second question. "I assume she just wants me there because I'm just about her only friend."

"It seems as though she followed your advice."

Fall Irmgard

Gep returned, followed by two French National border policemen.

"I'll have your papers, *s'il vous plaît.*" The older of the two demanded.

Gep took an immediate dislike the man's tone and quickly retorted, "We're in uniform and with the Armistice Commission. There's nothing more you need to know!"

Pulling his Wehrmacht identity card from his tunic, Rolf collected Addie's passport. Handing them both to the border flic, Rolf glanced up at Gep, smiled, and said in French, "If you would be so kind, Oberleutnant?"

Gep flipped his identity card in the air, forcing the French policeman to catch it.

When the border patrol agents moved on to the next cabin, Gep stated in German, "I admire a great deal about you, major." He gritted his teeth and shook his head. "But your infernal ability to match coyness with courtesy is well beyond me. How on earth do you do it?"

"I drink a lot?" Rolf quipped back in German.

Addie let out the briefest snort of a chuckle.

Rolf gave her a puzzled look.

"I was led to believe you didn't speak German."

She shook her head smiling, "I don't speak a word," she answered, then tapped him on the chin and added, "It was that ridiculous look on your face. It just caught me off guard."

Gep returned to his cabin, and Rolf had barely closed his cabin door when a knock sounded. It was another gendarme. He saluted and handed Rolf a telegram. Addie watched him pop the seal off the folded one-piece communication and read the note.

"It's from Luc in Paris," Rolf announced. "The inspector has discovered that Heht set up a brokerage account with the Lyon broker. But it wasn't in Heht's name." Then Rolf's shoulders sank and his entire demeanor wilted.

"What is it, darling?" Addie inquired, a troubled look in her eyes as she touched his shoulder.

Rolf's jaw clenched as he crumpled the telegram and stuffed it in his tunic pocket. He started out the door.

"Rolf, please. What is it?"

"It's not you, Addie," he said, looking reassuringly at her. Then, as he closed the cabin door behind him, she heard him add, "It's not you this time who betrayed me."

73

Thursday, 24 April 1941

Fischgeruch
L'odeur du poisson
The Smell of Fish

DAY TWENTY—Marseilles—Thursday, 24 April 41—8:34 AM
Yesterday afternoon Hans-Hubert von Hirschbach had taken the
grandest suite on the fifth floor of the Grand Hotel along the old port
of Marseilles. Last night he was driven to Monte Carlo for his
meeting with the American recruit. It had gone off perfectly. The man
answered every one of Hans' questions precisely and without
hesitation. His credentials were beyond question. He was a foreign
manager for an American tire company and was in France regularly
negotiating deals for raw materials in the Congo and French West
Africa. There could be no better man for the American operation.
Someone who was close to production and capacity figures. And not
just in regard to automobiles and trucks, but airplanes as well. Such a
man would be the perfect fit in his crew, which made Hans
suspicious. And if Hans-Hubert was suspicious, no doubt Admiral
Canaris would be suspicious as well. During the two-hour drive from
Monaco back to Marseilles, Hans realized any of the man's future
attempts at contact should be ignored.

But Hans-Hubert's interview with the American yesterday was
really more of a pretense. His true reason for being on the Côte
d'Azur was singular: Rutgers Heht. Or more directly, Rutgers Heht's
money. He fully expected Heht to be at the bottom of the
Mediterranean by now, having fallen victim to Kaspar Koch's
Ablegekommando, another Abwehr officer with dreams of slipping
away, rich and happy in some distant hideaway. Of course, how was
he any different? If Kaspar Koch had failed to get the information on
the Swiss account, then Hans-Hubert most definitely would. Must!

Hans left his Marseilles hotel this morning and went by taxi to
the warehouse district just off the huge freight harbor. Kaspar's
previously arranged meeting location turned out to be an empty and
now defunct fishery. He and his team had used the cannery a number

of times for rendezvous and exchanges. Well off the beaten path and dilapidated to such an extent, the only intruders likely to be around were rats, cats, and vagrants.

It took a few moments for Hans-Hubert to adjust his eyes to the dark.

"Koch!" he shouted, his voice echoing dramatically. "Are you here, Koch? Koch?"

"I'm here, major," Kaspar Koch called out, switching on a hurricane lantern in a far corner of the vast building.

"Yes, there you are, Koch. Now, where is this Heht fellow?" Hans-Hubert inquired, hastening toward the lantern. "I'm in a hurry. Does he have the money?"

Captain Kaspar Koch took a cigarette case from his beige linen jacket, lit a cigarette, and directed his open palm toward a small office in the back corner of the dim, deserted warehouse. Through the musty glass Hans could see a man with his hands cuffed behind his back wearing a black hood over his head. When Hans entered the office, the hooded man startled him by removing the hood himself. He was not handcuffed at all! Hans looked at the man's face and gasped to see his good friend Rolf von Gerz. Kaspar grabbed him from behind in viselike chicken wings. A look of disgust grew on Rolf's face.

"Why, Hans?" Rolf asked. "Why did you do it?"

"I'm quite sure, old man, I don't know what you're talking about. What is all this?"

"Heht told us about your part in the securities deal. About your connection with the rogue element in the de Forney gang, and you're having Heht put the money in a Swiss account. About his realization it could only be you who was pulling the strings when suddenly everyone involved had been eliminated."

"The man's a deserter, Rolf, and a trained deviate and assassin. You're not seriously taking his word on such a farfetched fantasy?"

"No, Hans," Rolf said as he forcefully slapped Hans' hat off his head and Gep slipped the black hood over him. "We searched your hotel room, where I found all the evidence I need to prove his charges accurate."

Gep hit Hans' neck hard with the syringe of phenol as Hans struggled, throwing them all into the wall. Presently, he went limp and they all loosened their grip on Major Hans-Hubert von Hirschbach, watching him slump to his knees, then tumble to his side on the floor.

In the struggle Kaspar Koch's finger was smashed against a doorknob.

"If you'll help me get him in my trunk, I'll await your orders on how to deal with him," Kaspar said, kneeling to put handcuffs on Hans and stabbing his bloody knuckle into his mouth in an effort to sooth the smarting. It was, of course, the same finger Ruti had dislocated in the Mallorcan cabin.

"I've had him transferred to Libya," Rolf told Kaspar. "Where he will be 'missing in action' next week."

"Then I assure you, major," Kaspar replied, then spit blood over his shoulder, "this fellow is not to soon be seen again."

DAY TWENTY—Marseilles—Thursday, 24 April 41—10:47 AM
Hans-Hubert's hotel room was packed with suitcases. In his briefcase Gep found a steamer ticket to Martinique with a sail date of 29 April. And another one from there to Buenos Aires, as well as an Argentine passport and visa in his name. In three of Hans-Hubert's suitcases, Rolf and Gep counted over seven hundred thousand francs. Money he had bilked from Sturekov and the Reich, skimmed from army purchases through his Bureau Otto operation. As Mélina told Addie the entire story of their recent Mallorca intrigue, Ruti asked Rolf if they could go outside on the balcony for a smoke. Realizing there was no doubt the boy wanted to impart information out of the earshot of his wife, Rolf consented and Gep joined them.

Ruti stopped and bent over to kiss Mélina. "I'm just having a smoke." His handcuffed hands cupped her worried face and he kissed her. "But I am with you always." He tenderly patted her stomach. "Always a part of you."

Once out on the veranda, Rolf offered cigarettes around.

"Mélina said you were a man of your word," Ruti said, as he leaned against the stone balcony banister and measured Rolf. "If that's true, you'd no doubt be the last of that breed left in Germany."

"Tell me how you let this happen, Leutnant," Rolf replied, lighting Ruti's cigarette.

"Have you ever been in love, major?"

"Yes, I have."

Ruti took a deep draw on the cigarette and blew the smoke high in the salty air.

"It's debilitating, isn't it?" he said.

Rolf looked away, cast his gaze out over the harbor when he replied, away from Gep, "I suppose it could be. If we let it."

"You see, I guess I had never been in love before," Heht continued. "Because I would have never allowed myself to make such impertinent decisions. As German officers we were taught to be like Krupp steel, weren't we? Strong, cold, true blue. Turn a blind eye to normal human emotion, our own and others'. And I assure you, major, no one was better at that than I was. When ordered to, I took human life without regret of any kind. Then I fell in love."

He moved his cuffed hands up to take another drag.

"The theft was just an impulse. My cut for delivering the securities was a hundred thousand francs. I leased the land and cabin in the Mallorcan mountains two months ago. My plan to desert and marry Mélina was set for the summer, when the war was supposedly going to be over. Then she told me she was pregnant. I panicked. I was sure I could make it work. I've been on the side of the hunter. I was sure I could disappear where others had failed. I'd seen their mistakes. Their presumptions and unfounded confidence. I knew how to stay small and insignificant. Or at least I thought I did."

"The heart makes poor decisions," Rolf stated, to himself as much as to Ruti.

"Indeed," Ruti replied, nodding continually. "Indeed."

The high and low wail of a siren called in a distant quarter of Marseilles. Gulls dove and barked in the harbor. Taking another drag on the cigarette, Ruti looked at it. "Ernst Udet. My father smokes these," he declared, holding it awkwardly in the handcuffs.

He gazed out to sea.

"I didn't know Herr Ritter originally. What I am about to tell you came from Hans-Hubert. It all started last fall. The occupation was causing shortages. By the time winter arrived, coal was virtually nonexistent. Food, too, was becoming scarce. Desperation was causing people to sell family treasures to survive. Evidently for some time Herr Ritter had been helping such people emigrate from Germany. Word got around in Paris, and the little broker Lemay contacted Ritter. Ritter put together a few investors he knew in Paris. Men, mostly connected to the automobile industry, who were forward thinking enough to know that once the Paris stock market reopened the markets would escalate. So a number of securities were sold by desperate people at bargain prices. And more importantly, sold for cash, or gold or diamonds, or traded for documents, for freedom. Ritter was a good man, major, doing what he could to help people."

"His only mistake was trusting Major Hans-Hubert von Hirschbach. Bringing him in on the second, even larger deal. Nothing unseemly happened at first. But three weeks ago, Hans told someone in the Paris underworld and the broker Lemay was approached, threatened in some way, I don't know. But he felt the rest of the securities in his family vault were in jeopardy. He contacted his remaining clients and convinced them to let him sell off the remaining stocks before the gangsters could extort them away."

"A fellow broker friend of his in Lyon put some Vichy investors together, and Hans brought me in as the courier. The deal was valued at no less than eight million French francs, over a hundred million francs worth of securities. But the Lyon investors would agree to just six million. My take was a hundred thousand. Hans was to get the same. It was all completely above board. Everyone was in agreement. There were bills of sale. The securities were to be registered, once sold, by the Lyon investors. Then Hans suddenly decided the money should be held in a Swiss account for at least six months to keep Deutsche Bank detectives as well as the Paris underworld figures from getting wind of it. I was to set up the account, and Hans and Lemay would handle distribution to the Paris investors in small doses next winter. Ritter didn't like it. He didn't trust Hans. He was insightful."

"It was smelling badly of fish to me then as well. But I went along. Then the little broker Lemay was killed. Next I telephoned Herr Ritter, only to find that he was dead. That night, one of Guy de Forney's goons came after me. That's when it all changed for me. I knew Hans was stealing it all for himself. And I decided, better me than him."

Ruti flipped off his cigarette ash over the banister and turned to Rolf.

"Major, I accept what will happen to me. I broke the law and I must suffer the consequences. But I must know that Mélina is blameless. She did nothing other than enter Vichy under false pretenses. Prisons would overflow if such transgressions were all prosecuted."

"That will be a matter for the French authorities." Then Rolf smiled and added, "But I have new friend at the préfecture. I'm sure I can convince him to show her lenience."

Ruti smiled gratefully.

"I dislike farewells, major. I'm going to give you the account number and pass code to the Swiss account I set up in Basel. Afterward, I want you to take me immediately away. And for whatever it's worth, I prefer being shot to being hanged."

"I will try to arrange that," Rolf stated, respecting and appreciating the boy's pragmatism.

"I want you to tell my wife I wished to spare her the pain and indignity of another sorrowful farewell. Tell her only that I loved her, probably far too much. And that from where I'm going, I'll be watching over her and taking care of her and our child for the rest of her life. Will you do that for me, major?"

"Yes, Leutnant, I will."

Ruti kicked off his left shoe, reached down, and handed it to Rolf.

"The stitching along the inside of the insole is loosely repaired and reglued. You should be able to slide your knife in and break the sole loose from the shoe. You'll find the account number and pass code penciled on the inside of a folded gum wrapper. The account holds most of the six million francs."

"And the forty thousand Swiss francs?" Rolf asked.

"You're thorough." Ruti smiled. "I bought a car, furniture, clothes for my wife."

"A very expensive car!"

"I was in a hurry."

Rolf examined the shoe closely. If there had been a repair, it was masterfully done. There was no sign of restitching of any kind.

"Ernst Udet is a good cigarette," Ruti said, then he effortlessly threw himself headfirst over the banister to his death six stories below.

74

Friday, 25 April 1941

Letzte Kleinigkeit
Derniers détails
Loose Ends

DAY TWENTY-ONE—Paris—Friday, 25 April 41—7:58 AM
Their train back to Paris arrived at Gare de Lyon just after one AM.
Mélina was interned in the very room where Addie had been arrested
two weeks ago. Addie stayed with her throughout the night,
comforting and consoling her as best she could. Just after sunup the
sedatives Mélina had been given finally kicked in and Rolf released
Addie to return to her apartment to get some sleep herself.

Rolf had telephoned from Marseilles for another meeting with
the general at his office, but had received instead a message to meet
Stülpnagel at his hotel. Once in the foyer of the Hotel Prince de
Galles, he had the sense of being in a library. The silence was eerie.
Other than a few inconspicuous guards, blending in to the floral
arrangements and the art on the walls, the hotel seemed completely
empty. A uniformed orderly finally entered the room and greeted
Rolf. He was led to the dining room, where he was seated at an empty
table in the center of the vast room. When the orderly left, Rolf was
completely alone in the rich, gilded, and quite cavernous dining
chamber.

Soon, the general appeared and took his seat.

"So?" he asked.

"It's all still being sorted out, sir. A search of Hans-Hubert's
hotel room in Marseilles turned up a briefcase bulging with nearly a
million francs. Money he'd evidently skimmed from Bureau Otto
transactions for the army over the past months. There was also an
Argentine passport and visa. He had planned his escape from Lisbon.
His hand was played in a most unclever way, general."

Reluctantly, Rolf related his personal history with Hans-Hubert.

"We came up through the ranks together. His father was of the
tradesman class and dabbled as a vagabond investor of some sort,
backing long shots with big payoffs, and of course, a few losses. Hans
was always cash-strapped. I don't believe the man ever paid for even

404

a cup of coffee. Then his family lost everything in the crash. None of us were really aware of how devastated he was. He had always breezed through on his good looks and guile. But over time he must have grown destitute. I've uncovered some large debts in Berlin, and I believe he owed Ritter as well."

The general chewed on what Rolf was telling him. He had obviously already made his decision on the direction he would take in regard to Ritter's murder.

"It all makes no sense to me, general. I don't think taking flight was a part of his plan until the end, as everything started folding in on him. Otherwise, if escape was always his intention, why go to the trouble to kill anyone? Obviously, he planned to end his little escapade with the only witnesses dead, no trail to follow, and as much as six million francs in a Swiss bank account. But he failed to anticipate the rogue actions of Leutnant Heht."

"One of our own?" General Stülpnagel asked, in passing, drumming his fingers on the table. "Devastating."

"Ritter's actual assassination was carried out by rogue elements of some underworld gangs led by de Forney and Sturekov. Men that Hans-Hubert worked with in acquiring goods from the black market. I doubt that Hugo Sturekov or de Forney knew a thing about it. Sturekov was definitely an investor in the first securities purchase, but I'm convinced the theft and the elimination of both Ritter and the broker Lemay was all done without his knowledge."

"Sturekov is a very important and highly regarded man to the Wehrmacht and to the Reich." The general was convincing himself as much as Rolf. "The most well-protected Jew in France, I would think. With von Hirschbach eliminated and the two true assassins dead, what I fear I must do, von Gerz, is let Kruder's fantasy of a British terror plot stand. It's already been reported to Berlin. And it prevents needless retaliation that would surely upset the peaceful nature of the occupation."

"I dislike it as well, general," Rolf said. "But it does indeed seem the most prudent of options."

The general rose from his seat and walked over to Rolf, who followed Stülpnagel's lead as he was escorted toward the door. "Who is aware of these recent developments?" the general asked.

"Other than myself, there's my adjutant, and Leutnant Heht's girlfriend, or wife, may know something. And the French police inspector. The girl is easily controlled; she fears possible arrest anyway. My adjutant is as tight-lipped as any man, and I've developed a close relationship with the inspector. I don't see him wanting to expose any Frenchmen to execution unnecessarily, even Sturekov and de Forney."

Stülpnagel patted Rolf's shoulder as they came to the dining-room doorway.

"Let's then, shall we," he said, pursing his lips and smiling unconvincingly, "not ruin the Führer's nice birthday present!"

After Rolf shook the general's hand and left, General Stülpnagel looked at his aide-de-camp, Professor Baumgart.

"Wars, professor, are managed and won by officers with a keen mind, a strong stomach, and a heart as cold as Krupp steel. Lacking in any of the three can lead only to defeat. Von Gerz has the sharp mind and his constitution seems sound, but he unfortunately possesses the heart of a dreamer, probably a dilettante. And that alone shall spell his doom."

The general shook his head and turned to leave. His fleeting voice could be heard in the hallway. "The man is nothing like his father."

DAY TWENTY-ONE—Paris—Friday, 25 April 41—10:21 AM
There was sunshine outside, in the sweet world upstairs. The Club l'Heure Bleue was empty and dimly lit from the stairwell leading up to the street, where the door into the little courtyard was propped open by a wedged chair, letting some of last night out. The only sound was a faint flutter of Édith Piaf on the radio wafting down the long hallway from the kitchen.

The baker at the Bistro Bruno had trained in Berlin and profited from a percentage of the sales of his cake and candy specialties in the glass case at the restaurant's entryway. He was also highly skilled in keeping Bruno and Sabina supplied with small, sweet gifts each day.

Sabina sat alone at a two-top and untied the silky blue bow around the small cube in front of her, wrapped in shiny ivory paper. She unfolded the wrapping and smiled at the square of lusciousness before her, a *Kalter Hund*, with alternating wafer-thin layers of dark and white chocolate cake, and dusted on top with powdered sugar.

Bruno poured himself a sip of schnapps and brought it over to where she sat. She sliced the chocolate *hedgehog* in two and gave him his bite.

"Have you seen Xavier?" Bruno asked, popping it into his mouth and swishing the sugar from his fingertips with his thumb. She just shook her head and he added, "I haven't seen him since . . . When was it? Wednesday, I saw him last?"

Bruno sipped the schnapps and relished its bite for a second with a taut-faced smile.

"He'll turn up," she answered.

"There's no one around, Sabina," he said, taking her hand. "We need to talk about Suzi. What are we going to do with her?"

"I'll take care of it, Bruno."

"How?"

"I'll take care of it." She took her hand back.

"I know what you're up to, Sabina," he said, taking a few perfunctory puffs on his cigar to bring it back to life. "I want you to let me help you."

"I don't have a clue what you're talking about." She threw back the balance of her gin and stood up to leave, stuffing a fanned-out Dutch pulp romance under her arm.

"When you disappear the way you do sometimes"—he reached up and gripped her arm as she walked past him—"I know what you're doing."

"Oh, really, Bruno," she barked, cocking her hip and looking down at him with tired, worried eyes. "And what exactly is it you think I'm doing?"

He took the cigar out of his purple lips, looked down for a second, then smiled knowingly up at her and said, "Making me proud."

DAY TWENTY-ONE—Paris—Friday, 25 April 41—10:30 AM
Rolf had Mélina released after Luc-Henri consented to drop all charges against her. She went straight to Addie's apartment and knocked on the door. When the door opened, Addie threw her arms around her and felt her nearly collapse in them. Mélina was helped into the room, and they sat on the sofa.

"Addie, if it weren't for my child, I would kill myself. I truly mean it."

"No, darling. Don't ever say such a thing. Ruti would want you to be strong for him."

"Why did he do that, Addie?"

"He did it for you. He didn't want you to see him go through imprisonment and then be hanged."

"But how will we live, Addie? How will I raise my child alone? I can barely feed myself."

"I'm going to tell you something, Mélina. A very dark secret."

Mélina dried her eyes with the heels of her palms and listened intently.

"Remember when I was seated next to Ruti in the car? He put this note in my pocket. I don't know what it means, but he was sure you would."

"What does it say, Addie?"

She handed it to Mélina. *They are not rhinestones,* it read.

Mélina gasped. She looked in her purse for the porcelain ring box. In searching for it, she felt an envelope slid into the lining. In the envelope she found a stack of Swiss francs. Then, from her purse, she withdrew a small oval white porcelain box decorated with roses and a silver locket. The beautiful box he had purchased for her in Barcelona. Around the outside edge of the box was a ring of twenty-two shiny rhinestones. That were actually one-and-a-half to two-karat diamonds.

75

In der Stille der Nacht
L'obscurité de la nuit
The Dark of Night

DAY TWENTY-ONE—Seine Valley—Friday, 25 April 41—8:54 PM
Two plump young things had been beheaded, plucked, and soaked to perfection in brine. The chef at the ancient estate overlooking the idyllic Seine River Valley then prepared his own treasured recipe, stuffed their gutless insides with fennel, rosemary, raisins, and chestnuts, and baked the crisp skin on their tender, juicy flesh to a perfect golden brown. The smartest table was laid out. Two bottles of the cellar's best wines brought up. For this haughty country villa, formerly owned by a titled English family, would once again host a pair of guests tonight. No doubt, another German officer and his French trollop.

But by the time the big, beautiful yellow automobile pulled up the tree lined drive, the two scrumptious young chickens were dried out and cold as ice. Because this German officer and his coquette arrived nearly three hours late! And neither of them was even the least bit interested in eating. The German had simply whisked up the two bottles of the cellar's best and two glasses off the exquisite dinner table, and stolen away with his beautiful whore to their bedchamber, not to be seen again.

And so, the embittered chef, his wife (the manager of the house), the chambermaid, and the gardener ate cold chicken and all the cold wonderful trimmings, paired with quite agreeable local table wine. *Magnifique.*

DAY TWENTY-ONE—Paris—Friday, 25 April 41—10:30 PM
It was ten thirty before Bruno's car pulled up behind the Chinese laundry truck parked in the alley behind the café in the 4th. Curfew was at eleven. And the next set at the club would start at ten forty-five. If Sabina didn't make her curtain call about five minutes later, questions would be asked, suspicions might arise. Bruno knew Enrico was worthy of stalling, but it wouldn't take too many barking Wehrmacht wolves to push his nerves beyond their limit.

"Hurry, Sabina," he demanded, opening his door slowly enough to catch and hold down the spring-loaded button that automatically tripped the interior dome light.

Sabina helped Suzi out of the car. She was dressed like a boy, in baggy dungarees, a wool sport coat, and a tweed flat cap. She limped along, leaning on Sabina's shoulder toward the back of the truck.

"You'll be taken across the border by a German friend of mine. He'll be quite rough and frightening. But it's just playacting. Your being frightened will just help serve his purpose. You'll be taken into the countryside where you can convalesce for a few weeks. Then someone will contact you to take you on to Spain."

"I never dreamed you'd be so wonderful to me," Suzi whispered.

"Oof, all I ever wanted, my darling, was to see you leave." Sabina tossed the knapsack in the truck. "Either way, I'm rid of you, ma chère. Couldn't just let you die, could I? I'd have to find a way to dump your body and cope with all that foul air."

"You saved my life, Sabina."

"That really has yet to be seen."

Suzi hugged her neck and kissed both cheeks.

Sabina turned another cheek to her and tapped softly on it, adding, "You owe me a kiss. I'm Dutch." Suzi gave it with a sweet smile.

"Come, come," the little humpback Chinese driver whispered, clapping his hands softly. "Chop, chop!"

Gingerly, carefully, Suzi was helped into the back of the truck, and the driver covered her in stacks of linens.

"Sleep, sleep," he told her. "Sun come, we go."

With Sabina back in the car, Bruno slammed the thing in reverse, and the transmission whined as he zipped out of the alley and back to the club. The band had played a second and then third chorus of "Wenn es Draußen Dunkel ist," which gave Sabina and Bruno just enough time to sneak into the club through Bruno's office in the bistro. Sabina quickly shed her coat, straightened her gown, unpinned her hat, and fluffed up her hair. When she stepped on stage to wild applause, no one knew she had ever been gone. She jumped flawlessly back into her sultry character singing, "Liebe ist ein Geheimnis!" No one suspected that even without her former partner, Konni Ritter, Sabina van der Gorp had once again helped another

410

enemy of the state escape to Free France and, hopefully, onward to true freedom.

DAY TWENTY-ONE—Paris—Friday, 25 April 41—11:03 PM
The burlap Hussar sack had been bobbing just under the water since sunset, when it was first reported to the police. It had evidently floated from somewhere upriver and become wedged in some rocks at the point of the Île-de-la-Cité. If it contained what the gendarmes expected, it was probably launched from the rail yards around the Porte de Bercy. It certainly wasn't cats.

The flics pulled it out of the water with boat hooks, and one of them cut it open. No, it wasn't cats. Perhaps instead a boy. His wrists and ankles were cinched up together with twine binding that cut deeply into the flesh, exposing bone. A flour sack was cinched over his head. Dead probably two days, surmised one of the flics with experience in fishing corpses from the Seine. Another policeman cut away the flour sack to reveal not a boy at all, but a tiny man, balding, his blue face contorted, his mouth frozen open, displaying hideous yellow teeth clogged with beige goo and decay. He was barefoot but wore a full suit of clothes. However, on closer inspection, the jacket and pants were unmatched, evidenced by faint pinstripes in the pant material.

76

Saturday, 26 April 1941

Unsere letzten Tage
Le dernier de nos jours
The Last of Our Days

DAY TWENTY-TWO—Seine Valley—Saturday, 26 April 41—1:10 PM

By early afternoon the brilliant sunshine was baking up a perfect day. Addie met Rolf in the sunroom at the back of the nineteenth century villa wearing Capri pants and a pinstriped white cotton blouse with an absinthe-green cashmere sweater tied around her shoulders. A blue silk shirt clung to Rolf's chiseled form. He looked so normal in his pleated slacks and cordovan wing tips. For these short few short hours, they were any continental couple on holiday in the French countryside.

They had missed breakfast as well. The *dame de manior* permitted her kitchen staff to box up the breakfast and take it home after they prepared their houseguests a picnic lunch. With a basket sprouting chilled champagne, baguettes, and gerbera daisies on his one arm and Addie on his other, Rolf led the two of them through a meadow of wild flowers and a rolling sea of green spring grass whipping in the wind. They found a remote hill at the back of the estate.

"What a glorious day," Addie exclaimed as she helped Rolf spread their picnic out on the grassy slope of the hill. The view of some village and the rolling countryside below was idyllic. Farther on down the valley, they could see the Seine and watch as a long train of barges chugged upriver toward Paris.

Rolf twisted the wire loose from the chilled bottle of Laurent-Perrier.

"You're so handsome in real clothes," she said, watching the breeze play with his collar. "I've only seen you in your uniform and your birthday suit!"

He had to think a moment, then smiled at her joke.

"Which is your favorite?"

"Pour the champagne and I'll show you."

Addie had had two lovers in her life, and with both there soon came a point where cracks of doubt crept through her girlish mind. She'd discounted them in each case as being held up to a fickle, unrealistic ideal of exactly what love should be. Nonetheless, indeed, each soon crumbled from her favor.

No such doubt with Rolf. Not even the slightest.

"It's our last day together; I commanded it be the most perfect we have known," he said.

"Oh, Rolf, darling, if you do possess such powers, then command an end to the war and stay here in France with me."

"I would if I could."

They finished their lunch and toasted Konni Ritter, whose unfortunate death had forced them together. Then Addie squirmed. "It's such perfectly charming weather. I think I want some sun, Rolf."

The buttons of her blouse were loosed one at a time, and she slithered out of it and turned her back to him. Rolf grinned as one hand worked masterfully at unclasping her brassiere while the other fumbled at his belt.

"Your skin would take the sun well, I think," he said.

"Oh, darling, I keep the most glorious tan all summer long," she said over her bare shoulder. "You'd simply adore it!"

"I'm certain I would," he said, shedding his shirt.

She lay back in the chilly grass and arched herself, unzipping her pants at her side and pulling them down.

He bent over her and kissed her, and they tirelessly made love in the warm sun on the cool spring grass.

Afterward, wearing nothing but sunglasses, they lay on their backs as the blazing day grew wondrously hot. Now and then they would turn to their bellies to warm their backsides. The ground still full of winter was refreshing on their cooked flesh. Sometimes, they took an elbow, and Rolf would pour warming champagne as he tried to etch Addie's lovely form in his memory.

"Your skin does take the sun well," Rolf said. He downed the last of his wine still peering sideways at her. He laid his head on his arm and placed his hand on her naked hip. And drifted off to sleep.

Rolf awakened to birdsongs and the glowing burn of his sun-scorched skin. He rose up and looked over to Addie. Asleep as well, lying on her stomach, her cheek was resting on her folded arms. Sunlight exploded a kaleidoscope of umbers and reds in the highlights of her brunette hair. Rolf surveyed her nude body, the curves of her back and waist, her cute, firm rump and long, elegant legs, all toasted rosy pink. The one eye he could see was closed. His fingertips followed a spiral of blond peach fuzz to the center of her back.

The beautiful eye opened. And she smiled at him.

His fingers softly slid her hair off the side of her neck. A swarm of tingles rushed down her spine and swirled as tickles and tinges danced amid the cool breeze and the fluttering blades of grass between her naked thighs. She rolled over to her back and saw herself in his sunglass lenses. Her empty arms reached out to him, stretching and closing her fingers wantonly as tears welled in her eyes.

Imprints of the cold blades of grass appeared in the soft flesh of her stomach and breasts. When he moved close enough to her, she pulled him forcibly to her lips. They both tasted of sweat and tears and dread. Then, one last time, in every way possible, they made desperate love to each other—awkwardly, clumsily, urgently, and ultimately unsuccessfully, their worst performance to date. But it would be the one they cherished. As they had each given it all either of them had left to give.

For a final few moments, they lay intertwined, comforting each other from looming dread. Repeatedly each of them glanced at Rolf's cruel wristwatch, watched its second hand whip around its oyster shell face, rapidly devouring their precious remaining hours together.

DAY TWENTY-TWO—Seine Valley—Saturday, 26 April 41—8:06 PM

The drive back to Paris was painful. Wordless. The car owned the highway. Addie clung to Rolf as if they were on the edge of some sheer cliff above a torrent of anguish. The sunny day was dreadful. The most perfect and despicable spring day either of them could remember. They both lamented its wonders, wished it was cold and dank and miserable. "God is such a cruel prankster!" Addie had once exclaimed, sobbing.

When they arrived at Hans-Hubert's villa, Gep and the driver were waiting for them. Rolf pulled the striking sports car into the garage, tossed Gep the key, and went into the house to change back into his uniform. Addie joined him in the bedchamber. After donning her pale-blue winged-collared blouse and navy traveling suit, she helped Rolf dress. Straightening and folding his lapels down, her hands, wet with tears, softly smoothed out his tunic over his big,

414

square shoulders. Then she broke down and wept, falling into his arms one last time.

"Yes," Rolf softly said. "Yes, get it all out now. While we're alone." He held her so tightly to him, he was sure he heard her tiny ribs cracking. "You must show courage when we are at the airport."

"Oh, Rolf." Her words were muffled into his chest. "Please know how much I love you. No matter what terrible things happen to us over the next days or weeks or months, please know that I shall never love anyone as much as I love you. Tell me you know that."

"I know, Addie."

She looked up at him, desperation etched in her face. Her knuckle pushed tears from her eyes.

"No, you don't. Truly, you don't. But I need to tell you. I want so to tell you something. I should have told you before. I've kept it from you, because I wasn't sure how you'd take it. But now, I simply must tell you."

"Tell me what?" A frown came to his face.

She looked at him. His grimace concerned her, and she looked down again.

"Tell me what, Addie?" He pulled her chin up.

"You won't understand. You'll think me horrid."

"What is it, Addie? Tell me this instant."

"I . . . you . . . you're the only man I ever went to my knees for."

The blast of a snickered sigh exploded from him as he smiled and pulled her to him again.

"And I'll never do so for another man, Rolf. That's how deeply I love you. Please tell me you believe me!"

"I believe you, you beautiful thing. And I love you, as much as I ever loved my dear wife. I want you to know that yourself, as well."

She closed her eyes and gritted her teeth, burying her face in his field-gray uniform.

Once again, she couldn't tell him. She just couldn't go through with it.

77

Auld Lang Syne

DAY TWENTY-TWO—Paris—Saturday, 26 April 41—9:26 PM
Dusk stole away the beautiful day. A cold, still night nestled itself in
as a sea of fog rolled and chopped twenty meters over Paris. By
morning it would settle in completely, cloaking the city's beautiful
nakedness in its gray blanket of gloom. The limousine's platter-sized
headlamps were reduced to drowsy blackout slits by cardboard inserts
and blue bulbs. The long, regal machine moved cautiously along the
highway north of the city toward Le Bourget and the airport. Addie
and Rolf sat in the backseat, their hands in each other's desperate and
cloaked embrace. Gep sat up front with the oblivious driver. The
wordless silence was uncomfortable. Just the deep rumble of the
finely tuned machine and the monotonous double thump of the tires
on the joints in the concrete highway. Gep reached over and pushed in
the automobile's tortoiseshell cigarette lighter button.

At a small incline, the car suddenly jerked. The driver groaned.
The clutch peddle had gone completely soft all the way to the floor.
The clutch was blown! But this was no more than an inconvenience
for such a man as him. He was well practiced at using the engine's
RPMs to ease the car in and out of each gear. A little pressure on the
shifter and a little gradual acceleration, and the car would softly jump
into gear. It all brought a smile to Gep's face. A special respect for
men who were good at their job, regardless of how insignificant it
may seem.

The lighter popped out, charged. Gep withdrew it, and a soft
orange patina filled the front half of the car's interior. His lips popped
in the eerie silence, and his stern face glowed and ebbed devilishly as
he lit his cigarette.

The limousine pulled up to the gate, and the driver gave one of
the two guards their identity cards. The long metal arm went, up and
they pulled onto the tarmac just as the plane from Lisbon was landing.

"You'll land at Portela Airport, some distance outside of
Lisbon." Rolf finally broke the silence. "The pilot will see that you
get to your hotel."

With the car parked and switched off, Gep and the driver went
into the terminal while Rolf and Addie said their final good-byes in

the car. Displays of affection on the tarmac were something Rolf wouldn't abide.

There had been enough tears from Addie. The past day. They both tried to stay in control. They kissed and held each other tightly, saying very little. Neither wanting to release the other and end it all.

"Oh, Rolf. Can you ever know how much I hate this bloody war?"

"The war will be over someday, Addie." With the swipe of his thumb, he caught a tear that streamed down her face in another's rivulet and smiled at her. "A year, perhaps. When it is, I will come to you, Adelaide Bridges. Wherever you are in the world, I'll find you. And I'll propose marriage to you."

"And I will be waiting, Rolf, my darling. One year, a hundred years, I will be waiting."

They kissed one last excruciating time. And Rolf opened his door and went around and opened hers.

The Lufthansa Junkers JU-160 had been commissioned by the army to make daily diplomatic courier runs and Foreign Office personnel transfers between Paris-Madrid-Lisbon. The all-metal, ten-passenger, single-engine monoplane had taxied to a stop, but the doors remained closed until the pilot received orders from the major to proceed.

When they'd composed themselves, Addie and Rolf joined Gep on the tarmac. Rolf motioned for the pilot to open the doors and disembark the trainees for the American espionage operation Gep would now take over in Hans-Hubert's absence.

Addie turned and hugged Gep. He politely kissed her hand and clicked his heels.

"Au revoir, mademoiselle."

Then she turned to Rolf. She wasn't one to parade her emotions, yet a single tear trickled around her red nose to melt on her trembling lips. With restraint she gave him a quick hug and kissed his cheek. Customarily, he took her hand in his and kissed it, bowing and clicking his Prussian heels as well. Their eyes were glued to each other as she started backing away. Her soft fingers lingered reluctantly in his, just as they had the first time he'd touched them three weeks earlier.

She turned and hurried toward the plane as the door opened and the two American espionage trainees started down the steps. As she passed them and scurried up the stairs, she stopped suddenly and froze for a second. Mysteriously. Then quickly boarded the plane.

417

The second of the two trainees, a man in a brown fedora, furrowed his brow and turned to watch her disappear into the silver fuselage.

Addie's face showed in the airplane window and melted into trepidation as the man in the fedora stopped at Rolf and Gep.

"Excuse me, gentlemen," the man asked as he approached them. "But is that woman's name Adelaide by any chance?"

"Yes, it is," Rolf stated, somewhat aghast.

"I thought so. I thought that was her. We were old school chums, she and I."

"You and Miss Bridges?"

"Bridges?" The man's brow lowered and a snide smile grew on his face. "How rich, *Bridges*. I suppose that might translate, mightn't it? But no. No, that's not her name."

"It's Brückner, isn't it?" Rolf sternly interjected, never taking his eyes off the terror-stricken face in the airplane's window.

The trainee just laughed, infuriating both Rolf and Gep.

"Brückner, well. I guess that would sort of translate as well, wouldn't it? But no. No, gentleman. That young woman is none other than one Miss Adelaide *Dupont*. Yes sir, Miss Adelaide Irmgard Dupont!"

Gep quickly grabbed the startled trainee and brandished his finger in the man's face while Rolf stood frozen, fuming, dazed. Bridges. Brückner. *Dupont!*

"You will forget you ever saw that woman, is that quite clear?" Gep shouted at the American. "She is a part of a secret mission for the Reich, and her life is worth far more than yours ever will be! You are to say nothing to anyone about her. If we find that you have, I assure you will wake up with an ice pick in your eye. Am I making myself completely clear?"

The mortified trainee started shaking uncontrollably. Nodding, he assured Gep he would never disclose to anyone that he had seen Adelaide Dupont. During it all, Gep kept a tight hold on Rolf's coattails to ensure he didn't run off and try to stop the plane.

"Now, go and join your comrade and tell him you asked us whether you would, I don't know, be staying in Paris tonight or traveling on to the training facility. You'll do the latter. Now go!"

Like a frightened schoolboy, the man did as instructed as Gep grabbed Rolf's arm.

"We must stop that plane!" Rolf demanded, oblivious to Gep, to the entire situation. Stunned.

"Let her go, major."

418

"You're quite insane, Gep. I'll have none of it!" Rolf turned to him, a pitiful look on his face. "The woman is a spy!"

"You have to let her go, major. We have Heitner. He's the spy. We don't need her."

"But it's our duty, Gep!"

"Yes, Rolf, it *was* our duty!" Gep had to almost scream as the plane's engine was started. Infuriated, he twirled Rolf around and barked, "Just like it was our duty in Warsaw. Our duty to not let ourselves become so enamored by some beautiful woman that we let her manipulate us like sideshow puppets. Let her make goddamn fools of us." The engine whined and whistled. "So yes, we have to let her go, Rolf. Let this goddamned spy escape so she can't put you in front of a firing squad and ruin my fucking career!"

Rolf's spirit was completely dashed by Gep's frank words. Like the forlorn boy he'd once been, standing against the chastisement of his father, he stared coldly at Addie's pleading, tearful face through the airplane window. He could interpret her frantic words, "*Je t'aime, Rolf. Je t'aime!* I love you!"

Rolf's jaw clenched. Bitter pangs of anger and scorn blazed within him, shackled to the pragmatic restraint of Gep's bombast. He jerked his arm free from Gep's grip as the airplane's starboard brake gripped the tarmac and its engine raced, starting its jerky, bouncy turn toward the runway.

Gep grabbed him again and screamed against the deafening noise and sudden blast of wind from the propellers.

"Do what you will, Rolf," he barked, releasing his grip forcefully and giving up his on good friend entirely. "Stop the damn plane if you must. I'll take these men to von Gröning's people and meet you back at the Lutetia. You decide. When I get back to the hotel, I'll know then whether we simply part ways as friends, or, if she's with you . . ."

He started buttoning up his overcoat as he turned to leave.

" . . . I'll arrest you both!"

419

78

Eine kleine Sehnsucht
Un petit peu de nostalgie
A Little Bit of Longing

DAY TWENTY-TWO—Paris—Saturday, 26 April 41—11:29 PM
Rolf met Gep in the second-floor hallway at the Lutetia. With raised
eyebrows and a whisper, Gep asked him only if he were *alone*. Rolf
gave a halfhearted nod, and within a few short, silent moments they
were outside strolling down the boulevard Raspail.

"How did she do it, Rolf? How did she move so freely between
Paris and Switzerland?"

"After you phoned from Berlin and told me about the Brückner
woman"—Rolf lit a cigarette and went on—"I went to Addie's place
of employment, an American bank. They were without records of any
sort, everything having been moved to Vichy at the collapse of
France. Most of the bank's former managers were no longer in Paris
either. The manager I talked to said, among her other duties, she had
done some work off and on as a courier. A courier for an international
bank would have little difficulty moving in and out of Switzerland.
And obviously, between Switzerland and Germany, she had the
Brückner identity old Ritter had obviously procured for her. I had
planned to pursue that further when I got word from you the Brückner
woman was deceased. With your call it all became just a silly
coincidence for me and I put it out . . . intentionally out of my mind.
Far too intently. I guess the real question is how Ritter was able to
pull off this fantasy of her death so plausibly."

Gep lit a Chesterfield and blew the smoke high into the still
night. "I'm sure, if we were in a position to pursue it, we would find
that Ritter had ties of some sort to one of the records keepers at
Ravensbrück. Duplicate passports were obviously no problem for the
crafty old fellow. Getting an old friend to create a simple index card
and match it to the demise of one of the nameless souls at
Ravensbrück would not have been that terribly difficult."

"You're probably correct." It was painful for Rolf to take the
conversation in the next direction. Reluctantly, though, he did so by
simply blurting out, "What of us, Gep?"

"I would suggest you remain here in Paris, major. I'm sorry to say this, but I think the laissez-faire military culture here in Paris suits you much more than myself. I'll report back to Warsaw and take those duties over, with a recommendation from you, of course."

"I'll give no such recommendation, Oberleutnant. You're the one who should remain here. This American operation needs your experience and cleverness. I'm the one who must do his duty in Warsaw and in the east."

"Forgive me for saying so, major, but I really feel you lack the strength of military character to return to the lion's den. You'll be consumed by those SS vermin in Warsaw. And I won't be there to . . . intercede."

"And you shouldn't have to be, Gep. This was my last straw. Hans-Hubert and now Addie. Two more people I cared for and trusted. Who betrayed me. It won't happen again, Gep, my friend, I assure you."

"We parted at the Warsaw train station to those exact words less than a month ago, Rolf."

"Like you said, Gep. This time I won't have you to protect me, will I? I'll have to do it on my own."

"Then as you wish. I'll leave for La Bretonnière in the morning. I'll go through von Groening's training with these two Americans who arrived tonight." Gep cocked his head to one side, then looked squarely at Rolf.

"One last thing." No other way to say it than to be harshly blunt. "Your wife is dead, Rolf! You'll never see her again. Not in the look in this woman's eyes or in the way that woman holds her cigarette. You must stop trying to find her. Bury her. And apply yourself to once again being the strong and steely soldier and officer you once were. If you don't, I fear your daughter will lose her father as well."

Gep stopped and placed his hand out to press Rolf's.

"Adieu, my friend." Gep shook his head. "My very good and far too noble friend!"

Rolf shook Gep's hand and nodded. A hollow tinge of regret and a chilling sense of loneliness filled his soul as he watched his former adjutant turn and walk back to the Lutetia and out of his life. Probably forever.

DAY TWENTY-TWO—Paris—Saturday, 26 April 41—11:58 PM

The last bars of the song "Du habst gluck bei dem Frauen, Bel Ami!" ended with applause and blown kisses. Sabina made her way through the cheering crowd to the back of the room, to a banquette where Addie's handsome major sat alone, a full, newly delivered, and not yet touched Mirabelle next to the one he was drinking. He didn't see her slink up to him. He was deep in thought, wondering. . .

So, Operation Irmgard had nothing to do with the murder of Konni Ritter and everything to do with Miss Adelaide DuPont— Adelaide Irmgard DuPont—alias Adelaide Bridges, alias Edith Brückner.

But what was Herr Ritter's relationship with Addie? Was it just duty born of friendship? Or was it some *cinq-à-sept* love affair?

"Bonsoir, major, darling," Sabina said, startling Rolf. She slid herself into the banquette and ordered her regular from a passing waiter with the mere wiggle of her finger. "May I join you, mijnheer?"

Rolf nodded. "It seems you already have." Another swallow from his glass.

"What time does your train depart tomorrow?" she asked.

"Noon."

"So then, we have the entire night together."

He looked at her, a pensive, mindful stare. Then he felt is head nod slightly. What harm could there be in it?

"You look very sad, major. You loved her deeply, didn't you?" she chortled in a pouty, almost mean-spirited fashion.

Nothing from him. A cold stare into the smoky blue gloom of the club.

"Of course you did." She suddenly cocked her head to one side and furrowed her brow. A gleam grew in her beautiful eyes as she added, "But there's something more, isn't there?"

Rolf gazed coldly at her.

"She imparted some last-minute truth, didn't she? And in doing so, betrayed your love."

Before Rolf could explode, Sabina went on.

"Some husband she failed to mention, maybe? A pregnancy perhaps? Or did she turn out to be some crafty American spy?" A long vulgar laugh from her.

"What makes you say this?" Rolf firmly inquired.

"I'm a woman, and you, mijnheer"—she tapped him on the nose with her finger—"you are an open book."

Rolf had to change the subject. "I don't want to talk about her. Tell me about you, Sabina."

"Sabina?" she quipped. "Oof, Sabina is the vixen every man dreams about." The waiter brought her drink, and she stabbed the olive with the long, red nail of her little finger. Slipping it in her sexy mouth, she bounced it around her tongue as she added, "The vixen he dreams about while he fucks his dreary, motionless wife, *nicht wahr?*"

Rolf chuckled.

"You've come back to life."

Slyly, Sabina sashayed her soft self over to Rolf. She liked to sit close to a man and tuck her *my-hands-are-always-cold-as-ice* fingers snugly under his thigh, very high on his thigh. One set of her long fingers crept softly under Rolf from the outside and one set from the inside of his leg. The latter so close to his scrotum that her wrist nestled itself in the sensitive, very warm crevasse in his pants. There it would remain, squirming now and then as she pinned his upper arm between her breasts and her warm whispers frolicked about his ear.

"That's so much nicer, mijnheer. Wouldn't you agree?"

Uncomfortable at first, Rolf quickly realized there was no reason he shouldn't indulge himself in Sabina van der Gorp. She was, after all, the most stunning vamp he'd ever known. A simple cabaret slut, but she had never betrayed him, had she? So he would go along with and enjoy her flirtations. It would help him get through this horrible fucking night!

"I am adding a song to my next set. Just for you, major."

He nodded as he took another sip of his cocktail.

"'Eine kleine Sehnsucht.' A little bit of longing."

She kissed his cheek and whispered, "Sabina can make the longing go away, mijnheer. If only for this one night. Come upstairs with me when the club closes. You have so many long, lonely hours before your train leaves. Spend them with me, major. Spend them in my arms." Another kiss and she bounced around the banquette to hurry backstage.

A warm and wonderful numbness was settling in. The long line of drinks was working. Rolf's self-pity and shame was being washed slowly away, sip by sip. How had she done it so coldly? Kept herself in character, the flighty young American girl, caught up innocently in the war. So frightened and frail. But now, as it turns out, so crafty and diabolical.

He should have tossed her in jail when she ran away that morning. Gep was right. There was something in her that reminded him of his wife. That made him fall so deeply, so blindly, in love with her. Brunette hair just like Frieda's. The way she pulled it back only to have a cantankerous lock fall sinfully out of place over her eye. And then, the dimples. Those infernal dimples! Weren't those all just memories he had of his wife as well?

These were things he would no longer let himself dwell upon. She had betrayed him. And Gep was correct about one thing: He surely would have faced a firing squad if she'd have been arrested and the truth about her clandestine past had come to light. Never again. Never again could he let this happen to Major Karl-Rudolph von Gerz. He must be the soldier and Abwehr officer he was raised and trained to be. Strong! Impervious! Imperious to a cold, crass fault!

The music started, and Sabina moved out onto the stage to her normal late-night hoopla, only to come down almost immediately into the crowd.

Rolf's head was teetering on his neck. He found himself chewing the inside of his mouth, introspective. He could hear his father. His father's lesson: "If we have the wisdom to know our flaws, then must we have the courage to overcome them!"

In the blur of his drunken mind, Rolf's old military school creed came once again to him:

In sternest school of warfare bred,
Makes one day him the Parthian's dread.

Even a cabaret slut could read him like an open book! No more would anyone read Major Karl-Rudolf von Gerz like an open book. No one! Some men, the fortunate ones, were born stoic and aloof. But some must train themselves to become so. And with the help of the war, Rolf would do just that. The war would make him the Parthian's dread. The Bolshevik's dread!

Sabina moved past quickly tickled necks and mussed hair toward the back of the room where Rolf sat. She knelt in the banquette and scooted over to him on her knees, singing.

She pulled him to her, her lips to his ear. She kissed it and whispered, "I am *sooo* wet for you!"

Tomorrow Major Karl-Rudolf von Gerz would make his father proud. Make his Führer proud. He would go to Warsaw and fight his war. He would show no quarter. To anyone! But tonight? Tonight he would drink. Tonight he would forget. Forget people who were now lost to him forever. Forget Addie Bridges. Forget Hans-Hubert von Hirschbach and his good friend and adjutant Gep Fechter. His pregnant daughter. That lovely bitch, Tippi Rostikov. His dear, wonderful wife. He would forget them all. Tonight he would drink. Tonight he would fuck Sabina! And he would forget!

He must forget!

Epilogue

Charlottenburg, West Berlin
(British Zone)

Eight and a Half Years Later

9 December 1949
8:02 AM

The war didn't end in a few months. Not even in a few years. It dragged on for many more and escalated into a heinous, worldwide tempest of slaughter and destruction. It had been almost five years now since the war finally did end. Yet the city of Berlin looked as though it should still be smoldering. Huge snowflakes swirled and pitched about in the crisp winter wind. Darkness still clung to the cloudy morning as dawn, a hint of charcoal gray in the eastern sky, illuminated stark silhouettes, crags, buttes, and spikes of the bombed-out ruins and bullet-riddled remnants of Berlin, the Nazi Carthage.

Bundled against the cold, the crippled police inspector limped through the crunchy, refrozen slosh and fluffy new snow on the Bleibtreustrasse sidewalk. A cane in each wool-gloved hand, he made certain each foot was securely planted before every onward progression. He limped his way past whole blocks of former buildings that were now nothing but a mountain of naked sapling and dormant weed-sprouting rubble covered in ice and snow. He was joined by others plodding along with their lives, striving to squeeze normalcy out of incomparable ruin.

As he progressed through other blocks, occupied building ruins had stovepipes jutting through the boarded and blanketed window openings, spewing black coal smoke. Others that still had or bore new windowpanes glowed white or golden from lantern or candle light. Now mostly washed or worn away, every building's granite or limestone or stucco walls still showed ghosts of old notices:

> *K. Waldmüller, noch am Leben! Umgezogen zum Kaiserplatz, Cottbus!*
> *K. Waldmüller, still alive! Moved to the Kaiserplatz in Cottbus!*

426

Hundreds more such inscriptions were still visible where any building still stood.

He rounded the corner to the cozy kneipe, his daily breakfast stop. The door opened and the heavy leather drape in the anteroom protecting the pub from the frigid blast of winter billowed and danced. Once inside the inspector hung his overcoat, hat, and scarf on the cherrywood hat tree next to the door. Clumsily, he hobbled over to his regular morning table and took his earthenware cup from the shelves of cups and steins on the wall, leaning both his canes against the wall behind a chair. Once he was seated, the proprietor's school-aged daughter came over and picked up the cup.

"*Morgen,* Herr Inspector." The cute little pigtailed girl wore a dress handed down from some older sister or friend, a full three sizes too big for her. She dawdled at the table, wagging her little tail, twirling the dress back and forth across her bony knees. A tyke with some secret to impart.

"*Morgen,* Maria." The inspector cocked the horribly scarred right side of his face away from the lingering little lady, looking at her with his good left eye. "So, do I get coffee this morning?"

Maria's sweet eyes darted back and forth. Biting her upper lip, she nodded and took a dust rag from under her arm. She moved uncomfortably close, leaning up against him. As she feigned wiping the back of his chair with the rag, she whispered, "She's been waiting for you since seven."

A sideways nod of her little head and she smiled awkwardly and asked, "Will you be having the usual?"

He nodded with a furrowed brow, a bit confused.

With that, little Maria was off to the bar, shuffling along in stained saddle oxfords, too large for her tiny feet. She placed the inspector's cup under the coffee machine and flipped the switch.

The police inspector could then sense the woman, two tables down against the wall, hidden from view by another hat tree full of coats. He could see a pair of women's shiny black galoshes next to the rack, droplets of water around each. Then he could smell her. Familiar. Painful. Quelques Fleurs. How had he put it so many years ago? *Smells like his mother's garden party.* He could hear the echo of her chair scooting across the linoleum as she stood and crept around the coatrack like a frightened deer. He looked down. He refused to look at her.

"Rolf?" she said, timidly. "It's Addie."

He fumed, his fists and jaw clenched. Slowly, he shook his head. Then he snorted forcefully and looked up at her. Furious.

An uncontrollable sob burst from her. "Oh, my god, Rolf!"

The whole right side of his face was deformed and scarred like the skin of a cantaloupe. His right ear was gone, a cloudy blue right eye was barely visible through the slanted and curled slit of an eyelid.

Her heart told her to give him a sweet, albeit pathetic smile.

"I've worried about you every day since I left," she said in perfect German. "I worried that I might have put you in a position to be arrested or even worse. I worried so, Rolf."

"You should have."

She pulled the chair out and took a seat as Maria brought Rolf's coffee. The little girl looked to Addie's table and motioned that she would bring her coffee to her. Addie shook her head and handed her a five-mark coin. When Maria left she continued.

"I hired a man in Frankfurt after the war, Rolf. Hired him to find you. I heard nothing for nearly a year. Then finally, he wired to say he had discovered that you had died in a prison camp. I was so sick with grief I was hospitalized. Two months later he wired to say you were actually alive after all, and you were being interned in that prison in Belarus. It took us almost another year to get you out." She paused for a moment. Eight years to practice what she would say to him, and she had already skipped or forgotten so many points. "I'm married, Rolf. My husband is an attorney practicing international law. He was a part of the team that worked on reestablishing private ownership to companies in Germany, German and foreign. My husband and I became engaged in '45. I made him wait to marry me for more than a year after the war ended. I was certain you were still alive. And I was determined to find you. Explain everything to you and make you fall in love with me again. He was the one who got you out. You were traded for a Ukrainian scientist."

She reached across the table to touch his hand, but he pulled it away and rested it on his lap. She closed her eyes and inhaled. Then went on.

"I was there, Rolf. At the Club l'Heure Bleue one year to the day after the war ended. Just like we had all agreed. But I was the only one to show up. The club, of course, is gone. They turned it into a parking garage. It didn't last six months after we left. I went back ten or twenty times that day. I pinned a note on the door, praying that you might show up. But you didn't. You couldn't. No one came. Just me."

Fall Irmgard

Little Maria brought Rolf his breakfast, a bowl of muesli with a portion of raisins piled up in its center and three pieces of toast with a foil-wrapped cube of USA margarine alongside. Rolf smiled at Maria as she wrinkled her freckled nose and pointed to his cup.

"More?" she asked, raising her eyebrows. With his nod she took the empty cup, and as she turned, she smiled at Addie, then shuffled over to the coffee machine.

"I refused to believe you were dead. I forced the investigator to keep looking long after he had given up the search. But it was to no avail. So I went ahead and agreed to marry my husband. Then . . ." She wiped her tears away, but started crying again. "Then that hideous man found you, Rolf. Three weeks! Three silly weeks after I was married, he found you! I tried everything to get you released. I was powerless. But my husband, he was tired of having to share me with this German ghost I had pined so for. So he agreed to work with the embassy to put you on a list of prisoners to be traded."

Rolf looked up from his breakfast momentarily, then just snorted and looked back down.

"My family name is Dupont, but I'm not a DuPont. We are neither related nor connected to the Delaware DuPonts. My father made his own fortune in banking, but there is no doubt confusion about his last name probably played an important part in his success. It was the notoriety of that last name that required him to secure me a passport under a pseudonym. He was certain a single young American woman named Dupont would know nothing but grief alone in Paris."

"So I became Adelaide *Bridges*. It was prearranged that I be met at the docks of Le Havre by my uncle, my mother's older brother, Konni Ritter. My mother's name is Irmgard. I'm named for her. My mother and father met in 1913 at a banking congress in Frankfurt. My father fell hopelessly in love with her, and she moved away with him to America, where they were married that winter. And of course, as you can tell, I have spoken fluent German my entire life."

His head shook slightly and his jaw stiffened. Her German was flawless. *All that nonsense in Cologne,* he thought. *Feigning an inability to understand what was being said.* What a diabolical wretch she was. How completely she had deceived him. Every sickening word of German she now spat was like another piece of shrapnel in his hip. All the old anger came rushing back. He truly feared he would reach out and slug her if they were alone.

"Don't speak German to me!" he demanded in French.

She switched immediately to French, the language of her love for him. How warm and wonderful it felt.

"After Germany occupied the Rhineland Uncle Konni's movements between France and Germany became difficult. Then, as war became inevitable, I devised a plan to become an intermediary in Switzerland to smuggle paperwork out of Nazi Germany. I was engaged at the bank as a courier and went to Bern almost fortnightly. Through Konni's contact with the artisans at Kunsthorn Heitner, he turned me into a Swiss woman with a high-level travel visa related to banking policy manuscript production. I carried the most boring and ludicrous volumes of banking and insurance mumbo-jumbo. And in these manuscripts, I would smuggle important documents: patents, deeds of ownership, formulas and the like for foreign companies, mostly American companies with holdings in Germany. I can only guess what was in there. Conditions were such that these companies feared they would be nationalized, taken over by Hitler once America entered the war. And I suppose these documents would have kept that from happening somehow."

Rolf nodded slightly. No doubt just an affirmation of something he suspected. But he was at least still listening to her.

"It was all just a lark really. A way to show my father I was more than just a silly girl. Then Britain and France declared war on Germany. After that, there was no reason to believe we weren't committing high treason. That was also when Werner Heitner forced us to move some phonograph records into Switzerland for him. He discovered our little game and threatened to expose me. I have no idea what the purpose of the recordings was. I merely brought them in as though I'd purchased them in Berlin, with a bill of sale and everything. I would deliver them to a record shop in Bern, saying they were scratched and asking for an exchange. I did that four times. That was the extent of my espionage activities. I never met Heitner, but through Uncle Konni I knew the man to be a devout Marxist and no doubt working in some fashion or other for the Russians or the British or both."

Addie folded her hands on the tabletop and struggled against the impulse to reach out and touch Rolf's arm.

"But I just wanted it to end. And Uncle Konni found a way. He killed me off, Rolf! He had a retired business associate who worked in Ravensbrück invent my arrest and demise. He told me all this after the fall of France when he started coming back to Paris regularly. When I was free. Free to be just Addie Bridges again and fall in love

430

with you. You know the rest. Except how difficult it was not to be able to open up to you and tell you everything. Each lie I told you, Rolf, was another needle in my heart. You have no idea how many times I almost gave up the ghost and told you everything."

"I must finish my breakfast," he coldly said, chewing a bite of his muesli, talking to her like some bored husband talks to a doting wife. "I have to report at nine."

"I'm so sorry, Rolf; please know how sorry I am." She wiped her red nose and dabbed a tear from the corner of her eye, as well practiced as any woman at doing so without disturbing her mascara. "There was just so much I wanted to say. So many things left unsaid when I boarded that plane that night."

"You've said quite enough." He put his spoon down and took a sip of his coffee, glancing indignantly at his wristwatch again.

An icy chill coursed through her. This wasn't her Rolf. The Rolf she had known was indeed dead! He'd died on the tarmac that night in Paris. And in that vile war. This piece of stone she was talking to was just his embittered ghost, void of the warm emotion she so loved to watch in his estimable eyes.

"You can go now." His jaws clenched as he took another insulting bite of his breakfast, interjecting as he looked to the same folded piece of his newspaper he'd been feigning interest in for the past half hour, "Don't come back."

"No, Rolf. I won't." She sobbed. "I won't ever come back. But you have to know this. You have to know . . ." Her words came laced with more sobs. "You have to know, all those years, through all my fear and dread and worry, you have to know how the warmth of your memory was so worth its sting!"

Rolf knew far more than she ever would the meaning of those words. Her memory, as well as his wife's, had saved his life. He had been assigned to the intelligence branch of the general staff of Foreign Army East in '42. Its commander, Oberstleutnant Reinhard Gehlen, was an old friend from staff officers' college. In July 1944, as the Red Army surrounded Minsk, Rolf and a small detachment of staff officers took refuge in the ruins of an office building. A barrage of Soviet incendiary grenades were launched into the building, and Rolf was blown from the second floor into a pile of rubble in the street. Splatters of the tacky incendiary tar fried him, spreading blisters of blaze deep into his uniform and flesh, up and down the entire right side of his body. Shrapnel had shattered his right hip, and the fall had fractured and cracked his legs in multiple places. He would have burned alive right there had it not been for two nuns who rushed to his aid with a blanket, ultimately smothering the resilient sparks.

A year in the prison hospital in Minsk, gasping for each painful breath of life. Nearly two more in a Belarus prison camp with only the stinging comfort of her memory to keep him alive on a frozen floor of stone, as cold and hard as the insolence he now persisted in displaying.

Hurriedly, Addie rose and grabbed up her galoshes, fighting to dry her wet cheeks with the back of her hand. Hopping and stumbling, she slipped them on. There was so much more she wanted to say. Needed to say. Planned to say. How many times had she gone over it these past eight years?

There was Gep, who had survived the war in a POW camp in Fort Reno, Oklahoma, where in '43 he and two other prisoners had made all the national newspapers by escaping and going on the lam for twelve days, causing a national FBI manhunt. It had turned out the three men were moving at night toward Mexico, and ultimately, suffering from dehydration and starvation, they turned themselves in to a postmaster in Big Spring, Texas.

And Mélina, who had given birth to a redheaded little girl. She was living quietly with her mother, helping with the laundry and ironing while she raised the tyke and cared for her invalid, war hero first husband, with the help of nearly forty thousand Swiss francs and a handful of diamonds.

And Bruno and Sabina, who had been arrested after the war, having both been severely injured by vigilante street mobs in Paris. They were released in '46 and moved to Schäftlarn outside Munich, where they opened a small restaurant and did very well until Sabina's stroke just this last summer, when Bruno sold the place, moved her into an asylum in Garmisch, and bought a house a few blocks away so he could be with her every day and nearly each night.

So many things that would go unsaid. Especially the news that she was pretty sure she was pregnant and had decided if she had a little boy she would name him Rudolf and call him Rolf. But what good would it serve telling him that? Hadn't she hurt this man enough? This had all been so brief. So wrong. And there were so many questions she had for him. Questions that would go unanswered.

Her overcoat buttoned and scarf wrapped snugly over her ears and nose, reluctantly she donned her fur hat, took her gloves from her pocket, and started to leave. As she passed Rolf, she stopped to look one last time at him, to watch the short hair at his temple flare and fall as his strong, square jaw moved with each chew of his breakfast. On this side of his face, he still looked the very same, exactly as she remembered, so handsome and imposing. How she wanted to touch him. As he sat there cruelly and deservedly oblivious to her, her fingers crept toward his curly brown hair, hair they had once so loved to explore. To adore. But before they could, she closed her fingers into a fist, shut her eyes, and with a sob pulled the gloves on as she rushed toward the door.

In the huge, fractured wall mirror at the back of the kneipe, Rolf watched her leave, watched the maroon leather wind-block slowly swallow her. When the door opened and the bell rang, the heavy leather curtains danced in the fierce winter wind, and one of Rolf's canes slapped loudly like a gunshot as it fell on the cold linoleum floor.

das Ende
Fin
The End

About the Author

Rand Charles is a writer of historical fiction who haunts the archives, pubs, and cafés of Europe; researching and pounding out copy on his next book. Alternately, he lives a quiet life in the American Southwest with his wife and her sissy little dog. *Fall Irmgard* is his first full-length novel.

Acknowledgements and Further Reading

I must begin by thanking Monsieur Desjeunes, former head concierge at the Hotel Lutetia in Paris. Monsieur was employed at the hotel just after the war ended. He worked very closely with and listened for years to the endless stories of Monsieur Arrau (now deceased) who was concierge during the German occupation and the Abwehr's installation in the hotel. That rainy December day I spent with Monsieur Desjeunes in 2009 was truly the inspiration to start serious work on this novel.

Further to my story finding solid purpose, I want to acknowledge Kim Oosterlinck, Professor of Economics at the Free University of Brussels. My interviews and correspondence with him in regard to the economic aspects of the occupation were undeniably important. Kim was quick to point out that the Paris Stock Exchange actually reopened for security trades in March of 1941. Conversely, a novelist can't let a silly thing like facts get in the way of a good story, so I evoked my fiction license and manipulated the date. I'm quite certain Kim, a serious researcher and author of important, well-documented papers and books on wartime economics, will forgive this indulgence.

Additionally, I want to thank Helga Schier, my writing coach and editor, and Lindsey Alexander, my copy editor. Both of them worked their professional magic to turn a simple storyteller into a novelist. Thanks as well to Audeline Leroisse for her help with my French.

And finally, gratitude to my wonderful wife, my muse and devotee, who believed in me and my story to its completion. I was always encouraged at virtually every daunting turn, as well as granted the freedom I needed to flee my everyday world regularly and bounce around Europe, writing.

Further Reading

Americans in Paris: Life and Death under Nazi Occupation 1940-44 by Charles Glass. Harper Collins

April in Paris. By Michael Wallner. Nan A. Talese Doubleday

The Collapse of the Third Republic: An Inquiry into the Fall of France in 1940. By William L. Shirer De Capo Press

The Fall of France: The Nazi Invasion of 1940. By Julian Jackson. Oxford University Press

France under the Germans: Collaboration and Compromise. By Phillip Burrin The New Press - New York

Occupation. The Ordeal of France. 1940-1944 by Ian Ousby. St. Martin Press

Trading with the Enemy. The Nazi-American Money Plot. By Charles Higham. Barnes and Noble Books

The Unfree French: Life under the Occupation. By Richard Vinen. Yale University Press

Fall Irmgard
Songs Mentioned
(In order of Appearance)
Many of these period songs are available on Amazon or iTunes

"Où Sont Tous Mes Amants ?"
Charlys
Maurice Vandair
"Ich Weiß Nicht, zu wem ich Gehöre"
Friedrich Hollaender
"Shorty George"
Count Basie
"Vous Qui Passez Sans Me Voir"
Johnny Hess
Paul Misraki
"Pavane"
Gabriel Faure
"Simplemente-Triste"
Bernardo Stalman
"J'ai Deux Amours"
Vincent Scotto
"Keiner weiss, wie ich bin, nur du"
Friedrich Hollaender
"Sagt dir eine schöne Frau, Vielleicht"
Nico Dostal
"J'Attendrai"
Dino Olivieri ("Tornerai")
Louis Poterat
"Les Roses Blanches"
Léon Raiter
Charles-Louis Pothier
"Albénitz Tango"
Issac Albéniz
"Schreib mir einen Brief"
Franz Grothe
"Nachtexpress nach Warschau" (Night Train to Warsaw)
Ehrhard Brauschke
"Ungarwein" (Gypsy Wine)
Helmut Ritter

"Musik! Musik! Musik!"
Peter Kreuder
Hans Fritz Beckmann
"Bei dir war es immer so schön"
Theo Mackeben
Hans Fritz Beckmann
"Regentropfen"
Emil Palm
"Schönes Wetter Heute"
Franz Funk
Heinz Niepel
"Le Cheland Qui Passe"
Caesare Bixio
de Badet
"Rhythmus"
Willy Berking
"Nuages"
Django Reinhardt
"Si Petit"
Claret & Bayle
"La Chapelle au Clair de Lune"
Billy Hill
Henri Varna-Lelievre
"Des Abends"
Robert Schumann
"Andante favori"
Ludwig van Beethoven
"O Haupt voll Blut und Wunden"
J S Bach
"Evacaçâo"
Heitor Villa-Lobos
"Ihr Kinderlein kommet"
Johann von Schultz
"Der Glocken Ruf"
Eduardo Bianco
"L'accordéoniste"
M. Emer
"Liebeslied"
Fritz Kreisler
"Wenn es Draußen Dunkel ist"
Gerd Gerald

Fall Irmgard

"Liebe ist ein Geheimnis."
Karl Amberg
Franz Doelle
"Du hapst gluck bei dem Frauen, Bel Ami!"
Theo Mackeben
Hans Fritz Beckmann
"Eine kleine Sehensucht"
Friedrich Hollaender

-FALL IRMGARD-

Made in the USA
San Bernardino, CA
11 March 2017